THE ALABASTER BOOK OF OCCULT FICTION

Brian Stableford's scholarly work includes *New Atlantis: A Narrative History of Scientific Romance* (Wildside Press, 2016), *The Plurality of Imaginary Worlds: The Evolution of French roman scientifique* (Black Coat Press, 2017) and *Tales of Enchantment and Disenchantment: A History of Faerie* (Black Coat Press, 2019). He has translated more than three hundred volumes from the French, mostly in the genres of *roman scientifique, contes de fées* and Romantic and Symbolist fiction. His recent fiction includes the visionary science fiction novel *The Revelations of Time and Space* (2020) and its sequel *After the Revelation* (2021); the last in his long series of "Tales of the Genetic Revolution," *The Elusive Shadows* (2020); and the comedy fantasy *Meat on the Bone* (2021), all published by Snuggly Books.

SNUGGLY BOOKS

THE ALABASTER BOOK OF OCCULT FICTION

EDITED, TRANSLATED
AND WITH AN INTRODUCTION BY
BRIAN STABLEFORD

CONTENTS

INTRODUCTION

THE history of French occult fiction in the nineteenth century is closely associated with the evolution of the Romantic Movement that developed after the trauma of the 1789 Revolution and its turbulent aftermath. By the time the Revolution had given way to Napoléon's Empire the French Movement was in full swing in poetry, but prose fiction was, as is usual with literary movements, somewhat behind the trend. The French movement was a trifle belated itself, its prose component taking considerable influence from Germany and England, where the symptoms of the parallel Movements had included a vogue for what came to be known as "Gothic" fiction. The heart of Romantic philosophy was the notion that the intellectual evolution of the eighteenth-century Enlightenment had put too much influence on the development of scientific thought, emphasizing rationalism and materialism at the expense of spirituality and emotion, and Gothic drama and fiction attempted to excite the emotions rather than aiming for cool analysis; the German movement was notoriously characterized by *sturm und drang* (storm and stress).

The literary analysis of emotional and psychological turmoil lent considerable impetus to developing theories of the unconscious mind and irrational aspects of human thought and behavior, and entered into a kind of symbiotic relationship with scientific or pseudoscientific investigations of such ideas, encouraging speculative writers and proto-psychologists to explore ideas relating to hidden wellsprings of human motivation. That led to a re-examination of many ideas that the philosophers of the Enlightenment considered superstitious and puerile, which acquired a new interest as they came to be seen as something requiring exploration and explanation rather than simple dismissal. In that context, not only was a renaissance of supernatural fiction inevitable, but it was also necessary that the supernatural would be addressed in the renascent fiction with new attitudes of mind, and that its enigmas would be thrown into sharper focus.

In consequence, the essence of the occult fiction that blossomed in the early years of the nineteenth century in France was not simply the representation of supernatural motifs but the attempt to address those motifs rationally—to lay foundations for an understanding of the seemingly-incomprehensible, however paradoxical that endeavor might seem. The contents of the present anthology, the early inclusions of which are arranged in approximate chronological order of publication, provide an illustrative snapshot of the progress of that quest.

An intense interest developed in the early nineteenth century in such phenomena as hallucination and somnambulism, and the traditional notion that dreams must have meaning and might be revelatory came under more sophisticated scrutiny. The traditional "occult sciences" of astrology and alchemy had long since given awkward birth to the authentic sciences of astronomy and chemistry, but the transitional separation had never been complete, the older ways of thinking being maintained not only by the persistence of popular superstition but also by the interweaving of both major branches of occult science with the practice of medicine, which was still in the Golden Age of quackery at the end of the eighteenth century, complicated and confused by the competition offered to traditional herbal treatments by the evolution of "chemical" medicine, popularized in the sixteenth century by such rebel practitioners as Paracelsus but now being investigated with the aid of the scientific method. In the aftermath of the 1789 Revolution new unorthodoxies developed in France in rapid profusion, the theory of "animal magnetism" swiftly generating intense interest in the practices of "hypnotism." Mystical protopsychology was inevitably entangled with the development of new religious movements of various kinds, in the context of a fierce defensive war being waged in France by the Catholic Church against the reckless spread of "heresies" on the one hand and the undermining of faith by skepticism on the other.

Consideration of that complex philosophical background has to be combined, if the evolution of nineteenth-century occult fiction in France is to be fully understood, with an awareness of the pressures of the literary marketplace in which writers had to operate. Prior to the 1789 Revolution royal licenses had been required for licit publication, and although the repression of printers and booksellers had not been able to keep pace with the sheer abundance of presses and the profusion of contraband publications, it had been difficult and often dangerous in the run-up to the Revolution for writers to produce material of which the royal censors—whose policies were partly determined by politicians and partly by Churchmen—were likely to disapprove. Reaching an audience was not a simple matter. History has, of course, blurred the effects of that situation considerably; many of the books that we now consider to have been the classics of the era were initially published illicitly, in the teeth of stern armed resistance, while many of the licensed publications issued and marketed by the official royal printers are completely forgotten. The Revolution put an end to the licensing system, but not to the prosecution of publications deemed offensive to the Church or the State, which became even more fervent at times but far less predictable, as French politics evolved through the Empire, the Bourbon Restoration of 1815, the July Revolution of 1830, the Revolution of 1848, the *coup d'état* of 1851 and the fall of the Second Empire in 1870, which gave birth to the problematic Third Republic.

It was difficult throughout that period for any writer to know for sure where he or she stood with regard to the creation of material that might be regarded by the authorities of the time as touchy, on political or religious grounds. It was particularly difficult for writers associated with the Romantic Movement, who were always in danger of being regarded as dangerous radicals on both counts. In considering the stories assembled in the present collection, it is as well to remember that their imagination and publication cannot have been unproblematic and might, in at least some instances, have been regarded as risky and courageous. Charles Nodier, the great pioneer of Romantic prose fiction in France, was banished from Paris for ten years after publishing a satirical poem deemed offensive to Napoléon while the latter was still the First Consul, and when he was allowed to return in the early 1820s he was probably kept under police surveillance for the rest of his life. That was a matter of considerable importance for the Movement, because the weekly *cénacles* that Nodier hosted at the Bibliothèque de l'Arsenal after his return—the creative powerhouse of the Movement—must have been monitored. The publications launched by members of the Movement were routinely shut down during the Restoration, when many of the leading figures in the Movement were suspected—correctly—of Republican sympathies, and often of "Voltairean" (a term routinely, albeit incorrectly, used as a synonym for "atheistic") sympathies too.

One such publication that survived for longer than most was the *Mercure du XIXe siècle*, founded in 1823, which did not actually die until 1830, although it was effectively castrated after a couple of years. In its early years it only published one series of prose works, by the pseudonymous X. B. Saintine (Joseph-Xavier Boniface), who employed the strategy employed by almost all the writers active in the next fifty years of setting the vast majority of his works in the past or in exotic geographical locations, where they could only engage with questions of contemporary political relevance by means of cunning indirection. He wrote little occult fiction in the 1820s, but his *contes philosophiques* were remarkably adventurous.

The pressure of censorship relaxed considerably after the replacement of the Bourbon monarchy in July 1830 by their cousin Louis-Philippe, who was expected to be more liberal, and whose parliament tried desperately to steer a course between the Republican left and the Royalist right, aiming explicitly for a *juste milieu*—which, inevitably, satisfied nobody and became a target for fierce satire in its own right. The situation of writers eased, but the threat of prosecution and imprisonment did not disappear, and the police surveillance of writers regarded as potential trouble-makers continued. Many previously-paralyzed literary careers began to make progress again after 1830, but not unproblematically.

Numerous new publications associated with the Romantic Movement were founded in the early 1830s, and a few thrived in spite of routine harassment, most notably the *Revue de Paris* and the *Revue des Deux Mondes*. Two that enjoyed unusually long careers were *L'Artiste*, the chief stock-in-trade of which was reportage of the annual Salon where the artists of the Academy displayed their wares, and the pioneering fashion magazine *La Mode*, which was also heavily illustrated (not an easy matter in a pre-photography era when paintings and costumes had to be cleverly copied and expertly engraved). Both publications featured fiction, in moderation, and both initially showed a marked preference for fantastic material, including occult fiction, although their editorial policies soon shifted dramatically, for unknown—or at least unpublicized—reasons.

The early contributors of fiction to *L'Artiste* included Henri Martin, Alphonse Brot and Jules Janin, all regular participants in Nodier's salon; of the three, Martin was initially the most prolific, and almost all of the fiction he contributed to the periodical was fantastic, but he gave up writing fiction almost entirely when he began to work with "P. L. Jacob the bibliophile" (Paul Lacroix) on a popular history of France, and became a specialist historian thereafter. Lacroix became one of the pillars of the *Revue de Paris*, but it was the *Revue des Deux Mondes*—which published very little fiction in its early years—that became the more significant locus of Romantic narrative history, and also of popular articles on protopsychology.

La Mode was one of a stable of publications founded by the ardent Republican journalist Émile de Girardin, who married the darling of the *cénacles*, Delphine Gay, and established her as the hostess of another influential salon, from which he recruited his editors, including Jules Janin and the pioneering folklorist S. Henry Berthoud. The early work of both writers included a considerable amount of fantastic material—a preference also reflected in their editorial policies and Girardin's own inclinations in the occasional fiction he published in his pioneering popular newspaper *La Presse*—but all of the relevant publications gave a much greater emphasis to conventional naturalism as time went by. That was a very common pattern, seen in the careers of several of the most prestigious Romantic novelists, including Honoré de Balzac and Victor Hugo and all of the periodicals that dabbled for a while in fantastic fiction. The most commercially successful of the Romantic prose writers, including Alphonse Brot and

X. B. Saintine, initially made their money and their reputations writing for the stage, as Alexandre Dumas did before he and Eugène Sue, building on foundations laid by Honoré de Balzac, demonstrated the circulation-building potential of newspaper *feuilleton* serials in the mid-1840s and ushered in a new era of popular fiction in France.

Following the general trend, Balzac, Dumas, Sue and all their imitators all expelled the supernatural from the majority of the work they aimed at a wide audience, although Dumas and Sue tried stubbornly to reintroduce it semi-covertly and many of the leading members of the movement, including George Sand as well as Dumas, Nodier and Alphonse Karr, took advantage of the special license granted by the evolution in the 1840s of publication for children, notably by Pierre-Jean Hetzel, to attempt a regeneration of fantastic fiction. Attempts to extend that regeneration into fiction marketed for adult readers—where occult fiction had to be concentrated—were, however, rare and mostly tentative.

It was, nevertheless, within the context of the Romantic Movement that the French "Occult Revival" of the latter half of the nineteenth century gathered its initial impetus. Romantic historians, who approached the narrativization of history—especially French history—with a new emphasis on the history of ideas, not only paid more attention to the hypothesized emotions of the actors in history but also imported a considerable verve and passion into their own representations; their collective endeavor reinterpreted French history as a series of heroic fantasies, from the fragmentary records of local resistance to the Roman invasions of "Gaul," through ready-Romanticized accounts of the establishment of the Frankish kingdom of Charlemagne to the supposed exploits of Jeanne d'Arc in the Hundred Years War. Some Romantic historians, including Henri Martin and Edgar Quinet, wrote fiction as well; others, like Quinet's friend Jules Michelet and Martin's friend Jean Reynaud, were content to remain within the flexible bounds of scholarly fantasy, but found an even greater license therein to test the limits of plausibility in their more adventurous endeavors; Reynaud's *Terre et Ciel: Philosophie religieuse* (1854) and Michelet's *La Sorcière* (1863) were among the foundation-stones of the Occult Revival and helped to provide justificatory arguments, and also to inspire, a great deal of occult fiction.

The gray area between scholarly fantasy and literary fantasy was extensively explored by several writers associated with the Movement, including Henri Martin, S. Henry Berthoud and Alphonse Esquiros. Berthoud edited Émile Girardin's pioneering *Magasin des Familles* for some years, running it as a didactic vehicle for Romantic history, before being sacked for publishing a story suggesting that humans had evolved from ape-like ancestors, and he subsequently became a leading pioneer of the popularization of science during the Second Empire. Esquiros followed Girardin into politics, and became one of the several leading members of the Movement exiled from France after the 1851 *coup d'état*, along with Victor Hugo, Alexandre Dumas, Edgar Quinet and P.-J. Hetzel. Those who were allowed to remain in France and to continue their careers as best they could—including X. B. Saintine, S. Henry Berthoud and Jules Janin—were, like those who accepted amnesty and returned, effectively working in a straitjacket throughout the 1850s, the laces of which were only gradually relaxed in the 1860s.

The foundation stones of the Occult Revival were laid by a series of scholarly fantasies published during the Second Empire, of which the most influential included the two titles already cited and the works of the "Spiritist" Allan Kardec. The most influential of all, however, or at least the most notorious, was the work of "Éliphas Lévi," formerly Alphonse-Louis Constant, who had previously harbored literary ambitions and had been briefly associated with Théophile Gautier's coterie of Romantic *littérateurs*—known as the *petit cénacle* while Charles Nodier's salon was still the heart of the Movement but effectively replacing it even before Nodier's death in 1844. In 1848 Lévi had married the aspiring writer Marie-Noémi Cadiot, who subsequently made a name for herself, pseudonymously, as an art critic, and although it is difficult to identify any influence that she had on her husband, or he on her, it is interesting that she published a landmark collection of fantastic fiction in 1856, under her pseudonym, Claude Vignon, the first edition of which appears to have been suppressed, although it was swiftly reprinted in an edition advertised as being restricted in its distribution to territories outside France. If nothing else, the incident illustrates the difficulties with which would-be writers of imaginative fiction had to contend in France during the Second Empire.

Censorship was easing markedly before 1870, but the siege of Paris by the Prussians was briefly followed by the rule of the Commune, which was swiftly and brutally put down by the French army as soon as they were not otherwise occupied. The Third Republic that took over thereafter was not as repressive as Napoléon III's Empire had been, but it showed its repressive colors from the very start, and in large measure it simply shifted its targets of persecution slightly; no longer able to define its subversive enemies as Republicans, it characterized them as Communists, Socialists or Anarchists—and once again, many Romantic *littérateurs*, especially the younger generation of neo-Romantic writers, found a considerable natural sympathy with adherents of those creeds. Félix Pyat, one of the leading activists of the Commune, had been one of the early contributors to *L'Artiste* in 1831, although he had quarreled famously with his fellow-contributor Jules Janin, while the pioneering Anarchist journalist Jules Lermina had only escaped direct involvement with the Commune—and subsequent execution or exile to New Caledonia—because he was in jail when the fall of Paris was threatened and was drafted from his prison cell into the National Guard and sent out of the city to fight the advancing Prussians.

The entanglement of the new radical left with the unorthodoxies of the Occult Revival was by no means straightforward; many of the leading figures in the nascent Occult Revival had aristocratic delusions and located themselves at the opposite end of the political spectrum, but still opposed to the Third Republic. On the other hand, many leading Communards and Anarchists had a mystical streak, embracing "utopian socialist" ideas descending from followers of the Comte de Saint-Simon. Although Jules Lermina's involvement with the Occult Revival was partly accidental, his involvement with occult fiction was not, stemming from a profound admiration for Edgar Poe, whose work was translated into French by Charles Baudelaire—an admiration shared by several other unorthodox theorists of Anarchism, notably "Han Ryner" (as Henri Ner began spelling his name after his conversion to that philosophy). The political spectrum of the Occult Revival was thus both wide and confused, and that width and confusion are prismatically refracted in the fiction earnestly produced in the shadow of the Revival by such offbeat scholars as Gilbert-Augstin Thierry—the nephew of the prestigious Romantic historian Augustin Thierry—Victor-Emanuel Michelet (no relation to Jules) and Jules Bois, as well as temporary fellow travelers whose principal interest was or became purely literary, such as Jane de La Vaudère, Gabriel de Lautrec and René Du Mesnil, Comte de Maricourt, who preferred the abbreviated signature "R. de Maricourt."

It is arguable that the reason that the classic scholarly fantasies of the Occult Revival escaped censorship during the severe years of the 1850s was that they seemed to the censors to be politely neutral, or sufficiently esoteric to be harmless—and that the freedom granted to their circulation was a significant factor in making the French Occult Revival so forceful and so idiosyncratic. Although the Revival was international, the shape it took in different nations was heavily dependent on local circumstances. Thus, the French "Spiritism" popularized by Allan Kardec strove to differentiate itself from American Spiritualism and British "psychic research," in spite of its focus on identical phenomena; one of the principal nuances of difference was a much heavier emphasis in France on the fusion of theories of the survival of the soul after death with theories of serial reincarnation, often with an interplanetary dimension—an idea previously popularized in French literature and scholarly fantasy alike by such pre-Revoltionary writers as Nicolas Restif de la Bretonne, and taken up during the Second Empire by the astronomer Camille Flammarion before being incorporated into adventurous occult fiction by such writers as Jane de La Vaudère and Han Ryner. That difference in intellectual tradition is clearly reflected in differences between French, English and American occult fiction, in their skeptical as well as their credulous dimensions.

The intimate involvement in France of Romantic history with Occultism inevitably colored French responses to and extrapolations of the elaborate imaginary history developed by Madame Blavatsky and integrated into Theosophy, which became the second of the three major branches of the French Occult Revival in the 1870s, between Spiritism and the neo-Martinism of the 1880s, which absorbed and took over the idea of the Hermetic tradition trumpeted by Éliphas Lévi. French political involvements in the Far East also colored the attitude of French writers to the mysteries of the East in general and to Theosophist ideas in particular, in both scholarly fantasies and literary fantasies, in a fashion markedly different from writers in Britain and America. Although Madame Blavatsky undoubtedly became the principal influence on the incorporation of Eastern mysticism into French occult fiction, she had been heavily influenced herself by such French scholarly fantasists as Fabre d'Olivet and Louis Jacolliot, and news sent back to France from voyagers in India and military adventurers in Indo-China also fed abundant fuel to French occult fiction.

That flow of information also lent considerable support to the influence on the development of French occult fiction, especially in its proto-surrealist aspects, of the medicinal and recreational usage of opium and cannabis. Publicized by some writers sampled in this anthology, notably Charles Nodier and Gabriel de Lautrec, suspicious readers might well be able to infer the covert influence of hallucinogenic narcotics in several other inclusions. In occult fiction, what Charles Baudelaire called (ironically) "artificial paradises" are often displayed, as well as the artificial infernos more typical modern generic occult fiction, which has always made extravagant use of the central lesson of "Gothic" fiction: that terror is a stronger emotion than amour, although the combination of the two has a particular hybrid vigor.

It is not without reason that the most popular subgenre of occult fiction is nowadays marketed under the terse label "horror," and Edmund Burke showed considerable acumen in his pioneering *Philosophical Enquiry into the Origin of our Ideas of the Sublime and the Beautiful* (1757) in arguing that the idea of the "sublime" is grounded in terror. Burke's essay laid intellectual foundations for his later *Reflections on the Revolution in France*, which Revolution laid ideative foundations in its turn for all of the "sublime" fiction produced in France in the long wake of the violent demise and subsequent resurrection of the Bourbon monarchy, at the historical heart of which was the Terror. The history of occult fiction since the end of the period covered by this anthology, for which the Great War of 1914-18 posted an obliging boundary-marker—has not simply been a matter of continuing trends begun in the nineteenth century, but the seeds of that history were all planted and nourished during the heyday of the Romantic Movement, and various phases of their germination are illustrated and mapped out in the careers of the authors sampled herein.

The contents of the present showcase anthology demonstrate that not all "occult fiction" is "horror," although some of it certainly is—and how—but that its appeal to the esthetic sensibility of the sublime is never without a particular emotional thrill, which is quintessentially *occult*. Although it can only represent a very tiny sample of the work produced during the period of its interest, this sample nevertheless provides a sketch, or a shadow, of the thoroughly Romantic history of the genre in its infancy, with all the features that hindsight allows us to recognize as premonitory signposts to things to come.

—Brian Stableford

THE ALABASTER BOOK
OF OCCULT FICTION

ONE O'CLOCK
OR, THE VISION

by Charles Nodier

I had a heart full of bitterness and I sought solitude and the night. My walk had scarcely extended beyond Chaillot's gardens, and I usually only began it after eleven o'clock in the evening had chimed; but I was obsessed by such sad thoughts, my imagination was nourished by so many dire reveries, that often, in the state of involuntary excitement that is familiar to souls in pain, I had had to repel I know not how many illusions at which a moment's reflection would have caused me to blush.

One day, I had gone, later than usual, to the accustomed place; and, either because the more obscure darkness had deceived my design, or because the succession of my ideas, more unequal and more fortuitous, had caused me to lose sight of the goal of my nocturnal course, the bell of the village church was striking one o'clock when I perceived that I was no longer following my familiar route, and that my distraction had taken me into an unknown path. I hastened my steps toward the place from which the sound had come. At a turning in a narrow passage, a shadow rose up before my feet and disappeared into the hedge. I stopped, shivering, and I saw a long stone in the form of a tomb. I heard a sigh; the foliage trembled.

The following day, preoccupied with that adventure, I sought the same place at almost the same hour; the apparition was reiterated, and the phantom brushed me in passing; its footsteps resounded on the stone; the dry grass rustled behind it, and at intervals, I saw it fleeing, like a dark cloud, between the nearby willows or at the corner of a path. Always following the light and uncertain trace, I arrived at the old monastery of Sainte-Marie; but, wandering from one heap of rubble to another, I no longer found anything.[1]

That dilapidated convent offers one of the saddest sights that can strike the human eye. Nothing remains of the church but large isolated pilasters which bear the debris of a destroyed vault in places. When the moon lets its light fall through those columns and owls ululate on the cornices, as one reaches the summits of the uncultivated terraces and advanced among the high walls, stumbling among the ditches, and descending the broken stairways overgrown by poisonous plants, such as henbane and celandine, one ends up at buildings that are utterly degraded, of which nothing subsists but menacing sections of wall and eaves suspended in an almost-miraculous manner. When one is conducted by hazard to that funereal avenue, which leads via a rocky slope beneath damp arches to the ancient catacombs, and by the light of some dying lamp one can read on the scattered stones the names of the chaste women whose bones were deposited there . . . there is no human strength that can resist similar emotions. They absorbed all my faculties to such an extent that I forgot, in a way, the strange motive of my research; it was not until the next day that I felt the desire reborn more vividly to penetrate the mystery of the being whose encounter had troubled me, and which had made the great sepulcher a habitation as mysterious as itself.

---

1 The ruins of the convent of Sainte-Marie, near Chaillot on the road to Passy, have long been swallowed up by the expansion of Paris, but in the 1820s the area was still rural.

At one o'clock, holding my breath and walking silently, I arrived at the tomb, and I recognized the specter.

He was sitting, with his eyes fixed on a certain point in the sky. It was a young man, thin and very pale, clad in poor rags, whose unkempt hair fell back in thick waves. On seeing his gaping mouth, his extended neck, his stiff arms and his entire occupied attitude, one might have thought that he was delivering himself to a grave contemplation; but a sob escaped him, and I presumed that he had not seen what he appeared to be seeking.

He perceived me then, and leapt up in order to flee. Then, stopping immediately and looking at me mildly, he said: "What do you want with me?"

"To know you, and perhaps to console you."

"You're a man," he said, "and your heart is made like theirs. I don't like that species; there were some in my early days who were sympathetic to the suffering of others; they were noble hearts loved by God; things are very different now."

He shook his head and wiped his eyelids.

"There are still some now," I said. "Don't close your heart to your brothers."

"I no longer have brothers; do the unfortunate have any? Look how wan and withered I am; Look how soiled I am. I'm hungry during the day; during the night I lay my bones in the mud and the water of marshes. God has given me bad days. There are moments when my eyes are troubled, when my teeth join effortfully. My breast rises, my nerves vibrate like the strings of a harp; I sense tears that are trying to escape, a chill that runs through my limbs, and an inexplicable malaise that grips me by the throat. It's said that I'm a maniac and an epileptic, and people pass by, letting a smile of disdain fall upon me. That is what I am."

He sat down on the tomb, and I sat down beside him.

"I can recount to you . . ." he said, suddenly. "She won't come tonight, anyway. Do you see that black cupola rising up there in the blue depths of the sky? And that star, shining above, floating in such a pure light. Do you see it? She's there, in truth, since she told me so; but she no longer descends.

"I was almost as rich as Octavie, but the heir of a great house presented himself, and her parents refused me. Two days before the wedding, I was walking under the trees of the Luxembourg and I was embracing my dolor. What dreams did I not have! 'I shall take a sharp dagger into the banqueting hall,' I said, 'and I shall give eternity to my beloved and myself; or I shall throw fear into the temple and I shall abduct Octavie from the midst of her consternated friends; or I shall mingle the horrors of a conflagration with the preparations for her hymen; and in the trouble of that scene of terror, I shall steal her, dead or alive, from the crime of a new amour.'

"She passed by. The satin of her dress rustled. I shivered all over; a red cloud obscured my sight; all my blood flowed to my heart. She had recognized me, my Octavie. 'I'll come back soon,' she said to those surrounding her. 'The calm of midnight must be more delightful here. I'll come back soon; perhaps I'll come tomorrow.'

"They resound like such sweet music, the words of the woman one loves. They resound for a long time. All the faculties are gripped by them; the soul identifies with them; it seems that in carrying away her last thought, one is bearing her away entirely.

"I went away repeating: *I'll come back soon, perhaps I'll come tomorrow*. Perhaps tomorrow, she had said. But she didn't come.

"One o'clock chimed. Then a lugubrious bell, struck at long intervals, filled the air with a symphony of death.

"I would not have been able to define the emotion by which my senses were surprised, but it was as if it emanated from the sky. Whatever it was, an action of will of which I had not taken account drew me to Octavie's house; and, cleaving through the crowd of domestics, I stopped at the disarray of the apartment that she occupied.

The windows were open. Behind the curtains, shadows and torches could be seen passing by turns, and I know not what stifled cries were rising from the depths of the room.

"'She's dead!' I cried.

"'No,' replied her father, clutching me convulsively in his arms. 'She's asleep.'

"She was lying on her bed of red damask; there was a candle on her nightstand, a book at her feet; a priest was motionless beside the bed; her mother had fainted on the floor. Eulalie was weeping copiously, and a man dressed in black said with a ferocious sang-froid: 'There's no more hope; I knew full well that she wouldn't get out of it.'"

"I have forgotten the entire year that followed that evening, for I was ill, people said, and my malady excited repugnance and horror. Since Octavie's death, there was no longer anyone who loved me.

"A year later, to the day, I was going up the Rue de Tournon by the light of the illuminations of a public festival; I had passed slowly through twenty groups who afflicted me with the outbursts of their vulgar joy when one o'clock chimed. If the stroke of the clapper had hit me, it would have wounded me less rudely than it did in making that bell groan. Why was that hour—the hour whose last murmur had covered the sounds of your agony—not removed from the cycle of time?

"Then an adolescent with an angelic face saluted me with a moist and luminous gaze, and disappeared into the crowd, indicating the Luxembourg to me.

"I hesitated; I could still see him; a tear slid down his face, glistened and fell.

"I went into the gardens, very emotional—me, who had never known fear—and the dust that rose up in my passage, and the rays of moonlight that sprang forth between the leaves, and the distant tumult of the crowd returning home, all filled me with disquiet and alarm.

"She finally appeared to me, dressed and veiled in white, as on the beautiful evening when we had traversed all the quais of the Seine on foot, and I saw distinctly that she was floating in a vapor as gentle as the dawn. I lost consciousness, and Octavie did not draw away from me. She leaned over my motionless body, and her hot breath warmed my breast. Her kisses fluttered from my mouth to my eyelids and from my eyelids to my hair. Her arms enveloped me softly and rocked me in a region full of light and perfumes. There was a burden of voluptuousness upon all my organs. But when my reassured mind began to enjoy more fully that scene of intoxication; when my anxious eyes sought Octavie around me, I could no longer distinguish anything but the trace of her flight, a pale and trembling furrow that extended all the way to that star, and which gradually faded away.

"I don't know why she no longer comes, but if she doesn't come, I shall go . . . I believe I shall go," he repeated, in a low voice.

Such was the story that the epileptic told me, and after that, I enquired at length, but fruitlessly, regarding his fate. I had despaired of seeing him again, when hazard informed me that someone similar had been seen in the infirmary at Bicêtre. I went there, and had myself taken to his bed. He was little more than a cadaver, almost totally fleshless, and frightfully livid. His eyes still had a little fire and moved quite rapidly in their sunken orbits, but his gaze made one feel ill.

After having reflected for a few minutes with the air of a man trying to fix confused reminiscences, a bitter smile creased his lips slightly and he leaned gently in my direction.

"I knew full well," he said, "that I would go. I shall probably go tomorrow. Octavie came to invite me there, and I've already received a pledge from her of imminent alliance—for it's good," he added, "Octavie's hand, which extends thus toward me at any hour; it isn't a hand desiccated by death. It isn't a black and hideous hand like those of skeletons that have grown old in the tomb; its form is sweeter than the hands of angels. It's true that I can't touch her yet, but when the moment is ready to be accomplished, that hand will seize me and draw me beyond the sky."

As he finished speaking, he started staring at his pillow with a fearful joy, and cried out in a muted and alarmed voice: "There she is, there she still is, and there's her oval onyx with a little circle of gold.

"I shall go tomorrow," he said, smiling.

Capricious aberrations of a vivid or credulous imagination! He did not seem to see the straw on which his head was resting, and the coarse sheet that covered him was depressed by the weight of Octavie's hand, conserving its imprint.

How do I know, an unfortunate they call mad, whether that pretended infirmity was not the symptom of a more energetic sensibility, a more complete organization, and whether nature, in stimulating all your faculties, does not render them more apt to perceive the unknown?

That idea still occupied me when I arrived the next day. I approached the epileptic's bed and I did not see him, but a shroud thrown over him allowed me to divine his body. There was also a little candle burning there, and everything else was as it ordinarily was.

When the evening had advanced somewhat I went to the place where I had encountered him previously and I sat down on the tomb where we had sat together. It had been disturbed, perhaps with the intention of taking it away in order to form the boundary-marker of a field or the cornerstone of a building. I heard one o'clock chime and I calculated that that night would be the second anniversary of Octavie's death.

The sky was not pure; at first, a dull and stormy cloud hid the star where her friend had so often looked for her, but it emerged slowly from the darkness, and seemed more resplendent.

"Poor madman!" I said aloud. "What is the price of your discoveries now, vain science of the earth? There is nothing obscure for you in so many marvels that make the astonishment of sages; and if some cloud has veiled your days, you are freed therefrom, like that star, in order to resume in a new life your primal grace and your original beauty."

THE SORCERER'S CHILD

by X. B. Saintine

If human beings arrived at the point of perfection of which they think themselves capable, their relationship with the rest of nature would immediately cease.

(Aristotle, *Rhetoric*)

THE celebrated necromancer Maugis left a part of his secrets to one of his disciples, named Sirvax, who soon astonished the astrological schools of Seville and Toledo by his profound knowledge of the double magic, and especially by the audacity of his attempts.

"The transcendent and sublime science that we glory in cultivating," he said one day to the initiates of Hermes enclosed with him in the cavern of Salamanca,[1] "will never attain the summit of the luminous column as long as human senses, the only instruments by means of which we analyze and decompose

---

1 A legend popularized by Miguel de Cervantes alleges that the Devil once taught necromancy in the Cave of Salamanca, which had previously been the crypt of the Church of Saint Cyprian. Maugis is the name of an enchanter featured in more than one *chanson de geste*, including the story of the four sons of Aymon; that and the fact that the events of the story predates the founding of Stockholm might suggest that the story is set in the eleventh century.

objects, have not arrived at a more exquisite delicacy of their own accord. In the great work, God has taken hazard as his aide; he contented himself with dispersing the seeds of human creatures over the globe, matter has done the rest.

"Different combinations of metals and primitive earths formed the envelope of the first individuals, and produced the existing varieties of our sickly race. The same seeds formed black men and white, Circassians and Laplanders; but the blind instincts of brute matter have diversified their forms and enclosed the celestial rudiment of human beings in a narrow and uncomfortable prison, where their reason and senses cannot develop. Hazard, in sum, has paralyzed the initial jet of supreme intelligence.

"Since that time, children have been born with the infirmities of their parents, and the sciences threaten to stop at the barrier that the weakness of our organs opposes to them. I want to open a limitless route to genius and reason, and give human thought, not a wretched dungeon for a dwelling, but a vast palace where it will reign without shackles."

A slight murmur rose up in the assembly; but Sirvax, raising his head proudly, cried: "I have spoken! A new family of beings, nobler and more perfect than us, will owe its existence to me. And who will oppose that? Does not the sun shine now as in the first days of the world, and will the great Maugis have left his sublime and mysterious science to his pupil in order for it to remain slavish and sterile in his power?"

Entirely devoted to his project, he soon left Spain and retired to one of the numerous deserted islands that cover Lake Meler. Sweden, rich in metals and mineral products, seemed to him to be the land most appropriate to the experiments that he was meditating.

Several years went by without any one hearing mention of him; then, suddenly, the rumor spread that, by the power of his art, a man had been born without having been conceived in the womb of a woman. Curious to verify such a phenomenon, I embarked on the Baltic, went up the Meler, and, after leaving behind me the enormous rocks on which Stockholm has since been built, I visited almost all of the islands covering the surface of the lake, and finally discovered the one on which Sirvax lived with his magical child.

Sirvax was on the shore; on seeing me he took on an expression of sadness and constraint that astonished me.

"Well," I said to him, "you've succeeded, then?"

"Yes," he replied. "He's alive, he thinks and he speaks; you can see and judge for yourself." And his brow darkened again. He seemed to head for his habitation then, and I followed him, heaping him with questions.

This is what I can remember of his replies:

"Twenty times human ashes, desiccated bones and the black liquor of old sepulchers passed through my crucibles, decomposed by me. The envelope of human beings is the same as that of pebbles.

"The *magicum carmen*[1] is the deposit of the high sciences; but the sciences are mothers of the truth that enlightens us and the pride that leads us astray. I had noticed on the island of Malta a rock struck in the three sacred epochs of the day by the sun's rays, to which it doubtless owes its existence, for light made the world. I detached fragments of it, which, crushed and mixed by me with the purest gaseous fluids, took on form . . .

"Alas, it is necessary to admit that the proportions and the arrangement of human organs also reveal a sublime intelligence; I suspected as much and I blasphemed. I spent five years of my life trying to alter the dispositions and give my work more perfections and harmony in its movements; I did

---

1 The Latin *carmen* refers to a ceremonial utterance, usually but not necessarily in song, so the phrase *magicum carmen* refers in occult literature to incantatory spells or evocations.

nothing but err for five years. The arms have to be placed thus in order to protect the sources of life contained in the breast, to bring before the eyes the objects that they need to contemplate and to the mouth the nourishment that it must receive.

"The last-named function satisfying the need that is felt most imperiously by humans, the organ of smell needs to be placed directly above that of nutrition, in order to savor even before the palate; and the eyes, active sentinels, also need to survey the materials offered to the mouth in order that no hostile body slips inside unknown to the sense of smell.

"But if I have been forced to respect those principal dispositions of the human body, I believe that I have at least found the means of improving them by complicating them. To the natural means of human respiration I have added to mine aspirant arteries like those of birds, and stigmata imitative of those of insects, in order to give his blood a warmth and activity that that his thoughts ought to feel. Our feeble eyes cannot distinguish forms and colors at too close or too great a range; his have such an extent that three leagues of distance does not impede them. Finally, I have given his senses such a development that I ought to expect anything of a reason directed by such motors."

"But how," I said to him, "after having planned all the mechanisms of that body, were you able to make life enter into it?"

"That is the secret of my art," he replied. Then, unrolling before me a long parchment covered with Oriental characters, and indicating them to me with his finger, he said: "The blood of a young bull stifled at the moment of its first amours, and the liquor of euphorbia and henbane, extracted at a certain time, would have been sufficient in combination to enable the intervention of the aid of the demon, but the demon was not a guest worthy of such a lodgment. I was able to constrain one of the intelligences that inhabit the mixed worlds to come and inhabit and direct my material creation."

Sirvax suddenly stopped at that point in his discourse, and then, with a long sigh and resuming his thoughtful expression, he went on: "In any case, you can judge for yourself; but let's be silent, we're approaching the place where he reposes, let's beware of waking him up too abruptly."

I was gripped by a sort of terror that I could not explain, as if alerted by instinct to an imminent danger. Although the sound of our footfalls was barely audible, a muffled and prolonged groan greeted us immediately. Then, a deformed and gigantic being appeared before me, raising with difficulty an enormous head that was balanced on broad shoulders. His eyes, yellow and earthen in color, seemed only to dart oblique glances; his skin, pale and dull, was not colored by the movements of blood; and his hair, or rather his mane, of a grayish hue, scarcely hid two large ears, which, fashioned like shells, shared with those of hares the property of rotating in the direction in which a sound was audible.

"Who comes to trouble my repose?" he cried, turning haggard eyes toward us. "Is the day not made for sleeping?"

"Be quiet, Mudloch," Sirvax said to him, his forehead covered with a sudden blush. "What use do you make of your reason? Have I not already proven to you that only the exquisite sensitivity of your sight, until now, has opposed your being able to support the rays of the sun like other men?"

At this point the sorcerer's child seemed to be seized by frenetic transports. "False reasoning," he said to him. "You raise your voice with such force that my ears are torn by it. The daylight only gives birth to darkness, your mind only gives birth to lies."

Having said that, he turned his back on us, without even perceiving my presence, and he went to lie down again on an enormous pile of heather.

"His senses still abuse him," murmured Sirvax. "Time will rectify that, but what keen senses of smell and hearing!

In darkness, what surety of gaze! He senses the opening of a flower on one of the neighboring islets; he can hear the sound of a falling leaf six hundred paces away; and he can hit a nightingale with an arrow at a distance that scarcely permits us to distinguish the tress on which the bird is perched."

Toward dusk, Mudloch came to knock on the door of Sirvax's habitation and demand his breakfast.

"My friend," the latter said to him, moderating the tone of his voice, "the evening meal is not a breakfast; we're about to have supper, come and eat with us."

"Breakfast is breaking a fast," replied Mudloch, "my night has just gone by, the day is commencing, and I've come to take my first meal. Cease, then, incessantly trying to make me adopt words that are contrary to my ideas. The senses are the organs of the intelligence, as you have told me yourself; you'll agree that mine have a perfection that yours cannot attain; my reason is therefore superior to yours; admit the insufficiency of your means, serve my breakfast, and have breakfast with me if you think it appropriate."

An enormous Halland salmon was set before him, but, having tasted it, he quickly pushed it away, complaining about its excessively strong flavor. I ate some; it seemed almost insipid to me.

However, I was able to attract the confidence of Mudloch by not opposing him in any way. After the meal I accompanied him, almost groping, in his nocturnal course. For three entire nights I became the companion of that man of darkness, about whose existence I wanted to know. His sight had a prodigious range, but the intermediate spaces escaped him; he could only see what he could not touch. The perfume of a flower seemed to give a dolorous quiver to his entire body, and the slightest sound held his mind in suspense.

In accordance with his senses, he conceived space, number, shape and movement, but occult causes, the possible, instinct, the future, and the sudden revelations of the soul all escaped him. His thought did not launch forth beyond a cold reasoning based on external sensations. His organs enclosed all of his intelligence, abused by them. His was a body that lacked a soul, a reason deprived of instinct. Without foresight, without enthusiasm, without imagination, disinherited of his divine part, of ideas coming from the heavens, he was the human being as Locke has since presented him to us, he was the man of science—in sum, the man of man.

"What do you think of him and me?" Sirvax asked me, one day.

"I think," I replied, "that in order to complete your work, you need to make a new world for your new man, but never hope to see that earth of your creation shaded by the branches of the tree of genius. Reason alone does not invent or discover anything; your Mudloch is deprived of any species of imagination, and even in the physical sciences, it is by means of that faculty that one arrives at the highest truths. One begins by inventing, and when, by experiment and reasoning, the means of verification, one has succeeded in giving bases and supports to one's theory, one believes that one has discovered it. One has created it.

"Instinct and imagination, in human beings, are like memories of a prior existence, and the emanations of a world of light that humans doubtless once inhabited; they owe to one their natural beauty, to the other the extent of their genius and preeminence over the other beings of creation. Your Mudloch, the son of matter, cannot possess either of those two sublime faculties."

While I was conversing thus on one of the shores of the island with Sirvax, who was seeking to combat the disadvantageous opinion that I had conceived of his favorite, we saw a small vessel approaching the strand, from which several men and a young and beautiful woman soon emerged. Sirvax seemed desolate at this further increase in the population of his island.

"On the contrary," I said to him, "thank Providence; it has sent you today the surest means of testing the human sentiments to which the child of your art might be susceptible. The sight of a woman ought to act immediately upon his heart, and develop emotions thus far dormant there."

We went to meet the disembarked newcomers, and Sirvax recognized them as some of his friends from Salamanca, curious, like me, to verify the reality of his promises.

Nightfall soon brought Mudloch to the sight of the young woman. He gave no evidence of attraction or surprise; his heart remained cold, his face impassive, except that his scornful gaze seemed to reproach her for being the weakest of the individuals surrounding him.

By means of their multiple questions, our philosophers from Salamanca had soon obliged Mudloch to explain the theory of his sensation himself. At first they all seemed very surprised by the eccentricity of his ideas, but when he came to invoke the superiority of his organs over those of other humans, he cited in his favor the axioms of their own school, *intellectus in sensu*, several of them began to doubt.

However, it still seemed difficult to them to admit that the day was consecrated to sleep and obscurity. One of them said: "It's during the day that birds sing and flowers open; the sun is the torch of nature; everything that vegetates or respires is reanimated, vivified and guided by its light."

"Absurd sophisms!" cried Mudloch. "The feeble light of day can suffice for your weak sight, dazzled by the luminous glare of night. The sun dispenses heat, the moon dispenses light; heat dilates the fibers of the body, enfeebles ideas and invites repose; who can deny those incontestable verities? Night reanimates the flowers that the sun withers; it is during the night that they exhale all their perfumes, that myriads of moths, more numerous than those of the day, flutter around them; it is during the night that the nightingale sings, that the races of the most noble among the birds agitate; do not the bear, the wild boar, the anteater and thousands of animals wander by night in our forests? By what right do you judge by yourselves? Do the osprey and the owl not have eyes as good as the warbler and the finch? Do you dare to compare your sight with mine? Abjure ancient errors, therefore, the moon alone is the torch of nature; everything that breathes is reanimated, vivified and guided by its light."

The balance was beginning to tip strongly in favor of the new speaker. The discussion was then taking place in obscurity, and our sages were no longer astonished that they could not see. The magical influences of the moon and darkness on the minds of mortals and the guests of tombs were retraced in their thoughts, and were reinforced by the theories of the motherless man in favor of the night. Sirvax, in whom pride had already subjugated reason, appeared triumphant, and addressed his colleagues:

"Perhaps my promises will be accomplished," he said, "and a new era is commencing for science; let us not hasten our judgments; let us examine before deciding. I shall try to see it in the night, insofar as my feeble means permit me to do so. It even seems to me that my eyes, less abused, can distinguish objects in the obscurity that surrounds us . . ."

And while that cabalistic family was arguing thus in favor of darkness and sensual intelligence, the young woman, who had retired at the beginning of the evening, came back in, carrying a blazing resinous pine branch.

Mudloch, dazzled and furious, had got to his feet, raising a threatening gesture toward her, when Sirvax threw himself in front of him. "What are you doing, raising a hand to a woman?"

"What is a woman?" said the monster. "What! Is this the companion of man about which you have spoken to me? If that is so, this woman is mine . . ."

"What is he saying?" cried all the spectators of the scene simultaneously, gripped by terror.

"She cannot belong to you," added the disciple of Maugis. "Society imposes laws upon us, which must be respected."

"What does society matter to me?" said Mudloch, roaring with fury. "I only know the laws that my senses, the organs of my reason, impose on me."

"But does this woman love you? Can she love you?"

"I do not know love and do not require it. Does the inhabitant of forests talk about love when he retains his indocile companion beneath his claws? Society! Love! Barbaric words invented to paralyze reason and strength! She is mine, I tell you; the countries from which you come must produce others for you, but, alone of her species on this island where I was born, she is mine!"

And, with his eyes filled with a somber gleam, and his mane bristling, with convulsive movements, he advanced toward the pale and dying creature. I leapt toward her and took her in my arms, while Sirvax, taking possession of the blazing pine branch, which she was till holding, presented it to the monster's face and forced him to retreat before the light.

We succeeded in calming the young woman's terrors, and were seeking a place where we could shelter her from further attempts by Mudloch until daylight, when we perceived that Sirvax had not returned to us. Anxious about his fate, we resolved to go in search of him, equipped with weapons and torches.

Shrill cries soon guided us to a part of the island where the unfortunate sorcerer, chained to a tree, was being heaped with maledictions and blows by the child of his art, who was reproaching him for raising an obstacle to his natural and reasonable desires. Seeing us armed, Mudloch seemed frightened and tried to flee. We stopped him in order to reproach him for the infamous treatment to which he had subjected his benefactor and the author of his existence.

An infernal smile appeared on his lips. "What do I owe him?" he said to us. "Has he created me for my benefit? What pact was I able to conclude before being born? I have served his projects in making use of his gifts; what more does he demand? Is he not obliged to me? He is triumphant today, since he sees that my reason has sufficed to convert yours, and that my strength has vanquished his. But for you, he would be subject to the punishment that any being deserves who is in contradiction with himself, any being cruel enough to harm his own work, to stop the effects of which he is the first cause. He knows my will now; he knows my strength and my skill; let him satisfy me or he will tremble!"

As he finished those words he plunged rapidly into the darkness, and disappeared.

"See, then, the results of the superior reasoning on which you want to found your new science," I said to Sirvax. "Believe me, let us abandon his fatal island as soon as possible, and let us leave that beast with a human face, that veritable lycanthrope, to bury his barbaric intelligence in this solitude."

He resisted, but we dragged him toward our boats, still moored to the shore.

"No!" the unhappy sorcerer soon cried, detaching himself from our arms. I want to see him again! He's my son! He's my work! He's doubtless already repenting . . ."

As he finished speaking, frightful laughter burst forth from a great distance behind us. Sirvax had just fallen at our feet, pierced by an arrow.

We forgot all the danger in order to surround him with the most tender cares, but his blood was escaping in floods; his wound was mortal, and he ordered us himself no longer to think of anything but our own safety.

"Have I been punished for having dared too much? Is it, then, for our wellbeing that nature has placed limits on our senses and covered her designs with a veil of bronze?" he said, gazing at the ground. Then, after a moment's silence: "I divine . . . God be praised!" And he exhaled his last sigh.

Gripped by horror and pity, we quit that bloody shore, and my companions soon returned to Salamanca, to frighten with the story all the disciples of Hermes who, since Sirvax's supposed success, were no longer occupied in anything but making men and correcting the imperfect works of God.

It is said that Mudloch succeeded in traversing the Meler, that he traveled through several countries, always at war with the protective laws of society and the mildest instincts of nature. Finally, weary of others and himself, he wanted to visit the rocks of Malta from which he had been drawn, and ended his days voluntarily there, without remorse for the past and without hope for the future.

His body was not subject to the effects of carnal dissolution; by virtue of a singular phenomenon, it returned to its primitive state, while conserving its hideous and terrible form; and the Maltese still show travelers that petrified cadaver, separated from the rock, suspended over the abysms of the sea, which is commonly known by the name of *il fratre impiccato*.

It is also said that, in the course of his errant life, he became a father, and that his monstrous race acquired a rapid increase. The same reports certify that from him is descended the host of men who mistake darkness for light; those beings deprived of instinct and imagination who glorify themselves in enjoying a mechanical reason, a mineralogical sensibility; the multitude of atheists, of materialists who, doubtless deprived of a soul like the author of their origin, are obstinate in refusing one to other men. People say that; I have difficulty believing it.[1]

---

1 In later versions of the story this last line is amended to: "People say that; but what do they not say?"

THE ANTIQUE RING

by S. Henry Berthoud

> Oh, tell me that it's a dream.
> Isn't it true that all of this
> is a dream?
> *Owen*

> Poor human reason,
> which cannot distinguish dream
> from wakefulness, or illusion from reality.
> *Alfred Mercier*[1]

MY dear Édouard, for fifteen years the most devoted amity has linked us to one another; which is to say that, for fifteen years, you have sustained me and consoled me; that for fifteen years, you, so grave, so positive, so superior to the impetuous distractions of our age, have listened patiently and consoled with perseverance the chagrins of an unhappy young man whom a disorderly imagination has dragged incessantly far from the real and the reasonable, whom an irresistible, deadly, extraordinary force never wearies of delivering to the

---

1 These citations are presumably false—Berthoud had a habit of inventing headquotes—as "Alfred Mercier" cannot possibly refer to the American poet and physician of that name born in 1816, although it is not impossible that he had Louis-Sébastien Mercier in mind.

consequences of a Romantic sensibility full of exasperation.

Édouard, Édouard, now more than ever I have need of that amity.

Listen, for I shall write to you; I dare not go to find you to tell you in person, so ashamed am I. I shall write you a story which you will not be able to believe. It gives birth to laughter and scorn on the visage of anyone who hears it; they treat me as a madman. But you, my friend, you won't laugh, will you? You won't tell me that I'm a madman, a maniac, a dreamer; that would hurt me a great deal, and you're so afraid of hurting me.

Then again, it doesn't matter that they call me by all those insulting names, which drive me to despair and make me clench my firsts in rage and stamp my foot on the ground; it doesn't matter that they slander my belief; I still experienced what I experienced, and I still saw what I saw. Oh, if it were permissible, for me, to call it into doubt . . . but the memory of that execrable scene pursues me so relentlessly . . . I can't get away from it . . . it's impossible. It's there, always there!

You know, Édouard, when one is suffering as I'm suffering, one has every right to lament that no one can believe in his suffering! Yes, yes, one has every right to complain!

My friend, you don't know everything about my difficulties. You know about the obstacles that were opposed to my marriage to Laura, and how they became more numerous and more insurmountable every day, but what you don't know is that the young woman was frightened by seeing love accompanied by so many torments. She raised her eyes with terror toward the future, and then she looked behind her with regret. I read it in her heart; she preferred a negative but peaceful happiness to the bitter intoxication of a sublime and ardent tenderness full of trouble and agitation.

In consequence, I took the decision to suffer alone, and not to associate that frail creature with the bleak destiny that weighs upon me. I wrote to tell her that I was renouncing her, since my love was causing her so much anguish. She replied in a letter moist with tears, in which she accepted my sacrifice.

Oh, I offered it to her in all sincerity; Heaven is my witness! And yet, Édouard, my dear Édouard, I cannot tell you how much harm she did me by accepting that sacrifice!

You have often told me that a good deed, a great act of courage, sustains the soul and renders the sacrifices imposed by duty less harsh. I confess, my friend, that that has not been my experience. But at least I have recognized the justice of another of your observations: that study is the only charm that soothes mental troubles. When one identifies with imaginary individuals, when one appropriates their chagrins, when one makes them weep over their misfortunes, when one softens sensations and torments that have become communal to them and us, it seems that one is not alone in suffering, that one is pouring out one's suffering into the bosom of a friend and that a secret voice is sympathizing, encouraging and consoling.

Two months ago I was spending the night writing beside a blazing fire. My ideas were flowing rapidly; pages covered in my large untidy scrawl had piled up on my desk. They were full of lugubrious thoughts, bizarre events and inconsequential, conflicting sentences of no interest to anyone but me, or you—you, Édouard, to whom a unique friendship has rendered my extravagant ideas, the impetuosity of my imagination and my fits of despair familiar.

When morning came, my blood was not refreshed and my head had not become any less heavy, but I had escaped from myself for a whole night, and that was a good deal. The day before, I had ordered that a bath be prepared for me, Dr. Fernand having recommended me more than ever to make frequent use of it. I only just had time to go into the bathroom because my lamp, for lack of oil, was about to go out, and I was scarcely in the water before it threw off one last gleam and left me in complete darkness.

Here, my dear Édouard, I renew the plea I made just now: don't laugh at me, don't call what you're about to read into question, for you'd be doing me an injury!

I didn't take long to relax into the comfort of the bath. A soft warmth refreshed my limbs, tensed by long sleeplessness, by relaxing them. My forehead, burning with chagrin, was enveloped by a benevolent moisture. My ideas were suspended, without ceasing entirely, and my eyes closed under a gradual drowsiness.

I had been in a delightful situation for a few moments, when I thought I could hear a vague murmur somewhere in the vicinity. It even seemed that some unknown light was visible through my eyelids, although I felt so content that I didn't have the strength to open my eyes, to move or to stammer a single word; however as astonishing the commotion might be that was happening close by, I could not pluck up the resolution to discover the reason for it.

A shock burst forth like a thunderbolt, but sharper and more harrowing.

I woke up with a start; in front of me stood a mocking and intimidating individual. He was looking at me as no human eye has ever gazed.

The sight of him suffocated me; it made me suffer indescribably.

He advanced his left hand and showed me the antique ring that, as you know, I bought from a Jew.

Then the specter passed the ring before my eyes, as if to prove to me that it really was mine; he gave me time to consider the fluting of the large ring and the two animal figures engraved on the black stone.

After that he raised his right hand; he showed me three fingers; he pronounced the word "three," struck me hard on the head and disappeared.

When I recovered consciousness I was in bed, surrounded by people who were caring for me. Attracted by a piercing scream, they had come running; I had been found in the bath, half-drowned; a few seconds later, and it would have been all over. Why, alas, did they bring me back to life?

My first words were to ask my manservant for the casket in which my jewelry, including the fatal ring, was kept. On receiving that order, he went pale and trembled in every limb. A bitter laugh contracted his features.

"May Satan strike me dead!" he stammered. "You know everything!"

I thought that the wretch was referring to the dream I had had shortly before, because I still thought that it was a dream.

Then, suddenly, another idea—an absurd idea—passed like a flash of lightning through my imagination. I clung to it urgently. The apparition of a little while ago was a joke, played by one of my friends; they must have involved Antoine.

"Yes, I know everything!" I exclaimed. "You shall be punished as you deserve."

Antoine went out, in despair. Five minutes later I heard an explosion. I ran to my servant's room. He had blown his brains out.

He had left a note for me: *Monsieur, I'm a wretch. I've stolen your jewels. I'm dishonored; I shall die.*

On reading that, I was overtaken by an unbearable distress, and a fever. I had to take to my bed, in a pitiful state.

Édouard, as truly as I believe in God, the figure that I had seen the night before leapt to my gaze all night long—except that he only showed me two fingers, and his vibrant voice pronounced the word "two."

Now, his mysterious speech and gestures were only too clear to me. The fatal ring was to cost the lives of three people. One of them had already met his fate.

During my convalescence, I was told that a young woman, poorly dressed and carrying a small child in her arms had come several times to ask for me. She begged insistently that she be allowed to speak to me. I ordered that she should be brought to me if she came back again.

An hour later, she was shown into my room.

Casting my eyes over that unfortunate woman, pale, save for her eyes reddened with tears, hardly able to stand up, I understood that she had suffered a great deal, even more of moral troubles than physical ones.

"Antoine loved me," she said—and her knees buckled underneath her; if an armchair had not happened to be there, she would have fallen on the floor. "It was for me that he stole. It's because of me that he's dead. I'm . . . this is his son . . ."

The poor young woman's sobs broke my heart.

"Here, Monsieur, take this ring back. It's the only gift of his that I have left. I hadn't yet sold it in order to live. Take it back, Monsieur, but don't denounce me to the law. What would become of my child, the only thing that remains to me? What would become of Antoine's son, if they threw me in prison?

She handed the ring to me, and I, overwhelmed by the memory of my vision, despairing in the realization that she had told the truth, chilled by fear at the thought of the misfortunes that she was still anticipating, remained motionless, absorbed by my lugubrious thoughts.

Poor creature! She thought that I was rejecting her supplications; she threw herself at my feet, seized my hand and bathed it with tears.

The unfortunate woman's agony brought me out of my reverie. "That ring must be destroyed," I exclaimed, "in order that it should not be deadly to anyone else. Hurry up, give it to me!"

The child had taken it from his mother's hand, in order to play with it; she had surrendered it listlessly. He had raised it to his lips.

Suddenly, he uttered a groan, stiffened convulsively and fell back. His mother was no longer holding anything but a cadaver.

The ring enclosed a mortal poison in its gem.

And the horrible figure that was pursuing me appeared above the despairing mother. This time, he did not speak, but his long finger held up a single digit.

Who will the third victim be?

Édouard, this is an idea that has lit up within me for the first time: an idea inspired in me by Heaven, I'm sure of it.

What if I were to put an end to the misfortunes caused by that infernal ring? I've lost everything that attached me to the earth. Existence weighs upon me; it has burdened me. What if I were to deflect the fatality that threatens someone else and draw it down voluntarily upon my own head?

The phantom has predicted it, and I am only too forcefully compelled to believe its predictions. It still needs another victim—only one! Will Providence punish me for sacrificing myself in this situation?

Already, for a long time, I've wanted to free myself from life. The fear of celestial wrath held me back. Now, God will bless me for dying.

Look! Here's the phantom coming back; he's giving me a sign that I can die.

Adieu!

THE EVIL EYE
A TALE OF THE KAHVEH KHANEH[1]

by Henri Martin

There is no shield that resists your eyes
—Asdjedy[2]

THE first fires of dawn were blanching the citadel of Gamdan on the high hill, and causing to spring forth luminously from the obscure masses of the great Sana the square towers of minarets and the large domes of mosques, when several litters borne by slaves emerged from the labyrinth of gardens that surrounded the royal city like an immense flower-bed. Traversing the delightful valley of Rodda, they headed toward the mountainous region of the Djiabal.

Oh, no man who parted the pink silk curtains of the first litter would have traded what they hid for all the treasures of Ima in Yemen.

He might have seen, floating over a neck whiter than a jasmine flower, tresses as black as musk; he might have seen, leaning over a small and delicate hand, a gracious forehead

---

1 Author's note: "Kahveh Khaneh: literally, coffee house. It is normally in coffee houses that Oriental storytellers make their stories heard."
2 Asdjedy, or Asdjedi, was a poet of the tenth-century "Persian renaissance," contemporary with Ferdoussi, or Firdausi.

50

of fifteen years, and two lowered eyes veiled by long lashes, which raised their elongated almonds with azure irises toward him. If a smile had suddenly appeared between those pursed and pensive lips, pearls more precious than the pearls of Bahrein enlaced in the young woman's braided hair, doubtless the indiscreet stranger's reason would have fled with his heart; he would have sworn to possess Leila or to die!

But the virgin's gaze was not lifted; her lips did not part in order to smile, and the gleam of tulips disappeared from her cheeks before the pallor of lilies.

Whence comes that melancholy, then, under which the charming head of the daughter of the Emir Farhan is bowed, who had once frolicked through life, as insouciant and light as a gazelle of the Nedjed? Her past was all joy and innocence; her future . . .

In the mountains and in the plain, from the shores of Aden to the rocks of Khaulan, there was no daughter of a sheikh or emir who did not envy the fiancée of the rich, powerful and handsome Mansor, the proud dola of Sanhan! She had seemed to receive her father's orders with a satisfied soul, and more than once she had followed with an attentive gaze the dola's long-maned mare when he passed at a gallop before her jealousy.

However, this is not the sweet reverie of a fiancée who trembles with emotion and hope at the moment of crossing the threshold of an unknown world; there is suffering in that languor, anxiety and a kind of somber presentiment in that mild physiognomy. For an entire month she has not been behind her loophole to watch the dola and his brilliant escort pass by, and a kind of fear contracts her features when her father talks to her about the approaching marriage.

She has been thus since a stranger has seen her face at the hour of morning prayer.

One day, when she was walking on the balcony of her father's palace, shortly after the muezzin had summoned the faithful to the first prayer, she chanced to lift her head toward a minaret adjacent to the corner of the terrace where she was walking. The muezzin was no longer there, but in his place a hadji was standing, leaning on the balustrade of the tower. At first Leila wanted to withdraw, frightened by seeing a stranger at that dominant point, to which only blind muezzins have the right to climb. An irresistible force retained her; in any case, the stranger did not seem to perceive her presence. He was tall and slim; his face, which she could only see in profile, was handsome and sad, like that of a Peri thinking about the Eden from which his race was exiled. One might have thought that the iron fingers of fatality had furrowed that noble and as-yet-young physiognomy with profound traces, thinning its angular contours by tightening them.

Leila was gazing at him with an indefinable constriction of the heart when he suddenly turned sideways and lowered upon her two large dark eyes, profoundly sunk in their orbits, which emitted a strange and somber flame like the cavities of a double crater. It seemed to her that the rays of the hadji's gaze had penetrated her breast like two burning arrows; a sensation that was both an unspeakable dolor and a delirious pleasure caused her entire being to shudder; everything vacillated around her and she fell against a trellis, palpitating and almost fainting. But although all the other objects were floating confusedly in her gaze, she could still see the stranger distinctly. He leaned toward her, hiding his forehead in his hands; then he straightened up, made a movement to return to the interior of the minaret, stopped momentarily, darted an oblique glance at the young woman—and, striking his breast with a gesture of despair, he disappeared into the stairway.

That is what has caused Leila's melancholy.

And this morning, she is more absorbed than ever in her thoughts; for she knows that she is returning as a virgin for the last time to her father's country house, and that she will only see the royal city again on her bridal camel. So she is gazing indifferently at the fresh hills covered with rich plantations of coffee-trees, the elegant groups of date-palms with large fans, and the sand dunes where trees of Judea make their pink bouquets shine amid the foliage of the cheerful acacias: gracious landscapes that she once loved to see passing by turns alongside her litter.

Silence! Who is brushing the branches of the balm-trees thus? Are those brown heads that are parting the leaves the malicious faces of apes that have come to grimace at the travelers? The slaves have stopped; the eunuchs are whispering and putting their hands on their sabers. Disaster! A troop of men with grim faces launch forth from the bushes, muskets in hand. Their black hair, circled by a simple cord, and their muscular bodies, naked save for a loincloth, make them recognizable as Kobaïls from the mountains of the North. Disaster!—for pillage, devastation and death are the companions of the Kobaïl.

A cry of distress rises in the little caravan; a discharge thunders, and three eunuchs fall under the devastating bullets of the muskets. The slaves flee; Leila's women throw themselves out of their litters and disperse. Abandoned by all those who surrounded her, the daughter of Farhan invokes the Lord and his prophet in the depths of her heart and flees like a young antelope surprised by a cruel panther.

Alas, the avid eyes of the marauders have seen the pearls shining in her hair and the gold of her rich necklace; they all run after her. Their rapid surge devours the distance that separates her from them; their iron leg-muscles will soon have wearied the frail and gracious legs of a young woman accustomed to the slack idleness of the harem. Exhausted, breathless, she feels her knees buckling beneath her; she gets up again to resume her course, totters and collapses on the burning soil.

She sees the Kobaïls arriving, without being able to make an effort to escape the fate that threatens her. Horrible! A horrible moment! Here they come, here they come! They are bounding and howling, already extending their arms, tensed by impatience and rapacity.

At that moment, a man clad in the long white garment of a hadji emerges from a clump of palms and places himself between the mountain men and the daughter of Farhan.

An electric flame ran through Leila's veins; she had not seen his face, which was turned toward the Kobaïls, but she understood well enough that it was him!

He was wearing a trenchant dagger in his belt but he did not draw it. Leila saw him fold his arms and stand still, only imprinting a slight movement on his head, as if he were looking at all the marauders one after another.

The latter stopped in mid-leap; their fixed gazes were suspended on that of the stranger; the passions that swelled the muscles of their faces had given way to a bleak stupefaction. Then the hadji raised his right arm and extended his index finger toward a clump of coffee bushes that rose up some distance away. The brigands gripped their scimitars angrily, grinding their teeth; their breasts swelled, and they appeared to be making a violent effort to tear themselves away from the unknown force that was nailing them to the spot, in order to hurl themselves forward; but the hadji's finger made a more imperious gesture, and they recoiled slowly, following the direction that he imposed on them, and finally disappeared into the coffee-trees.

Then he turned toward the woman he had just saved. She got to her feet; not knowing what she was doing, and, incapable of sustaining herself, she let her head fall on the shoulder of her liberator. He shivered; his eyes were shining like those of a lioness who has just fought for her cubs; but their gleam was as sharp and as penetrating as on the day when it had been fixed on Leila for the first time. Leila felt her heart pierced by a strange pain—but she would have given her entire life for that instant; she would have died without a plaint!

Suddenly, the stranger uttered a dull groan, and pulled the hood of his ample marlotte over his face.

"Daughter of Farhan," he said, in a low and compressed voice, "I shall take you back to your father."

Leila did not reply, but she covered her head with her almizar, and they set forth silently.

They went for a long time in that manner; the hadji's bosom rose convulsively, but his tongue was mute and his head was bowed—and yet, if he had looked at the woman who was walking behind him meekly he might have discovered treasures of joy in the blue eyes that were shining behind the transparent gauze of the almizar.

A delightful scenery was deployed around them; a light breeze was refreshing the burning atmosphere and murmuring melodiously in the branches, carrying through the air the multiple perfumes of myrrh, jasmine, incense, cinnamon and coffee; a thousand birds were singing, hopping and fluttering among the verdant masses of foliage, the red clusters of the date-palms and the white flowers of the mimosas. Everything was sighing, embalming the air and undulating vaguely, bearing upon the heart.

The hadji finally spoke, and his voice was sweeter than the sound of the vina, sadder than the song of a bird of paradise at the moment when it expires.

"Do you understand, young woman, the embalmed breeze that is agitating your veil as it passes? It is the amorous breath of nature, which warms and perfumes the nuptial bed of all creatures. Look: green snakes are enlacing their flexible coils and embracing gently under the branches of thee acacias; turtle-doves are moaning in an excess of happiness, intoxicated by endless kisses; red grouse are calling to one another breathlessly under the cinnamon trees. Everything loves, everything unites under the sky, without fear and without remorse! I alone am rejected by that concert of amour and harmony; for me alone to love is a crime."

"Why?" said Lela, naively.

"Why?" repeated the stranger—and his tone became hoarse, as lugubrious as a death-rattle. "Don't ask me that, young woman. For pity's sake, don't ask me that. You are here, beside me, confident and tranquil, like a little bird under its mother's wing. Do you want to flee me, then, with more horror than a squirrel of the palm trees flees the murderous gaze of a snake?"

"I won't flee!" she said, in a voice that was simultaneously firm and infantile.

He threw himself at the young woman's feet with a stifled cry and embraced her knees forcefully. Then, getting to his feet, he said, impetuously: "Oh, don't speak to me in that soft voice, don't say such things to me, for the frightful sacrifice would become impossible for me—and yet, it's necessary, it's imperative that I quit you forever, that I submit to my destiny alone, that I save you from me!"

A second *why* expired on Leila's lips.

At that moment, cries became audible; they were calling "Leila! Leila!" and several men, yataghans in hand, ran toward the young woman. They were Emir Farhan and his man, who had learned from fugitive slaves about the attack on the escort and had come running to rescue the young woman they supposed to be a captive of the mountain-dwellers. They gazed with astonishment at the hadji.

The latter advanced toward the old chief.

"Emir Farhan," he said, "here is your daughter, whom I have saved from the hands of the Kobaïls; I replace her in yours, pure."

"Peace be with you!" cried the old man. "May the blessings of the prophet accompany you, O faithful Muslim!

56

Would you like my most beautiful mare and the lightest of my dromedaries? Would you like half my hills, green with odorous coffee bushes, and my most beautiful garden in the valley of Rodda, with its rose- and lilac-bushes and its jasmine arbors? All that is yours, if you wish, O saintly hadji, who has returned my unique child to me!"

"I am not a saint before the Lord," replied the stranger, in a grave and somber tone. "May Allah recompense you for your generous offers, but I cannot accept them; I have no use for the wealth of this world."

And he drew away slowly, leaving in the souls of Farhan and his men a singular impression of respect and dread. For Leila, when she no longer saw his blue mantle between the trees and could no longer hear the sound of his footfalls, it seemed that a mortal silence had succeeded the countless harmonies that had filled her heart a moment before, and that a dull and colorless veil extended over all of nature.

The days went by, and with them Leila's sadness augmented. Her eyes, often moist, shone in her sweet face like violets in a field of snow. She begged her father to withdraw the promise that he had given to Mansor, but the emir's brow became severe, and he asked whether she wanted him to break his word, like a kafir who does not believe in God, and he ordered her to prepare to be the wife of the dola, who was already her husband in the eyes of the law—for he had seen her without her veil—the following day.

The emir did not know that he was not the only one!

Leila withdrew, pale and unsteady. She plunged into the darkest shade in the garden, and wept.

She heard a rustle in the bushes, and a man dressed as a slave came to prostrate himself before her. A slight blush colored Leila's features; a smile parted her lips momentarily—but only momentarily, for it was immediately succeeded by a movement of alarm.

"Oh," murmured the stranger, "forgive me! I wanted to see you again one more time before going away forever. No, don't look at me! No, but let me hear your voice! A word, a single word, and then I'll go, and you can expel from your memory this lugubrious apparition, which will have disappeared before becoming fatal to you—but speak to me once more! Oh, you're trembling, I see; it's your good angel that is warning you. It is right; but I shall not engage you to close your ears."

"Adjem,"[1] said the young woman, in a hesitant voice, "if I'm afraid, it's for you! Alas, if they catch you here, they'll cut off your head with their yataghans, without my being able to defend you. Go away! The idea of your danger is causing me to die in advance!"

"I would have liked to finish thus," he replied, "but since you do not wish it, be tranquil; I have nothing to fear from men. The savage Kobaïls are not the only enemies that I am able to tame!" And his smile was as proud, as ironic and as sad as that of a rebel djinni. "Alas," he went on, "I'm accursed for having sought to trouble your life again, but I don't have the strength to resist. Pardon me—I love you so much!"

"I love you too," she said, placing her little hand on the stranger's shoulder.

He threw himself on that hand, which he covered with kisses and burning tears.

"Oh, woe betide you, daughter of Yemen! For pity's sake, don't pronounce that word!"

"I love you," she repeated, "but the other is marrying me tomorrow!"

The hadji leapt backwards, like a tiger; then his head slumped upon his breast.

---

1 Presumably the author's rendering of the Arabic word more usually given as *ajam*, in this instance meaning "Be quiet!"

"Marry him," he said, in a dull voice, "marry him, and send me away, for my love is a gift of Hell!"

"Yes, I want you to leave here—but you won't depart alone. Who would wipe the dust of the journey from your brow then? Who would veil your face when you sleep in the sun? Adjem; you must take me with you tomorrow."

"Do you know to whom you want to deliver yourself, poor imprudent gazelle throwing yourself foolishly into the lion's mouth? Do you know the wretch who is before you? Listen . . ."

"It's futile! It's too late. Your first gaze engraved you in my heart in ineffaceable traces. The sight of you pleases and lacerates me, plunges me into a bleak abatement and then enraptures me with ineffable transports. I don't know whether you will be deadly to me, as you say, but it's necessary that I go with you, for it is written!"

"Are you weary of living, then, young woman? So much youth and beauty sacrificed to one accursed, like me? No! I cannot!"

She took a short, light stiletto from her belt, a frail and delicate ornament that could have shone in her hair if necessary, like a great golden needle with a head of turquoise and onyx.

"Do you believe that a woman's hand can weigh enough upon this blade to make it reach her heart? You will abduct me tomorrow, or this dagger will have touched me before Mansor. Do you not have a mare as rapid as a mountain eagle?"

"Yes."

"Well, be ready with it near this garden; sound a trumpet to warn me of your arrival. In the midst of the tumult of the celebration, when my companions prepare to place me on the bridal camel to take me to Sana, I'll escape from the nuptial cortege; I'll flee through the gardens, which won't be guarded, and I'll be yours! No response: go quickly, for the eunuchs are about to make their evening round. Adieu! Until tomorrow!"

She had disappeared.

The hadji pressed his breast forcefully with both hands.

"Yes, it was written!" he said.

The next day, at dawn, numerous horsemen arrived at the country house of Emir Farhan Nothing could be seen in the distance along the road but the sheiks of Téhama clad in long abas as white as camphor, djiabalys in broad striped chemises, magnificent caftans, and large turbans of undulating muslin. There was a continuous file of horses, camels and litters, between the curtains of which heads veiled by embroidered almizars appeared.

All her companions are clustered around the beautiful bride. They have already brought her from the bath; they have ornamented her neck with brilliant golden chains, and her head with a rich turban, from which bandlets of silver gauze are suspended; they attach balls of ruby and opal to her ears and pass gold circlets around her slender arms and legs; they paint her nails with carmine and henna, blacken her eyelids with powered kohl and perfume her beautiful hair with benzoin and civette. She allows them to decorate her like the marble statue of some divinity, less white and less cold than her. All of her blood has flowed back to her heart; but if some slight noise rises up—the cry of a samarmog perched in the branches of a sycamore, the whinny of a mare, or the whistle of a camel-driver summoning his dromedaries—she shivers and her pale cheeks are suddenly inflamed by a red tint, like clouds at sunset.

She listened in vain; the trumpet had not projected its clear and prolonged voice through the noise of the fête. She went up to the high terrace and gazed into the distance, with a gaze as piercing as that of a swallow searching for her stolen chicks; but the vale was silent and deserted; nothing whitened in the sunlight between the nopals and the fig-trees.

Then she slipped her dagger, which she had hidden in a jasmine, into her bosom and went down toward her companions, who led her away, mute and docile, into the courtyard, where a camel was waiting, caparisoned with bright carpets, its head ornamented with floating ostrich plumes. Its neck enlaced by garlands of flowers. The bride was seated on the camel and the joyful caravan set forth for Sana to the song of hautboys, tambours and cymbals.

Leila took once again, with her cortege, the route that she had traveled with another company. She saw again the hills covered with coffee-trees and the boscage were the birds were singing amorously; and when she passed close to the palm trees from which he had emerged in order to save her from the Kobaïls, a bitter regret seized her heart.

Why had it happened? Everything would be finished now! The noisy marriage feast would be celebrated in the emir's palace, and when evening came, after the young women had danced to the tambours and sung the praises of the bride, after everyone had begged Allah and his prophet Mohammed to bless the union of Mansor and Leila, to give their sons the courage of Antar and the wealth of Karoun, and their daughters the beauty and virtue of Aïesha, and to preserve the two spouses from the evil spells of enchanters and the gaze of the evil eye, the assembly would conduct the married couple to the nuptial chamber and leave them alone there.

The men would wait for a long time in the banqueting hall for the husband to come to announce his victory to the relatives and friends; the women would wait in the harem for the young bride to come and join them, confused and blushing, to pass the rest of the mysterious night among them.

No one appeared; they listened; a mortal silence reigned in the spouses' apartment. They called out, but obtained no response.

Anxiety took hold of all the witnesses; superstitious terrors agitated minds. People ran to fetch the father of the bride, who, in accordance with custom, had drawn away during the supreme hour of his daughter's virginity. He seized a cornelian consecrated by the talismanic names of protective angels and, opening the curtains that separated the fatal chamber from the next room, he hurled himself into it, his heart constricted by suspense and anguish.

By the red radiance of the torch he saw the bed, empty and in order. A little further away, a confused mass lay on the floor. He approached; it was the dola Mansor.

Leila had disappeared,

Farhan cried out; everyone cane running; Mansor was lifted up. He was only unconscious and bore no trace of any wound.

When he came round, nothing could be obtained from him but vague and incoherent words, imprinted with a profound terror; his reason had departed forever.

The moon is asleep over the great desert of Djilof.

Under a solitary dune that rises in the plain, the rim of a somber cavern opens; one of Phingary's rays slides through the nopal and basilics that block the mouth of the lair and extends far enough into the depths to repose upon two immobile but living objects. Is that a lion lying on dry palm leaves with his royal companion? No, it is a pilgrim of Mecca who is hiding his face under the folds of his marlotte. It is a young woman brilliant with the jewels of a bride.

Is that lair of wild beasts of the desert, then, the palace in which the wedding of the daughter of an emir will be completed?

"Why are you remaining silent, my beloved?" murmurs the virgin of Yemen. "Since we have seen the domes of my natal city disappear, you have been as bleak and silent as an angel of tombs; you have not addressed a word to me to reassure my uncertain soul."

"How could I have words of consolation on my lips, when the thoughts of my heart prophesy mourning and death?"

"Is that my recompense, ingrate? If you're pursued by a regret, it's that of having snatched me from the death that I was about to give myself; the misfortune that your thought prophesy is the tedium of being burdened with a poor girl whose aspect importunes you."

"Leila, Leila, I love you more than the blessed, whom I shall never see, love their divine houris. I would have given my share of paradise for one of your kisses, when I had one for which to hope."

Leila had only listened to the first part of his statement. She tipped back her pretty head on the stranger's knees, and her little hands seized the falling creases of his hood.

"Don't hide your face thus, like an Imam when he comes to the tent to pray on Friday. Look at me with your mad eyes."

"Oh," stammered the terrified hadji, "child, do you want to take a scorpion in your soft hand, to play with a sharp damascene blade?"

But she had already uncovered the hadji's pale face, and her hands, crossed over the stranger's nape, drew his face toward hers.

The stranger's reason was troubled; he threw his arms around the young woman, and in their long ecstasy his gaze devoured her with all their flames. Their cheeks touched, their mouths united, quivering; then he lifted his wild gaze again in order to contemplate her anew. Leila sometimes felt sparks springing forth in her arteries and setting fire to her entire body, their sharp darts starring in all directions, sometimes a heavy cold gripping her heart like an icy hand; sometimes she was agitated, prey to an extraordinary delirium, sometimes she fell back, dying and annihilated.

He got up abruptly, passing his hand over his brow like a man returning to his senses after an agitated dream. Leila was sitting on the palm leaves; her head fell back, exhausted, against the wall of the grotto; her lips were discolored, and the vivacity of her beautiful eyes, ringed by black circles, was seen to fade away gradually.

He uttered a cry, a cry so terrible and superhuman that wandering lions responded to it in the distance with fearful roars, and, falling full length, he rolled at Leila's feet, biting the earth and tearing it with his fingernails.

"I've killed her!" he roared. "I've killed her! The prediction is accomplished! It was written! Malediction upon the angel who has written it in the iron book! Malediction upon the prophet and his race! Malediction upon me!"

Leila raised her languid head.

"What's the matter with you, my husband?" she said to him. "You don't know what I'm experiencing; my heart is going away; but why do you say that it's you? Why are you blaspheming the holy name of the prophet?"

"Listen!" he cried. "I am the enchanter Il Haboul;[1] versed in the sciences that reveal to the physicist the most hidden secrets of creation and submit it to the occult forces of nature, I succeeded in giving my gaze the irresistible power of fascination. I used it to seduce the wife of a descendant of the prophet!"

A profound sigh interrupted him; Leila's head slumped on to her breast. "I seduced her," he cried, in a heart-rending voice, "but I didn't love her."

Leila raised her eyes toward him again.

---

1 Il Haboul is a character in one of the continuations of Galland's *Mille-et-une nuits,* but the name had also been employed by the mystic proto-Romantic Jacques Cazotte.

"The outraged Emir knew my crime; he could not kill me, but he cursed me. 'Go,' he said to me, 'your gaze, which fascinates hearts, will not lose its fatal power. You can still make yourself loved, but you will give death when you love. Go, take with you the evil eye!'

"I was returning from a pilgrimage to Mecca, undertaken in order to try to obtain mercy from the prophet, when I saw you for the first time. And I've killed you! I've killed you! You're going to expire before my eyes, and your last thought will be a thought of horror for me, for the monster that has withered your youth, who has devoured your life, like a hideous vampire!"

"Come here," said Leila, in a faint voice.

He dragged himself to her on his knees.

"Have you ever loved anyone but me?"

"No."

She put her enfeebled arms around his neck.

"I forgive you, friend. You can see that I'm not suffering; it's a very mild death. I don't regret dying thus. Isn't it better to die young than to go slowly with the years, to feel love ebbing away slowly from a heart chilled by age? I've loved you; I've been happy, I have no complaint now. I'm only sad because of you, for you'll be unhappy when I am no more."

He burst into sobs, bathing her with tears, and clasping her to his bosom, with anguish, as if to dispute her with the angel of death.

She spoke to him thus for the rest of the night, more gently and more tenderly as she felt the flame of life dying within her by degrees; and when the dawn appeared she closed her eyes, collapsed in her lover's arms, and her soul departed with the first rays of sunlight.

He gazed at her for some time in silence; then, suddenly, uttering a discordant and insensate burst of laughter, he cried: "Ah! Ah! Imbecile emir, you forgot the best of your vengeance.

You did not think of the means to prevent me from following her!"

And, drawing his dagger, he plunged it to the hilt into his heart.

A few days later, a desert Arab, having chanced to go into the cavern, discovered the bodies of the two lovers, still holding one another in an embrace. Transported by avaricious joy at the sight of the young woman's rich ornaments, he was about to bear a sacrilegious hand to her remains when a cry of terror escaped him. He had thought that he had seen the other cadaver gazing at him with fixed and flamboyant eyes. He withdrew, tottering, seized by a strange vertigo.

The evil eye had conserved its power, even in death.

FAUST

by Alphonse Brot

I

IN the year 1420, at the extremity of the theater of Berlin there was a promenade mentioned by the chronicles of the era, which now only exists in the memoirs of a few German historiographers or alchemists. That promenade was nearly a quarter of a mile long and just as wide; it was there that amorous couples wandered during the intervals, in order to escape profane gazes, as curious as indifferent.

On one beautiful evening in April, when the air was as sweet as a young girl's breath, the blue mantle of the sky was strewn with gold spangles, and beautiful red tints, surging forth in the distance, illuminated the horizon, reminiscent of the meditative gaze of an ardent chariot drawing the divine spirit in limitless space, instead of raising their gaze to contemplate the munificence of the Eternal in his works, the citizens of Berlin, by virtue of a rather ordinary habit, had lowered them on leaving the spectacle toward the sign of the one-eyed horse that decorated the tavern of Master Martin, and had allowed all their thoughts to be obstructed by the honest taverner's casks and beer.

"*Demonio! Demonio!*" cried a privy councilor, struggling in the midst of a dozen pots of ale, which he had emptied during the evening. "*Demonio! Demonio!*" Then he accompanied those strange words with gesticulations that became so unfavorable to his purse that, when it was necessary for him to pay, he did not have enough money.

Further away, at an oak table, were two Germans; after having enjoyed their mistresses, they were enjoying the casks.

It is not our intention here to give an exact account of the pots of beer, barrels and Berliners gathered in Master Martin's tavern; we shall go peacefully to sit down with the two gentlemen placed at the furthest extremity of the counter.

"Yes, Doctor, I've arrived at no longer understanding it; there are several opposed natures in me, a fire that undermines me, a hurricane that stimulates it and a torrent that quenches it. I desire, but when I possess, I become cold again. Doctor, if you knew what I contain of the immoderate, the bizarre, the ardent, the satanic and the divine, your eyes, instead of passing over me placidly, would spring out of their orbits! I am a summary of grandeur and baseness, idealism and materialism. The universe is too narrow for me, and yet its immensity crushes me; the air is not heavy enough to nail me to the earth, and yet I am choking under its miasmas; the heavens, those cataracts of the air, only give me a feeble idea of the Creator, and yet, seeing that my gaze only measures a meager span, I do not know what to think; in my chagrin I am scornful of everything that is, and at the same time I establish my altars everywhere; I kneel before everything and I sweat admiration through all my pores!"

"Ha ha ha," sniggered the man clad in red with the long vigorous face who was placed before the student.

The latter continued: "Doctor, for two months you have been directing me, I had a soul; you have remade it for me; I had sensations, you have quintupled them; I had passions, you have given them a voice; now I'm in love, what do you reserve for that?"

"Ha ha ha!" grunted the stranger, twisting his mouth.

"If you cannot satisfy it," added the student, "at least teach me a spell that will cure me of it, for it is not only a single object that I love; my passion embraces everything. I am like a universal echo; everything resounds within me: the arts, the sciences, crimes and virtues. If I go to spectacles, my forehead, which contains the lava of a volcano, ignites; my eyes sparkle, my breast swells, I'm no longer myself. My existence is bound to everything that surrounds me. A thousandth part of the great whole that lives and moves, I would like to be that whole, with its thoughts, its heartbeats, its admiration, its stamping feet, its convulsive hands. I would like to improvise in a low voice what the author is going to say, to know what inflection to give to the actor's voice, to analyze the entrails of the audience. What do I know? Jealous of everything that is called sensation, I would like to be, by myself, the author, the actors and the spectators; I would like to be the torches that illuminate them, the echoes that repeat them, the theater that embraces them, the city that contains the theater, the world that contains the city, God, who contains everything!

"Well, Doctor, am I still an ordinary young man? Doctor, if I had not studied medicine for some time and it had not demonstrated to me perfectly that no one can have more than one soul, I could almost believe that I had received one for each of my passions."

The younger man, the one placed at the corner of the table, appeared to be twenty-five years of age at the most. His features, although handsome, did not have the antique regularity that fatigues and importunes; his pale physiognomy bore the seal of strangeness that excites so forcefully nowadays, and a few wrinkles that furrowed the young man's forehead indicated that, for want of years, mental toil or the abuse of pleasures had furrowed it prematurely. Add to that a slender stature, an elegantly frail body, blue eyes, and you will have a living portrait of the enthusiastic student.

As for his drinking companion, he was one of a kind, and either by virtue of art or fascination, he could not be analyzed. Everything about him was clad in strangeness, without it being possible to take account of him. He did not appear to be German, but his coat, cut in the latest fashion, would have enabled him to pass for a Berliner. His language, although it was only comprised by exclamations and sniggers, was horribly intelligible for everyone. As for his complexion, perhaps the reflections of the lamplight gave it that nuance, but it was green-tinted, and without a few colors that animated it, one might have thought him a death's-head articulated on living shoulders, which a miraculous calm preserved from putrefaction.

Eleven o'clock chimed; the student shuddered on his bench, as if the timbre of the bell had communicated an electric commotion to his table.

"Pardon me, Doctor, but that movement escaped me involuntarily. A child, I am only in my first amour, and I believe that the beloved—who, in order to summon me to the rendezvous, is communicating her voice to that clock—is making a greater impression on me than I have ever felt, or ever will, even when the voice of God summons my soul to his throne of azure and radiance . . ."

The green-tinted face of his companion now took on an expression of frightful mockery.

"Yes, Doctor," the student continued, "the voice of that clock is so powerful that but for my fear I would say to it: 'O voice, what are you, then, to disrupt my soul, to labor therein and break my desires as if with a plowshare, to communicate to a single passion more existence than twenty others would demand? Avid a little while ago for everything—science, arts and virtues—envious of the power of the universal creator; I now sense all of that extinguishing. Have pity on me, Doctor; like the fallen angel, I am tumbling from Heaven!"

"Ha ha ha!" replied the man with the green face.

"I am very unworthy! To sacrifice everything that is beautiful to the love of a woman! But you know that amour kills all the arts!"

"Or the arts kill amour!" said his companion.

"Malediction!" cried the young man, his eyes swollen, his face taut and the veins bulging on his forehead. "You have just pronounced infernal words, Doctor!"

And they both left.

When they were outside, Master Martin, approaching a man who had lost his wife at piquet, said to him: "Who are those two men? I've forgotten their names."

"One, the younger, answers to the name of Herr Faust."

"And his companion?"

"His companion has only been living in Berlin for three months; as for his name, no one knows it."

"If that man were yet to be baptized," said the tavern-keeper, "one might call him Satan."

And the conservation stopped there.

For a quarter of an hour, a young man had been walking in the avenue that ran alongside the theater, and that young man was our friend from the tavern, the guest of Master Martin, Herr Faust.

You know that the twenty-four hours that separate the condemnation of a criminal from his execution last for years; well, the instants that separated Faust from his rendezvous seemed even longer to him. In his amorous rage, I believe that he would have given a week to age by a second, a year of joy to be older by a minute, and yet his life was precious to him, to a man who spent his evenings in scientific works, in future works of genius.

A few moments later a young woman was trembling beside him. She was dressed in black, as if she wanted to wear mourning in advance for the arts and works that her friend would doubtless sacrifice for her.

"Alice, Alice," said Faust, clutching her in his arms as if in an iron vice; "Alice," Faust cried to her, reddening with his first kisses the chaste forehead of the young woman; "Alice," Faust cried to her, devouring her amorously, analyzing her perfections one by one; "Alice," Faust cried to her after deflowering her with his gaze! His beloved had no voice, for scarcely had she parted her lips to respond than he closed them with countless caresses.

"Do you love me?" he said to her, finally.

Alice drew away, chagrined, and shedding abundant tears. Faust contemplated that spectacle with delight.

"Alice, do you want to kill us?" he added, his eyes charged with passion and felicity. "Alice, we are exhausting in a few minutes the happiness of two long existences, do you want to kill us?"

Alice nodded her head affirmatively and threw herself into his arms.

Alas, thought Faust, *to die thus would be beautiful, but the sciences, but the arts . . .* Aloud, he said: "Alice, you love me amorously; I'm content with you!"

There was an interval of silence then. The young woman trembled and hid her head in the bosom of Faust—who, similar to the spirit of Evil, looked down at her from his full height and strove, by virtue of pride, to cool the internal volcanic fire that was consuming him.

However, in spite of his efforts, amour prevailed.

"I am entirely yours, and only yours," Faust murmured, clasping Alice convulsively.

"Only mine?" she said.

Yours alone, Alice, yours alone!"

She continued: "So, to all those brilliant dreams that men form, those dreams of honor and wealth, you prefer me?"

"Are you not above all that?" responded Faust, deliriously.

"So," she added, in an infantile tone, "those distant voyages of which you spoke to me, those voyages over the Ocean, the depths of which you wanted to fathom, you prefer me to all of them?"

"Yes," murmured Faust, in a less affable voice.

"So, if you learn to sculpt marble, it will only be to reproduce me therein; if you pick up paint-brushes, it will only be to give me an endless existence on canvas?"

"Yes, yes," Faust pronounced, tremulously.

"If you lift the veil that weighs upon the sciences, upon alchemy, upon necromancy, upon medicine, theology and jurisprudence, you will bring everything back to me alone?"

"Alice, what are you asking me?"

"Faust, I love you above all things; I want to be loved in the same way. That you might pass your time elsewhere than by my side would seem a Hell to me; I would be envious of the marble that your chisel would fashion, the paintings that your hand would produce, the writings that your imagination would dictate. Faust, Faust, I need for myself alone as much amour as you accord to all the sciences."

"Well, so be it!" cried Faust, whose voice had taken on an ironic and funereal accent. "So be it; I shall do nothing if you are not beside me. You shall be my inspirational demon; you shall follow me to the theater, in my excursions, into the woods, over the sea; you shall follow me in my thoughts, in my dreams; you shall even follow me to our public lectures, into our amphitheaters of medicine; you shall be beside me when I study the needs of living nature on dead nature; in short, you will never quit me!"

"God be praised!" murmured the young woman.

Faust, his gaze scintillating and baleful, drew her to his heart, and after having lavished on her everything that the truest passion can invent, after having spoken the most ardent words that can be suspended from the lips of a beloved lover; after having contemplated her with all the frenzy of a first amour, Herr Faust, his gaze still scintillating and baleful, threw his hands around Alice's beautiful neck as if to play with her hair, and strangled her.

"The arts kill amour," said a voice.

"Yes," replied Faust, firmly; then he added: "A new sensation for a crime is still a great deal!"

"Ha ha ha," sniggered the same voice, while Faust carried the cadaver of the young woman to his home.

II

Thirty-one years after Alice's death, on a winter evening in 1451, the entire city of Berlin, illuminated, was swimming in an atmosphere of clarity that made a nebulous sky stand out more. That day was the anniversary of the birth of the emperor of Germany, Frederick III,[1] so the nobility of the land had been invited to a celebration that the young Duke of Alberg, one of the princes of the blood, was hosting. No solemnity had ever been more extraordinary, according to contemporary poets; all the marvels of art, all the refinements of pleasure, had arranged a rendezvous there; immense drawing rooms,

---

1 The Holy Roman Emperor Frederick III (1415-1493) was not crowned until 1452, but he was already King of Germany, having been elected in 1440, as Frederick IV. The historical Johann Faust, on whom the legendary figure featured in the chapbook of 1587 is alleged by some commentators to be based, was not born until 1480, but the Johann Faust who assisted Johann Gutenberg in the invention of printing was certainly alive in 1451, a year after the first press apparently went into use; he lived until 1466. The other characters named in the story are entirely fictitious.

constructed by the famous architect Sorretius, resounded under the feet of a thousand elegant dancers, under the echoes of the rarest instruments, under the turbulent gaiety of innumerable guests, under a deluge of happiness.

While pleasure, with its cries, with its flowers, with its resonances of joy inundated one part of Berlin, at the sinister extremity of the city, on a camp-bed faintly illuminated by a lamp, there was a man whose bones jutted from his emaciated face; the austerity of his features and the pallor of his hollow and flaccid cheeks proved that serious labors had worn away his body, perhaps even his soul.

The furniture of the mansard into which we have been transported was no less bizarre than the man himself. To disguise the absence of leather on the walls they had been charged with several layers of dark paint, with the result that, without a few rays of daylight that entered the room via a narrow and dirty skylight, one might have believed oneself to be in the hold of a ship. In the foreground were several tables laden with compasses, set-squares, world maps and instruments of mathematics and physics; further away one distinguished a doctor's medical bag, scalpels, pincers and bone-saws; even further away, on the floor near a human femur, lay a stuffed owl; to one side was a pitcher of water and a Hebrew manuscript of the Holy Bible; on a hunk of brown bread was the partly-dissected head of a horse, and nearby, naïve sculptures by Bendocci the Florentine and a charming Medieval painting representing Mary Magdalen in tears.

In the background, through the shreds of a tapestry the color of fire, a few armfuls of straw scattered in a heap on the floor proved that the master's bed was reduced, at the most, to a poor mattress.

However, a great idea penetrated the apparent disorder of that environment, that bizarre mixture, that bitter derision of sciences and arts; and that idea translated into an intelligible language the superiority of man over all the marvels of creation; the idea in question elevated to the height of God that same man who—a creature become a creator and a God in his turn—in his pride, did not even touch with his foot his works, more durable than him.

Facing the skylight, on an oak sideboard—which, if necessary, served as a table—alongside several mathematical instruments, were wooden boxes bristling with innumerable little bars of lead; further away, in a vase, was a thick black compound.

Although that apparatus offered nothing solemn, and nothing even curious, it extracted such frequent exclamations from the master of the camp-bed that one might have taken him for the demoniac of the Gospel.

"To work, to work!" he cried, his eyes scintillating. "A few more minutes and what you have created will make the tour of the world and traverse the centuries.

"To work, to work! Exhaust all that you have received of genius, all that you have received of soul, all that you have received of science! What does genius matter when its strong sap does not overflow? What does the soul matter, when it is not communicated? What do the sciences matter when they are not multiplied tenfold?

"To work, to work, ardent worker! God has constructed the world; you who call yourself his equal, make him envious; construct in your turn, even if your frail offspring breaks like glass, or your brain will languish, exhausted henceforth!"

Then the man fell silent, and his gaze was illuminated again; his respiration became more difficult, his cranium was on fire; he trued to walk, but inspiration gripped him so forcefully that he could not; in the end, breathless and exhausted, but still struggling victoriously with his genius, which obsessed him, he cried:

"I have found what I sought!"

In fact, Doctor Faust had just discovered the printing press.

That sensation, still new for him, was so powerful that he fell backwards, unconscious.

A few minutes later, the man of genius was contemplating proudly a painting of a woman placed next to his bed, and he said to it: "Have I not told you that you would follow me everywhere, in my dreams, in my courses, in my creations?"

That portrait of a woman was of Alice, strangled thirty-one years before. In order to keep his promise, Herr Faust, ready to throw the cadaver to the worms, had extracted the eyes; then his satanic hand had nailed them to the painting that was to eternalize the poor young woman.

"Alas, I loved you very much," he continued; and his voice lost its harshness, his gaze its flame. "I loved you, but why, feeble creature, did Heaven make you with thoughts that did not befit a woman? Why did it give you an immeasurable soul, enough amour to consume the life of a man in its grip, and enough egotism to bring everything back to you alone? Poor Alice; your possession would have been paradise for the rest of the world; why did your amour want to settle upon the only man who possessed the strength to annihilate it? Why, Alice, did you demand more idolatry for yourself alone than I accorded to the arts, the sciences and to God himself?"

At this point a distinct noise became audible on the staircase. That noise, which resembled footsteps, grew louder, and then a light hand rapped on the doctor's door. The latter remained motionless with amazement for a moment. In fact, in the six months that he had resided in the house, no one had yet entered his abode.

A female voice murmured: "Herr Faust, are you there?"

And that voice made Faust tremble; it had been almost identical to that of a young woman he had once loved ardently. Nevertheless, he opened the door.

Juana came in with a casual step, and without giving the doctor time to greet her, she slammed the door shut.

You might perhaps think that the strange furniture of that hovel, which she was seeing for the first time, would cause her some fear, or even some surprise, but she looked at everything with insouciant eyes.

What astonished Faust was seeing the young woman, after having contemplated the stuffed owl for some time, throwing it to the floor and laughing like a madwoman—but what surprised him even more was hearing her translating the Holy Bible into pure German.

"Sire," she said to him then, pointing her finger at the penitent Magdalen, "you have there one of the finest creations of Aventorius; that painting is worth at least ten thousand thalers."

"How can you know all that?" murmured Faust.

Without paying any heed to the stupor imprinted on the doctor's face, the young woman went on: "Maestro, I see that everything that I have been told about you is true; you are a scholar." Then she took a compass and a world map, considered them with attention, and added: "Do you know what a beautiful thing astronomy is? To force the sky to open its portals of light and gold; the stars to teach us their march, their influence; the planets their immobility; the sun the time of its revolution on its axis; God, the mystery of his works . . ."

Submissive to the power of Juana, Faust already saw his discovery of the printing press as pitiful, and was perhaps thinking of annihilating it. Juana took him by the hand.

"After all, Doctor, however beautiful astronomy is, is it not a theft that we commit on the divinity? So, more powerful than us, the divinity lets us wander in the sky, that limitless space; we want to follow the stars in their courses, but we draw away from their progress; we give them an influence, which perhaps they don't have; we believe the sun to be an inhabited globe of fire, but perhaps the sun is only the inferno and its turbulence; we believe that the earth doesn't rotate, but why shouldn't it be mobile?"

"Who are you, then, young woman, who know science and debase it," exclaimed Faust, "who talk about medicine and astronomy, who know Hebrew, who sets a price on the painting of Aventorius—in sum, you who build and destroy?"

"Sire," she replied, laughing, "my name is Juana, and I'm a Bohémienne."[1]

"You're scarcely twenty years old, Juana, and yet you're more knowledgeable than a woman would be if she spent two centuries on earth."

"Doctor, I'm scornful of the sciences and the arts; that's why I've studied them."

"I'd give twenty years of my life to comprehend that woman," Faust murmured, progressing from surprise to surprise.

As for Juana, she looked at everything, touched everything and then laughed loudly, saying; "The doctor only knows this?"

Faust was tempted momentarily to smash her skull with the half-dissected horse's head, but Juana was so beautiful that he spared her. He thought privately: *I hate this woman*; and a few minutes later, his soul fascinated, he said: "What do you want from me, my charming Juana?"

"Nothing, Doctor."

Faust became thoughtful again. The young woman continued to overturn the instruments scattered on the table.

She finally broke the silence: "Maestro, are you not a sorcerer?"

"I've studied necromancy a little," the doctor replied.

____

1 I have left the term "Bohémienne" as it is rendered in the original; it is presumably intended to imply that Juana belongs to the Romani people, whose presence in Germany was first recorded in the 15th century, rather than a subject of the kingdom of Bohemia, although a woman of the time would certainly not have used it in that sense.

"Are you not an architect?" she continued.

"I've occupied myself with architecture during my voyages," he replied again.

"Are you not a naturalist, an antiquary, a physicist, a mythographer, a jurisconsultant and a theologian?"

"Yes," murmured Faust, confused.

"There only remains, then," she went on, laughing, "one more thing to know, and that is there most curious of all; that thing, Doctor, is amour."

"Amour!" said Faust, in a changed voice. "In fact, I once interrupted the study of that science."

"Look," Juana continued, "see how Alice's eyes sparkle!"

"Alice! How do you know her name?"

There was then a long interval of silence; the Bohémienne had crossed the space that separated her from the painting with the human eyes, and was contemplating it with all the avidity of a child. As for Herr Faust, placed in his immense wooden armchair, his gaze frantic and his cheeks on fire, he seemed to be meditating an infernal work. The combat that he was delivering internally must have been of a strange nature, for the veins in his neck were visibly blue-tinted, the air that penetrated his lungs was roaring like the breath of a tempest, and his bones were creaking over his breast.

Finally, in that struggle in which the love of the sciences, that avidity to know everything, disputed Faust's heart with tender and carnal love, Juana prevailed. Weeping with shame, despair and frenetic passion, he fell at the Bohémienne's feet; she gazed at him, laughing like a lunatic.

The doctor opened his mouth, and the young woman's noisy gaiety was immediately extinguished.

"Juana, I would not put myself at anyone's knees for an eternity of happiness, even if God ordered me to do it with his powerful voice. Juana, I would not kiss the feet of a woman for the empire of the earth, for that of the seas, and for that of the heavens! Juana, what God and Satan could not have obtained from me, you have obtained! Juana, thirty years ago I was in love, but Alice wanted me to prefer her to the arts, to the sciences, to everything, and I choked her. Understand, then, the immense amour that I bring to you, since I prefer you to everything."

The young woman lowered her eyes innocently, and Faust took possession of one of her hands, covering it with caresses.

"Juana, Juana, I will love you with an amour that will put that of other men to shame, an amour that will make God envious!"

Juana's bosom swelled with sighs.

Faust, still on his knees, drew nearer.

"Juana, you will be the goal of my thoughts; if you wish, I'll abandon my work for you, I'll break my instruments and I'll annihilate my creations!"

"I don't believe it," the young woman replied, smiling.

"See, then!" cried Faust; and with a fatal hand he overturned and destroyed everything that charged his tables; already, he was about to destroy his latest masterpiece . . .

"Enough!" said the Bohémienne, stopping him. "Let the centuries to come at least conserve that creation of your genius."

"No, no, let everything that comes from me die, except my ardent amour!"

"And what do you want me to do with it," replied Juana, "since I don't love you?" And she accompanied those words with strange laughter. A red-hot iron bar, so to speak, traversed Faust's head.

"She doesn't love me!" he cried, bearing his hideous gaze over everything that surrounded him. Then he added: "I will constrain you to love me, Juana. Tremble! I know the occult sciences, I shall have recourse to them! Tremble! I conserve manuscripts of sorcery, I shall delve into them! Tremble! You shall not have made me abandon my work to satisfy your coquetry! At whatever cost, I will possess you entirely; if God will not aid me, Satan, I invoke you!"

"Another already possesses me, Doctor. Now, *au revoir*," said Juana, throwing him by way of an adieu a burst of ironic laughter.

"*Au revoir*," Faust responded, closing his door again.

"Ha ha ha!" pronounced a resounding voice.

III

The ancient hospice of Sainte-Marie, of which nothing remains today, was then situated in the center of the city of Berlin.

Although the building had been constructed without any elevated architectural thought, if it still existed, as a monument it would put to shame all that Berlin has of masterpieces. Firstly, the hospice of Sainte-Marie was not crushed by narrow streets intersecting to infinity, but built of paltry appearance only asking to collapse. Secondly, nothing on the square that served it as a pedestal disharmonized it. You know what silence descends into the heart from the cupolas of our churches; well, the same majesty surrounded that edifice; there was no clamor of drunkards, no rumbling of carriages, no whinnying of horses around it, as if Berlin did not want a joy that death could so easily stifle. It was, therefore, with gratitude, hands joined, that people came from neighboring cities to admire the beautiful architecture of Sante-Marie. You know that an artist would spend time ecstasizing over the masculine beauties of the cathedrals of Reims or Notre-Dame; well, the hospice of Berlin fascinated to the same degree; hours or days were spent in contemplation before its severely colored façade; its slightest details and its boldest conceptions were adored while kneeling. The columns, colonnettes, entailed ogives, triumphal arches, figurines and bas-reliefs were all solemn and grandiose; everything exhaled an odor of the Middle Ages.

Eight o'clock in the morning had just chimed; in a few more minutes the cold hall of the amphitheater of Sante-Marie, with its gray walls, its parquet of black stone slabs and its semicircular steps would fill up with curiosity-seekers and students. A surgeon came to announce that the autopsy demonstration would take place at nine o'clock; that news excited violent murmurs.

However, the chief physician of the hospice, Herr Faust, had been in the amphitheater for some time. On seeing him pacing back and forth in that somber enclosure, and hearing the noisy sighs emitted by his breast, it was easy to understand that something unusual was happening within him.

The door at the back opened; the man with the green face who had been drinking in Master Martin's tavern twenty-one years before came in; the doctor received him with open arms.

"Have you not been waiting for me impatiently, Herr Faust?" said the man whose name was unknown.

Faust allowed a gesture of astonishment to escape.

"You see, Doctor, there is a line in your face whose alteration I alone can comprehend. Since a certain apparition you have suffered greatly. Don't interrupt me. Now, give me your hand. You have need of a physician, my dear Faust, but not a physician who might study, analyze and stitch bodily wounds; the malady is elsewhere. The immoderate love of the arts, the desire to know everything, to fathom everything, has killed you mentally; universal science has developed another soul in you, that soul has other needs, other passions; those passions speak to you, and you cannot satisfy them. Do you know what you need at present, Doctor? It's the enjoyment of everything."

Faust nodded his head.

"But what do you expect? Your greatest folly is to have commenced where the rest of men finish. Tell me, what good would it have done me to enable you to love a woman when you were young and handsome? You preferred set-squares, world maps and stuffed owls; and then, when she tried to make you abandon such futilities, you strangled her."

"Who told you that I strangled her?" Faust interjected.

The man with the green face went on, placidly: "A woman violated by death! By Hell, that isn't a game, after all! But what is unreasonable is that now you're ugly, decrepit and valetudinarian; now that you have skin as jaundiced and wrinkled as old parchment, and you cause disgust, you reject science and want amour."

"Who told you that?" Faust interjected, again.

His companion continued: "To be sure, Juana is a beautiful child, a novice heart; she has only given herself as yet to a simpleton. Juana contains more amour than your fibrous heart; she alone can reheat your blood, give you life again, remake your sensations, rebuild centuries of felicity for you!"

"Mercy, mercy!" cried Faust. Then, violently seizing the arm of the man with the green face, he added: "Do you know that I have sworn that she will belong to me?"

"My dear, Juana doesn't love you!" the other replied, laughing.

Faust strode back and forth in the hall; his mouth was foaming, his eyes sparkling and his voice blaspheming.

As for his companion, his face was suddenly striped with several colors; his jet-black coat became red, his body grew by half a foot, his gaze took on an expression of triumph, and he sniggered in a frightful fashion.

"Why are you laughing?" said Faust, turning round.

"Because Juana doesn't love you, and yet you'll possess her within the week."

"A week!" repeated Faust. "What derision!" Then, surprised by the other's change of costume, he added: "When you arrived here, it seems to me, you were dressed in black?"

Noisy acclamations, like the creaking of several doors that someone was trying to break down, were heard then. Blood rose to the doctor's face; his entire body was trembling with anger, but he contained himself.

"Would you like me to make the walls of Sainte-Marie collapse on your students?" said the man dressed in red, suddenly.

"Let them struggle at their leisure against the doors and the bolts," Faust replied.

"Would you like me to steal the electricity from the clouds and strike your accursed students with lightning?"

"Can you, who command lightning to strike and walls to collapse, not make Juana love me?"

"Have I not told you that you'll possess her within the week?"

"Oh, by the fever that's consuming me and desiccating me, don't talk to me in that way! You don't know, then, what the words you're pronouncing signify? You don't know that there's more than life at stake for me, that there's my felicity on earth and in Heaven?"

"You shall possess Juana, Doctor."

Faust drew nearer to him then, looked at him with avid eyes, then gripped his hand convulsively and murmured: "You must be very infamous to say such things to me seriously, or you'll have to swallow your words." Then drawing him to the window, he added: "Do you see through these dirty windows the sky resplendent with radiance and azure? Except for God, what being has furrowed this world with vapor? Well, what if I told you that, with the aid of insufflation, I can force the air to carry me, and the winds to serve me as wings? You would recoil in astonishment, you would admire me, wouldn't you? For myself, I look at myself pityingly, for if I wanted to surpass, in the waves of the heavens, the limit that a superior intelligence has fixed for me, lacking breath, I would suffocate.

"It is the same with Juana; her body, which I could possess, is the portion of air that obeys me; but her soul and her amour are the higher regions that, placed between the sky and my human will, forbid me to go any further. It isn't Juana's body, with its thousand perfections, that I desire so ardently to possess, but the soul that inhabits her body; it isn't her lips that I want to press, her hair that I want to inundate me, and her breath, a pure essence, whose perfume I want to savor, but the will that gives them to me, the passion that purifies that gift!"

"Juana will love you amorously, I tell you."

New cries made themselves heard then; the immense arches of the Hôpital Sainte-Marie were agitated under the stamping feet and the redoubled cries of the students, who, having finally broken through the doors of the amphitheater, were flooding into the autopsy hall and then, silently, placing themselves on the steps destined for them.

The man with the green face opened the door and almost went out.

"Remember that Juana must love me," Faust said to him.

"Yes, Doctor, but it will be on condition that you avenge yourself for the scorn that she has shown you."

"Ah! I sensed that I had something there more fatal than amour!" Faust replied, grinding his teeth and tearing his breast.

IV

If we went back to times past, and especially to the fifteenth century, we would be surprised by the violence of the medical students of Berlin. The love of science, in that epoch of sap and vigor, animated the soul more forcefully than in our day, so the need to know everything spoke a more virile language. Today, our students of surgery and law at the Sorbonne travel on horseback, change mistresses like furnished rooms, play politics, run up debts and form mobs; in the epoch that we are retracing, students understood their mission.

Doctor Faust, his visage calm and cold, although a tempest was in his heart, advanced to the middle of the amphitheater, leaned on the stone table, and demanded a cadaver in an imperious voice.

A valet came in, carrying an inanimate body over his shoulder, which he threw heavily on to the table.

Having cast his eyes over the cadaver, the doctor recoiled in fear. When that first impulse had passed, he approached, examined the subject attentively, turned it over, examined it again, and then said, insouciantly: "Messieurs; this man has been poisoned."

"Poisoned!" repeated the pupils; and they looked at Faust as if to ask him if he knew the author of such an unusual crime. But the latter, without taking the trouble to interpret their expressions, ordered the student Jonathan to open the cadaver. Jonathan armed himself with a hatchet, struck the cadaver with it, and opened the dorsal spine.

Then, although there were at least a hundred students of all ages, all fortunes and all characters in the hall, one single thought dominated the witnesses of the scene; that thought, rooted in the soul of each of them, Faust could have destroyed with a word, so highly-considered was his science, but he repeated:

"This man died poisoned." Then, his voice weakening as if he were ashamed to confess his ignorance, he added: "The poison that was used having left no trace, Messieurs, my science is surpassed."

Then he fell into a profound meditation; but, by the tremors that agitated him and the nervous movements that constricted him, it was easy to see that a somber despair was devouring his soul. Finally, he ordered the opening of the brain, in order to seek the traces of the poison there.

A student was already manipulating the scalpel when the door of the amphitheater opened abruptly and a woman ran in.

"Horror! Horror!" she cried, falling at the feet of the cadaver. "They've killed him!"

A few students, believing her to be mad, wanted to expel her from the hall. She had attached herself frenziedly to the mutilated body; and as they were still trying to drag her away, the body fell on to the floor, and a faint gasp was heard. It emerged from the breast of the cadaver.

All the students shivered with fear, and gathered in a circle around the stone table.

"Profanation! Frightful profanation!" cried the disheveled woman, at the sight of the blood that was running from the opened skull of the dead man. "Profanation! They've killed him!"

In vain they tried to put an end to that horrible scene; like a tigress gazing jealously at her family, threatened by a hunter, the young woman had passed her arm around the man she had loved, and seemed determined never to be separated from him.

A student seized her forcefully in order to lift her up, but the fury bit the hand that retained hers; then, after having spat the shreds of flesh that she had borne away in the face of the young man, she threw herself on the cadaver again and wound herself around it like a serpent.

Meanwhile, Doctor Faust, placed on a high step, contemplated that scene in a stupor. One might have thought, judging by the convulsive moments of his entire body, that he wanted to interrupt an infernal dream. He was tearing his garments, striking his breast and forehead, as if to assure himself that everything offered to him was the terrible reality.

"Leave me this cadaver!" cried the young woman.

That voice woke Faust up; he descended precipitately to the stage and then placed himself between Juana—for it was her—and the students; his gaze scintillated, and his arm lifted imperiously, indicating that he wanted to protect her.

Juana cast her eyes over her defender and uttered a scream. Soon, subject to the power of fascination that surrounded Herr Faust, she dragged herself toward him, crying: "Doctor, Doctor, save me from these cannibals, these monsters who have stolen happiness from me with my Wilheim! Help a poor woman!"

At the same instant an infernal snigger was heard in the hall; Juana turned round.

"It's him who gave me the opium in order to calm Wilheim's suffering," she said, hiding on Faust's heart—and she pointed at the man with the green face.

The cadaver gasped again, for the last time.

"Have I kept my word?" murmured the hideous stranger, approaching the doctor.

"Yes," Faust replied, extending his hand.

"I don't want your hand; you aren't yet at my level," said the other, and launched a long scornful glance at him.

V

"Death to the sorcerer!" was cried from all parts. "To the pyre! To the rope with the sorcerer!"

"You're wretches!" Faust responded, backed up against a wall, trying to rid himself of the rabble that were abusing him. "For you I have used up my youth, day by day and hour by hour; I have traveled the world in order to learn everything and to ameliorate the fate of my homeland; I've invented printing—and now you're accusing me of sorcery!"

"To the pyre with the necromancer!"

"Woe betide anyone who raises a hand against me!" cried Faust. "And may it wither like that of the impious man in the Gospel!"

"Satan is quoting the Gospel; to the pyre, to the pyre!"

They were no longer clamors but howls that were heard, and the crowd whirled around the doctor. However, no one dared touch him, so great was superstition in that era, which emerges like a transition between two distinctive characteristics of German mores: barbarism and civilization.

"Jacob Blumm," said a voice, "will you promise to have a mass sung for me every year, and to burn four candles with my intention if I die?"

"Yes," replied Jacob Blumm.

Immediately, the populace opened up, and a man of tall stature, with broad shoulders, advanced boldly toward the doctor.

"Hurrah!" cried the populace.

"May the demon blind you!" murmured Faust, preparing to defend himself.

The colossus threw himself upon him, but the combat was not of long duration. A few seconds later, the workman was rolling on the ground uttering frightful howls, writhing with rage and biting the pavement. The doctor had put out his eyes with his lancet.

"He entertains commerce with the demon," said the fearful populace. "To the fire with the sorcerer!"

Meanwhile, Herr Faust, still backed up against his section of wall, awaited the denouement of the scene anxiously, which he did not desire greatly. A few butchers, having taken up the pavement with the aid of pickaxes, threw enormous blocks of stone at him, accompanying that new genre of attack with gesticulations and howls.

"Saints in Heaven," murmured Faust, "is it you who will save me?"

At that moment, a fragment of pavement nearly crushed his skull.

"In default of God, Satan, I invoke you!" he murmured, feebly.

Immediately, a thick smoke surrounded the hall; then, through the swirls of fire that sprang from the ground, the doctor distinctly perceived demons with heads devoid of eyes and ears, which, making use of their mouths like fireplace bellows, stimulated the flames. An invisible hand pushed him forcefully into the midst of the populace. He saw at first, fearfully, that everyone had an arm extended, armed with a paving stone; but he remarked afterwards that the arms were motionless and that the rest of each body was nailed to the ground. He passed between their ranks and continued on his way without accident.

When he was ready to reenter his home someone tapped him lightly on the shoulder; it was the man with the green face.

"Good evening, Doctor," he said, and then added: "Isn't it tonight that Juana is coming?"

Faust made no reply, and went back into his hovel.

With the exception of an old bed placed behind the shreds of the flame-colored tapestry and an oak chest of drawers backed up against the skylight, nothing had changed in the doctor's room. The instruments of physics and mathematics, a manuscript Holy Bible and a recently printed Psalter could all be seen scattered on the parquet of yellow tiles. Herr Faust quit his mantle and his doctor's equipment bag. and, as tranquil in his soul as if he had not run the risk of the rope or the fire, he murmured these words:

"Juana, you can come and inundate me with seductions and amour. I shall play with your seductions, I shall bear them all the perfumes of my mouth, and then I shall blow upon them like soap bubbles! I shall smile at your amour, I shall open my arms to it, I shall draw it to my heart, and I shall stifle it!"

Then he set to work with a strange fervor. Sweat ran over his body, and yet he did not slow down; one might have thought that a diabolical power was multiplying his strength tenfold. Before him was a heater filled with oil and aromatics; and although he drew from it continually, it was not emptied. After an hour of toil he pushed the heater away with his foot, saying:

"To dispute her prey with Death, to prevent a cadaver from rotting, is beautiful, O Egypt; why have you not also ripped up the frightful pact that betrothes man to death for eternity?"

After having sewn up in several places the pale and bizarre envelope that he had perfumed with aromatics, he enclosed it in the sideboard. Then, taking a few steps back, he lifted an immense tile and placed a pump there, which was connected by means of an iron pipe and a valve to the bottom drawer of the chest.

Having finished those preparations, he replaced the tile and placed his foot on top of it. Immediately, a sound similar to that of the wind being engulfed in the opening of a chimney was heard; and as the doctor agitated the parquet more forcefully, the noise grew louder. Advancing a few feet then, he opened the drawer in the chest.

His first sensation was one of amazement, so bizarre was what he saw. But soon, as if ashamed of that weakness, he approached, saying: "Juana, my complete beauty, Herr Faust is waiting for you." He sniggered as he pronounced those words.

Then, as he lifted the tile again, a loud noise emerged from the chest of drawers, a noise similar to that which escapes from a punctured bladder.

The creak of footsteps resonated on the staircase, and then a white hand knocked on the door. It was Juana. The doctor felt all his blood flowing away from his heart, and his lips trembled. However, he said to himself: *It's Juana, let her wait!* Then he headed for the alcove and addressed the portrait of Alice:

"My poor friend, although infidel, I shall always love you." And as it seemed to him that Alice's eyes were veiled by sadness, he unhooked the portrait and approached it to his lips.

"You're weeping?" he added. "My beloved, you're foolish to be sad." And as real tears ran abundantly over the cheeks of the portrait he drank those tears amorously.

Faust continued: "Alice, all the passionate words that I say to that woman are only addressed to you; when my arms surround her, it's you that I shall believe I'm embracing; when I bury myself in her hair, when I exclaim in lust, when I inundate her with amour, when I die of the fire of her caresses, your name alone will spring from my lips; you will always be my beloved, Alice."

The portrait agitated then, as if to demand something.

"Alice, I understand," Faust replied. "All that I have promised you by means of this kiss, I swear to keep." The doctor hugged her, and he trembled, sensing that Alice's lips had parted and that a sweet breath had emerged.

"It's bad of you to have made me wait for so long at your door, Maestro," said Juana, as she came in. And without leaving him the chance to respond, the Bohémienne had thrown her arms around Faust's neck; and clasping him passionately, she murmured: "Doctor, I beg you, teach me the fascination that your gaze has, the talisman that your words have. Oh, please, Maestro, don't look at me like that; you who can do anything to others, order your eyes to soften, your voice to embroider tender sermons, and your heart to have only one beat for each of mine." And as she accompanied that ardent prayer with delightful smiles, engaging caresses and naïve seductions, Faust forgot his resentment; his eyes lit up, his speech became almost gentle; his soul was intoxicated by Juana's kisses and all the young woman's amour.

A sigh sprang from the alcove. The doctor—who, a quarter of an hour before, had promised Alice to laugh bitterly at Juana's passion—did not even quiver.

The portrait sighed again, and again Faust did not hear it. In fact, what man, if he has exhausted his life in work, if he has only known amour through a prism, if his body has not lost its sap, his soul its juvenility and its impetuosity . . . what man, when every instant distances him from his dreams, if he encounters an angel on his route who extends a hand to him, would refuse her many gentle caresses, would coldly order his sensations to be silent and his amour to go back to sleep in his heart?

"Dear Maestro, at least have the goodness to unhook me," said Juana. And she laughed like a lunatic, seeing the doctor's clumsiness. "Dear Maestro, we're not going to be parted again, are we?"

"No, Juana," murmured Faust, trembling with amour.

"So, Maestro, you don't know what is charming in a woman's toilette?"

"Juana, I know it now," replied the doctor, in an altered voice, "but please don't make fun of me!"

Then came the delicate words, the persuasive promises, the friction of lips encountering one another, kisses that succeeded one another.

"Maestro," said Juana, "I love you, Maestro, I love you, oh, I love you!"

And Faust, intoxicated, pressed her forcefully to his heart, inundated her with caresses, and cried: "Mine alone, my

Juana! Her love for me alone, her perfections for me . . . her soul for me alone!"

"Yes, Maestro, I'm entirely yours." Then she added, tremulously: "Faust, I can hear your breast swelling, sobs emerging from it!"

"You can hear my sighs!" replied the doctor, passionately.

"Faust, I tell you that they're sobs."

In fact, the sobs were emerging from the alcove. And Faust, to calm Juana's fear, cradled her in his arms as a mother does her child, lavishing upon her all that true passion has of the sweetest, all that caresses have of the most extravagant. Juana, stunned by so much sensuality, intoxicated by so many kisses, dying of the refinements of pleasure, her hair in disorder, her bosom swelling and breathless, her heart bounding and her mouth on fire, writhed like a bacchante, enlacing him in a powerful embrace, biting him in an amorous fury.

Suddenly, she shuddered, and, trembling with fear, said to Faust: "Maestro, you scare me with your predictions."

"My Juana," Faust replied, "I only have tender words for you."

"Maestro, I can see clearly that you don't love me, for you have no pity for me."

"To Hell with the Bohémienne!" cried a voice emerging from the alcove. "To Hell! Satan will be her spouse, the fallen angels her lovers, the damned her progeniture. To Hell with the Bohémienne!"

"Mercy!" murmured Juana. "Have pity on me, Doctor!"

And Faust, to calm her fear, had recourse to his caresses again; but the voice, having become even louder, was still singing: "To Hell with the Bohémienne! Satan will be her spouse, the fallen angels her lovers, the damned her progeniture."

Juana squeezed the doctor's hands forcefully, and, shedding bitter tears, demanded pardon for having delivered herself to him. And the loud voice sang:

"Bohémienne, may the tar and resin of Messire Satan's boilers consume you for all eternity!"

Juana, beside herself, her brain ardent and boiling like a furnace, embraced the doctor's feet and said to him, sobbing: "Maestro! Don't you love me any more?"

Faust drew her to his heart, and swore to her that he would love no one but her.

"He blasphemes," continued the deafening voice. "He blasphemes!"

Juana drew away from Faust again and rejected his caresses.

"Juana," said the doctor, "I only love you."

"And Me—so you don't love me?" continued the voice.

"Juana, my Juana, I only love you."

Further heavings of the breast were heard, further sobs, but more forceful, more distinct than the first.

"Faust, my hair is impregnated with your tears," murmured Juana. And, supporting herself on her elbow, she wrung her hair, and the water that emerged therefrom streamed over the tiles.

"Juana," the same voice was still howling, "he is playing with your amour as Satan plays with the damned!"

"That's an infamous lie!" cried Faust.

"Juana, near the skylight there is an oak chest of drawers . . ."

"Juana," murmured Faust, "Juana, I love you with all the powers of my soul!"

"Light a torch, Bohémienne," the resounding voice continued, "go to the chest of drawers and open the bottom drawer; you'll see that he is playing with your amour like Satan with the damned."

Juana leapt from the bed, in spite of the doctor's efforts, and said to him: "Mastro, where do you keep your torches?"

"Behind the door," murmured the voice.

"You lie," replied Faust.

"Now, where do you put the briquette?" said Juana.

"In here," the voice continued. And when Juana approached the alcove, the left eye of the portrait of Alice sparkled in a horrible manner. "Approach the torch to my eye," added the same voice.

Palpitating, Juana approached the torch to Alice's left eye, and the torch ignited.

"Juana, my beloved!" cried Faust, whom an infernal power nailed to the bed. "Juana, come back to me."

But Juana headed frantically toward the chest of drawers, and as it was necessary, in order to arrive there, for her to walk over the yellow tile, scarcely had she set foot upon it than a noise like that of twenty bellows in motion was heard. The Bohémienne remained motionless with fear for an instant. Finally making an effort upon herself, she opened the drawer in the oak chest. She uttered a cry of dolor, and dropped the torch, which went out.

And the voice cried: "Bohémienne, let my eyes serve you as torches!" Then it added, more softly: "To Hell with Juana! Let Satan be her spouse, the fallen angels her lovers, the damned her progeniture."

And Juana, in the midst of lightning bolts that sprang from the portrait of Alice, perceived the body of her first lover. At first she turned away, but, submissive to the force of a fatal power, she returned her gaze to Wilheim. Then she saw him as he had been before: his eyes were open and blue, his face was pink as if it no longer belonged to a cadaver; and, to complete the horror, his breast was swelling continually, the respiration trying to emerge from it, and his heart was palpitating.

That sigh rendered to Juana her first amour.

"Wilheim!" she cried, throwing herself upon him and embracing him. "Wilheim, poor friend, dead or alive you are still dear to me." And as Wilheim's breast continued palpitating, Juana added: "Is it my presence, poor friend, which makes your heart palpitate thus? For pity's sake, respond to me, Wilheim; who, then, has saved you from death?"

"And me," murmured Faust, who had placed himself behind her. "Do you love me?"

"You fascinated me for a time with your eyes; now I hate you," Juana replied. And, throwing herself on Wilheim again, she embraced him. "Poor friend," she went on, "speak to me; don't remain cold to my kisses. On seeing you, there is no doubt of your existence, but by your silence, one could mistake you for a cadaver!"

"Juana, what is the point of speaking to Wilheim? He cannot respond to you. Juana, what is the point of covering him with kisses? His lips won't part. Juana, it's me who has returned an artificial life to that cadaver, it's me who has communicated breath to it!"

"Horror!" cried Juana. "Horror!"

That moment of despair passed, she took Faust by the hand, coldly, and designating Wilheim with her finger, added: "You've done well, for he is your son!"

"My son!" repeated Faust. "That's a glaring lie; I have never had a son."

The portrait placed in the alcove murmured: "Wilheim was born of our amour."

In his wrath, the frightened doctor broke the tile and the mechanical instruments that communicated air to Wilheim's body.

"At least I've possessed you!" cried Faust, turning toward Juana.

"Thanks to me," added the man with the green face, suddenly surging forth.

"Who are you, then?" Faust said to him.

"You'll know later, when we seal our bargain . . . ha ha ha!"

EBN SINA

by Alphonse Esquiros

I

EBN SINA[1] was an old alchemist of the fifteenth century who sought, like Geber, the universal remedy, and the method of making gold, like Raymond Lull. Old histories attribute the honor of the discovery of that science to the first angels, who were supposed to have been amorous of the first women; the story is not very gallant, since, according to it, even the angels would have needed to have recourse with women to a certain gift in order to make themselves welcome; but that fable was not invented yesterday, and nothing prevents us from thinking that women have changed considerably since those times.

Throughout his life, which had been long and turbulent, Ebn Sina had only ever had one passion, which was science. Like all mistresses that are courted too ardently, however, science had shown herself to be completely intractable. He was reaching his eighty-third year and he had never spent a day without leafing through his books and lighting his fur-

---

1 This name is an obvious appropriation of that of Ibn Sina (c980-1037), the great Persian physician and polymath known in the West as Avicenna, but the character in the story bears no resemblance to the actual Ibn Sina.

nace; more than five heritages and a few considerable legacies had disappeared in turn in ruinous experiments; flame had worn away its tongue licking the contours of the crucible; the bellows had no more breath, and still the operation that advertised itself as rich in gold only give birth to a little ash.

No other patience would have held firm, but instead of breaking his furnaces and disemboweling his old asthmatic bellows, the scholar, after a vain experiment, tranquilly postponed success until tomorrow. Nothing disconcerted that faith, as old and unbreakable as rock. Every day Ebn Sina invented new methods, and as those methods were always found in default, the scholar concluded that it was necessary to begin again.

Meanwhile, a certain odor, described in the books, escaped the ardent crucible in the middle of his operations, and announced to him that he was on the track of his discovery. Ebn Sina became old and ill, but he continued his attempts nevertheless; the fire would become weary of burning sooner than he would weary of blowing.

For several days, however, the scholar seemed to have been plunged in an absorbing meditation; his disciple Emmaus, a young man seventeen years old, with a brow already pensive and silky blond hair, no longer dared to interrupt that formidable silence, which had to be brooding some great creation. Emmaus was one of those handsome adolescents who attach themselves to some aged hermetic scientist in order to take care of him and to be initiated under his direction into the secrets of the *magister*. Melancholy and mild, with eyes the color of the sky, the disciple composed poetry while sitting on a stool in the venerable hovel of science. His pretty head leaned gravely on his hand and formed with the severe head of Ebn Sina, lying horizontally on a mattress extended on the ground, a contrast full of grace.

The old man was thinking, the child dreaming. Nothing was heard in the humble cell but the intermittent sound of their breathing and the murmur of folios stirred by the wind. Sometimes, a bird came to perch on the window, open in the fashion of a skylight near the ceiling, with a grille of iron bars corroded by rust. Emmaus lifted his head then, but the old man did not hear it.

Ebn Sina was in the state of mental enchantment that a Greek artist has depicted on a bas-relief by representing Jupiter with a sober expression, whose forehead Vulcan has just struck with a hammer.

Ebn Sina had never gone so long without putting his hand on his instruments; the round-bellied flasks, the alembics with slender and tapering necks like those of storks, and the curved madrases seemed to be astonished and to lament that abandonment. The furnace, which had fasted for a week, opened its empty maw in a corner. The bellows crouching in the middle of the room no longer gave any sign of life. Every day dust descended on the earthenware jars; a little more, and spiders would have spun webs there.

"What is the master doing?" the cold crucibles seemed to be saying. "Has he renounced his dreams of potable gold? What was the point, then, in wearing away our flanks with the bites of flame? If the science is only a chimera, let him say so and let us take our leave! He will not be the first, then, to extract gold from the vein of molten metals and who will make of that friable gold and elixir whose effect is to postpone death for more than a thousand years. Courage, Master! Get up! Take care that death does not come to surprise you before you become immortal; hurry up and become a god."

There were such mysterious relationships between that family of chemical instruments and the paternal heart of the scholar that the reader ought not to be surprised if the flasks, the furnace and the crucibles took the liberty of addressing speech to him.

One day, when he woke up, Emmaus saw a ray of June sunlight descending between the bars of the skylight, which summoned him outside; the sky was blue and the soul of the spring that rejuvenates the world was tangible in the air. The disciple darted a glance at his master. Ebn Sina was still in the contemplative and reflective position that the statues lying on the marble tombs in our churches have. Emmaus got up quietly and, after having adjusted his garments, opened the door gently and went out.

Left alone, the scholar did not appear to perceive Emmaus' absence, but after a few moments of silence and immobility he raised himself up on his elbow and, putting his chilly hands together he said: "The daylight is bright today." Then, turning to the Orient with a solemn air, he added: "Spirit of Solomon and great Hermes, inspire me! Have pity on the last of your sons, who has sown mercury in the fields of Gomorrah and whose wizened hands have only ever harvested ashes. Enable your servant, before dying, to see the salvation that you have prepared for the children of science. And you, Sun, universal fire, soul of nature, principal of all metals, allow to fall from the long lashes of your eyelids a single one of your rays, to fecundate my virgin crucible today!"

According to the ancient hermetic scientists, gold is sunlight in the solid state.

Having said that, he stood up and washed his hands carefully in an earthenware vase; the science is a jealous and simple divinity that one ought only to approach with clean hands. Then, loading his furnace with charcoal, Ebn Sina addressed it in these terms:

"And you, furnace, recipient of the fire that is the secret agent of nature, Vulcan with the lame foot, I adjure you by Averroes and Mithra, the two princes, to do your duty. Burn, my son, and remember the fortunate furnace of Ab Selamim,[1] which, for having perfected the Great Work, remained lit for a thousand years!"

---

1 Selamim is a Hebrew term meaning "peace-offering," or "sacrifice."

We cannot say whether the furnace was sensible to that exhortation, but the truth is that it did not take long to catch fire. Ebs Sina did not spare, to that effect, the short and unequal breath of the old bellows, which had resumed its service in the scholar's hands When the incandescent surface of the furnace permitted him to apply the crucible to it, the old man sat beside it on a stool, with the solicitude of a surgeon watching over a woman in labor. In Ebn Sina's mind, the crucible was pregnant with gold, but the poor instrument had already had so many stillbirths that it could not be watched too carefully.

It was a grave and singular spectacle, worthy of the pencil of Rembrandt: the scholar in that somber cell, his face illuminated by the glow of the brazier. The deep wrinkles on his bald forehead stood out rigid and dense, like the creases of his lips, folded in parchment. His head was titled forward and his eyes were covering with mute attention the molten metals.

For that man, at that moment, there was no sun, no spring and no nature; the birds sang in vain over his head and the gentle waves of the Seine kissed in vain with a soft sound the strand inundated with strollers; his sun was his lighted furnace. A cloud of thick black smoke rose furiously from the crucible and spread a suffocating odor throughout the cell, which drew a dry cough, tenacious and hoarse, from the old man's lungs several times over. But what did that cough matter to him, who could already glimpse immortality through the fumes of the crucible and the darkness of the science?

At each precipitation, every time the substance in labor quit its primitive color to take on a new one—which the ancient alchemists designated by the name of metamorphoses—the face of the scholar brightened with hope. Already the *corbeau* had changed into the *colombe* and the *colombe* into the *épervier*; which is to say that the contents had passed from black to white and from white to yellow. The experiment was on the way to success. All the characteristics furnished by the book to announce the preliminaries of the transmutation had been produced; Ebn Sina was definitely on the path, this time, to the great arcanum.

Meanwhile, the moment for the final precipitate had come. Ebn Sina reanimated the force of the furnace by giving it a further ration of fuel to devour. Then, seizing the bellows and compressing it violently, he said: "Blow, my old soul, blow! We're approaching the solemn moment; we're about to make gold. You will be greater than the god Aeolus, the great ventilator, whose exploits were celebrated by the poet Virgilius in his book."

The bellows, doubtless flattered by that comparison, filled its cheeks with air and emptied them impetuously over the charcoal in the furnace, the combustion of which it stimulated. An acidic vapor spread through the room, but the scholar paid no heed to it. Having done that, he charged the ardent and hissing crucible with new substances, which foamed as it worked like a charger. The bellows continued to spur on the flame, entirely out of breath, but its master said: "Courage, my friend; hold firm; we're about to reach the terminus."

O miracle! A reddish powder, the true projection powder described by the ancient alchemists—it was impossible to doubt its color—escaped from the crucible in a fine and friable rain. At that sight, Ebn Sina, seized by a lyrical transport of which he could not moderate the shocks or the surges, said:

"Oh! Gold! Here's the gold! A little of that powder in water and I shall be immortal for at least a thousand years! The world is mine! I shall found cities and buy women. Have you not done well, Ebn Sina, to keep your heart apart until now from the pleasures and passions of the crowd? When you were young, old scholar, while you withered away deciphering the pages of the grimoire, the world laughed, danced and feasted around you. It's your turn now! You shall be adored; you shall be a king.

"You will travel to the Orient, to the land of the magi, where pearls emerge white and mat from the bosom of the sea, where the sun warms and the women are beautiful. You will build a palace that will make Solomon's forgotten; the Queen of Sheba will come to visit you from the extremities of the earth, and all peoples will prostrate themselves before your face. Rejoice!

"Gold is, in any case, only a symbol; this crucible is only an image of the great crucible in which you will melt the entire world. You will change and transmute nations. Gold is glory. You will shine like Moses, the great alchemist, who had received the science of the Egyptians and who bore two horns of light on his head. Henceforth, the science is your vassal and your servant; all those figures of mystery, Isis, Mithra and Osiris, who hide so obstinately from other mortals, will let their veils fall before you. With your gold you will forge a key that will unlock all the secrets of nature. O Ebn Sna, bless the star under which you were born!"

The scholar tried to get up, but his head was heavy. The chamber was full of carbon vapor, for Ebn Sina had forgotten to open the window of the skylight. Three times he tried to drag himself to the door and three times he fell back on to the stool, stiff, nailed to the spot; his stiff and wrinkled hands extended toward the furnace in order to bring back to the edge a little of the powder that enabled one to live for a thousand years, but they could not reach it. A cloud extended over his eyes, his tongue stuck to his palate, and he felt himself becoming as hard as stone.

II

Meanwhile, Emmaus, the beloved disciple, had been to refresh his lungs, burned by sulfur and carbon, with the air of a spring day. He came back along the Seine cheerfully. Emmaus was

more of a poet than a scholar by nature. He had studied alchemy because of the beautiful blue figures heightened with
gold that his fingers encountered with delight on the pages
of the grimoire. He loved the myths of the science, Orpheus
torn apart by the bacchantes, and the fire of heaven stolen by
Prometheus. Often, he still told himself that it was better to
surprise the secrets of nature in herself than to pursue them
sadly in the gloom of a laboratory. He took pleasure among
trees and liked the sunlight. In the evening hours when, like
women vanquished by the heat of the day, nature become more
confident and more communicative, Emmaus liked to interrogate her in the depths of woods or on the banks of rivers.

This evening, the sun, having descended behind the city,
red and incandescent, resembled an immense furnace over
which the somber mass of houses was posed like an alchemist's crucible. Emmaus stopped. He said to himself that
perhaps the dreams of hermetic science were like the horizon
of solid gold that was about to be extinguished and vanish.
The disciple even wondered internally whether the hectic
research of material wealth was worthy of a man. His mind
hesitated as to whether he ought not to detach himself from
his covetousness in order to elevate himself to nobler designs.

"Instead of tormenting matter in every direction," he exclaimed, "in order to extract a little gold from it, might I not
do better—might we not do better, O Ebn Sina—to devote
the faculties that God has entrusted to us to informing our
fellows and discovering the great secret of intelligences? Even
if the philosophers' stone is not a chimera, even if you are
on the point of discovering it, Master, do you not think, as I
do, that it would be better to civilize men than to transform
metals and brute substances? I prefer a kind thought to all the
gold of which you dream."

Emmaus lingered for a few more minutes on the quay
watching a window obscured by curtains. The disciple had

amours more human than his master. The window was that of Thérèse, a beautiful young woman of eighteen who sometimes took the air on her balcony in the evening. Emmaus loved Thérèse and was loved by her, but the young woman had the misfortune of being rich, and like the disciple, she was counting a great deal on the science of Ebn Sina to facilitate their union.

That evening Thérèse did not appear on her balcony; Emmaus only saw a light shadow outlined on the mist of the curtains, which blew him a kiss with its hand.

The disciple returned to his master's dwelling at sunset. His young head was full of dreams of amour and poetry; he stopped for a moment to collect himself before going back into the obscure sanctuary of the science.

Ebn Sina's house was bizarre and tall; a roof opened out in the middle in a sort of terrace permitting the course of the constellations to be followed from there; a chimney with a long neck ordinarily discharged thick smoke into the sky in intermittent gusts that resemble the respiration of a volcano, but this evening no serpent of fumes unwound its fleecy coils over the starry transparency of the sky. Night had fallen; the quays, surprised by the warm and emollient obscurity of a spring evening, wound their sinuous lines silently, over which the line of the houses could scarcely be seen any longer.

The curfew had rung. Emmaus therefore decided to go back into the old scholar's tower; he climbed the steep spiral staircase, plunged obscurely in its stone cylinder, with a light step. Having arrived at the door of the cell, the disciple put his ear to the disjointed planks that sealed the entrance; he could not hear any sound, not even the light murmur that the wind rendered as it was engulfed by the skylight. He concluded that Ebn Sina was asleep and opened the door to the room cautiously.

It was very dark. A ray of moonlight illuminated coldly the face of the scholar, lying on the floor. Emmaus contemplated him silently. His master still had the same attitude of profound and blissful meditation in which he had left him that morning. As Emmaus was an artist, he paused for a few moments to follow with an attentive eye the strong and severe lines that designed the configuration of that remarkable head.

The scholar was lying on his back; his hands, folded over his breast, seemed weary of trying to grasp the void; a white beard descended in thick waves from his chin; his forehead was tilted forwards, drawn by the weight of the head and his staring eyes seemed to be studying an object that was standing out confusedly before him in the darkness.

Emmaus lit a wax candle. On following the direction of the gaze that the scholar was attaching to the floor he discovered an extinct furnace charged with a cold and empty crucible, which designed an exaggerated shadow on the wall.

Oh, he said to himself, *the master has blown today; the acrid and caustic vapor spread through the room is perceptible.*

At the same time he opened the window of the skylight to let in some air, which caused the light of a group of stars to enter the cell.

Meanwhile, Emmaus tried to interrogate at closer range the results of the chemical experiment that appeared to him, at first, to be like all the others, only having ended up swelling the volume of ash with which Ebn Sina enriched himself every day, with a persevering joy. The instruments were in the disorder of an interrupted action. The forceps extended their immobile fingers next to the extinct furnace. The flat and collapsed bellows were lying on the floor on the other side. Flasks and metal debris strewn on a table announced an endeavor completed; the crucible was empty.

O surprise, however! By the vacillating light of the candle, the disciple distinguished around the furnace a light red powder that his master had once mentioned to him, and which, according to learned alchemists, must be projection powder.

At that sight, Emmaus went pale with joy, and, accumulating on the floor a fine and ideal pinch of that dust, he rubbed a copper coin with it; the coin became gold.

"My master has found it!" cried Emmaus, putting his hands together with intoxication.

Then, holding his breath for fear of blowing away the admirable dust, Emmaus began to consider it silently.

"You are great," he said, turning toward Ebn Sina. "You will reign for a thousand years, like Methuselah, and you will be adored like the god Baal. Master, have pity on your disciple, who is not even worthy to untie the laces of your sandals. His heart, young and carnal, is not, like yours, purified of the weaknesses of nature. While you were making gold, O incomparable one, he was picking flowers by the roadside and gazing at the radiance in the foliage. Do not show him for that a severe face, O Ebn Sina; he is not, like you, a solid and positive mind able to watch over a furnace for forty years. Being rich, have pity on the poet!

"We shall be happy, Thérèse and I; I shall sew diamonds in her dress; I shall attach solid gold bracelets to her wrists, so fine that they will be mistaken for the coils of a snake. We shall have slaves and marble baths! Bring us flowers! The walls of our palace will be covered with paintings and bas-reliefs, like the walls of a cathedral.

"To work, master! Here I am; let us recommence the experiment. Is it necessary to relight the furnace? Is it necessary to blow? Let's spend the night making gold. Tomorrow, we'll be richer than the king of France. I am at your orders, Ebn Sina. If you no longer have the strength to shift the instruments or precipitate the substances, indicate them to me and I will carry out your instructions. One word, and we are masters of the world. You have vanquished the Sphinx, Ebn Sina; you have extracted from the bronze mouth the fatal word of the enigma; repeat that word to me.

"Come on, what is it necessary to do? I'm waiting. You can reflect another day, Master; but today time is pressing. Take care that your memory doesn't fail; let's make haste, let's make haste."

Seeing that Ebn Sina made no sign or gave any response, Emmaus, struck by a horrible presentiment, passed the flame of the candle before the scholar's lips; it did not stir.

"Ebn Sina! Ebn Sina!" cried the young man, in a desperate voice, into his master's ears. The master did not raise his eyes.

Then the disciple touched his master's hands; they were cold.

"Dead!" said the distressed disciple. "And the secret?" he thought, aloud. "Who will tell me the secret? The furnace and the crucible are still here, but they have both forgotten it. The walls are mute; and this old man . . ."

Beside himself, Emmaus started shaking the scholar's cadaver furiously.

"Speak, then, dead man!"

The scholar's head, agitated by his hand, made a formidable movement, but soon resumed its center of gravity on the breast.

Emmaus ran around the room like a madman, imploring all the objects with his gaze to speak to him, collecting the powder strewn in the ground in tiny quantity in order to submit it to analysis. In fact, he reanimated the extinct furnace and tried the virtue of solvents in order to lay bare the substances contained in the projection powder; but all his efforts failed; the powder evaporated under the action of heat; all his gold went up in smoke.

The mystery, which had emerged momentarily from the murky profundities of nature, had returned there, perhaps forever. The scholar was dead, and his secret had died with him. Emmaus had questioned the crucible and the old man in vain; the one responded by devouring the last traces of the victory, the other, his mouth irrevocably closed and his jaws clenched, imitated the silence of statues; science had taken back its secret.

Emmaus could not determine himself, however, to release the wings of the gilded chimera that he had held in his hand a little while ago. He returned impetuously to the old man.

"The secret, Master! Tell me the secret! You're not dead, are you? Haven't mages been seen, in any case, to sit up in their tombs in order to instruct the living? Theodose de Meun, having been buried with an incomplete manuscript that contained, under cabalistic figures, the secrets of magistery, continued his work after his death; and when his tomb was opened, after half a century, the blank pages were found to be covered with writing and images. Can you not come back, great Ebn Sina, you who have vanquished the mystery of nature? Can you not slide the key to the enigma into the ear of your disciple? I won't confide it to anyone, Master, I swear to you. The science has killed you in order to punish you for having violated its secrets; try to grasp the expression of them with your cold lips; avenge yourself! One word, Master; speak! Speak!"

Emmaus accompanied these arguments with a flask of an alkali, from which he disengaged corrosive scents into the flared nostrils of the scholar.

Ebn Sina slowly closed his eyes, reopened them, paraded around him a stupid and dull gaze, and then fell back into his inexorable silence.

"You're alive!" cried Emmaus, transported. "You're alive, Master! We're saved! Make an effort, Ebn Sina! Try to unclench your stony jaws; one gesture, and I'll understand; give me a sign, and I'll remake for you the elixir that cures death."

The disciple presented the flask again to the old man's nose, but this time Ebn Sina did not make any movement; he was asleep forever.

Emmaus was devastated, and maintained silence, but eventually he turned toward the scholar's crucible and utensils.

"Adieu," he said; "I'm quitting you forever. The goal of our ambitions was immoral; heaven has reckoned with Ebn Sina and me as a punishment. By dint of pursuing the progress of chemical substances, we had lost sight of the development of our nature. Like that bellows, which uses its breath against flame, we only aspired to perishable treasures and we blew to fatigue the elements. A truce! Mind, virtue, intelligence, I'm returning to you; I'm returning to more durable riches; receive a disciple who repents and is breaking his earthenware idols today!"

Emmaus crushed the scholar's crucible underfoot.

"Insensates that we were," Emmaus continued, "to believe that all progress was material and to seek human grandeur therein! That wealth is only an illusion; it's a wealth of the poor, for the true wealth resides in the depths of the mind and the heart. If the science of gold ever penetrated into societies, it would become an incurable poison there, and sick humankind would only be cured, like me, by a return toward justice and conscience."

THE MAGNETIZED CORPSE

by Jules Janin

WITH regard to good stories, here is one that was told to me by a trustworthy man, who claimed to be the friend of a friend of an eye-witness who played a significant role in the drama that I am about to relate to you briefly, not without making the ardent wish that the story in question might be honored before long by an adaptation for the theater—which is, as everyone knows, the greatest honor that can be desired nowadays.

Not six weeks ago, a young Englishman named Belfort was dying, quite simply from a bad chest and a few crazy years recklessly spent. The young man, although he was nearing the end, did not regret losing his life too much, for he had had his fair share of amours, duels, bad debts, picnics, and even fine sermons—in short, his fair share of all the Parisian joys.

One of his friends, a man of science but a good enough fellow regardless, seeing that Charles Belfort would soon render his last breath, came to say to him, in his softest voice: "If it wouldn't displease you too much, my dear invalid, I'll use my abilities to magnetize you, and I'll choose the moment when you render up your soul; it seems to me that it will be a fine experiment, and that there's nothing about it likely to displease you. What do you say?"

"Not only doesn't your experiment displease me," the other replied, "but it seems to me to be very amusing and interesting, and I thank you for having thought of me for the proof, which will be decisive. Count on me, my dear doctor; you'll be content with my patience, I hope, and I'll be sure to let you know when the moment comes."

With those words, the two friends shook hands and separated, saying that they would see one another again soon. They were both full of hope, and it would have been difficult to decide which of the two was the more content, the moribund or the magnetizer.

Two days went by—two centuries—while the magnetizer waited impatiently for the final agony, which did not seem to want to arrive for good and all. The dying man, for his part, lost patience, and he said to his friend: "Damn it, my dear chap, it's not my fault if death is treating me with such ill-will, but what consoles me is that you won't lose anything by waiting, and I'll be a magnificent subject."

On the night following this conversation, the sick man had a final crisis and fell into a comatose ecstasy; he started sketching fantastic spider-webs with his finger, and yet, in the midst of the most abominable grimaces, he still had the presence of mind to say to his comrade: "You have to lift my head, to hide the light that is hurting my eyes."

The other obeyed. He propped his moribund up in a sitting position, took away every importunate light and set about the operation; which is to say that never, absolutely never, had such beautiful passes and counter-passes—the whole customary apparatus, in short—been performed. The magnetizer was in the swim; but in the end, when he had enveloped the moribund—who lent himself to it with exemplary willingness—with his all-powerful fluid, and saw that his subject had arrived at magnetic perfection, the magnetizer started to interrogate him.

"How are you doing, Belfort? Where are you?"

"My dear friend," the other said, "I'm just dying; you've caught me just at the moment when the breath was leaving my body, and now it depends entirely on you to let me finish the job or to keep me here, suspended between being and non-being, which doesn't seem to me to be a disagreeable state, so far."

"Let's wait," said the magnetizer. "There's no hurry, Belfort, my friend." And with that, the magnetizer went to dinner, without taking the trouble to demagnetize his friend.

The next day the maker of magnetism reappeared in the mortuary chamber; everything was in its place, including the cadaver.

"Belfort," said the scientist, after a few preliminary passes, "what have you been doing since you died?"

"In truth, my dear chap," the dead man replied, "I've been obliged to follow you everywhere you went."

And with that, the dead man told the living one everything that the latter had done the day before: he had dined in a cheap eatery, and from there he had gone to stand on the steps of the Café de Paris; he had been given a ticket to the Vaudeville and he had seen some young women who were pretty enough, but some of whom sang out of tune; finally he had gone back home, and read a little of a novel that he had picked up on the way.

"And if you'll permit me to make an observation," the dead man said, "so long as I'm attached to you by a thread that only you can break, eat better, I beg you, remembering that I'm sharing the experience. You know that I like music, so don't expose me to hearing quavering voices that would spoil the most beautiful faces. All alone here, I'm getting bored, and I wouldn't be sorry if you were to read a good novel from time to time, but at least, for pity's sake, read it all the way through. Finally, if you please, don't go to bed so late; I become irritated not sleeping, because for twenty-four hours, I ought to have been sleeping eternally."

With these words, the man slumped back, and the magnetizer left the room, slightly discomfited by the strange spy that was dogging his heels.

The next day, the living man came back, and found his dead man a trifle numb. He warmed him up with a further dose of magnetic fluid, rendering him, if not life, at least a little color and the ability to speak.

"Ah!" said the dead man, raising himself up. "You're not showing me any charity. What! You go to see such hideous sick people, and I have to hear them coughing, spitting, howling, moaning and all the rest! In the street you follow a horrible woman reeking of musk, a woman in old shoes and a dirty skirt, and I have to keep you company counting the holes and the stains of the filthy creature! Then you go to meet up with some young people, and you tell them about your good luck! You make the streetwalker into a duchess, and a cotton apron into a silk skirt! When you're dead, you know, lying makes you feel ill. And what makes you feel even worse, when you're dead, is stupidity—some quip that would have made me laugh when I was of this world appears to me to be utter nonsense now that I can hear your mind with the ears of my own. So try to talk better my dear chap, and, if it's all the same to you, I'd be obliged if you didn't get drunk on adulterated wine; my throat's been torn apart by the alcohol you've swallowed."

Who do you think pulled a face? It was the living man, who was beginning to think that his dead man was damnable hard to please—because, after all, the previous evening's indulgence hadn't been deserving of such scorn. As for the lady with the worn-out shoes, the living man hadn't noticed the shoe, but only the foot and a little bit of the leg. However, he was fond of his dead man, and he resolved to keep a better eye on himself, in order not to give poor Belfort further reason for discontentment.

When he came back two days later, he found the deceased in a state of incredible excitement. The dead man was sweating copiously, with indignation legible on his distressed face.

First of all, the magnetizer set about trying to calm that anger; he blew his most soothing breath upon those irritated nerves, and appeased that motionless and frozen heart as best he could, which beat in memory.

"What is it, Master Belfort? Who has upset you? And for God's sake, what's the matter with you?"

"What's the matter with me?" replied the cadaver, after a long pause. "What's the matter with me, imbecile that you are? A curse upon the brazen threads that attach me to a fool like you! What's the matter with me! But my dear chap, for two days you've been going from one stupidity to another. The day before yesterday, it's true, you were well-groomed and well-dressed, but you'd fastened your belt too tight and I nearly choked. Your boots—or, rather, our boots—were well-polished, but they were too small, and if I could still walk, I'm sure that I'd be limping with my right foot.

"I've nothing to say about the lovely salon to which you took me; it was pleasant and it was calm; the clothes weren't at all garish; the mature ladies kept to their place, leaving the foreground to the young women; no one played the slightest sonata or read the slightest sonnet; people only spoke in even voices, neither too loud not too quiet, and said the nicest things—trivial but light, benevolent and sonorous. In brief, had it not been for your belt and our footwear, I would have blessed you for having taken me to such a beautiful place. But good heavens! Could you have been any more gauche, maladroit and absurd?

"In a corner of the little room to the left, a more beautiful woman than I ever saw with my mortal eyes was sitting; by dint of attention and will-power, via your terrestrial intermediation. I had attracted the benevolent interest of that amiable lady; already she was looking at me with a certain tenderness, and she was about to smile at me; our two souls were no longer any but one, and we were about to fall in love, when you turned your head like an idiot to greet I don't know what starchy spirit. Then the image of my beautiful lady fled, and if you live for a hundred years you won't find either another face as beautiful or another heart as noble.

"Idiot that you are, having done that, what do you do next? You know that I've left some glaring debts, and that I don't even have a tomb. You haven't a sou yourself; you live from hand to mouth; your rent hasn't been paid and never will be; in brief, you're as poor as a poet and an actor rolled into one—which is to say, abominably poor! Well, you sit down at a card-table, tremulously risk a wretched pistole, and, having won the hand, you pocket the money and run away like a thief!

"Now, do you know what you did there, Monsieur Idiot? You renounced getting your hands on a round sum of four lovely thousand louis d'or, for you'd have won the next thirteen hands, my son! With your four thousand louis you'd have had a carriage and I'd have had a first-class funeral. You'd have had a new suit and I'd have had an embroidered shroud. You'd have gone to seek your supper in the chorus of the Opéra, and I'd have gone to look for Monsieur Gannal.[1]

"Damn your feeble intelligence—you can't make use of what little sense you have, but you amuse yourself dragging

---

1 Jean-Nicolas Gannal (1791-1852) was the pharmacist and inventor who founded and developed the modern techniques of embalming in the early 1830s, winning the Prix Montyon three times by virtue of the benefits thus provided to human society. In 1837 he obtained a patent for his embalming fluid and set up a commercial laboratory in the Rue Saint-Hippolyte.

another man's intelligence around with you. Go away—you make me sick, wretched living individual that you are!"

When our magnetizer finally understood that whatever he did would surely attract criticism or sarcasm, he fell silent. Now that he felt that he was being followed and observed at close range by some invisible entity that he had retained on the boundary between the two worlds, the scientist dared not take a step in the street; he scarcely dared answer yes or no to the simplest questions that were addressed to him; it was as if he were deaf and dumb. At times he wondered whether he might be the magnetized man and the magnetizer that great motionless—but not speechless—cadaver, the mere sight of which had ended up making him shiver.

An idea, a thought, is such a powerful thing, even independent of life! An idea pursues you, obsesses you, more tenacious than a shadow, as eloquent as remorse or hope, full of starts, excitations and perils!

However, our man went back to his friend Belfort three days later. This time, once again, a great change was evident in his inanimate face; pure and simple scorn had replaced indignation and anger. The half-closed eyes seemed to be saying: "Away with you!" The tight lips were expressing an indescribable disdain. Every muscle, taut from top to bottom, held a contempt suspended from every thread connecting it to the soul.

"What's the matter now, my friend?" cried the living man, "You seem dazed. You can't say this time that I've done or said anything stupid, because I've stayed at home, alone, entirely given over to my thoughts."

"Oh, my dear fellow," the dead man said, "it's the contemplation of your thoughts that's giving me nausea. Motionless as you were, I was forced to look into the depths of that chaos you call your soul. But what kind of animal are you to occupy yourself with so many ignoble, frivolous and shameful things?

When I was alive and I called you my friend, everyone said that you were a gallant fellow; you had a reputation for keen, even eloquent wit; you were credited with philosophy, probity and tact.

"For three days, unable to help it, I've been watching you very attentively—but my dear fellow, you're a complete mess! What you know, you know poorly; what you don't know, you replace with words as empty as your head. Your generosity is a certain organic weakness that ends up making your eyes red, and that's all. Your intelligence is represented by a few mechanical cog-wheels that rotate of their own accord like the wheel of a water-mill incessantly repeating the same tick-tock. Your courage—I've seen all the way to its depths, your courage!—is a cardboard mask that frightens children. Your probity—let's talk about your probity!—is written in the margins of the commercial Code and the penal Code.

"Shame upon your vices, those of a badly brought-up child! I wouldn't give four sous for your vices; they make me sick, your wicked shameful vices: they're like a kind of boasting! As for your virtues, they're so worthless I wouldn't even give them to my lackeys; there's something limp and vain about your virtue, which bears some resemblance to a badly-cooked broth. Oh, I advise you not to lay bare the inside of your brain and your heart—it's not a pretty sight, although, on the other hand, it's very sad.

"And what ideas you have about other men! What thwarted ambitions! And I don't envy your work at all, my poor sir! What! You aren't ashamed, even of your castles in Spain, when you amuse yourself rambling on for entire hours in petty daydreams?

"Anyway, Monsieur, let's leave it at that—but I'm damnably sorry that I ever called you my friend!"

It would not have taken much on this occasion for the magnetizer to destroy his work and liberate himself from the unwelcome thought that was obsessing him. He left the mortuary chamber in a very bad mood, and on the way home he said to himself that it was, after all, quite an accomplishment to have stopped Belfort's discontented soul half-way.

Then again, the living man said to himself, sadly, *what good has it done me to have retained that dead man in the edge of his grave? To have myself told such rude home-truths, to hear the story of my everyday life told in such a cruel and grotesque fashion, no longer to be alone with my conscience, my thoughts, my ambitions, my self? If the clairvoyant that sees everything were, at least, to indicate some unknown science to me—a remedy for the gout or some hidden treasure easy to extract—I'd be rewarded for my troubles, but no! For having carried out the most difficult task, the most excellent miracle that magnetism has ever accomplished, here I am dragging behind me a bilious inquisitor who isn't content with anything, and who'll end up making me disgusted with myself.*

Thus the clever man reasoned; he was very annoyed, and firmly resolved to put an end to his dealings with such a miscreant, no matter what it cost.

As he was unable to sleep, the magnetizer went back to Belfort's house that same evening, at midnight.

Belfort watched him come in, and without waiting to be interrogated—for the magnetic fluid becomes, it seems, a habit, and replaces life as a well-lit candle replaces with winter sun—the dead man cried: "I'll tell you what you've just done, amiable doctor! You've quite simply decided to murder me! Yes, you're jealous of this artificial life, you're furious at my revelations, and you've decided to extract me abruptly from magnetic sleep in order to return me to dust and silence!

"That's handsome of you, Monsieur, it's glorious, what you're doing, coming to murder . . . a dead man! Coming to trouble a cadaver in his coffin! Attacking the thought of a man because the man, having become, thanks to you, a part of eternal life, is no longer able, and no longer wants, to flatter you!

"Well, get on with it, then, and turn me to dust—but that dust, when you've cast it to the wind, will summon to its aid another, bolder thought, to follow in your tracks, another gaze, even more clairvoyant, to read the depths of your soul, another avenger, even more implacable: remorse!"

At these threats the magnetizer fled, but, in his distress, he left the door ajar.

The neighbors of both sexes, who had initially kept their distance, took the chance, one after another, and finally all together, of coming to greet and interrogate the dead man, and picked up, here and there, some of those fine verities—I mean a few of those eternal, ever-living truths—that only the dead know how to voice appropriately. Husbands, wives, children, tenants, owners, masters and servants, the rich and the poor, all the way to the porter, each obtained a parcel of justice addressed to them.

The dead man spoke true words and expressed true notions, and what he said was, admittedly, cruel. If you asked him where fortune lay, he would point out a wart on the end of your nose; if you mentioned ambition to him, he would talk to you about modesty, economy and bonhomie. The female neighbors found him so ungallant that they slammed the door violently.

That was all that the late Monsieur Belfort wanted.

A week went by without the magnetized and the magnetizer seeing one another again; they were sulking, but it was obviously not up to the dead man to make the first move. The scientist finally understood that, and came back to his subject's bedside.

"I've thought about everything that has happened," Belfort said to him, "and I'd be glad if you were to carry through the plan you made the other day. You're right: wake me up, so that I can finish dying quietly. It had made such a good beginning, when you came along to disrupt it, that I'd already be devoured by worms and returned via the thousand pores of universal decomposition into the ocean of life and light. Wake me up, then, and I'll die entirely—and joyfully, for, this time, I'll amuse myself by gazing, not at your soul, which isn't beautiful, but at your body, which is very ugly.

"Only the other day—I caught you in that agreeable occupation—you were telling yourself how fortunate you were before, but please, where are these women who can look lovingly at an ape like you? You're badly-formed; you always have one shoulder higher than the other, this one over that one or that one over this one. Your hair started falling out a long time ago, and what's left is hanging on to rotten roots, like last year's thatch after the winter. Your eyes can still see, but I can see some sort of pellicle extending over your line of sight that doesn't augur anything good.

"Oh, if you could see those layers of yellow chalk encrusted in the joints of your fingers, which are corrupting your bones and are going to break them bit by bit, like the boot of torture, but more slowly, more insidiously and with a more obstinate verve!

"Your heart is swollen, my dear chap, and the point is being torn by some viscera or other that is wounded in its turn. Your left lung isn't much better than my right lung. Gradually infiltrating between your skin and your softened tendons I can see layers of thick fat which makes you resemble some sort of sea-cow. Your teeth are already turning yellow; they're loose in their bloody cavities. In your brain I can see veins swollen with apoplectic blood, ready to burst. You're doomed, you see, and—give me your hand—you're dead!"

On hearing those lugubrious words, the magnetizer begs the magnetized for mercy, pity and forgiveness. And, in order to free himself from the vision that is obsessing him, to expel from his mind that voice, which is pursuing him with such bruising stubbornness, in order not to remain exposed to that mockery and those prophecies of misfortune, the magnetizer sets about countermanding the magnetic fluid and destroying that artificial life.

The dead man resists, but in vain; it is necessary that a corpse, which is dead, should yield to a man who is still alive.

Gradually, the voice fades away. It utters one last gasp, and then Belfort, so eloquent a little while before, is no longer more than I don't know what, that which I don't know how to name in any language . . .

It was, in fact, for three weeks already that death had had possession of the cadaver, and now the magnetic breath had ceased, corruption and the worm took hold of their prey again and did not let go.

One shivers at the mere idea that the magnetizer might have died before having demagnetized his friend Belfort. How long eternity would have seemed to the latter then—unless his thought, obedient all the way to the abyss, or to Heaven, had followed the soul of magnetizer.

That would be another trial to attempt!

THE GUEST OF THE DEAD

by Claude Vignon

THE emperor Frederick Barbarossa, duly reprimanded by the Grand Council of Venice, came after many refusals to render homage to the sanctity of Pope Alexander III,[1] who, as penance for his rebellion and a host of other detestable sins, sent him to the Holy Land to fight the infidels.

When he had decided to depart, Frederick sent throughout his empire a large number of heralds-at-arms to summon, first all of his high barons and liege-men, and then all the good burgers of his good cities, and finally all his loyal and faithful subjects: nobles and commoners, burgers and villains.

Many came at the first call and took the cross with great heart in order to follow their emperor to Palestine; but many required the summons to be repeated, because they liked sowing their fields and cleaving to their hearth better than riding over mountains and valleys in unknown lands, and preferred to earn indulgences by saying *Ave Marias* under the porches of their churches rather than pursuing the Saracens toward Damascus and Saint-Jean-d'Acre.

Gradually, however, whether they liked it or not, all good Germans in a condition to bear arms were brought under the

---

1 The Holy Roman Emperor Frederick I, nicknamed Barbarossa, acknowledged Alexander III as the true pope—having previously supported the antipope Victor IV—in 1177.

orange and black banner of Barbarossa and took the road to Asia, to go and be decimated by famine, plague and Greek fire. And in the meantime, during the long years in which Germany waited for her children and her emperor, who was never to return, everything went from bad to worse in the empire.

To begin with, strong arms were lacking in the fields to labor the earth, and the crops cultivated by the old men and the children did not grow well; in the towns and in the fortresses the lords, always at war with one another, destroyed edifices and ruined commerce; on the Rhine, communications were cut everywhere and navigation was interrupted. To complete the misfortune, it seemed that all the maleficent spirits that haunted the Germanic lands in those days, without any regard for the pious devotion of the crusaders, had redoubled their rage and skill in order to torment the infirm old men and the poor widows.

Never, perhaps, had the gnomes and sprites of the forests of the Hartz and the Niederwald showed themselves so restless and played such malevolent tricks on the housewives who had sole care of their cottages or on travelers delayed on the roads; never had the fays and the loreleys been crueler and more deceptive to fishermen and boatmen; never finally, had the phantoms, stryges and vampires of the banks of the Danube slept less tranquilly in their tombs. In sum, there was a veritable desolation.

Fortunate still were those housewives neglected by their spouses who saw growing beside them some handsome lad, already strong, and soon capable of being the head of the family! Those gathered their courage, in the hope that better managed affairs and a more firmly conducted plow would soon bring back ease to their house. But what dolor, also, was there if those sons, the last hopes of an entire family, showed bad sentiments or gave themselves to vice and idleness, for want of a powerful hand to support or chastise them.

And that is why two poor women of the village of Arnsberg, situated in the confines of the Black Forest, were weeping and lamenting.

"Ah, Barbel my friend," said one of them, wiping her eyes, "What have I done to Heaven to have a killecroff [1] in my family; for, God forgive me," she added, making the sign of the cross, is it not evident that Fritz is a killecroff, on seeing the manner in which he eats, drinks and beats his brothers, and all the children of the village?"

"Margareth, my good Margareth," replied the other, sobbing, "Don't blaspheme God and don't curse your son. Alas, if Fritz were a killecroff, my son Hermann would also be one, for throughout the country he alone is capable of matching Fritz in the matter of brutality and gluttony; but everyone knows that killecroffs, or changelings, are the spawn of the devil born of possessed girls and introduced into families by henchmen in place of veritable children. Now tell me, what have you and I, poor widows whose husbands are in the Holy Land fighting the infidels, done to see our sons exchanged by the devil for his own?"

Margareth sighed. "Oh, my dear Barbel, perhaps never have so many killecroffs been seen in Germany as at present! Do you remember the one in D*** who ate as much as two workers, cried and beat the neighbors all day long, and was only able to laugh when misfortune struck the house?"

"And the one in K*** near Halberstadt, Margareth, who, from birth didn't leave a drop of milk in his mother's teat for his twin, and dried up another five nurses! But, thank God, we were soon rid of that one, for his father took the good ad-

---

1 As the text explains, a *killecroff* is a kind of changeling; the term had apparently been introduced to French Romanticism by Gustave Brunet in his 1844 translation of Martin Luther's table talk; it was subsequently recycled in X. B. Saintine's oft-reprinted collection of *La Mythologie du Rhin* (1862; tr. as *Myths of the Rhine*) but was still esoteric when the present story was published.

vice of his friends and relatives, and took him to Halberstadt to devote him to the blessed Virgin Mary. And as he passed over a bridge devils started to dance on the water and to call 'Killecroff! Killecroff!' The child, who was in a basket and had not moved or proffered a word until then, being scarcely six months old, started to agitate and to cry 'Oh! Oh! Oh!'

"'Killecroff, Killecroff where are you going?' shouted the devils.

"'I'm going to Halberstadt to have myself cradled,' replied the infernal nursling—on seeing which, his father, who was a good Christian, recognized the genealogy of the brat, signed himself devotedly and threw the basket into the water, infant and all. Then he returned to do penance."

The two devotees signed themselves in their turn and raised their eyes to the heavens.

"Ah, Lord God," murmured Margareth, picking up her spindle, which she had dropped, "no, my dear Barbel, it's necessary to hope that our children aren't killecroffs . . . !"

To be sure, if some sage rector had initially found the judgment of the two prudish women regarding their children severe, he would have ended up thinking like them merely by seeing the surly and grim faces of the two boys, occupied at that moment in administering forceful slaps and punches.

They really were the two most frightful fellows that one could see and the two most diabolical scoundrels in the entire country. They were fighting then over the cadaver of a vulture, which each of them claimed to have killed, and blows fell as thickly as hailstones, accompanied by insults and blasphemies.

The elder was sixteen years old and the younger fifteen; but they were singularly strong for their age—which did not make them any better, said the two poor mothers, for they only employed their strength and skill in wringing the necks of their neighbors' chickens to make a meal, in stealing pitchers of beer and playing nasty tricks.

Fritz was a big, strongly-built and bony fellow with a flat head and twisted, almost limping, legs. Thick red hair fell over his forehead and mingled with his bushy eyebrows, which only allowed a glimpse of the wild pupils of two wandering eyes of different colors. Beneath those eyes a nose like the beak of a bird of prey surmounted a twisted mouth with overlapping teeth, which completed giving poor Margareth's son a horrible physiognomy.

Hermann, the younger of the two scapegraces, was a stout boy, square from top to bottom, whose face was more bestial than grin. His heavy head, supported by a thick neck, was illuminated by two faience-blue eyes shaded by a magnificently tangled shock of coarse hair. He had bulging highly-colored cheeks, pale blond eyebrows and lashes, and thick lips. Gluttony and drunkenness were his principal vices, and for a pot of beer and a slice of bacon he sold himself body and soul to Fritz the bandit.

On an empty stomach, when he saw his mother weeping and his little neighbor Ketha, Fritz's sister and his own promise, he swore to mend his ways, but that repentance did not last long, for that miscreant Fritz, who had never been able to touch holy water without swearing, taught him to profit from that moment of confidence to steal coins and victuals and drown the repentance in some frank mouthful.

When the two mothers, having run out of sermons and weary of tears, had recognized their total impotence to put their sons on the right path, and when Ketha had begged her mother to send her as a novice to the convent rather than give her in marriage to Hermann, the parish priests of the neighborhood got involved, and with a great reinforcement of holy water adjured the devil to abandon the killecroffs. But Satan held tight to his property, for neither prayers nor exorcisms changed the miscreants. Every year they seemed to become more prolific drunkards, more prolific thieves and more malevolent.

Often, strange noises had been heard in the hovel where they made their lair, ill-sounding for a Christian son of a good mother; so everyone in the village desired ardently to be rid of the killecroffs.

They poached, pillaged and started fires. They pursued young women, threw excrement into the holy water and profaned cemeteries. But seigneurial justice was finally stirred by so many crimes. Fritz was seized by the Baron of Halberstadt's men-at-arms after killing a gamekeeper, and shortly afterwards his body, hung high and short, was swinging on the gibbet, to serve as an example to his companion.

After the execution, Hermann judged it prudent to decamp and to give some proof of repentance. That is why he went to the town to learn his father's trade, who had been a weaver before departing for the Holy Land.

Fritz's cadaver was left suspended from the gibbet for a long time, as evidence of the power of the lord of Halberstadt, but the executioner finally took it down and buried it, with neither benediction nor prayers, in an old abandoned cemetery.

When Hermann came back with his mastery as a weaver, the memory of the execution was still vivid in all memories; he understood that it was necessary not to attack people or property if he did not want to rejoin Fritz. He had, in any case, passed his nineteenth year and he knew that the doctors affirmed "that killecroffs, or *suppositii*, never attained the age of twenty."

On his return, therefore, he passed himself off as best he could for a good, tranquil and adroit weaver, and quickly produced his aune of cloth. He seemed to have forgotten in the town his habits of violence and rapine; but he was incapable of containing himself in confrontation with a pitcher of beer, or of seeing the sign of a tavern without going in to sample the Rhine wine, and he hardly ever came out before his troubled head and his tottering legs had lost their power, the former to guide him and the latter to carry him.

In spite of those appearances of conversion, Ketha did not decide easily to marry her fiancé. She wept a great deal, but it was necessary to provide a support for her mother; it was, moreover, pious work to complete the conversion of that strayed soul.

The marriage took place discreetly, and the young couple went to set up home in the house of Hermann's father, who had died in the Holy Land. That house, constructed some distance from the village, was constructed on piles and only had a very narrow entrance on the ground floor, which formed the cage of the staircase and a kind of dark cellar where provisions were stored. At the top of the staircase was the unique living room of the poor dwelling. A large four-poster bed, a dresser, a broad fireplace, above the mantel of which a few rusty weapons were hung, and a loom formed the entire furniture. It was there that Hermann's ancestors had lived, father and son, all weavers by profession, and it was there that Ketha and her husband were to live and work like humble manual laborers.

All went well for some time. The mothers had enriched the young household with all that remained to them, and the weaver earned a few écus making cloth; but such good conduct could not last long on the part of the former companion of Fritz the hanged man.

Soon, Ketha remarked that the loom remained motionless for entire days; her husband went to the town to obtain thread or take cloth, spending more in one day on drink than he had earned in a week. Gradually, penury replaced ease, for remonstrations exasperated the weaver instead of converting him.

In the meantime, Margareth, Ketha's mother, died and Barbel came to take a place at the hearth. Then Hermann, seeing one more mouth to feed in the abode, took his house and his family in horror; he only came there to drink and eat when he had no more money, and to carry away anything that he could sell to pay for new orgies.

The poor women prayed and wept.

When Hermann came back, drunk, staggering and brutish, after entire weeks of absence, it was to pass through his house like a scourge, to beat Ketha, who had no money to give him, to insult his mother, and to make the entire village curse because of his debauchery and his depredations.

One evening, Barbel, old and stooped, less by age than by chagrins, counted the family's last resources, groaning. "Oh, my dear child," she said to Ketha, "the Lord has reserved rude proofs for us, and his hand has been heavy upon us. Consider your good mother Margareth, who died of chagrin for having seen the body of her killecroff son suspended from the gallows for six months, and am I, great God, destined to die too of shame and dolor? For if Hermann continues to live as a miscreant, I shall certainly see his cadaver too swinging in the wind at the tip of the gibbet."

"Dear mother, don't despair thus," said Ketha. "God will touch Hermann's heart once again. May God protect him! For seven days and seven nights I haven't seen him, but when he returns, do you believe that he can be without repentance, on hearing our plaints and seeing our dolor?"

At that moment, a hoarse and whiny voice became audible in the distance; that scarcely distinct voice was soon recognized by the two women. It was intoning nasally an old Bacchic song, a sort of drama with two characters, one a penitent and the other a drunkard, who, having met, were trying mutually to convert one another, one to the virtue of anchorites and the other to the free expansion of the swine of Epicurus.

> *"Who are you, you who are singing?"*
> *"Who are you, you who are bored?"*
> *"I am a penitent,*
> *Who goes through life weeping."*
> *"I weep endlessly!"*

"Your motives are pious?"
"I mean when the wine
Emerges through my eyes!"

Barbel and Ketha made the sign of the cross, weeping; they sensed that the hoarse, trailing, halting voice belonged to the ultimate degree of drunkenness; that the weaver's unsteady legs were following an uncertain route, and that the ignoble song was often interrupted by hiccups.

Gradually, however, the voice approached and the words became more distinct.

"Do you know that it's necessary to die?"
"I want to die . . . at table!"
"Dread a sad future,
That isn't a fable!"
"I only dread thirst!"
"You ought to dread death."
"I drink as long as I'm thirsty
And when I've drunk, I sleep!"
"Dream, then, about dying!"
"I dream of it when I think of it."
"You ought to remember it
And do penitence."
"I very often do it . . ."
"You never do it!"
". . . When I have no more money
Penitence I do!"

Soon the poor women, trembling, heard heavy and unequal footsteps striking the pavement of the courtyard, and the door screeching on its hinges.

Hermann climbed the stairs. He shoved the door rudely and made his entrance staggering; then, without seeing his wife and without saluting his mother, he went to fall like an inert mass on to a stool. His garments were ragged and soiled with wine and mud; his tearful eyes darted a vague gaze around him.

"Hey, wife," he cried, cursing, "where's my supper? I want my supper! Haven't you had time to set the table, Madame Lazybones?"

Ketha wiped away her tears and tried in vain to find the strength to respond.

"What, preachy beauty, have you the pip? Or has the Devil done me the favor of tying your tongue so that you can't say a word?"

"My son," said Barbel, finally, after an effort, "shut up and let your wife be. You've supped too much, and far from home, where you don't worry about filling the bread-bin!"

"Hum! What's this?" growled Hermann, without paying much heed to the maternal admonition. "Am I or am I not the master of the house? No cackling, women, and serve me a drink!"

"Shut up yourself, my son!" cried the indignant Barbel. "Your wife and your mother are ruining their health spinning all day long, and can't succeed in earning the daily bread. The time has finally come to resume work and make a few good aunes of cloth! This isn't a drinking den, and there's no cause for rejoicing, since, far from becoming a good Christian, you persist in remaining a filthy drunkard without pity or respect for us."

"To the devil with the mother and the wife!" shouted the furious drunkard, making the entire house shake with a formidable thump of his fist on the massive table that occupied the middle of the room. "Now, which of you is going to fetch me a drink, you old hags?"

That exclamation was followed by a moment of silence, and that silence had something solemn about it; the old woman was rotating her spindle beside the fireless hearth with a feverish movement; Ketha was trembling and weeping, hesitating between obedience and revolt.

"Will you obey me, finally, instruments of Hell?" roared Hermann. "Obey me, or I'll thump you!"

Old Barbel raised two glaucous eyes to the heavens, in which two bloody tears were pearling. "Don't move, daughter!" she said, in a tremulous voice to Ketha, who was rising to her feet.

Herman bounded like a ferocious beast, launching himself at his mother, seized her by the shoulders and threw her on to the stone staircase.

"Thunder! It's you, then, old fay, old witch, who teaches insubordination to my wife! Get out! Get out, and quickly! Run to the Sabbat and may Satan roast you, you and your broomstick!"

And as the poor mother got to her feet, with difficulty, he lifted her up again, dragged her down the steps, half-dead, and threw her outside, cursing; and, in spite of the cold and the darkness, he slammed the door shut.

"To the devil!" he said.

He went back up to the room.

"You, now, pretentious beauty!" he said, seeking Ketha with his gaze. "Obey, and find the route to the cellar for me, quickly! But damn it, has she gone already? I'll have to make those spouters of paternosters feel the bit! I can't see her!"

At that moment, the drunkard's foot collided with an inert body; that was Ketha, who had fainted with horror, on the tiles.

Then Hermann, alone in confrontation with his inanimate wife, felt himself marked with the sign of Cain; fear enabled him to see through the fumes of drunkenness, and he fled like a man accursed.

Some distance from his abode he encountered his mother, exhausted, bruised and bloody, who was hanging on to the brambles by the roadside in order to go to die outside the house of the village pastor. The poor old woman lifted a hand toward the heavens on seeing Hermann, and in a voice full of prayer she murmured: "God forgive you, my son."

The drunkard wandered for a long time in the countryside, prey to a kind of delirium in which images of reality were mingled with phantoms engendered by the vapors of drunkenness.

Sometimes, it seemed to him that a thousand demons were pursuing him with discordant cries and hideous grimaces; sometimes it was his mother and his wife, pale victims who were imploring his pity or, weary of praying in vain, were asking God to punish their torturer; sometimes, finally, it was the gibbet of Halberstadt that loomed up menacingly before him, and Frtitz's cadaver that was writhing at the summit, as if in the anguish of an eternal agony.

Soon, that last hallucination achieved a strange empire over his mind. It seemed to him that the fatal gibbet was attracting him invincibly, and that, in spite of his will and his efforts, every step was bringing him closer to it.

Then, when he was very close, he saw Fritz suddenly detach himself therefrom by dint of his gesticulations, and he felt the hand that had struck his mother grasped by the stiff, cold hand of the hanged man, as if by a vice.

Then he was dragged into an immense round in which thousands of fantastic and terrible figures were dancing furiously. It was as if all the dead people that the gibbet had borne had arranged a rendezvous for an infernal orgy by the dubious light of the moon, which was about to set.

All the bandits were there who had once desolated the country, and whose skeletons were rattling with the grating sound of horrible laughter; and also the murderers, whose bodies were utterly fleshless, while their arms and hands retained the appearance of life, still soiled by ineffaceable blood; and also infanticide girls, who seemed to be condemned eternally to give their living breasts to their dead children.

All those specters vomited by Hell were dancing with rage an irregular, mad, jerky dance, as if convulsive.

Hermann was dragged away by the killecroff, without the strength to resist, devoid of will and energy. Screaming, he followed the vertiginous round, which unfurled in a spiral at the foot of the gibbet.

Exhausted, bruised and out of breath, he finally fell. Then it seemed to him that there was nothing but specters around him, dancing and sniggering. He thought he could see their bony, livid fingers designating him as a victim or a prey, and the circle tightened to envelop him completely. They spun without stopping or slowing down, as if moved by a mechanism. Herman soon sensed space and air lacking, for the cold limbs of the specters were pressing upon him and choking him. There was something like a circle of ice around his head, something like a horrible weight upon his breast. He lost consciousness.

The cool of daybreak calmed the anguish of the weaver. He opened his eyes painfully and found himself, with horror, lying under the gibbet of Halberstadt.

His first impulse was to flee far from that sinister place, without choosing his direction and without looking ahead.

Gradually, however, his senses calmed down and he disengaged from the visions of the night the frightful reality. Far from being seized by repentance, however, and a need for expiation, he only experienced a brutal horror for everything that reminded him of his crime. From the place where he was, he could still perceive his house and his village in the distance. That sight was odious to him, and, only listening to his bestial instinct, he drew away from the locale rapidly.

This time, as he was hungry, he followed a direct route and did not make detours to avoid seigneurial justice.

In spite of his haste to arrive at the goal of his journey and the precipitation of his march, Hermann only reached the edge of the Black Forest toward the middle of the day. He engaged in a dark path vigorously hollowed out by diluvial rain, where the shadow was so dense, even in broad daylight, that he could scarcely see far enough to recognize a traveling companion at ten paces.

After a few moments of rapid march, he stopped outside a wretched woodcutter's hut and knocked vigorously on the door three times. A decrepit old woman with glazed and squinting eyes stuck her head through a hole lined with straw, which served as a window.

"Come on! Hurry up, my dear!" he cried, as soon as he perceived her. "Open up, and quickly, if it pleases your cousin, the devil!"

The old woman came down the few steps that separated her from the ground as quickly as her age and her infirmities permitted; then she lifted the wooden latch that barred the door internally, and Hermann precipitated himself into the room.

His first movement was to sit down at a big table soiled with wine and bordered by benches, and as he found that the old woman was not hastening enough to serve him, he struck it with a vigorous blow of his fist.

"Thunder! Get the rust out of your old carcass, firebrand of Hell, and serve me a good meal! I've been marching quickly and I'm hungry."

"Lord! Master Hermann," said the old woman, terrified, "how agitated you are! But don't get angry, for here's the remains of my men's soup; the bacon is sliced, the beer's in the pots and I can hear my Antoine calling out from the entrance to the sunken path. He's your good companion, and you can wait for the time of an *Ave Maria*."

While making that speech, the old woman took a few pewter pots from a large dresser and a few wooden spoons, and set the table, in order to assist her guest to be patient.

During those preliminaries three men arrived, and after having rid themselves hastily of their weapons and their cloaks, they sat down by Hermann's sides, cursing the ingratitude of the weather.

Those three men were Antoine and his two sons. Perhaps Master Antoine and his sons feared God and said their paternosters, but they had a strange reputation in the region. To begin with, for charcoal-burners, they were more often seen hunting and marauding than cutting wood, and their house, kept by an old woman who was half-witch, had become a rather ill-famed drinking-den, where the bad lots of the neighborhood got drunk during the day. It was said in low voices that several foreign travelers who had gone astray in those parts had never seen their homelands again, and that their cloaks had sometimes been recognized on the shoulders of the charcoal-burners.

At any rate, fairground merchants and traveling peddlers did not like to stop after nightfall at Master Antoine's inn; but no one accused the charcoal-burners out loud, for the father and sons were reputed to be redoubtable to their enemies and made them pay dearly for ill-sounding words.

Hermann maintained his habits of idleness and debauchery in Master Antoine's house. To continue that life, the weaver was capable of anything, and Antoine had understood that, so he helped him obligingly to spend the last coins that remained to him, knowing full well that once he was hungry and devoid of a frederick, the drunkard would belong to him entirely.

When, therefore, after copious draughts, Hermann dared to boast about his exploits of the previous night and recount how he had put his house in order, Antoine applauded that energetic action wholeheartedly.

"A plague upon weeping and moaning women," he said, "who don't know how to do anything but complain and recite paternosters! You'd have done well, my master, while they were going on, to clear out the place completely by throwing the wife out with the mother. It would have been good riddance."

"And I dare say," said Hans, his elder son, "that with a pretty maidservant, very mild and very obedient, which I'm holding in reserve for you, it would be a pleasure to make your house into a nice inn like this one, where, by feeding your guests, you'd be able to feed yourself, drink for free and make merry for the rest of your days!"

"Damn! Advice has its price, and the proverb is right that says that a good mother's son doesn't lie!" Antoine put in. "Hey, old woman! Something to drink, and better! There, Master Hermann, my colleague, drink, and don't forget not having supped at home yesterday!"

Hermann swallowed a full goblet of *eau-de-vie* in a single draught. "Damn!" he cried. "You're right, fellows! Out with the wife! And we'll soon be hanging the cooking-pot over a bright fire, for my old trade as a weaver is up in flames, I swear to you."

It was with a good heart that the charcoal-burners lavished wine and *eau-de-vie* upon their guest, for they had dreamed for some time of forming an association of rapine with him;

in fact, his house, transformed into an inn, would make an excellent subsidiary of their own. In addition, Herman had broad shoulders and solid fists; they could lend one another a strong hand if the occasion arose.

The old woman seemed to have divined the intentions of her masters, for while distributing Rhenish wine and cherry brandy around the table she did not neglect to fill Hermann's goblet twice rather than once.

As the weaver's drunkenness was augmented, his head was excited further against poor Ketha, His ignoble passions, over-stimulated by the drink and the encouragement of the charcoal-burners, drew him toward new crimes, and he was now yearning to return to the house that he had fled with so much horror, in order to throw his wife out.

Antoine's sons continued to design and excite his brutal instincts; suddenly, he got up and tipped over his goblet, still full, cursing.

"Damn it!" he cried. "No need to wait any longer to be master in my own house! It'll still be daylight for another hour; in any case, I know my route, and if you please, my good companions, we'll sup together tomorrow in my place!"

Upon which, the old woman having brought a good flask of *eau-de-vie*—for, she said, it was a lantern to light his way— he picked up an iron-tipped staff, staggered out of the hut, and advanced into the country.

At first he followed the route traced by a winy but rapid stride, as if a determined will had dominated momentarily the fumes of drunkenness.

Although it was already late, as the day had been fine, the last rays of sunlight were shining with a splendid glare, and the country was still illuminated by the fugitive light that gilds the atmosphere for a few moments before sunset. Crimson-tinted clouds, mingled with yellow and leaden hues, enveloped the star ready to disappear over the horizon, seemingly presaging an imminent storm, but until then the gold of its rays only made the shadows stand out more darkly.

Gradually, the action of the air completed the weaver's drunkenness; his ideas become confused and he stumbled over the stones of the road.

It was in vain that he tried to remember his route and to follow it with a firm stride; his unsteady legs seemed only to be lending him their service regretfully, and his mind no longer had any but a vague perception of exterior objects.

In the meantime, dusk enveloped the earth entirely in its gray veils; the blue mountains on the horizon were only separated from the sky by a line of fire, and the accumulated clouds were colored by coppery reflections, while the distant rumble of thunder announced the storm.

Hermann tried to increase his pace, but all his efforts only ended in making him turn about in the middle of a road that he no longer recognized. By the fugitive gleam of lightning flashes he perceived the towers of Halberstadt in the distance and the bell-tower of his village, but when he tried to orient himself in order to go in that direction, the towers and the belfry immediately changed location and appeared on the opposite side, as if to mock his efforts. The whole surrounding country, of which he had known every corner and viewpoint, every field and roof, since childhood, seemed to be spinning around him in order to multiply his uncertainties and astonishments.

It was like a vast circle shaken by an inexorable movement of rotation, and as darkness descended more thickly over the earth, the circle shrank, the more distant or less obtrusive objects faded into obscurity, and nothing any longer remained standing around the weaver but the fantastic silhouettes of pointed steeples, high keeps or gigantic oaks.

The storm was approaching with desperate rapidity; the clouds were crowding together and the lightning flashes were ever more frequent in their torn flanks. The wind chased dry leaves along the roads with strange noises, and swirled, whistling, in the high branches. At every turning and corner of the hedges a thousand fantastic forms appeared to the drunkard, which agitated in all directions to bar the route he traced, leading him astray in the long grass and laughing at his efforts.

Hermann became irritated against the obstacles, and swallowed further mouthfuls of *eau-de-vie* at regular intervals in order to sustain the futile struggle. He struck out angrily with his iron-tipped staff at all the real or imaginary barriers that hindered his progress.

"By the dead God!" he cried, furiously, "the devils have made a pact against me! Can't I finally find my house?"

And while stumbling, he went astray between the stunted trunks of a few old willows that bordered a stream, whose gnarled crowns seemed to make the hideous faces of gnomes appear periodically behind elder and privet bushes. At every step he hurled another horrible oath at the sky and made a more desperate effort, until, battle-weary, he returned toward another exit in order to search for his route. And it was pitiful to see him, tottering, marching at random, turning painfully in a circle that he had already explored twenty times over.

Sometimes, stiffening himself by means of a residue of lucid will, he launched himself at a run and crossed a large space with a single bound; sometimes, he fell, exhausted and bewildered, at the foot of a tree or into the mud of a ditch. He stayed still for a moment and then, brutalized and stupefied by ever thicker vapors of drunkenness—for at every pause he had recourse to his flask of eau-de-vie—he got to his feet again in order to search for his route through the paths that divided up the countryside and seemed to him to be multiplying infinitely and intersecting in an inextricable tangle, like the confused threads of a ball of silk.

Suddenly, without knowing how, he found his legs hindered by long grass, and stuck from time to time, as if by barriers hidden under creepers of terrestrial ivy and climbing plants.

The storm was imminent. The clouds intercepted the moonlight completely. The thunder, coming closer and closer, formed the dull rumble that precedes a downpour. The wind was swirling furiously in the trees and curbing them like reeds, and the earth exhaled the bitter odor that announces rain.

By means of a last effort of will, Hermann tried to hasten his steps and to free his legs from the bushy and tangled grass; but at each of his movements he seemed to receive a violent blow of a stick against his legs, and the more he agitated, the more the blows multiplied.

"May Satan come to my aid!" he cried, finally, in a paroxysm of fury. "By Fritz, my old friend, who danced so well for me yesterday, does Sire Lucifer not have in his domain a poor little blue flame at my service, to light my route?"

At that moment, large raindrops began to fall. Suddenly, a little blue flame, which cast no light, shot forth from the ground and described unknown forms on the wet ground. It danced with a magical rapidity, circling the weaver, licking his garments without burning them, and touching his feet without enabling them to feel any heat.

Hermann repeated horrible oaths a hundred times over; he struggled like a madman, but, soon embarrassed by the creepers, he fell face down on the ground. As he fell, he tore up violently one of the sticks that was striking his legs with redoubled blows. He raised it swiftly to eye level, and uttered a cry of malediction.

It was a black, worm-eaten cross. He had gone astray in the middle of an abandoned cemetery.

"Thunder!" he cried. "You're bad jokers, Messieurs the dead! By the devil!! Since the fires of Hell give no light, isn't there one of your old carcasses that wants to get up to show me my way?"

The rain was falling in torrents.

Hermann's foot struck a grave still freshly dug.

"Hola, all of you! Is there no kind companion here who wants to help me? If some good son of Satan will come with me, I'll keep him to supper! I'll slake his damned thirst with my last bottles of Rhenish wine, and then guide him back politely to his lodgings, in order that he can offer me as much!"

And the drunkard accompanied those blasphemous words with cynical bursts of laughter. But suddenly, a malediction expired on his lips and the laughter caught in his throat. He had just felt himself gripped by an icy hand.

That stiff, bony and hooked hand sank into his flesh by means of a horrible pressure and shook him with a superhuman violence.

His head cleared as if by magic, and all the blood flowed back toward his heart.

In the midst of the horrors of overturned nature, the fury of the storm, the claps of thunder and sinister lightning flashes that embroidered the clouds with fiery festoons, a specter loomed up, motionless and terrible.

Hermann raised his eyes swiftly, and suddenly closed them again. A lightning flash that had just lit up the sky from the orient to the occident had struck the hideous head of the specter; it was the weaver's old companion, the killecroff accursed throughout the land, Fritz the hanged man!

Hermann fell to his knees, chilled by horror, paralyzed by fear.

The blue flame, having vanished momentarily, had just returned; it launched forth, bold and incompressible, before the specter and enveloped it like an infernal circle. Its faint light only projected phosphorescent reflections over it, and Fritz stood out against the thick darkness like a pale blue silhouette.

It really was him, such as the inhabitants of the region had seen him for a long time, attached to the gibbet of Halberstadt.

His stiff, long and green-tinted body was dislocated at the joints. His horribly contracted features mimed the grimace of the scaffold; his red hair stood up over his forehead as if by virtue of a supreme anguish, and his round and bloody eyes protruded from their orbits.

But so much hideousness, once attenuated by the dull reflection of death, now contained the flame of a supernatural and diabolical life. His limbs agitated, as if put to work by a spring, and slowly bent at the joints with an automatic movement. The ardent color of his hair was heightened by gleams that resembled jets of fire, and his eyes, veiled by his thick eyebrows as if by a necessary shadow, resembled carbuncles and launched flashes of lightning.

He was motionless. and he plunged that terrible gaze all the way to the utmost depths of the weaver's soul. The latter remained fascinated, as if by an invincible power; a muted gasp exhaled from his throat; his teeth chattered; he remained nailed to the ground by a supreme terror.

This was not the nightmare of the day before but a terrible reality!

By means of a slow movement, the phantom lifted his right arm and extended it toward the horizon. Far away, in a straight line from the end of that arm, a light was shining, like a star in the night. By the intermittent reflections of the storm, Hermann recognized his house, where Ketha was still awake.

Completely sobered up by terror, he bounded out of the cemetery and started running desperately through the countryside.

He ran with a prodigious rapidity. Neither the beating rain that lashed his face nor the gusts of the west wind that almost lifted up the earth stopped his hectic course. Launched forward by the omnipotent force of terror, he traversed woods and precipices, in spite of the obscurity, without collision, without drawing breath and without looking behind him.

And the further he went, the faster his flight seemed. One might have thought him, not a man traveling over the ground, but a demon flying to the sabbat on the clouds of the sky.

Finally, the rain ceased momentarily and the clouds parted, letting a few rays of moonlight escape. Harassed, out of breath, exhausted, unable to do any more, Hermann let himself fall like a mass at the foot of a tree.

He propped himself up in the wet grass and lifted his eyes to see where he was.

Great God! He was at the foot of the gibbet of Halberstadt, and Fritz, the hideous specter with the green-tinted limbs, the twisted mouth and the flamboyant eyes was before him, upright and impassive, his arm extended toward the horizon.

Horror rendered the weaver a new energy; he resumed his desperate flight.

The fields, the meadows, the mountains and the valleys disappeared in turn behind him, mute witnesses of distances crossed.

From time to time he turned round, vanquished by fatigue; then he saw Fritz, who was still following him, always at an equal distance, always at the same measured and automatic pace.

In vain he took more forceful strides, in vain he leapt across unusual spaces; in vain, in his superhuman course, he scarcely skimmed the ground. The specter, in spite of the slowness of his march, did not lose an inch of ground. Sometimes, Hermann even thought that he was on the point of being overtaken and seized once again by the terrible hand of the hanged man. Then fear lent him wings. He ran without looking back for instants that seemed to be hours, and when strength failed him and obliged him to catch his breath, he still found the phantom behind him, and there was not one pace more between them, nor one pace less.

The night had advanced; the rain, having become finer, was still cold and penetrating; a mortal silence reigned in the region. But the infernal voyage continued its course relentlessly. The weaver was still traversing woods and fields, and yet he never reached the end of his journey. It seemed that distances all took on fantastic proportions and extended immeasurably.

The unfortunate man, within sight of the village, shouted and called for help, but his voice expired in his throat, stifled by fear, and his teeth were chattering with a violence that did not permit him to formulate a prayer.

Finally, exhausted, dying, at the end of strength and courage, Herman arrived at the threshold of his house, seized the door-knocker and agitated it frenziedly, uttering howls of fright.

Ketha recognized her husband's voice and came down the stairs, recommending her soul to God.

Hermann struck redoubled blows; he heard the inexorable march of the specter behind him, and the seconds appeared to him to be centuries of anguish.

Finally, the bolts emerged from their sockets and the door opened.

Hermann leapt into the house, his head lost, his eyes haggard, like a madman. He pushed the bolts again with all the force that he could still find and looked around.

But the specter had not come into the house.

"Wife!" he cried. "Quickly, quickly . . . ! Bring everything here . . . everything that we have . . . quickly . . . quickly . . . the furniture, the casks . . . everything, everything!"

And, tottering, he leaned on the wall.

Ketha remained immobile, not understanding. Hermann opened the judas-hole in the door and showed her Fritz, who was still advancing.

The poor woman uttered a scream of horror.

"My brother!"

Then, understanding her husband's idea by means of a rapid intuition, she launched herself into the cellar.

In an instant, the ladders, the vats and the barrels were snatched from their places and heaped up before the door in a formidable barricade.

In the common room, at the top of the steps, they closed the door, bolted it again and forbade access by means of a pyramid of furniture that they prepared to sustain with their bodies.

When the last fortification was complete, the weaver collapsed, exhausted; Ketha threw herself to her knees beside him and implored God.

But the footsteps of the accursed killecroff approached continuously. Soon they were heard making the pavement of the courtyard resound under their sonorous impact.

Ketha seized Hermann in her arms and said a supreme prayer. She had forgiven, and prayed to God to forgive also.

Suddenly, the footsteps stopped; there was a moment of silence, and the door-knocker, slowly lifted, fell back again with a dull thud.

They both leapt to the interior door and stiffened themselves, sustaining the furniture that defended it with all the force of their taut limbs. Then, motionless, their respiration halted on their lips, they waited.

After a few seconds, a second blow was repeated by the echo.

A solemn silence reigned in nature. A third blow, stronger than the first two, made the exterior barricades tremble.

Ketha felt faint.

"My God, what does he want?" she asked her husband, in a voice so faint that he only divined by the movement of her lips what he could not hear.

"I blasphemed . . . I invoked Satan . . . I challenged the dead to show me my way, to send me a guide . . . I invited a damned soul to come and sup here . . . I promised to follow him thereafter. And Fritz came . . ."

The weaver's voice expired in his throat, for the hammer struck the door three times, at equal intervals, and at the third stroke, the first barricade shook, while two barrels rolled on the floor.

There was an inexpressible anguish; the patients felt their hair stand up on their heads and all their blood froze in their veins.

The blows were still resounding, and at every impact an item of furniture fell, clearing the entrance to the house. Soon, the bolts themselves opened without resistance.

Then the specter's slow footsteps struck the steps of the staircase at regular intervals. When he reached the last one, his bony fingers struck a dry rap on the panel of the door, and the wall trembled.

As at the first barrier, every blow overturned an obstacle; as at the first barrier, when the last obstacle fell, the door opened by itself, and Fritz the hanged man appeared on the threshold.

At that horrible sight, Ketha fell in a faint; Hermann fled into the darkest corner of the room and huddled against the wall, as if he hoped go find a refuge there. But the pitiless specter marched straight toward him, gripped him with steely fingers, lifted him off the floor and sat him down facing him at the dining table; and when they were both seated, he darted his flamboyant eyes at his former companion and struck the table with a curt blow to demand the promised supper.

Hermann uttered a despairing cry and shook his head in a sign of refusal. "In the name of God, go away!" he murmured feebly, trying to make an impossible sign of the cross.

But the killecroff remained immobile, maintaining his funereal rictus and keeping his damned soul's eyes fixed on the weaver. He struck the table a second time, more imperatively

Then, in a choked voice, the weaver appealed to his wife: "Ketha . . . !"

The poor creature lifted herself up painfully and opened her eyes slightly.

At the sight of her husband and the specter of her brother, she let out a shrill cry and fell back, broken, like someone emerging from a horrible dream only to enter into a reality even more terrible.

The killecroff rapped for a third time.

"Ketha," murmured Hermann, "fetch us something to drink."

Moved by a supernatural force, fascinated by the terrible gaze of the hanged man, she got up, took a few dried fruits and a piece of ham from the dresser, and placed them on the table in front of the two diners; then she rinsed out two pewter goblets mechanically and put them alongside; then, still followed by those two eyes, which resembled torches lit by Hellfire, she went down to the cellar in order to fetch the last bottles that Hermann had left there.

When the bottles had been deposited in front of him, Fritz took his goblet and raised it in the air. Hermann filled it to the rim and replaced the bottle on the table.

But the specter's arms remained motionless and extended until Hermann had also poured himself a drink and had approached the wine to his lips, blue-tinted by fear.

Then the golden liquid seemed to descend the killecroff's throat as if through the plug-hole of an empty barrel; and while drinking, he still directed his fixed gaze at the weaver. Under that insupportable pressure, the unfortunate weaver was also forced to drink.

When Hermann put down his goblet, he found the extended arm of his guest before him again, requesting more wine. It was necessary to fill the empty cup again and renew the funereal libation.

And when the first two bottles were finished, Fritz, still pitiless, thumped the table to demand moiré.

Still under the killecroff's infernal domination, Ketha obeyed his signs without being conscious of herself.

Fritz did not eat, but he kept drinking. The wine seemed to circulate in his veins as in an avid and desiccated torrent, without animating his face, and without warming his rigid limbs or rendering them any more supple.

Finally, when the last bottle had disgorged its last drop of liquid, when the last goblet had been emptied, the specter stood up, and with an inflexible gesture, made a sign to the weaver to follow him in his turn.

With a bound that contained a supreme energy, the unfortunate launched himself to the back of the room and hung on with the force of his most powerful grip to the columns of the bed. Then, with a heart-rending cry, he invoked Ketha one last time as a protective angel.

With a movement more rapid than thought, the poor woman had thrown herself upon her husband to try to shield him with her body; but the killecroff ground out his sinister laugh and plunged his hooked fingers into the weaver's thick hair; with a single effort he lifted him away from that feeble aegis and threw Ketha far away.

Between the dead man and the living one there was a horrible combat, devoid of pity and mercy. Sobbing, Ketha clung on to her husband's garments; she invoked God and even begged on behalf of the dead man.

Hermann clung to the furniture, the walls and the steps of the staircase with all his strength; but the frightful specter did not seem to hear the prayers or feel the resistance. Having reached the exterior door, Hermann grabbed the doorpost and clung to it with his fingernails and teeth; Ketha threw herself across the path. Fritz kicked her away and went past, dragging his prey, without looking back.

Ketha remained unconscious on the threshold of the dwelling.

When she recovered her senses, the night allowed her to glimpse the first glimmers of morning, and a funereal bell was ringing the knell of the dead, for Barbel had just expired in the house of the rector of Arnsberg.

Then she went up to the upper room and knelt down to pray next to the open window.

The rain had stopped, the clouds were dispersing in the sky, and on the horizon the pale tints that announced the day were enabling the silhouettes of bell-towers and keeps to emerge from the blackness.

Far, far away in the countryside, Ketha was still able to recognize the phantom of the killecroff, dragging the inanimate body of her husband through the brambles and the stones.

And, so the legend says, Hermann was never seen again down here.

THE REDEMPTRIX

by Victor-Émile Michelet

> And there appeared a great wonder
> in Heaven, a woman clothed with
> the sun, and the moon under her
> feet, and upon her head a crown
> of twelve stars.
> (*Revelation* XII: 1)

OH, gilded flower of my ideal, you bloom too high for my hand ever to pluck you.

Certainly, my gaze has never quit you, but it is with an irremediable despair that from below—from below forever!—I see your silhouette flamboyant on the horizon of my dream.

And I go forth, I go through life, groping for obstacles, rubbing shoulders with men whose natal baseness I disdain. I march in darkness, the density of which oppresses me and stifles me. And I sense that the darkness will not be illuminated again, whatever happens, that I shall turn around in the obscurity of a funerary crypt.

Certain kabbalists claim that many men are dead, who believe that they are alive because they have conserved the appearances of life. Perhaps I am one of those men. My soul departed with *her*, when she disappeared. Oh, I felt the wing of distress pass over my forehead on that day, the day on which I saw her for the last time. Since then, I have been a dead man walking.

How can I talk about *her?* How can I express in words the impression that her presence gave me? It was the fête of my life. Her aspect multiplied my energies. Existing in her atmosphere, I was conscious of inhabiting a world in which the soul blossomed in bliss. Her person suggested joy, certainty and strength. On seeing her, I understood what theologians call the real presence.

I have lived. Now I am almost old. For having known that creature, what thanks do I not owe to destiny? Often, before the happiness of seeing her had illuminated my sad heart, I envied men whose powers permitted them to march in the orbit of a sublime being. To live in the radiation of a hero; to be a disciple blindly trusting a tranquil and strong master; to be a frail John whose head leaned on the serene shoulder of a Jesus—how many times did I sigh after that possibility?

I have envied you, poor fishermen to whom the mere gesture of the Nazarene Master opened the golden door of total Knowledge.

For I am not a demigod. Although my ideal is higher than that of other men, I remain at their level. I was a seagull whose wings devoid of feathers extended toward the immensity, without the power to soar there.

Now, *she* appeared. I approached her. And all the embryonic forces within me stirred. My most obscure virtualities were manifest in deeds. I cannot imagine an intensity equal to the one I felt in her radiation. Yes, I tell you, my sensibility had joy, my intelligence certainty, my will power. Who was she? An incarnation, a human appearance radiating Wellbeing.

In truth, to remember the man that I was before her coming it requires a painful effort. For I date from the friction of her dress on my life. I had suffered a great deal, I had studied a great deal. I knew all the science of scholars—which is to say, nothing.

I ought to note how my thought was occupied with her for the first time. In what fashion did I succeed in making myself understood? For me, whom she deigned to initiate with a gaze to the most inviolable arcana of life and death, for me, before whom her forbearance opened the five doors of light by means of which one enters the world of causes, for me, all the events contingent to her mysterious existence appeared in the lucidity of absolute logic. But would people understand them? I feel in regard to them like an older brother who is making a little child a portrait of the adorable deceased other whom his adolescence knew. No matter! I shall say how, for the first time, my thought was occupied with *her*.

There was an annunciation of her advent. One night, I had stayed up late poring over an old folio volume of anxious science. Two o'clock had just chimed on the clock of Notre-Dame-des-Champs, of which my house was a neighbor. The weather was stormy, heavy and oppressive. I had shut the window. Heavy Oriental drapes hung along the four walls of my room, in order to isolate my frequent meditations from the exterior world. At that moment I had pushed away my book in order to write notes. I heard a slight continuous rustle.

It's a moth, I said to myself, *which came in while the window was open.*

I lifted up my lamp in order to illuminate the whole room. Not having perceived anything, I resumed writing.

When I raised my head again, stupor held me motionless in my armchair. In front of me, in the lamplight, an extraordinary vision had invaded my room: a naked woman standing on a sphinx. I perceived all the details of that phantasm with an extraordinary precision. The sphinx appeared to be a living animal, of a volume almost equal to that of a horse. Oh, it really was the sibylline beast whose claw oppressed the courageous breast of Oedipus.

It was moving slowly through the air, its vast wings deployed with grace and strength. Its body, as white as marble, was quivering with tamed energy. My imagination, accustomed to represent that allegorical monster in the serene immobility that the sculptors of ancient Egypt attributed to it, was astonished at first to see the vibration of an intense supernatural life in that being, in that human head, of a dolorous and tranquil beauty, in its taurean flanks, in its lion's paws, an in its eagle's wings, which were bumping into the walls of my room as if impatient for limitless space.

On that mount, the young woman was standing calmly. Oh, the strange beauty! The slenderness of her body, the marvelous oval of her face, and, amid the dark undulations of her hair, the gilded pallor of her complexion! An expression of superhuman energy spread in a divine softness, an audacity of innocent domination radiated from that head, from the black profundities of the eyes, from the sinuosity of the lips and the heroic outline of the chin.

The Visitor was brushing the back of the sphinx with her placid feet as a goddess might caress the pale sphere of a world with an indulgent toe. A sidereal rider, she had tamed in the blink of an eye the pride of the hierogrammatic animal, which, abjuring any attempt at prancing and any whim of revolt, was prepared to carry the mystery of that victorious will into the infinite with a thrust of its submissive wings.

That conquering beauty invaded my entire soul with an irresistible and suave vehemence. She did not seem to me to be a woman. Her magnificent nudity did not awaken any amour or desire in me. Oh, I remember that, in that minute, an intimate revolution changed the face of my being. Immediately, I felt the analytical faculties from which I had drawn vanity abolished. My intelligence awoke in a renascence. My soul was washed by a lustral water, which impregnated it with enthusiasm, power and plenitude. Life enveloped it like a diaphanous mantle.

Certainly, that apparition, which was to have a definitive influence over my destiny, constituted what the vulgar call a hallucination. But what is a hallucination, if not the projection, on the visible plane, of an invisible reality obedient to the call of our imagination? My thought creates that which it affirms; and are the Platonists not right to consider ideas and images as alive, immortal daughters of the spirit, emanations of the eternal Word? In any case, the distinction that one is accustomed to make between reality and unreality seems to me to be an insult to the subtlety of intelligence so coarse that I shall not deign to linger upon it. Is not reality a subjective creation of the mind that perceives it? Oh, whatever you were, exalting vision, your mere proximity had overturned my soul.

O dominatrix,

You have entered, triumphant and mild, into my ecstatic soul like a beloved king into a village in fête. As soon as the revelation of your possibility, as soon as the caress of your image, as soon as your annunciation, I have cried toward you from the depths of my distress. A gesture of your right hand has opened my eyes. Into the field of my mind you threw the seed of a world. You were Royalty, Glory and Strength.

O liberatrix,

You have entered, triumphant and mild, into my ecstatic soul like a savior warrior into an enslaved town. In the darkness in which my servitude was languishing you brought torches and starlight. The demon of doubt that was gnawing my breast, you expelled with a sign, and your venerated hand has broken my shackles. You summoned Light to my forehead. You were the Truth, the Way and the Life

O consolatrix,

You have entered, triumphant and mild, into my ecstatic soul like a blessed hero into a city in dread. The intoxication of marching in the wake of your robe has charmed all my woes. Your gaze has melted the burden of the dolorous past, which weighed upon my shoulder. Your smile is the flower that confirms life. You were Joy, Hope and Amour.

From the day when that vision came to me, I no longer had any but one desire: to see that creature, whose existence in this world I sensed; to see her and attach myself to her footsteps. The goal of life was flamboyant before my eyes. The goal of life was to march in the circle of her gaze, was to be impregnated by her radiation, was to respire her emanation.

The irresistible impulsion that projected me toward that woman was not sexual amour. In the impetuosity of my youth, amour had watered me with all its delights and all its anguish; but this Unknown Woman had invaded me with a sentiment analogous to the one that believers have for their god, that of Magdalen for Jesus, that of Saint Theresa for the Crucified. For me she was the Divine made flesh. She was an abyss of light into which I rolled recklessly.

Where would I see her? For surely she existed. In what place in the world would it be given to me to approach her sublime silhouette? Sometimes, a horrible anguish gripped me. What if I were never to see her? What if she had manifested herself thus to me uniquely? To glimpse that mysterious mirage for an instant, to understand in certainty that she existed, and never to contemplate her sacred feet! Perhaps I was not worthy of her presence? I passed through all the graduated alternatives of hope and despair.

At all hazard, and even though an intimate voice cried to me that such a creature laughed at distance, that she was not enslaved, like the rest of us, by the norms of space, I was always ready to depart; I was always ready to run, at the top speed of present means of locomotion, toward the country that possessed her aspect.

One morning, I received an invitation to an intimate tea at the home of Madame X***. The name was unknown to me. I threw the letter on the table indifferently, with the intention of sending the woman my card. I had completely forgotten that incident of a mundane order when the appointed evening arrived. An irresistible need then invaded me to render to that invitation. I dressed in haste, and an hour later I arrived in the small town house in which Madame X*** lived, very close to the foliage of the Bois de Boulogne.

As soon as I crossed the threshold of the drawing room, an emotion took possession of me. *She* was there. Yes, this time it was really her, alive and similar to the apparition that had bowled me over. As on the night of the annunciation, I sensed a superhuman expansion within me, a heroic exaltation of my entire being. In less than a second, I perceived everything that was happening in the drawing room, and I penetrated its mystery. Why is it necessary for me, in order to try to give an impression of it today, only to be able to use the cold and impotent succession of words?

Isiah, your breath has vivified my breast. In order to speak about you, to evoke your essence, give your faithful follower the force of genius and the speech of the Prophets! In order to confide to the world a pale exoteric notion of what their gentle Master was, the four evangelists, the quaternary of disciples who accompanied the Lion, the Angel, the Eagle and the Bull have clad the esoteric allegory of their story in simplicity. Alone on Patmos, John revealed, under the veil of a higher symbolism, the fulgurant Word that only Initiates understand. Isiah, in order for your reign to arrive, others will announce your Word in the due form. I shall simply say what you enabled in me.

✳

Isiah spoke, standing up, in a circle of listeners avid for her voice.

She was dressed in a white robe of Chinese crepe, the admirable organization of which and the profound esthematic[1] would have discouraged the most expert Parisian couturiers. Over the right skirt, pressed by a very light gathering, ran the pleats of a bodice garnished with silver embroideries, the modern arrangement of which evoked a memory of the peplum. Delicately opened over the masculine beauty of the throat, the undulating pleats of that bodice permitted the body of the woman a sumptuous liberty of attitudes, seemingly maintained by a silver cord around the waist, the curve of which they accompanied in order to fade away along the skirt.

With the sudden lucidity that the proximity of that creature inspired in me, I understood the symbolism of that evening dress, marrying the vestimental forms of the Orient and the Occident, and charged with silver, the lunar and feminine metal.

A glance over the members of the audience alerted me to all their idiosyncrasy. There were some twenty men and women there, belonging to different social categories. Amid the

---

1 The slightly esoteric term *esthematique* [esthematic] is defined in Nicolas Bescherelle's 1845 dictionary as "pertaining to costume." It was briefly popularized by Octave Uzanne in the title of a history of French fashion, but Michelet's story predates that 1897 text.

luxury of that drawing room there were men of the people, and also those people that society calls *déclassé*, with foreheads too high to pass under the low doors that led to the cowsheds of the flourishing mediocrity, breasts inflated by an idea that only emerges in sobs! All had faces sealed by suffering; and I sensed that those men were my brothers.

Desolate hearts: some, on the threshold of a chagrined maturity had been tossed harshly by the swell of life; others, on the threshold of their adolescence, had resorbed their efflorescence, alarmed with a sacred fear by an intuition of the dolors of life. Oh, like mine; those hearts had groaned toward the serenity of a faith; they had all palpitated toward a master who would orientate definitively the nobility of their essential impetus, who would guide toward an unknown sky the quivering wings of their will.

There were sad young women. There was a weary courtesan whose soul no one had fathomed, and who ennobled the charity of having offered to the unfortunate the consoling flower of her beauty. There was a noble virgin, lamentable in not having encountered on earth the elect of her dream; and also a woman bewildered by bearing in her loins the immortal wound of her betrayed amour. There was a mother from whom the tomb had stolen seven children. And among them was the mistress of the house, Madame X***. She was a woman of about thirty, of an unhealthy elegance. I read in her faded blue eyes the dolorous secret of her past, and I bent over to kiss her meager hand.

A glory of morning magnified the foreheads of the men, whom destiny had treated differently. Some were simple, accustomed to daily labor. There was a pastor with eyes enlarged by the kiss of the stars; a pale miner whose deformed body developed the awkward gesture of nocturnal beasts; a sailor whose rude mask was resplendent with the nobility that the habit of braving danger imprints. Children of the sea, the earth and the sky; weary bodies, candid hearts, and new heads; no social hypocrisy, no conventional baseness, and no fallacious education had assaulted the august liberty of their instinct. Having known no other masters than nature and tribulation, their intact souls were ready to understand everything.

There was an orator, a generous homilist of revolt, who, shaking off the resignation of the poor and the oppressed, had clamored toward a vision of justice, had extended the anger of his vibrant fists toward the ignominy of the rich and powerful. There was a very young dreamer whose admirable solar beauty was radiant with genius. Others, in sum, whom life had disappointed: a flock of bleeding souls in quest of a pastor with saving hands.

We were twenty and one around Isiah, all still young.

Oh, that evening of my life embalmed me for eternity; I had the sentiment of being, in a glorious flesh, a divine soul. And likewise were the twenty companions of my ecstasy. A total revivification had effaced the anguishes of nature, as if Isiah's magnificent hand had extended toward their ardent nostrils the azure flower of nepenthe, from which one inhales forgetfulness. All lovers of an illuminative existence, we were liberated from Time, Number and Space and we were floating in the Eternal with the vertigo of eaglets trying their wings in the liberty of the skies.

And I heard *her* voice, her silence already expanded over me, with a torrential force, her infinite thought. But the music of that thought, that adorable speech, awoke in me the plenitude of a somnolent world. And I saw *her* body, a radiant symbol of her soul. She had given the scepter of her hand to our lips, a hand sculpted for power and superhuman audacity. Then I understood the charm with which she enveloped beings. In her, there was nothing that was not in accordance with the perfect Rhythm, rhythm being the most direct expression of the Word. She was all harmony, and her grace realized the immutable logic of her potentialities.

There was an organ in the room. Isiah sat down at the keyboard, and I had the revelation of Music, that angelic language capable of concentrating in a definitive formula the most mysterious vibrations of human being and worlds. For music is to speech what Amour is to Thought, what the eagle is to the cricket. Beyond speech, a narrow hood shaped to fit a single idea corseted with precision, it is a cloak vast enough to shelter the unlimited aspiration of being; it is the monstrous voice that sings the exegesis of the infinite.

But all the music I had known, what was it? An infantile stammer! The vehement fervor of Bach, the somber anxiety of Beethoven, the passion of Wagner and all those beautiful cries of genius in the parturition of a dream, how frail and frozen they appeared to me!

In that ineffable evening, my soul, in flight in the mysterious orbit of sonorities, perceived the total Revelation. Yes. I lived harmony. Rhythm carried me away, a bewildered corybant, into the sphere of the angels, and, my eyes dazzled by wild light, I rolled in the golden egg where the gods involve.

Scarcely had Isiah run her fingers over the keys than we all felt a solemn and vertiginous frisson run through us. That new music bathed us, washed away our past, enveloped us with rebirth. In order to uncover for us there and then the limitless horizon of her soul, Isiah spoke to us in the seraphic language in which the mystery of her essence became a parable. On the cheeks of my companions, pale with a sacred pallor, slow tears trickled, the dew of a spiritual dawn.

Who, then, would have the derisory pretention of analyzing that hymn? To begin with it sang, formidably, all our past sufferings, intimately precise and all fused together in the immensity of human dolor. But while showing us the withering memory, it transported us to a mountain of bliss, like prisoners contemplating from the height of a sunlit summit the somber city in which yesterday's prison stood. Then, launched from that black world to rise toward a world of whiteness, we had the sensation of soaring, spirits under full sail, through cycles of eternal wellbeing, which she filled with her triumphant presence.

The finale was vibrating within us when Isiah stood up. Every amorous emotion is made of a delight and an anguish. In our rapturous minds an anguish became sharp: was *she* about to quit us? After being manifest, a sun in the darkness, might she not vanish, leaving in our charmed eyes the regret of the adored vision? For none of us could any longer conceive life without *her*.

She calmed our dread with a smile, and spoke.

"Friends, we are going to live together, in a solitary land where no noise of the world will trouble our peace. You will be alerted when the time has come. Let serenity be within you, and strength, for you are the elect of a mysterious destiny."

A gesture of her bright hands and I no longer saw *her*. In the room, we remained mute, but the benediction of the creature lived within us, delectably.

A supper awaited us. No one dared raise his voice for fear of alarming the silence, full of dreams of having known her. I tried to interrogate Madame X***. She looked at me with consoled eyes, without responding.

The railway deposited us, on a light evening in spring, on the edge of a high forest extended over the side of a hill. We found one another again, the twenty and one companions of the memorable evening, in the delight of our common secret, and we exchanged the kiss of our gazes. We knew that it was necessary to traverse the forest. We walked along a winding path at a brisk pace without pronouncing a word. All vibrant with the same sentiment, it was not necessary to awaken the debilitated echo of it. And we had the intuition of being a single collective soul living the same thought, absorbing the same amour.

The shadow enveloped us. The woodland voices of which, in the course of my childhood walks, I had heard the sinister buzz, shivering—the intermittent voices in which are scattered the rustling of leaves, the creaking of stems and the noises of nocturnal insects—accompanied the beating of our hearts. And we raised our heads in the expectation of seeing, between the black masses of foliage, the flamboyant star descend that would guide our march toward *her*.

We reached the summit of the hill, from which we could hear the sea growling. There was a house among the trees. That was it. A door opened of its own accord, and we penetrated into the hoped-for refuge, shaking off with the dust of our soles all the anguish of the evanescent past.

Poverty, the poverty of human aspiration! When Psyche possessed Eros in nocturnal mystery, she had happiness. What did derisory curiosity matter? No, it was necessary that she abandon her heart in fête to the insidious demon of anxiety. And am I not, by virtue of natal impulsion, a simple soul? Why did the stars that scintillated over my cradle deprive me of heroic and credulous candor?

Isiah, when my bosom was resplendent under your gaze like a helm of steel under the fires of the sun, I occupied the supreme peace, the peace promised to men of good will. But your absence was the return of darkness. In the hours when I no longer sensed upon me the influx of your will, I yielded to the phantom of curious distress. I desired to know the key to the divine enigma that was You. I allowed the armor of my faith to be corroded. And that is why I lost the gleam of your trace.

*

It was during the morning meal on the day after our arrival in that blessed house. We were gathered around a vast table. In the frame of the windows, we perceived the sunlit sea. It seemed to us that we would have been able, behind *her*, to walk on those waves all the way to the horizon, beyond which the fatherland of our hopes might be resplendent.

She was wearing a pale blue robe, in linen cloth, the loose pleats of which broadcast quietude to us. Blue, the color of Amour, inspires calm in sick souls. A golden belt rose toward her breasts. She exercised her hospitality with a sovereign grace. Croaz, the sailor, was sitting to her right, Heliel, the handsome young poet, whose gilded eyes reflected the bewildered dream of being enchained to her gesture, to her left.

A glad silence floated over us. Who would have dared to break with a voice the charm scattered in our confidence? And we ate the bread as if her lips had said: "Eat, this is my flesh."

An impenetrable meditation darkened Isiah's beautiful forehead, but without tarnishing the golden radiation that our sharpened senses perceived around her dark tresses. A tear was suspended on the velvet of her eyelashes, and there was the heavy flight of a distress over us. Suffering, then, could bite into the marble of that bosom, in which our strength resided.

She had a divinely sad smile.

"Friends," she said, "children of my election, I am suffering your suffering. Forgive my forehead for being morose. I have woven a crown for it of all the thorns that will wound you. I am weeping for your future dolor in losing me. For you will lose my appearance. Alas, your curiosity will chase me away from you. Thus the Law wishes it."

We shivered. Heliel let his desperate hands fall upon the table. "Oh!" he said. "I believed in the eternity of seeing you!"

He expressed our sentiment; for our hearts were vibrating in unison, and each of us was a string of a unique lyre, of which the finger of Isiah revealed the harmonious soul.

"Heliel! What cloud is enveloping your genius? Have you forgotten, then, why you are here? Poet, gentle missionary of the Word, be able to support the bitterness of exile in a world where you are not heard. Your voice reveals beauty and amour, two of the highest manifestations of the gods. And since it announces the word of the gods, who will understand it among humans that have renounced the energy of belief? No matter; you will do your duty of a Hero. You will sing, like your brother Orpheus, among the beasts; you will reflect light, son of the Sun, upon the somber children of Saturn."

"Isiah! No, I can no longer forget the Causes. I was summoned to your presence in order that an inextinguishable enthusiasm should set my life as an apostle ablaze."

"None of your gestures is devoid of a cause, as none is devoid of an effect. If each of you was chosen to come to me, it is by virtue of immemorial reasons of which I know the origins. In all of you, dolor exalted life. Each of you is a link in a chain that still attaches me to the earth. I was sent here for a mission. I shall direct the course of the river of your allied wills toward the ocean of mystery."

"Isiah," I asked, trembling like a child, "Jesus of Nazareth was the son of God. Alas, we are no longer able to adore the bloody feet of Jesus. Are you, Isiah, the daughter of God?"

"Jesus, my supreme brother, has said: 'I inform you making use of the speech of the earth, and you do not hear me; how would you be able to understand me if I spoke the language of Heaven?' And I say to you: every man is the son of God; all living flesh is the symbol of a divine thought. Every man is an Adam summoned to become a Christos. He is three Adams.

Meditate, and you will understand the meaning of words. Now, beings are born who have a more profound revelation of the Truth. They arrive on earth, from time to time, delegated and sanctified, in order to show humans the increate Light. They do not fasten all the sails with which destiny covers them, for mortal eyes would be burned by their glare. When Moses descended from Sinai, having contemplated the increate Light, he knew that humans would be unable to support the dazzling reflection on his brow, and he hid his face with a flap of his cloak. The Revelators, his sacred brethren, the Buddha, Mahomet, the Báb and all the Messiahs lifted over the world, in their predestined fists, the torch that each of them had lit from the same resplendent hearth. But if they had unveiled the naked glory of the hearth itself, they would have blinded the eyes of races. To the unique and eternal Truth they built sanctuaries of different architectures. They sang the same hymn in various languages. And when they expired, voluntary victims, their last breath swept away one of the clouds interposed between the planet and the absolute. The supreme breath of the Crucified tears the veil that covers the Temple. He has given a part of the world the keys of the initiation."

Her voice carried us away like a river of force. Having reposed the gleam of her eyes in a vision, she went on: "I have come to you in order to put you on the path. Then I shall return."

Her head tilted toward her shoulder. Her beauty seemed to us more profound than the Heavens. Our hands came together, extended toward her. Sobs rose up from our group.

"Isiah! Isiah! Don't leave us!"

Her voice caressed us: "Friends, it will be my good fortune to suffer for you. The Law is ineluctable: the initiator perishes by the initiate."

Her smile melted our anguish. An enthusiasm irrupted within us, vaster than the blue sea whose waves we perceived through the window. Oh, to live, to live that hour . . .

The worlds were as transparent for us as globes of crystal, and we existed in the power.

Heliel's voice formulated our thought, our gratitude and our hope:

⁕

"O Revelatrix,

"I salute you outside Time, for I know you in the Eternal. You exist, O daughter of God. O supreme symbol of femininity. The Ancient of Days is your father and you were engendered in the womb of the Divine Mother. You are the silver cup in which my charmed soul drinks—Salut!

"O Salvatrix,

"I salute you, you come to us with hands full of graces and fingers extended for benedictions, bearing the ring of amour and the ring of forgetfulness that Moses forged. Between your breasts, suspended from your silver necklace, the seven talismans repose that caressed the vapor of perfumes flying toward the septenary of planets. And your eyes are gentler to wounds than oil and wine.

"O Redemptrix,

"I salute you. In tearing from our gaze the veil that hid the light, you charged your beautiful forehead with our heavy sins. All the weaknesses of our frail wills, you assume, adorable starveling of sacrifice; and the palest of our smiles to Sathan is an arrow that goes to pierce your bosom. Triumphatrix of suffering, I salute you in the glorious eternity in which you are enthroned, near Horus, to the left of Isis.

"Your Name is a Mystery. Your Age is a Mystery. You count thirty-three years; for you have meditated during the twelve hours and you have accomplished the twelve labors. Into the calm palace of your breast, the five infernal torments have rushed: Bitterness, Pain, Darkness, inextinguishable Ardor and penetrating Putrescence. And, smiling, you trample under your victorious foot the four demons of the elements who howl at the four corners of the world: Samael, prince of Salamanders; Azazel, prince of Sylphs; Azael, prince of Undines; and Mahazahel, prince of Gnomes.

"You are a Mystery yourself. You emerge from the heart of God in order to bring us back to him. Sons of the Fall, children in exile, we will rise again in your wake toward the bosom of our father. Eyes of the light of your glory, we shall evolve, through supracelestial cycles, having scorned the ambushes of serpents, dogs and fire. You will give us the strength to defeat the Dragon Nahasch, which guards the gates of Heaven, and we shall pass, clad in joy, through the sonorous flights of the Angels, the Cherubim and the Seraphim, toward the throne of musical gems where you reign, contemplating the repose of the cohorts of Fire."

The hours passed, as caressant as mothers. The hours! What scorn we had for that habitual human conception! Time, that lamentable division of eternity! We were delivered from its embrace. Our spirits moved in a limitless liberty, and our eyes were able to see effects in causes.

Her presence enveloped us in wellbeing. How sweet the air was in our lungs during walks along the sea shore, when her voice enchanted our souls; I would toil in vain in the attempt to evoke our bliss. Happiness is indescribable. I, who have known it, who have lived it, would not be able to awaken the palest reflection of it in the mirror of words that I present to humans. The most luminous poets and the most vertiginous musicians have blunted their genius on that impossibility. No matter how magnificently they translate the cry of dolor, none of them has been able to hurl in the face of the sun the triumphal hymn of happiness. The chain is mysterious that retains their flight in the song of felicity. If the most sublime of those heroes succeeded in incarnating in the living body of a poem the idea of the wellbeing contained in the heart of the infinite, if the Prometheus in question stole that flame from the bosom of the gods, the intoxicated earth would possess, enchained in form, the very soul of that wellbeing, and humankind would desert the path of suffering into which it has been forced by destiny.

One day, we were walking at the fall of dusk. A fresh sea breeze was blowing and the moon, still pale, surged forth in a mist that was softening the contours of things. I was giving my arm to one of our companions, an admirable redhead whose youth had mourned futile beauty. We were all waking in groups behind Isiah, whose meditation we were respecting. Our eyes never quit the silhouette, the juvenile magnificence of which was enveloped by a vague mantle of Aeolian lilac; and in the ash-blue evening, the pale scintillation of flecks of gold dotted in the mantle of lace caressing her dark hair, appeared to me to be the glimmer of a holy star over the sinister path.

We arrived in a ravine planted with bushes and brambles. Isiah was sitting on a corner of rock. We lay down around her feet. A disturbance was haunting me, but I dared not speak. She enveloped me with her tender gaze.

"You will be cured of your malady one day; you are suffering for having respired the surrounding air since birth."

"Your hand on my forehead, Isiah, has expelled all my illness."

"Learn Faith! Learn Amour! Learn to magnify yourself. Alas, you count on me too much, my friends, and your feeble hearts are suspended on my lips. You hope that my finger, striking the rock, will make the spring gush forth in which you can drink the living water, and you do not extend your strength toward the required effort. But my wings cannot carry you asleep into the heaven of your aspirations. No one is redeemed other than by himself. No one will attain the summit of universal life without having bloodied his feet on the stones of the road. I am showing you the way. March! Create your paradisal atmosphere, my friends."

Our eyes begged her. She gazed at the nocturnal vault in which the stars were lighting up.

"I exist to bring strength to your bosoms. You have suffered for having lived in a time of cowardice. For unbelief and absence of amour are daughters of cowardice. All skepticism is a weakness, as vile as fear. All Faith and all Amour are the courage of the will in parturition of its divine becoming. Osiris is a black god, but you will be gods if you wish."

She had risen to her feet. Now she stood out, a mysterious silhouette, against the velvet of the night. Her voice had the suave force of the music that she had revealed.

"Have Amour, and you will understand Number. On the day fixed by destiny, when a new Sign reigns over the earth, when the Four will be succeeded by the Five, when the Flamboyant star will rise over the sphere instead of the Cross, humans will disdain the vanity of thought for the evident Amour. They will possess the Amour that gives Sight, and they will see and hear, and currents that will girdle the planet that will ferry Amour. Friends, you to whom I have revealed the superhuman path, hurl yourselves into amour, recklessly. Amour, creator of worlds, is manifest in two powers, Belief and Prayer, the two supreme energies of will. The man in whom the Prayer lives will march, clad in joy over the seven Spheres, and *his flesh will become Word*. Prayer is the action of Will upon the world. It directs forces, commands the elements; it manipulates the lightning known to Seers alone. But those alone possess Prayer in the sanctuary of their breasts who accomplish the quadruple duty announced by the Sphinx: know, dare, will, fall silent. Those, Prayer guides, with its fulgurant glare, into the somber temple of mystery. O brethren of my election, love, believe and pray. You are twenty and one and we are twenty-two. There are twenty-two arcana. Unite in Amour and you will be the chain that will attach to the world the Sign that I bring in my vaulted hands. For humankind is led toward its ends by the virtue of Signs that it does not know."

During a pause, the face of the revelatrix subsided into a heroic anguish. A mysterious combat was taking place in the depths of her silence. A sharp intuition traversed my heart like a sword-thrust. It seemed to us that the evening breeze was bringing us, from the heart of the Invisible where all that exists is conserved, the total comprehension of the unspeakable dolor of which the solitary Garden of Olives was witness beneath the veil of a pale evening. Oh, all the majesty of an angelic suffering enveloped the beauty of that creature. In the glimmer of starlight, the infinitely subtle nuances of her flesh were effaced. Our gazes only perceived the black velvet of the eyes amid the darkened whiteness of the profile, whose pure design, superb in the slightly aquiline nose, audacious in the mouth, sovereignly strong in the chin, was outlined in a gilded glory bathing the hair. That was the duration of an eagle taking flight. The triumph of the will dressed that noble head with splendor, and those hands, those ghostly hands . . .

"The hour has come when you will not see me any longer. Friends, hold out your foreheads, that my hands might summon the caress of life, the clemency of death and the emprise of eternity thereto. Adieu, beloved hearts, human hearts that dolor has washed with its corrosive waves. Why is it not given to me to efface past wounds forever? Let my blood be the lustral water, the living water from which you emerge penetrated by invincible hope! Adieu, renewed hearts! I bless in you rosy Orients from which the sun of universal amour will surge.

"You are the beautiful thoughts of the earth, the earth that is a beautiful thought of the Eternal. Adieu, earth from which I am passing. May my trace remain in your flank, as luminous as a lighthouse indicating the port to its bruised children! Adieu, earth to which I came in order to suffer. May you erect on your horizon the vivifying Sign that I have the mission of revealing to you, washed with my blood as it was torn from my heart!

"Adieu, Earth; you seem a soiled fatherland; on your face, the genius is mocked, the just man torn apart, the weak crushed, beauty insulted, the gods blasphemed. The echo of your mountains sends back to the holy stars the clamor of the stifled poet, the flagellated saint, the violated virgin and the poor starveling. You are, however, a chaste fatherland. You nourish souls of devotion. I salute you in your prophets, your victims and your martyrs. You are a noble fatherland, for, to those born on your soil, you can give the crowns of genius, beauty, sacrifice and dolor. The heroism of a few of your sons intercedes for you in the visible; and I, with my mysterious brethren, who die on the cross, summon with my wounded hands the infinity of the increate Light upon our expanded bosom. Adieu, flower of the infinite of which I am bringing the perfume to the feet of God."

The day after that evening we did not attempt to look for her. We knew that her appearance was abolished. We exchanged gazes of a serene sadness. Oh, it was doubtless for us that her adorable flesh was suffering in some desert. Alas, with what ardor we would have offered our common soul to infernal torments, the very soul of our twenty and one forms, in order to save a hair of her sweet head! We did not see her again, but her presence lived in us like a star of force.

We wandered, souls in joy and in pain, over the sand of the shore.

It was the third morning.

We saw—yes, we saw, with our eyes from which the scales had fallen, the eyes of Seers. The sun was rising over the sea, a vaporous and gilded sun. The plain of the tranquil waves was spread out, an immensity of pale gold that volatilized at the horizon toward the light vault of the sky. On the rutilant and distant disk of the star, oh, vision of terror . . . her beautiful head was tilted over her shoulder, blanched by dolor; her hair was a mantle of mourning flowing toward her bloodless feet. And her body, that admirable body, was nailed on a cross, wounded, broken, stained with pale blood, weakening under the blows of torture and death.

Slowly, the crucial apparition sank into the waves.

Now, in the solemn ascension of the zenith, the entire circle of the sun emerged, flamboyant with red gold.

And there was a second vision.

Inscribed on the disk touching the marine horizon, a majestic silver star with five points appeared, like a section of a blazon of mystery. The star had a point at the top, two at the bottom, one to the right and one to the left. And upon that Sign *she* sprang forth, vertical, extending her marvelous horizontally toward the two points of the star. And the sun made an aureole for her glorious flesh, for her sacred nudity. Her head—oh, so luminously beautiful in her nocturnal hair—was held high, radiating triumph, ablaze with her gaze, directed toward the heavens, all of whose arcana she possessed, toward the infinity of worlds, her eternal fatherland.

Star of divine wellbeing . . .

And since then, I live, I march, passing nostalgically over this planet; and I am still waiting, waiting . . .

THE TALISMAN

by Gabriel de Lautrec

AT the hour when the twelve nocturnal crows fly away from bell-towers, I was dreaming among unknown faces.

People were standing in the middle of a room. They had the sadness of immemorial regret in their gaze; their enigmatic faces, although I had never seen them before, were frighteningly familiar to me.

We were looking at an object that one of them had bought and set down in front of us, with gestures of profound veneration. It was a rectangular tablet, longer than it was broad, with the approximate dimensions of a quarto sheet. Its shiny surface appeared to be made of ivory, or perhaps the bark of a tree with a very narrow grain, polished extensively. It obviously came from a distant and fabulous civilization, and who knew how many hands had held it respectfully before ours? On drawing nearer, I distinguished lines traced on the ivory. Everyone was admiring the delicacy of the design. But it seemed to me that the details were fluctuating before my eyes, as sometimes happens in dreams, without presenting any precise significance. I felt annoyance in consequence, and a sort of humiliation.

It seemed to me, moreover, on seeing their faces, that it was the same for most of the observers. Only two or three individuals, with wonderstruck expressions, remained plunged in an attention that allowed me to deduce that nothing of the scene represented had escaped them.

I took hold of the tablet respectfully, in order to associate myself with the sentiments of my companions; I held it up to the light that was coming from a high-set window, and which was lending everything an unreal yellow tint. I maneuvered it in all directions, trying to obtain some clear vision.

After my fruitless researches, one member of the company, drawing nearer to me with a sad smile, said: "That's not it. You could have turned the tablet in every direction and it wouldn't have become any more intelligible. I'll tell you the secret, for you have in your hands the summation and votive offering of long dead souls. It's appropriate to have a profound respect for that survival of the immemorial past. It's a talisman clothed with all the successive adorations of the scene it represents."

And I evoked visions of yesteryear on the black wall of my thought, imagining the hands raised in temples whose very dust no longer exists, the lips chanting supplications for the dead in a language forgotten for hundreds of centuries. There were gods. The most ancient known to us did not even suggest their names to us. Prayers were addressed to them. They were invoked in their anger, or, at other times, taken as witnesses to trembling desires of love. Who can name, in disappeared religions, all the ancestors of Eros?

The man who had read the tablet leaned towards it again, and by looking at it with me, enabled me to see it. The lines gradually became more precise. It was as if a picture were slowly emerging from the depths of the past. Born of vague undulations, a majestic river flowed between widely-spaced banks. On the banks stood trees resembling our palm-trees. And at intervals, between the trees, the ruins of temples could be distinguished, in various architectural styles, which moss and ivy had invaded. I glimpsed mutilated white statues beneath the sacred arbors, like those which we still venerate today in our museums. The gods are quitting the temples for the museums—but those marble fragments respired all the beauty and the dream created by the effort of generations.

There was no living creature in the landscape, but the river carried boats that seemed to be coming toward us. In their prows were idols, which did not have human figures like the gods of today. They did not resemble those of Egypt, whose features represent forms that we call animals, and which preceded us. Thus, when we have disappeared, the image of our gods will doubtless survive us for some time, perpetuating the memory of our present appearance, and future humankinds will retain idols after us. But those forms of strange and terrible aspect told of a fabulous epoch. They must have been contemporary with the earliest ages of creation. Sad muzzles leaned over the water of the river. Membranous wings flapped like veils. They still seemed damp with all the mud of the Deluge. And passing over their hideous faces, first sketches of humankind, like smoke dispersed by the wind, I saw the love, hate and anguish of the eternal becoming. I held out my hands, in supplication, toward the frightful apparitions. I knew that after the vision, it would not be possible for me to talk about them in terms capable of evoking them again.

And beneath the boats with the divine cargoes, sailing toward some unknown shore of nocturnal adorations, the river slowly rose and respired like a loving wave.

As one changes individuality in revelatory slumber, I had been one of the ignorant at first, then one of those who knew. I was now part of the scene that I had been contemplating a little while before, as if my fabulous ancestors had beckoned me to follow them in their headlong flight toward the future. The river overflowed its banks and I found myself borne away by the current. A limpid joy invaded me, along with the pride of reliving my most distant past. The anxious words of the people standing nearby still reached my distracted and disdainful ears, muffled by the water—but I finally faded away into an unconsciousness laden with sentiments and memories.

LARMOR'S REDEMPTION

by Gilbert-Augustion Thierry

. . . .

So I picked up the manuscript that my savant friend, poor Victor Longchamp, had bequeathed me—a very long manuscript, believe me, and entirely written in the hand of a deceased archeologist. At first sight it seemed to be incomplete and full of lacunae: here and there, several blank sheets interrupted the text; in many places, lines of dots served as a transition or replaced a chapter. The author had not had time to finish his work.

At the head of the first page there was a sentence traced in capital letters, a bizarre text, an epigraph of mysterious meaning:

BY VIRTUE OF THREE THINGS A MAN FALLS BACK INTO THE NECESSITY OF ABRED: THE ABSENCE OF EFFORT TOWARD KNOWLEDGE, THE MISUNDERSTANDING OF GOOD AND THE PRACTICE OF EVIL.

At that point, my savant friend had put an explanatory gloss in the margin:

"ABRED, *vulgo* the Inferno down below; rather, in my opinion, the Inferno down here. Thus, three things bring one back to the Inferno of life: ignorance, scorn of the good, and the practice of evil."

Very intrigued by such a logogriph, I struggled for a few minutes trying to comprehend the incomprehensible enigma. But, having been unable to succeed, I turned the page and I read:

I

It was in the month of April 1875 that the first volume of my *Essay on the Bardic Triads of Iolo Morganwg*[1] appeared from the academic publisher Didier et Cie.

To tell the truth, that book, whose sole defect is an overly modest title, could have been called *The History of Human Religion.*

A convinced adversary of Biblical traditions, I denied from the outset the divinity of Eloha, the mud-kneader of Eden, and I even mocked that strange God who "takes the air every evening, when the wind rises" on the banks of the river Pison and the river Gihon.[2] "No," I said to him, daring to speak rudely, "I refuse to bow my head before you, who forbade human beings to know, when the very essence of humanity is to learn; you, who have not understood that all good comes from science and that all evil is nothing but ignorance of the god. With your negative law, you might perhaps have formed the brute, but you never created human beings."

---

1 "Iolo Morganwg" was the "Bardic name" of the Welsh antiquarian Edward Williams (1747-1826), who is now believed to have forged many of the "triads" that he passed off as translations from Medieval Welsh.
2 Pison and Gihon are two of the four rivers said in *Genesis* to flow out of Eden.

After Eloha and his transformation into Jehovah I studied the Christian God. That illogical and unreasonable being, who chastises or recompenses the finite by means of the infinite; who, in his Inferno, does not improve the sin but avenges himself on the sinner—that inventor of the eternity of punishment—was proclaimed by me to be worthy of all human disdain. "Sorry creator," I also said to that one, "who, responsible for social misery, have only found for an excuse the remark that 'The poor will always be among you!'"

I dared even more. Not content with denying the Gods of the Church, I did not hesitate to attack all the deities worshiped at the Institut:

the Bel of Chaldea who, floating impassively in the azure of his Oriental sky, pours his radiance indifferently over the good as over the evil;

the Api of Egypt, the incarnate with the big round eyes, who contemplates the fellah without compassion and the Pharaoh without anger;

the Zeus of the Hellenes, that immortal born of Time, not of Eternity, who, by virtue of his passions, made himself more miserably human than humans;

and Allah, that other Semite, as infantile as all Semites, that fanatic of himself, who demands of humans not virtue, but faith.

Finally, the doctrine of Nirvana, the Buddhist annihilation, in spite of his followers, more numerous every day in Europe, extracted unworthy protestations from me.

Only one God appeared to me to be truly divine: the one who had been worshiped by the noblest of the Aryans, the Gallo-Cymri, our forefathers. With what admiration I exposed the religious philosophy of the druidic triads: the perpetuity of life through death; the necessary reincarnation of all beings until the final amelioration; the successive transformism of the soul, the complement of the transformism of the body, one by the selection of the Beautiful, the other by the selection of the Good; the redemption of a bad life by an unhappy life; poverty the expiation of wealth, tears of laughter and hunger of greed—in brief, the perpetual ascension of every animate being from world to world, though space, until the total annihilation in the One who is Light, Justice and Truth.

"I have crossed your summits," I cried, in a moment of enthusiasm, "O gigantic dolmens of Carnac and Gawr'innis, sepulchral mountains, glorious tombs in which the great chiefs with the necklaces of jade, the powerful manipulators of flint axes, slept inviolate for such a long time! And seeing you standing so high above the plain, I understood the meaning of your structure—emblems of Death dominating Life . . .

"But down there, sown in the heathland like the crop in the fields, I perceived the menhirs springing from the earth to launch themselves toward space, and I understood again, and I saluted in them Life, daughter of Death . . .

"Then, oh, then, a cry of admiration rose toward You, who revealed all these things to our forefathers; and I worshiped you on my knees; on my knees I wanted to love you, for you alone are my God, you who, by expiation, constrain human beings to become gods, O merciful justice, O implacable benevolence."

In any other land than our land of France, the appearance of such a book would have excited public curiosity violently. In Germany, that philosophical battlefield, applause or protests would have risen up from every university; Bel, Api, Zeus or Jehovah would have had their partisans or their detractors. Alas, very different was the welcome given by our population of *Welches*[1] to the Essay on the Bardic Triads. What an

---

1 The German word *Velches* or *Welches* [foreigners] was once frequently

icy silence and what indifference! Messieurs of the *Figaro* remained mute; even the messieurs of *Le Temps* maintained a strict silence. Only infimal technical journals devoted a few lines to my work, in order to pour criticism upon it, not to say outrage. In the *Année historique*, a colleague who prudently maintained his anonymity, declared that my "nonsense" did not merit the honor of an analysis, but he joked ponderously about the "poetics of my style" and the "flowers of my rhetoric." Two Catholic newspapers treated me as a "firebrand of Hell" and, in the deplorable style that is fashionable today among the French clergy, demanded that my book should immediately be placed on the Index . . .

And that was all!

The indifference of the public and the attacks of the malevolent produced their effects. The proprietor of the firm of Didier et Cie announced to me in a heartbroken tone that the edition of the *Essay on the Bardic Triads* was encumbering the cellars of his bookshop almost in its entirety; he had not even sold twenty copies! Furthermore, that timorous man declared to me that I must renounce the publication of my second volume. O dolor! Such, then, was the recompense accorded in my homeland to so much labor! And I fled; I ran away from Paris. On the first of August I was in Carnac.

The old stones of the old menhirs, friends so long cultivated by me, I was avid to see you again; I wanted to tell you about my sadness and receive your consolations, you who had informed me in your great silent language. Yes, I was desperate! And yet, the Persian poet says: "Let the bite of the envious be milder to your flesh than the kiss of the beloved woman." A sentence that is assuredly admirable, albeit formulated by an author who is perhaps apocryphal.

---

applied with scathing contempt to the French and Italians in particular.

II

. . . .

"Bonjour, Madame Lautrem!"

The mistress of the Hôtel des Voyageurs quit the fireplace with the vast mantle, where roasting meat was crackling, and came to meet the person who was calling to her.

"Why, it's you, Monsieur Longchamp! You've come back to us!"

"And for a long time, I hope, my good Madame Lautrem. Can you give me a room, then . . . the best of your rooms, if you please?"

The good Madame Lautrem put her hands together

"Jesus and Mary! A room? A room for you, all to yourself?"

"Of course."

"Oh, Holy Virgin! Typical of those men who occupy themselves with antiquities: always with the dead, never with the living. But look, my dear Monsieur, look out there!"

And the lady's finger extended in the direction of the square of the church.

The square was, in fact, overflowing with people, and a confused hubbub was rising into the air. A few Venetian masts, stuck in the ground, were allowing their tricolor pennants to undulate; a few fairground booths were exhibiting, with a noisy concert of big drums, two-headed calves, sword-swallowers or *odalisque-torpilles*;[1] and in front of the façade of the Mairie, was a stage hung with superb red calico. A buzzing Breton crowd was coming and going along the village's only street: men from Vannes in black jackets, men from Hennebont in blue jackets; men from Pontivy in white

1 The wordplay of this phrase is complicated; there was something of a fad in the late nineteenth century for the exhibition in fairgrounds of "electric boys" who could deliver electric shocks by means of static electricity. On the other hand, *torpille* [literally, electric ray or eel] had long been a vulgar term employed with regard to prostitutes, although "*odalisque-torpilles*" might simply be belly-dancers.

ones. And, just as joyful as the young men, the girls were clad in their finery, those from Auray with heavy bonnets and pigeon-throat aprons, and those from Elven with large saffron-colored headscarves; pretentious pretty girls from the Île d'Arz and tall prudish brunettes from the Île aux Moines; and others who had come from further away, from the region of Quimperlé, where every respectable young woman hides her hair modestly under a nun's head-dress and wears a folded collaret falling all the way to the hips. Everyone was drunk, prodigiously drunk, reeking of cider, hiccupping eau-de-vie—especially the women.

"The Agricultural Show!" I exclaimed, fearfully.

"Yes, the Agricultural Show," said Madame Lautrem, vaingloriously. "The Sub-Prefect is lodging here, in uniform, and the messieurs of the district council have come with him, three general councilors, a député, and the noblemen with their wives. The festival will last a week. The day after tomorrow, the speeches; this evening, dancing to the bagpipes. I don't have a single room free, but I can set up a bed for you in the grain-loft—and that, Monsieur Longchamp, only because it's you . . ."

"The Show!" I repeated again, fearfully. "Keep your bed, Madame Lautrem; I'm leaving, and right away, for Quiberon. I'll go to Saint-Pierre; there are the remains of an alignment of five menhirs there, and, above all, silence. Quickly! A carriage and a horse!"

The hotelier started to smile and shrugged her shoulders. "Oh yes, a carriage and a horse! But you won't find a carriole or a bourriquet in the entire region. The people at the Show have taken everything."

She saw my air of desperation, and doubtless felt sorry for me, because she added: "Tomorrow morning, but very early, Monsieur Gestas is going by sea to Quiberon. Do you know him?"

That name, Gestas, made me start abruptly. Gestas! What a bizarre name!

"Do you know him?"

"I don't know him." Then, gathering my memories: "Gestas? But, in our ancient mysteries, that's the name of the thief crucified to the right of Jesus Christ, the reprobate who was the first to be ransomed from Hell. Gestas! Gestas! What a strange name!"

Madame Lautrem looked at me disdainfully. "If you were a Breton, Monsieur, if you had fought with our lads at the battle of Le Mans,[1] you'd know the name of Monsieur Gestas."

I wasn't listening. The text of a Mystery Play had suddenly returned to mind: "'Gestas,' said the Lord, 'enter into Paradise.' Oh, adorable naivety of ancient authors! Oh, exquisite charm of . . ."

"Monsieur," said Madame Lautrem, a pious and stern woman, "I don't like hearing the good Lord mocked, the Holy Virgin, the saints in paradise and our Mother Church."

With that, the lady turned her back on me and went toward the fireplace to rejoin her maidservants.

"Madame! My dear lady . . ."

Bah! She was no longer listening, entirely occupied now with the difficult launch of an omelet on to the stove. I took out a visiting card and laid it on the table.

"Ask your Monsieur on my behalf for the favor of climbing into his boat tomorrow."

And I left.

While walking through the crowd, however, I repeated aloud: "Gestas! Gestas!" Like an obsession, the verse of the old Mystery Play harassed my mind: "Gestas," said the Lord, "enter into Paradise."

. . . .

---

1 The Bartle of Le Mans (10-12 January 1871) was a disaster for the French resistance to the invading German armies in the Franco-Prussian War. 25,000 French soldiers were killed and 50,000 deserted.

III

How desperate the voice of your bells seems, church of old Carnac, when, at the decline of the day, it awakens with its plaint the vast slumber of the torpid heathland!

Dusk was falling. The last glimmers of the sun were dying away in the ocean, setting the waves ablaze and speckling the sands of Quiberon with sparks. Toward the east, darkness was veiling the sky, already pierced by the scintillation of stars, and in the distance, the great fir-plantations of Kerlescant were filed with shadow and terror. The road that ran past the tumulus of Saint-Michel, that sepulchral mountain, was cluttered with joyful people; people were singing and shouting—the last echoes of the day's festival. The bagpipes were making their shrill notes heard, and reed flutes, the monotonous *bombardes*, were responding, even more highly-pitched. Soon, men taking one another by the hand were beginning to dance the *hroal*.

A strange farandole, the Breton hroal! In cadence, everyone balances on the left leg, and then on the right, leaps ponderously on both feet, and recommences the hop and skip. "Blow! Blow! Couëdic! Blow till you burst, old pagan!"

And he blew and blew, the old pagan, like a frank Devil's fiddler, without pausing for breath. Crouched on the ground, to either side of the road, the women watched the dance, motionless and silent.

With voices and gestures, our lads teased them. "Come on, come on, Yvonette, your four lovers are quivering with us! And you, Corentine the prude, are you so scared of M'sieu le Curé?" Wasted gibes; Yvonnette and Corentine don't budge; there's still too much light . . .

And the shadow enveloped us, denser from moment to moment, and the bagpipe and the bombarde whined their three notes with no truce or repose.

Finally, no longer able to stand it, a girl got up, and with a bound, threw herself into the dance. A clamor of joy welcomed her arrival. "Good for you! Good for you!" Then two, ten, twenty women launched themselves likewise; hands interlaced; the *hroal* unwound, snaking and twisting, black against the white dust of the road.

The voice of one dancer rose up, singing a ballad taken up in chorus:

> *In trouble, in work,*
> *In all amusements,*
> *I never forget my love,*
> *She's always on my mind.*

Lying in the heather, at the foot of a dry stone wall—the habitual enclosure of Breton fields—I allowed myself to be lulled by the chant, savoring pleasurably the great forgetfulness of myself.

O indelible vestiges of our primal origin, I said to myself, *one finds you everywhere. Is not the Breton* hroal *the syrtos of the Hellenes. Doubtless borrowed from the first Aryans, and by the Aryans themselves . . .*

"Darling!" murmured a voice nearby, in English. "My Bella, how I love you!"

"No, Harris," replied another voice. "No, you don't know how to love!"

I raised my eyes. A man and a woman were standing a few paces away. They were amorously enlaced, the man holding the woman by the waist, the woman leaning her head on the man's shoulder. Completely lost in the shadow of the wall, I could see them, but they could not see me.

"Harris O'Riordan," said the woman, in a mocking tone, "how courageous you are this evening! One can tell that *he* isn't here."

And that *he* was pronounced in an indefinable tone in which hatred, anger and scorn vibrated simultaneously.

"*He*," she continued, "is practicing at this moment one of his habitual sacrileges; he's evoking the dead and blaspheming the Omnipotent. Why haven't you gone with him, Harris?"

The man she had just called Harris O'Riordan replied: "He forbade me to go with him."

And a frisson appeared to agitate his limbs.

The woman laughed heartily. "How you're trembling, my poor friend, and how frightened you are!"

"Yes, I'm afraid," said the man, in a dull voice, gradually becoming animated. "I'm afraid because he's a terrible seer. Look around you, Bella, don't you recognize these places, about which he talks incessantly? This land where, he affirms, an O'Riordan, my grandfather, once lived. There's Mont Saint-Michel, the enormous tomb where the unknown dead, whom he knows, have been sleeping for so many centuries. Further away, there are the stones of bizarre form, and the heathland that souls take pleasure in haunting, where the living can converse with the dead. Look again: those dunes that are plunging into the ocean; isn't that Quiberon, the peninsula so often detested by him, and of which the seer has said: 'It's the land where Larmor must accomplish his redemption'? What is he, then, that man? Oh, how many times, back there in Dublin, in our house on Sackville Street, has he not described these places? And yet, he has never, ever seen them!"

"Lies," the woman interjected, shrugging her shoulders. "He has doubtless visited them, during the war in France, when, in his mad stupidity, he quit his homeland to go and fight under a flag that isn't his own."

"No! He hasn't seen them," said the man, forceful. "When he came to France I was with him, for everywhere he goes, reluctantly, I go. He hadn't seen them, for he said: 'I forbid you to see them before the time,'"

They both remained silent for a moment. The Breton *hroal* was agitating frenziedly, and the dancers were howling their refrain:

> *My love receives my letters.*
> *From the skylark of the fields;*
> *And she sends me hers*
> *By the singing nightingale.*

"Harris," asked the woman, slowly, "why, since you love me, don't you hate *him*?"

"He was my benefactor," replied the man. "He's my father . . . don't look at me like that, darling, oh, not like that! Oh, Bella before you arrived under our roof, I loved him so much! Why are you obliging me to repeat here what I've confided to you so often? Can I forget that he extracted me from the most abject poverty? Yes, yes, I was stagnating in the most abject poverty, and yet Harris O'Riordan, it appears, is of a noble race. My parents were dead and I had been confided, an abandoned waif, to a drunkard, a vagabond accustomed to the workhouse. My God, how I can still remember the day—a winter day of snow and ice—when he came into our hovel on Bathurst Lane in the Liberty district. My companion was lying dead drunk in a corner, and I had just stolen! Suddenly, the door opened; it was *him*! Without pronouncing a word, he walked straight toward me, contemplated me for a long time in silence, put his hand on my head and exclaimed: 'Poor, poor child, I've been searching for you for a long time!" I went with him. Who was he? I didn't know, and no one has ever been able to tell me. And I became his son, better still, his disciple. He taught me the Great Science; he revealed the terrible secret to me, the secret of life and death. Hate him? Bella . . . hate him, who has been so good to me!"

"And to me too," said the woman, angrily. "To me too—and that's why I hate him! Yes, he's been good to Bella. He picked me up too, miserable and famished, in a hovel in our city. In those days, my mother, my own mother, wanted to traffic her daughter and sell my flesh publicly. Well, she was hungry, my mother, and so was I. You're making a gesture of disgust, Harris? Well, *he* married me, the imbecile!"

She interrupted herself to utter a nervous laugh.

"He married me! Oh, truly, perhaps I ought to owe him gratitude! Gratitude? But who else but a starveling like me would have accepted him as a husband, that atheist, that somnambulist, that evoker of the dead, that damned soul who bears the stigma of Hell on his forehead? Gratitude? But since he loved me! Does a woman owe gratitude to all those who love her? Yes, certainly, he was good to me, and yet I hate him! Oh God, I hate him . . . as much, my Harris, as I adore you!"

And the woman brought the man's face toward her own, and I saw them kiss for a long time.

The singers of the hroal where still howling their refrain while dancing:

Not knowing how to read or write,
We read what is within,
There is within those letters:
Love me, I love you so much!

"You swore," the woman said, breaking the silence again, "you swore, Harris, on the eve of our departure . . . I've quit Ireland, a slave of that reprobate, and I only want to return there free . . . oh, to be free, and to be able to love one another without constraint and without remorse!"

"Without remorse!" said the man, in a dolorous tone.

They drew away together.

I saw them in the night, walking slowly, stopping, exchanging a kiss, and slowly walking on. Now they fell silent, holding one another tightly.

"Tomorrow!" said the woman, one last time.

And in an indistinct murmur, it seemed to me that the man replied: "Tomorrow."

IV

. . . .

The place that souls take pleasure in haunting, the man had said, the heathland where the dead can converse with the living. And a voice spoken within me, and said:

"Dare to see!"

. . . .

V

. . . .

The heath of Kermario extended into the distance, solitary; no human sound traversed the immensity of its silence. The night was hot—a blue-tinted night not variegated by any cloud; and in the profundities of the sky, stars scintillated in millions. No breath of wind passed over the plain; the gorse was motionless; nature entire was annihilated in a heavy slumber . . .

And looming up, seemingly sprung from the heather, stood the enormous menhirs, black against the luminous yellow of the flowers of the heath . . . and their lines stretched away as far as the eye could see, plunging fantastically into the distant mysterious mists.

For a long time, already, I had been contemplating the desolation of that solitude, listening to the great voice of the silence. Time went by. In the distance, the clock of Carnac chimed eleven. Almost immediately, toward the east, a glow lit up the horizon: the moon was rising. I started walking in order to return to the village, but the same voice in my heart that had said: "Go!" cried "Stay!"

I stayed.

Suddenly, from a farm lost on the heath, the whining of a dog rose into the air. Oh, the frightful sound, the dolorous plaint! How it was exhaled, sometimes muted, sometimes vibrant. How it was stretched out, lamentably, as it traversed space: the dog was howling mortally.

A frisson ran over my flesh.

The moon emerged then from the abyss of the horizon, spreading its whiteness over the ferns. Ah! A cry was strangled in my throat. There! There, before me, stood a man: a man exactly similar to some corpse rejected by the tomb; the pale rays of moonlight enveloped him like a shroud.

It was a man who was still young, but no one could have specified his age. His proud and arrogant features, his tall stature and the masculine breadth of his shoulders all denounced power and strength. Long black hair framed a beardless face—and so pale, so frightfully pale! His eyes, sunk in their orbits, were shining in the night; they were staring into the void.

Standing on a fallen menhir, the man remained motionless. Sometimes, a convulsive sigh lifted his breast, and his head immediately inclined, as if under the burden of an excessively heavy despair. Sometimes, too, he raised his hand swiftly to his forehead, and a cry of dolor escaped his lips. Then, when he parted his fingers, I thought I glimpsed, traversing his forehead, two red scars, exactly similar to tears, and also similar to two bloodstains . . .

And the hour fled, and the minutes of time fell into eternity one by one . . .

Finally, he broke the silence, and his voice reached me.

"Come," he said. "Oh, come, you who, in the circle of human existences, have known me, have loved me . . . you who are no more, and who are forever . . . you who, traversing death, have attained life . . . O too fortunate survivor of the proof, victor of the three victories, vanquishers by Science, by Amour and by Strength, of my brethren, come to me: I am reaching the end of my pilgrimage, and I am afraid!"

Fearful, chilled by terror, I had collected myself, and, crouched on the ground, hidden in the shadow of a menhir, I extended my head in order to see. From all points of the heath, were demons about to surge? Like a flock of birds, were the dead racing from the profundities of space, about to descend upon us?

But no; no murmur traversed the night, no breath of wind caused the heather to undulate. And yet, they must all have been there—yes, all of them, for the evoker went on:

"Tomorrow! Oh, tomorrow . . . ! Tomorrow, the anniversary of my crime and the term fixed for my expiation! Tomorrow, suffering wringing my heart and the death-rattle choking in my throat! Tomorrow, cold, stupor and annihilation! And tomorrow, the distant gleam, the increasing glow, the dazzle! Terror! Terror! What will be the sentence pronounced when, launching myself into the Night and wanting to plunge myself in the Light, I shall cry: 'I too have submitted to my redemption, I too am purified!'"

He fell silent, and the silent voices doubtless replied to him; then his speech became bitter

"Yes, I know; my crime was horrible, my sin infamous; but I have expiated, for I have suffered; O God, I have suffered . . . !"

And again, his lamentable sigh rose toward the sky.

"I have expiated," he cried, forcefully, "for I love and am not loved! I have expiated, for I am outraged and I refuse to chastise the outrage! I have expiated, for I hate, and I, the stronger, am not avenged!"

196

His face, contracted now, had become malevolent, and like the eyes of wild beasts, his eyes shone in the night. Soon, however, he seemed to calm down, like a child whom a softly murmured refrain lulls into somnolence, and then to sleep. A strange prostration took possession of him; his head inclined, resignedly.

"Alas, alas!" he said, again.

. . . .

Suddenly—had he perceived me?—he extended his finger toward me, and, terribly:

"Get away from here, sacrilege! Get back, you who have come to surprise the secret of my weakness and my cowardice!"

And abruptly rising to my feet, I started running, and I fled.

VI

The absurd dream!

Six o'clock in the morning chimed; the sunlight came in, bright and warm, through the window of my loft; I leapt out of bed, dressed in haste and went downstairs. In the kitchen of the inn, Madame Lautrem was already busy around her ovens, aided by the two maidservants with white bonnets.

"Hurry up, Monsieur," said the old innkeeper. "Monsieur Gestas has been informed; I'll introduce you to him."

At the same time, she opened a door and went into the dining room adjacent to the kitchen. I stopped on the threshold. In one of the corners of the room, three people were sitting around a pot of tea: two men wearing the costume of English clergymen and a woman clad in black.

"Monsieur Longchamp?" said one of the men, rising to his feet.

He headed toward me, and I remained motionless, as if petrified. I had just recognized the man on the heath, the evoker of souls. Yes, it really was the same person, with his black hair, his pale face and the two red scars traversing his forehead.

Without remarking my stupor, however, he said: "Monsieur Longchamp, the eminent archeologist, the author of the *Essay on the Bardic Triads?*"

I bowed, modest in appearance, although secretly committing the sin of pride.

"Be welcome," Monsieur Gestas continued, extending his hand to me.

Shall I confess it? I did not take it without a certain repugnance. What stupidity, though! It was, in truth, the hand of a man, an amiable and charming man, who had read my work, and who rendered me full justice.

"Be welcome," he said to me, for a second time, and, still holding my hand in his: "It's a long time, Monsieur, such a long time, that I've been waiting for you."

I looked at him in surprise, and swiftly disengaged my fingers from his grip. He did not even seem to perceive my abrupt movement.

"I'll introduce you to my wife," he said, smiling.

Then, turning to the lady sitting in a corner of the room: "Bella! Monsieur Longchamp, a friend of mine, known without him knowing me."

At the name Bella I could scarcely suppress a shudder; and while she looked at me with a disdainful moue, I studied her physiognomy. The woman might have been about twenty-five years old; her mat complexion, her chestnut-colored hair, and the large dark blue eyes illuminating her face all indicated her Irish origin. She lowered her head slightly, without addressing a single word to me.

"And this, my dear friend," Monsieur Gestas continued, still smiling, "is Harris O'Riordan, my adoptive child."

He pronounced the three words "my adoptive child" in a slow voice.

Bella launched a strange glance at her husband. Harris O'Riordan, a man of about thirty, with pink cheeks, clear gray eyes and pale blond hair, saluted me coldly.

"Now," said Monsieur Gestas, "let's go!"

And as we crossed the threshold, he added, talking to himself: "The announced witness has come; the pilgrimage begins."

Two Bretons in Sunday costume were waiting at the door of the hotel.

"Here are the boatmen," said Madame Lautrem, designating them.

They came toward us, and, taking off their broad-brimmed hats, bowed respectfully.

"Does Monsieur Gestas recognize me?" said the first of the men. "Léonnec . . . Jean-Paul Léonnec?"

"And me," said the second. "Little Corant . . . Corant of Ploermel."

Gestas looked at them. "Where have I met you, my friends?"

Léonnec started to laugh. "At the battle of Le Mans, of course, near the bridge over the Huisne. It was there that the shells burst and thundered! What misery! I was next to you. Oh, good God, you didn't have cold in your eyes. You said to us: 'Look death in the face, then; she'll be afraid!' Afraid? The slut! Bah, but in seeing you, a foreigner, fighting for France better than us, Frenchmen, I felt a great shame entering my heart. I was a coward, I became brave, Monsieur Gestas, you taught me to love the fatherland; I bless you."

"Right," said the second of the men in his turn, "and I too was in that bullet storm. It's there that I knew you, my dear Monsieur. German lead had put me down; I was howling in pain and appealing to the comrades. Faint hearts, the comrades! They had other things to do than listen to little Corant; they were running as fast as their legs could carry them. Only you heard me; you lifted me in your arms and loaded me on your shoulders; without you, old Mother Annette would no longer have a son. Monsieur Gestas, you taught me to love humanity; I bless you."

Gestas bowed, and replied, simply: "May I also teach you to love my God!"

We set forth.

"So," I said in my turn, "you were in Le Mans on that lamentable day?"

"Yes," he replied. "At the first news of the disasters in France, I quit Ireland in order to come and fight in your ranks. Oh, don't admire that; I had an imperious duty to do, but I could only arrive to witness the supreme defeat. Alas! Why did I not die that day? But no, the proof would have been too mild."

In silence, we followed the road that led to the beach. The two boatmen marched ahead, conversing in low voices; then came Gestas and me; behind us, Harris and Bella, both going at the tranquil pace of lovers who want to linger. Gestas was somber and taciturn. A nervous movement agitated him; sometimes he stopped abruptly, and immediately resumed walking just as abruptly. He did not turn his head once.

"And you have dared, Monsieur Savant," he suddenly said to me, "to write the sentence: *you alone are my God, you who, by expiation, constrain human beings to become gods!*"

"Certainly," I replied, "but long before me, and much better, the Druids, the first adepts of the Great Science, had said: 'Three things are necessary for the triumph of humankind: to suffer, to change and to choose.'"

"To suffer, to change and to choose," Gestas repeated slowly, in a tremulous voice.

"Yes, the formula of all redemption."

"Oh, redemption!" he exclaimed, dolorously.

A fugitive blush reddened his face, and he raised his hand swiftly to the two stains on his forehead.

VII

The heat was already overwhelming. No breeze traversed the heavy and inflamed air. The sea extended, a transparent blue, flat and polished, devoid of undulations and devoid of ripples.

"We can't hoist the sail," said Léonnec, the owner of the boat. "We'll have to row. Let's go!"

And, bending over the oars, the two boatmen began to beat the water in cadence.

Harris O'Riordan and Bella were sitting next to one another at the rear of the boat. I was not far away, and standing at the prow, Gestas, his head bare and his arms folded, was gazing. We were all silent.

The landscape was superb. To the left was the little isle of Houat, with its girdle of reefs, which the unfurling waves fringed with foam; in front of us, in the distant blue-tinted mists, Belle Isle seemed to be striping the horizon; to the right, flat, yellow and devastated, stretched the peninsula of Quiberon. Here and there, however, between its dunes, patches of dark green showed: a few stunted firs, which the great winter wind had curbed, twisted and tortured.

"In those days," said Gestas, breaking the silence, "those trees didn't even exist."

"They were planted not long ago," replied Léonnec, "but they weren't able to grow."

"Nothing will ever be able to grow on that accursed land," murmured Gestas. "Never, never!"

Again he fell silent. The boatmen were rowing laboriously; somnolence overtook me; Harris and Bella were smiling at one another; and Gestas was still at the prow, gazing.

"Patron," said little Corant to his companion, "the oar's becoming heavy; we're no longer going together. Sing something that will put us back in rhythm."

And Léonnec started to sing, on three notes, a monotonous ballad in the Morbihanese Breton that the purists of
Quimper call a dialect, and which I proclaim, myself as the
primitive Breton. That *complainte* was curious, even bizarre,
and I listened.

"Alleluia! From Auray to Pontivy the bells have rung, and
from Auray to Hennebont they are ringing still. And you,
lads, come out of your houses, ask for scythes, unhook the
carbine and bite the bullet: the beloved hour has come, the
hour of battle. *De profundis.*"

"What is that complainte?" I asked. "It certainly isn't in
the *Barzaz Breiz.*"[1]

"I can't tell you, Monsieur," replied Léonnec. "My father,
formerly of the village of La Trinité, sang it, and his father, it
appears, also sang it. I don't know any more."

He continued:

"Alleluia! The beloved hour has come, the hour of battle.
And they are gathered, quivering with anger, on the vast heath
of Elven. Georges is in the midst of them, and they surround
him, for the moment has come to chastise the insolent Gaul,
the infamous Blues, the men who drink the blood of men
as the drunkard drinks cider. The holy rectors and the good
priests are there too; they have blessed the arms; the Breton
who dies in these battles will go straight to paradise. *De
profundis.*"

An abrupt movement had made the boat oscillate; Gestas
had turned round violently, and he was staring at the singer
with bleak eyes.[2]

---

1 *Barzaz Breiz* [Breton Bards] (1839) is a collection of ballads and legends, in Breton with French translations, assembled by Théodore Hersart
de Villemarqué, which achieved a great success within the context of
the Romantic Movement, much as Iolo Morganwg's triads and James
Macpherson's Ossianic poems had in the British Isles; like them, its au-
thenticity is nowadays reckoned to be highly dubious.

2 Many readers, like Gestas, would have realized almost immediately that
the references in the fictitious ballad are to the Battle of Quiberon in 1795,

"Alleluia!" Léonnec went on. "The Breton who dies in these battles will go straight to Paradise. Georges has spoken to them.[1] 'Sons! The ships from England are coming to save us, ships in which all the brave have taken their places, all the knights, all your noblemen: O'Riordan, who was never afraid, Larmor the loyal, who . . .'"

"Larmor was nothing but a wretch," Gestas interjected, dully. "Let his name disappear from history, as his bones will be rejected from the tomb this evening!"

The silence became profound, crushing and strange again. We were advancing very slowly. In the distance, above Belle Isle, a small white cloud was rising, brightly, into the somber blue of the sky.

"We'll have a storm before nightfall," said Léonnec, who, leaning on his oar, resumed his *complainte* mechanically:

"Alleluia! There they are, swaying on their anchors, the ships come from England, the great black and white ships with gleaming canons. Jesus and Mary, here they are at last! To sea, to sea, the boat that will disembark the brave! And Puisaye said: 'The bravest is the man who touches land first.' O'Riordan replied: 'That will be me.' But already, Larmor has thrown himself into the waves, Larmor the loyal . . ."

"Shut up! Oh, shut up, then!" cried Gestas; and seizing the boatman's arm, he twisted it violently.

---

when émigrés returning from Britain joined Royalist "Chouan" troops under the command of Joseph de Puisaye, in the hope of launching a counter-Revolution. The English ships began disembarking troops on 27 June in the vicinity of Fort Penthièvre. The fort was betrayed to the Republican forces of Lazare Hoche on 20 July—by whom is unknown—and 6,000 Chouans were taken prisoner; instead of being treated as prisoners of war, 750 Royalist soldiers, including 430 noblemen, were executed as traitors by a Revolutionary Tribunal headed by Jean-Lambert Tallien. An expiatory chapel was built on the so-called Champ de Martyrs in 1829, and the Chartreuse [i.e., Charterhouse] d'Auray kept the remains of 952 men in a vault, with a list of their names.

1 "Georges" was the customary appellation of the Chouan leader Georges Cadoudal.

Bella stood up and, pointing at her husband, said: "That man is mad!"

"No," said Harris, as white as a shroud. "He can see!"

Gestas collapsed heavily on to his bench. His face plunged in his hands, he was silent, and I heard his labored respiration.

I touched his shoulder. "Monsieur, what is that man singing, then?" I dared to ask.

Then, letting his arms fall back, he replied to me in a harsh voice: "The legend of Quiberon."

VIII

The boat felt a slight shock; it had just touched the bottom; but only a few brasses separated us from the shore, and the tide was going out rapidly. In front of us, a little sandy cove extended, its yellow dunes dotted with black granite. To the left, a redoubt that had almost collapsed, the southern fort, allowed the mouths of a few old cannons to be glimpsed behind its parapet; to the right, the hamlet of Port Haliguen scattered its houses along the shore.

"It's here!" said Gestas, shaking off his torpor. "Here! Eighty years, already!"

He gave the impression of struggling against a will superior to his own, but, as if vanquished in that interior combat, he said:

"Listen, Harris, and understand! Larmor was cleaving the waves, racing toward the shore, in order to be first to land. A hand posed on his shoulder: O'Riordan was beside him, looking at him . . . as you're looking at me, at this moment. He was noble, very noble, Earl O'Riordan, from an Irish family that had taken refuge in France with James II, but no less noble as him was Baron Larmor, of the Larmors who were killed in the Crusades. Both of them, officers of the king, lived in neighboring seigneuries: O'Riordan in the château that you can see over to the right, lost in the heather, on the slope descending to the river at Auray; Larmor in that old lair whose disemboweled tower can still be seen on the coast of Morbihan, amid the black fir trees and the great somber oaks. Oh, how desolately the winter wind moans as it passes over those enormous forests, curbing them. How lugubriously the flocks of crows croak, in the days of Autumn, around those solitary ruins!

"And both of them were brave, very brave, Baron Larmor and Earl O'Riordan. It was already three years since they had emigrated, respiring the hatred of their homeland for three years. Now they were disembarking on the coast of France in order to cut French throats, wearing English coats with pockets stuffed with English pounds. Oh, woe to the sacrilege that cannot love you, you whose soil is made with the dust of our forefathers, you who receive the imprint of the first footprints of our children, twice sacred thing, great family, powerful mother, Homeland!"

I had drawn closer to Gestas and I contemplated him, almost with terror, that Seer for whom the past was so very present, that living man who was reviving the lives of the dead. Only Bella had remained seated, and, with a smile of disdain on her lips, she was tapping the planks of the boat with her umbrella.

Gestas went on:

"'Larmor,' said O'Riordan, tugging his arm, 'I hate you.'

"Larmor shrugged his shoulders.

"'Yes, I hate you, the earl went on, 'and again, you're going to steal my share of glory!'

"Larmor started to snigger, and thought: *Your share of glory, as I've already stolen your share of love, your allotment of happiness!*

"'One of the two of us,' said O'Riordan, 'is surplus to requirements; that one must disappear.'

"Larmor still kept quiet, but he thought: *It will be you*. An infamous idea had just sprung forth in his mind.

"Come," Gestas commanded, speaking rudely to Harris. "It's necessary, finally, that you know."

Then, leaping out of the boat, he started running toward the strand.

"Harris," said Bella, retaining the young man by the hand. "Earl O'Riordan, you have sworn!"

She drew closer to him, and whispered to him very quietly, two words in English:

"This evening."

[At this point the manuscript is interrupted; several pages left blank cut the text; then the story resumes.]

IX

. . . .

And we went.

"Giddy up! Giddy up!"

The driver whipped his beast with a sweep of his arm. The little Breton horse shook its head angrily and increased its pace. The cart made an enormous leap, and all four of us were shaken by rude jolts. What a strange equipage—the only one that we had been able to find in the village of Port Haliguen!

"Giddy up! Giddy up!"

Gestas had said to the innkeeper: "First, to the hamlet of Lenneiz; then to Fort Penthièvre; finally, to the Chartreuse d'Auray."

The innkeeper, while drinking his coffee laced with brandy, his "little tipple," had replied: "Today, August the second, daylight lasts until eight o'clock, so all that can be done, but you won't arrive before the storm . . ."

"Giddy up! Giddy up!"

The horse ran, flat out, and the landscapes succeeded one another rapidly before our eyes. Behind us, already, the town of Quiberon and its tall square clock-tower; to the right, now, the village of Saint-Pierre and its menhirs . . . oh, old and dear friends, you whom I had come to see again, was it thus that I was keeping the promise made to myself? But no, I was scarcely thinking about you; I too wanted to know what this Larmor was.

"Giddy up! Giddy up!"

The heath . . . the heath . . . the heath, with its spiny gorse, its green ferns and its variegation of pink heather and yellow flowers . . . the heath! Oh, what charms there are in your desolation! What beauty there is in your ugliness, earth of great poetry, Bretagne!

"Giddy up! Giddy up!"

The little white cloud that had been floating, that morning, above Belle Isle, was now spread out over our heads, black, sinister and concealing the storm. The wind was beginning to blow. To the right, the waves of the bay were splashing against the shore; to the left, the ocean, the "savage sea" was twisting its waves over the reefs and silvering with foam. Out there, at sea, the "howlers' reef" was replete with sobs.

"Giddy up! Giddy up!"

We had traversed the peninsula in its full length. At the place where a tongue of land soldered it to the continent, on a hill of sand and mud, stood a house . . .

"Stop!" commanded Gestas; and he was the first of us to leap to the ground.

X

It was a house of solid appearance, with cob walls slit by zigzag cracks, a thatched roof caved in and eaten way by moss. For a long time, no doubt, it had stood thus, solitary on the dune, and for a long time, the March winds and the November gales had harassed it with their bites and battered it with their swirls. A low wall of dry stones formed a narrow enclosure in which a few ears of buckwheat with glabrous flowers grew, undulating at the slightest wind. Outside the door, a dung-heap emitted its vapors and allowed a nauseating liquid manure to leak out, drop by drop. All that spoke of abandonment; all of it also reeked of poverty and hunger.

Gestas went into the enclosure. Suddenly, a dog crouching against the house got up and bounded toward us: one of those big sheepdogs with short hair, bloodshot eyes and enormous fangs . . . but it stopped dead, lay down on its belly, and started trembling in every limb. Gestas marched slowly toward the house. Then the dog started recoiling before him, step by step, uttering continuous dolorous howls—the same frightful plaint that I had heard the evening before in the silence of the heathland of Kermario. Harris, still very pale, picked up a stone and wanted to throw it at the dog.

"He won't shut up," said Bella, curling her lip in disgust, "he's sniffed a cadaver!"

The door was closed on the outside by a latch. Gestas opened it, and closed it behind us.

The interior of the abode was truly filthy. A single room formed the entire habitation. The beaten earth that took the place of floorboards was hollowed out by rain dripping from the roof on stormy days. On the walls, once whitewashed, smoke and dust spread large patches. A table scarred in many places by a knife and a few rickety stools were the entire furniture of the sordid redoubt. In a corner of the room, a bed seemed to be embedded in the wall—a Breton bed in the form of a cupboard, with crude sculptures, in worm-eaten wood. Two ragged calico curtains, closed off the bed. The daylight, already darkening outside, had difficulty filtering through the only dusty and greasy window; it was almost dark in the hovel . . .

No one!

Suddenly, a human voice similar to a death-rattle spoke in a corner of the room:

"The traitor! The traitor!"

Immediately, the red calico curtains agitated, and then opened, and a man appeared in the gloom, sitting on the bed: a tall old man of almost centenarian appearance. Long greenish-gray hair fell over his shoulders; the hairs of a white beard garnished the cavities of his cheeks in clumps; the rictus of his mouth allowed the sight of gums devoid of teeth; two large white leucomas extended over his eyes: the old man was blind. He extended a tremulous finger toward us and spoke for the second time:

"The traitor! The traitor!" he murmured.

Gestas marched toward the old man and placed his hand on his shoulder. "Yes, yes," he said, "eighty years have already been accomplished." And, in a tone of profound melancholy: "In those days, you entered into life in pain; and now you're about to leave it . . . from infancy you've returned to infancy."

"The traitor!" stammered the man sitting on the bed, for the third time, and bizarre words, phrases devoid of meaning, emerged in hiccups from the lips of the miserable idiot.

"General Hoche is here," he said, "sitting over there!" With his finger he pointed to a long Breton coffer placed near the bed. "At his side, the man who arrived yesterday has taken his place, the man with long hair, the man with the tricolor sash, the man of the Convention. Oh, sweet Jesus! Holy Virgin! What's going to happen? The general gets up . . . he's marching angrily.

"'No capitulation, then?'

"'No capitulation!' replies the man with the sash.

"'And everyone, everyone has passed under arms?'"

"'Passed under arms,' replies the man, again.

"Me, I look at my mother, on her knees beside the fireplace, preparing a meal. She's weeping. This morning, Father disappeared. He's gone to join the others, out there . . .

"The general stops again and says: 'For a fortnight, the émigrés have been masters of Fort Penthièvre; they're retrenched there; to take the fort will be hard.'

"'The fort will be taken,' says the man with the sash, simply . . .

"*Pif! Paf!* Rifle shots. 'What's that?'

"An aide-de-camp rushes outside and comes back immediately. 'They've just captured a clown who was prowling around the house. He wants to speak to you urgently.'

"'Send him in.'

"Aha! There he is. A large hat is pulled down over his face; he's wearing a jacket and britches like our peasants. The general asks: 'What do you want with me?'

"The peasant replies, and he talks in good French: 'For a fortnight the Whites have been masters of Penthièvre. They're fortified there; you'll be repelled.'

"'Is that all you have to tell me, spy?' cries the general. 'What's your name?'

"The peasant takes off his hat and throws it across the room. 'My name is Claude-Marie, Baron de Larmor.'

"'A former nobleman?'

"'Oh yes, a very former nobleman!'

"'What do you have to tell me?'

"'This. Tonight I'll be guarding the postern that opens over the sea. Are there fifteen hundred brave men among your Republicans?'

"The general shrugs his shoulders. Larmor goes on: 'Well, let them slip along the strand, tonight, as far as that postern, and they'll see what a former nobleman dares to do!'

"The general looks at Larmor suspiciously and interrogates the man in the sash with his eyes. 'And what recompense are you asking from us to pay for your service?'

"Larmor straightens up. 'Keep your recompense! I'm not serving your Republic, I'm serving my hatred!' Then, in a low, sniggering voice: 'O'Riordan is in the fort, and I'm his wife's lover!'

"Then the man in the sash, the silent man, the man of the Convention, Tallien, starts to laugh, and says: 'In that case, Penthièvre is ours!'"

XI

. . . And Fort Penthièvre appeared in the dusk, bleak and somber.

Out at sea, the storm, now unleashed, was raging. Lightning was streaking the horizon; thunder was rumbling dully. To the right and the left of the road, the waves of the bay and the waves of the savage sea were unfurling with a great murmur.

The door of the fort was open; the guardian was doubtless absent; Penthièvre was abandoned to us.

Gestas went in.

On the drawbridge, Harris appeared to hesitate. "Bella," he said, in a low voice, "I'm afraid."

"March," she replied, harshly. "It's necessary that you see."

Beyond the drawbridge, a round-path turned. To the left was a dilapidated barracks, to the right a high wall pierced by loopholes. Gestas set forth along the path.

The path descended in a slope parallel to the ocean and terminated abruptly in a stairway of several steps. At the bottom of the steps was a postern, and behind the postern, the roar of the waves beating the rocks was audible. At that moment, a flash of lightning lit up the night, and for a second we saw, as if in broad daylight, Gestas' livid face, his ardent eyes, and, on his forehead, the two red-brown stains that had surprised me so strangely the previous evening.

Gestas went down the stairs leading to the postern. Like a somnambulist, he went . . . he spoke . . . he listened . . . he heard.

"'Aha! The storm so ardently desired, the storm that will permit them to slip all the way here.' He looks at his watch. 'It's time! They can enter. The guard at the postern is me!'" He made the gesture of opening the door. 'Come on, come on! Hurry up beloved artisans of my hatred!' Here they are . . . they enter . . . they climb up . . .

"'To arms!' The general! The fort is in tumult. 'Too late, wretch, you're doomed!' Ah! An officer of the Loyal Emigrant comes running, lantern in hand. 'Fire! Fire on that one! It's O'Riordan!' He falls . . . is he dead?

"No . . . he's calling out . . . he has recognized . . .

"'Larmor! Larmor, my companion in arms, save me!'

"Larmor approaches, leans over the wounded man. He takes two pistols from his cloak. He leans over again, and discharges his weapons at point-blank range.

"'Ah! Larmor! Infamy . . .'

"And Larmor whispers in his ear: 'Yes, infamy, for it's me who delivered Penthièvre in order that you would die, and that I could return to your wife, your widow, my mistress!'

"Then O'Riordan raises himself up on one elbow; he dips his hand in the blood of his wounds, and two drops of blood have just splashed Larmor's face. 'Larmor, I don't know whether there is a God, but if he exists, may he chastise you, may he chastise you until you have expiated!'"

Exhausted, Gestas fell to the ground, on his knees. Sobs lifted his breast, but he was not weeping . . .

And Bella, approaching, extended her hands over the man's head, and without saying a word to him, but looking hard at Harris, she pointed with her finger at the two stigmata similar to two drops of blood.

For a long time, the three of them remained thus, silent in the midst of the howling of nature in torment.

XII

And our journey over the heath resumed, furiously.

"Giddy up! Giddy up!"

Damn the tempest, which now seems to be pursuing us determinedly! The lightning flashes blind us, the thunder deafens us, the torment shakes us, the rain lashes us.

"Giddy up! Giddy up!"

The night envelops us, thick and black . . .

Out there, in the gray vapors, lights scintillate and tremble. That's Auray.

"Giddy up! Giddy up!"

The vehicle traverses the town. The gallop of the horse strikes sparks from the pavement; the wheels resonate with a strident metallic sound . . .

The houses become rarer; the lights disappear; the heath again. Emerged from night, we reenter night.

"Giddy up! Giddy up!"

Abruptly, we turn left. A long avenue of fir trees extends, utterly funereal. The vehicle stops. In front of us, a little edifice with a Dorian portico.

"That's the ossuary," says the driver, and he makes the sign of the cross.

We get down.

"Go away!" says Gestas to the driver, and throws him a purse.

The other counts the coins by the light of his lantern; he laughs and says: "Thanks! Giddy up! Giddy up!" And the vehicle draws away.

Shivering under the downpour, I listen to the sound decreasing in the darkness. A gust of wind carries a "Giddy up! Giddy up!" to us . . . now, nothing more.

Gestas is still motionless, not daring to cross the threshold of the chapel. Harris looks him up and down.

"Larmor, I don't know whether there is a God, but if he exists, may he chastise you, may he chastise you until you have expiated!"

And the voice of that debilitated being resonates, menacingly.

"Yes, does he exist, that one?" asks Bella, with a cynical laugh.

Then Gestas bows his head. "He exists."

At a slow pace, he climbs the steps of the ossuary.

XIII

The door stood ajar, allowing a ray of light to filter out. Gestas pushed it; it swung on its hinges, without making a sound.

The chapel that we had just entered was an edifice of medium size, with walls sumptuously paneled with marble, the vault of which constellated with fleurs-de-lys; here and there, on the plaster-work, inscriptions stood out in golden letters, taken from the Scriptures. A vast mausoleum in the form of a catafalque occupied the center of the chapel, and a second door, of bronze, gave access to it; it was open. Still preceding us, Gestas slipped into the tomb.

There, a large square pit was gaping, and a ladder permitted descent into it. The smoky light of a lantern was projected over several death's-heads, and those heads seemed to be staring at us with their empty eyes and smiling their eternal smile at us.

Sitting amid that human debris was a nun, a very young woman, doubtless a novice. She was wearing the costume of the Soeurs de la sagesse: the robe of white linen, the white veil, the white wimple. Her pale, emaciated face had ivory reflections, and in the light of the lantern the forehead of that living person was as shiny as the foreheads of the skulls. Beside her was a bucket of water, and the little sister was washing the skulls with a sponge. While she did her repulsive work, thinking that she was alone, she was speaking aloud.

"Yes, yes," she said. "You'll all have your toilette . . . and a hundred!"[1]

She placed a cleaned head among others that were piled up.

"A fine toilette, for tomorrow is your anniversary, your feast day; tomorrow, the Dean of Saint-Gustan will come to say a high mass in your honor. It's necessary to be very clean, very genteel, for that day . . . a hundred and one."

The new head placed on the pile rolled on to the ground. The little sister picked it up.

"Uh oh, Monsieur Mutineer, what's this? You're playing the rebel!"

She took it in both hands and gazed at it pensively.

"Yes, you're my favorite, you. Oh, you must have been pretty, very pretty, once . . . big blue eyes, curly blond hair, a martial air, and doubtless a bad boy . . . a true Saint Michel! And now . . . uh oh! No matter, you're my favorite . . ."

Her hands approached the skull to her face, and her lips extended as if to give the hideous thing a kiss. But her movement stopped dead; she made a rapid sign of the cross, murmuring: "Jesus and Mary . . . !

"A hundred and two," she added, with a sigh, and threw the head among the others. "And you, Monsieur," she said, suddenly, "you who are trying to hide back there, I can see you! Come on, it's necessary to be nice and clean, like the friends. You can look at me with your nasty eyes, I'm not afraid. Oh, you must have been wicked, once!"

---

1 The Soeurs oblates de la sagessse, founded in 1859, were a silent order, so this one is a trifle garrulous.

She extended her hand and picked up another skull.

Suddenly, Gestas, who was watching all that with haggard eyes, uttered a strangled exclamation. The little sister looked up and perceived us. With an abrupt movement she came to her feet; a blush spread over her face, soon followed by a livid pallor. She was afraid.

"What do you want?" she stammered. "What do you want? Oh yes . . ."—she strove to laugh—"visitors, no doubt? But it's late, much too late!"

Rapidly, she came toward us. "It's much too late. The doors of the chapel close at seven o'clock, and ten o'clock has just chimed . . . ! Anyway, as you're here . . ."

Her teeth were chattering with terror; she could not finish her sentence. She paused, as if to pull herself together

"Madame et Messieurs," she said, in the monotonous tone of a cicerone, "you are in the expiatory chapel constructed in honor of the victims of Quiberon by Her Royal Highness Madame la Duchesse d'Angoulême,[1] and this is the crypt in which their remains are deposited, which remains sacred to the hearts of good Frenchmen, for the heroes of Quiberon died as martyrs for their God and their King. Now, turn your eyes and look. There, inscribed on the mausoleum are the names of the victims, nine hundred and fifty-two names, and among them the most illustrious in France: a Broglie, a Soulanges, a Sombreuil, a Talhouët, a Larmor . . ."

"What is the name of that traitor doing here?" howled Gestas, with a threatening gesture.

The little sister looked at him fearfully. "You can't stay! You can't stay!" she stammered. "Leave!"

---

1 La Duchesse d'Angoulême was the title employed after her marriage to the eldest son of the future Charles X by Marie-Thérèse-Charlotte of France (1778-1851), the eldest daughter of Louis XVI and Marie-Antoinette.

Gestas had approached the ladder and had already put his foot on a rung. Then, uttering a cry of fright, the little sister ran outside.

. . . .

"And that, I have seen, yes, I've seen it!"

Gestas let himself fall into the tomb, took possession of the head that the nun had been holding, and uttered a strident laugh.

"It's him! Him, Larmor!"

He came back up, holding the skull between his arms.

I tried to stop him.

"Infamous sacrilege, Monsieur! Horrible sacrilege!"

But he pointed at one of the inscriptions traced on the wall, and I read:

My bones like grass will germinate and be reborn.

XIV

And he went on, he went on . . .

The rain had stopped, but in the tormented sky great clouds were running, the gaps in which allowed momentary glimpses of a large crescent moon. Sometimes its rays, falling obliquely, spread a mat whiteness over the gorse and the heather; sometimes plunged to shadow again, the heather and the gorse resumed their sinister coloration.

And he went on, and on . . .

With his folded arms he pressed the skull stolen from the tomb against his breast.

The path descended steeply, muddy and eroded by the rain, an escarpment bristling with broom; to the left was a profound ravine where a stream swollen by the rain was howling, rolling from one waterfall to the next. To either side, mossy oaks with rugged trunks extended their branches toward us, as if in a gesture of menace.

And he went on, and on . . .

At the bottom of the slope, a stone cross barred the way. Gestas went around it and engaged in a long path of funerary pines that bordered an immense heath. In the middle of that heath a river ran, which the rising tide was driving back with little splashes. In the moonlight, that marsh, cut by pools of water, shone and scintillated. A lugubrious silence weighed upon the place; the desolation of the solitude extended as far as the eye could see . . .

And yet, from the distance, but very far away, the sound of human labor reached us. The river was dammed; a mill was rumbling slowly, and a red dot of light shone in the night. Out there, in the midst of that reposed and slumbering nature, a man was awake, a man was working.

Gestas stopped at the foot of a fir tree; he sat down.

We were grouped around him, Bella leaning impudently on Harris's arm.

"Larmor!" said Gestas, speaking to the skull that he was holding in both hands. "It is eighty years since, on this heath of Brech, more than nine hundred of your armed companions fell under the bullets. Traitors had delivered them, and you were the most infamous among those traitors.

"Larmor! It is eighty years since, on this heath of Brech, you too fell under the bullets. Captured with the others and clad in the royalist uniform, you were put before the council of war. Tallien refused to recognize you, and when you implored him he started to laugh. Had you not said: 'I'm not serving your Republic, I'm serving my hatred!' You had your recompense. That day, you, the skeptic, the atheist, died blaspheming, for you had just learned that a God exists . . .

"And for a very long time, Larmor, the voice of the One who chastises as recompenses has been speaking to me and saying to me: 'Go out there, to the land where your crime was accomplished; take from the glories of his tomb the bones of the unworthy, and disperse them in the same place where he expiated the first time—for it is there that he must expiate again . . .'

"I am obeying."

Then, getting to his feet, Gestas threw into the mud of the heath the last remaining bone of Claude-Marie, Baron de Larmor.

There was a long silence.

Finally, Gestas said, in a dull voice: "The pilgrimage is terminated. The expiation is accomplished."

But he was speaking in an ill-assured tone, like a man who does not really believe what he is affirming.

Harris placed a hand on his shoulder.

For a long time, the two of them looked one another in the face. They were not speaking, and yet they were listening; they understood one another.

With an imperious movement, the master pushed away his disciple's arm, and seized his hands in his own.

"Oh! Oh! Truly, Larmor has not expiated sufficiently? And it's you who dare to think so . . . you! You!"

He extended his finger toward Bella. "Larmor has not expiated sufficiently? Look at that woman, and dare to tell me that!"

"You know, then?" stammered the young man. You know . . ."

Gestas, raising his clenched fists and letting them fall back, was terrible. "I know that I could have crushed both of you!"

"Harris!" cried Bella, clinging to her lover. "Defend me and avenge yourself!"

He pushed her away gently; then, after a brief silence, he said: "Gestas, what O'Riordan, my ancestor, said to Larmor, I say to you: 'One of the two of us is surplus to requirements. Do you understand? Listen. The O'Riordans are not assassins, so it's a duel that I offer you, a duel without mercy, but honest. Are you ready?"

From the pockets of his cloak he drew two revolvers, gripped one of them, and held out the other.

"Give!" And Gestas, taking possession of the revolver, armed himself.

They stood facing one another, six meters apart, taking aim, ready to fire.

"You're the elder," said Harris, "begin!"

But Gestas raised his arm; the flame of anger that had illuminated his face had just gone out.

"No," he said, in a very soft voice. "I won't kill my son . . ."

"His son!" howled the young man, with a laugh full of rage. "Fire, then!"

"No," replied the new Gestas. "I won't kill O'Riordan." He dropped his weapon and kicked it away. Then, his eyes fixed his challenger, he marched toward him. "I won't kill the executor of the sentence."

Then, as if the master's gaze had twisted his wrist, Harris dropped the revolver.

But suddenly, with a rapid bound, Bella leapt forward, bent down, and picked up the weapon.

"Harris!" she cried. "Cowardly heart, which cannot love to the point of crime!"

Three times, at point-blank range, she fired at her husband. Gestas fell.

"Her . . . her!" he murmured. "So she is the executor of the sentence."

And he lost consciousness.

I ran toward him, and with loud cries, I called for help.

At the extremity of the heath, in the distance, in the direction of the mill, a light passed back and forth in the night; a rumor reached us. Someone had heard me.

Stupefied, Harris stood still, nailed to the ground. Bella approached the young man and, offering him her hand, only pronounced one word: "Finally."

Suddenly, as if revived by the sound of that beloved voice, the moribund man made a movement and opened his eyes. "Bella! My Bella?" he asked.

She clasped her lover more tightly.

"Oh, the poor woman!" stammered Gestas.

From the depths of the heath, lights advanced toward us, and cries drew nearer.

"What's that?" asked the wounded man.

"Help, Monsieur," I replied. "It's coming."

Then a bizarre change, a mysterious transformation, was operated in that man, almost dead already. His halting respiration became regular again; for a moment, the death-rattle ceased to strangle his throat.

Gestas freed himself from my grip and leaned back against a tree

"Harris, and you, Bella, go!" he commanded in a forceful voice. "Go, both of you, there's still time. Monsieur"—he designated me—"will attest that I committed suicide. Go back to the house in Dublin; you'll find my will there, which makes you the heirs of my petty estate. I forgive! One more word: your first-born will bear my name, and him too you will educate in the Great Science. I wish it! Now, come closer, my son."

Harris seemed to be struggling with himself, but, like a somnambulist. He advanced slowly and knelt down.

Gestas ran his hand over the forehead and then the eyes of his disciple.

"Harris," he said, affectionately, "in your hours of weakness and despair—they will be numerous for you, those hours, poor feeble heart—often, you will feel the same caress that your dying father is giving you. You will know then that old Gestas is nearby. Now, go!"

"Come on, Harris," said Bella, brutally.

They both drew away, rapidly.

Gestas raised himself up on his elbow. I supported his head, and silently he watched them draw away. At a bend in the path, Harris and Bella disappeared.

"She didn't even turn her head," said the dying man. "No matter. May she be happy. I forgive." Then, suddenly, and joyfully: "What! I'm weeping—me, who didn't know until today what a tear is! The redemption of amour is, therefore, accomplished by amour. Gestas has redeemed Larmor."

❋

Here the manuscript of the archeologist Longchamp ends. Nevertheless, at the bottom of the last page, my savant friend had written this comment:

> *Gestas buried in the cemetery of the little parish of Larmor, near Auray. No name on the tomb, but this text from the triads:*
> *Three victories redeem anterior and evil humanity: Science, Love and Strength.*

No other explanation was given by the author of this bizarre story, so full of incomprehensible strangeness. And yet, I closed the manuscript very troubled. I remained pensive for a long time.

THE SPELL-CASTER

by Jules Lermina

ALTHOUGH curious about the occult sciences, I am not naïve, and if my imagination sometimes carries me away, I am able to resist its traction by hanging on with all my strength to the sane affirmations—retrograde, if you wish—of cold reason.

Today, not daring to formulate a conclusion myself, I want in what follows to take the reader for a judge. I will not hide anything nor add anything to the strict truth, without omitting any detail; then I shall leave to others the care of conclusion—which is to say, of responding to the question: was the man of whom I am going to speak a madman or a criminal? Not only a criminal by intention—that would be a subtlety—but a criminal in fact; or to put it another way, although it is certain that he thought of a crime, did he actually commit it, and was he able to commit it?

First of all, who was the man?

I did not know him well, not having had with him any other relations than those sketched between young men who encounter one another in society. However, I cannot say that I had not noticed him; he was one of those who, for anyone slightly endowed with a spirit of observation, would have had difficulty passing unperceived.

His name is unimportant; I shall call him Gérald. He was very assiduous in the home of an important and very rich businessman, Monsieur Solmes, whose greatest pleasure was hosting quasi-princely receptions.

That millionaire was very affable, although I did not request any service from him; he testified a real amity to me, and a certain confidence, perhaps for the very reason of my independence.

One evening, after a concert that was prolonged rather late, he retained me, and after asking me to follow him into his study he said: "I'd like to ask a favor of you; I deem you to be a man of honest conscience and good advice, and I beg you to respond to me in all sincerity. What do you think of Gérald?"

Rather surprised by that interrogation and hesitant to assume a responsibility still ill-defined, I took refuge behind banalities. Gérald was a man of exquisite distinction and eccentric physiognomy, perhaps trying a little too hard to compose a physiognomy that the old romantics would have qualified as "fatal," but, in sum, intelligent and good company. The few words that I had exchanged with him had revealed to me an inquisitive mind, passionate for labor. Finally, without knowing anything positive about the matter of his pecuniary situation, his entire lifestyle indicated an ease almost amounting to fortune. Of his occupations I knew nothing; he seemed to me to be undertaking experiments in chemistry, or at least high mathematics. I had come across him several times in the street carrying books with old-fashioned bindings under his arm, dating from a previous century.

The millionaire interrupted me.

"Regarding those details," he said, "I'm almost certain. Gérald is rich—a consideration of only mediocre interest to me, my own fortune leaving me complete freedom of action in the present matter. I know that he leads a very regular existence, that he has installed a laboratory in his house in which he devotes himself to research in the natural sciences—or supernatural sciences," he added, with a half-smile. "Who knows whether he might not find the philosopher's stone? Much good may it do him . . . In truth, that ardor for the crucible will pass, and he might make a fine figure in the scientific world. All that, I repeat, is secondary . . . but . . . have you looked at his eyes?"

"His eyes?"

"Yes, his eyes, and to speak frankly, it's on that very particular point that I wanted to consult you. I deem you to be a good physiognomist, having sometimes collected observations from you of great accuracy. So what do you think of Gérald's eyes?"

I had difficulty in remaining serious. Do you see me called to make a profession of checking passports? His eyes . . . ? Evidently, they were . . . singular, which is to say, not exactly like commonplace eyes . . . let's see . . . wide open, with slightly raised lids, allowing the sight of a golden pupil—spangled, even—and a white circle . . . sometimes tarnished like a metallic oxide, sometimes, on the contrary, bright, as if a light were shining behind. Also, those eyes were not absolutely rectilinear; under the empire of an emotion they lost their normal axis instantaneously, as if afflicted by an intermittent squint. At those moments a kind of flash escaped from them, like—I'm explaining myself as best I can—the impact of two rays whose interference would have constituted an incandescent source.

As I was speaking, I realized that I had attached to those eyes much more importance than I had thought at first . . . and that I thought even more than I was saying, for, I don't know by virtue of what association of ideas, the words of the second Faust were resonating in my ear with a hoarse monotony: "The vision looms up, hollow-eyed, like a bizarre specter that troubles life and the mind."

All Monsieur Solmes said was: "Those eyes frighten me."

That radical formula did not astonish me unduly, but I attempted to protest . . . the eyes were neither crossed nor squinting; there was an unimportant singularity about them. "In any case," I said, not without a certain impatience, "what is the point of these questions?"

"Gérald has asked me for my daughter's hand."

I could not suppress a shudder; for at that moment, it seemed to me that everything in me was proceeding by revelations. I loved Camille—yes, I loved her, without ever having admitted it to myself. How could that be? Not that I was surprised by loving her, for she was certainly the sweetest and most interesting creature that I had ever encountered: as delicate as a winter flower, but not frail—robust, on the contrary, and almost indefatigable, as I had seen her in the interminable games of lawn tennis that we had played in summer at her father's provincial château.

Why had I not declared myself yet? Because I had not known that I loved her amorously and it had been necessary for me, in order to read my own heart, to learn that someone else . . . !

"And what have you replied?" I asked, in an almost imperious tone.

"I don't recognize the right to exert the slightest constraint over my daughter . . . however, I have, you understand, some influence over her, and I reserve that of directing her choice. I would, I admit, immediately have given some hope to Gérald . . . if it were not for his eyes . . ."

"Demonic eyes!" I exclaimed, involuntarily.

Monsieur Solmes looked at me, doubtless astonished by the facility with which I now found the characteristic epithet.

"Demonic," he said, shaking his head. "Certainly, for us, as skeptics, the expression is hazarded—and yet, it springs to my mind, as to yours."

"You've rejected him . . ."

"Between men of the world, one doesn't proceed expeditiously . . . I want to consult Camille. Women have ways of seeing different from ours. I've put off any response; that seems wisest . . ."

I breathed out, like a man who has just escaped a grave peril. Monsieur Solmes smiled, without my seeking to understand why. I have found out since. He let me go, thanking me, and announcing that he would take some time before coming to a decision.

I left his house absolutely metamorphosed; I was prey to a complicated sentiment, compounded of anger, joy and I know not what vague hope that I had never conceived before. At the same time, however, a hatred rose into my brain against that man, that Gérald, whose audacity had almost compromised the happiness of my entire life—as if my timidity and my insouciance were not the only culprits.

Oh, he permitted himself to love Camille! Who was he, anyway? What was he hiding behind his strange eyes, which now caused me both horror and terror?

I started to spy on him, with a tenacity that nothing deterred; I spied on his life. He almost never left his house, but I bribed one of his domestics and I soon knew that the studies to which he devoted himself were confined to those mysterious sciences whose secret seems lost, but which are today reinscribed in the register of human curiosity. I obtained from the valet that he would copy the titles of the works that Gérald consulted most frequently, and I was not astonished when, through the orthographic fantasies under which Latin words hid, I recognized the most evil works of the necromancers of old from the *Minerva Mundi* to the *Enchiridion*, and from the *Pimander* to the worst works of Paracelsus . . .[1]

---

1 *Minerva Mundi* is one of several titles attached to an apocryphal work attributed to "Hermes Trismegistus" and thus belonging to the *Corpus Hermeticum*, whose first item is *Poimandres*, or *Pimander*. An Enchiridion

He was a madman, and his eyes were those of a madman!

Monsieur de Solmes was absent; I was not belated in revealing those facts to him, before which a father had to hesitate. One does not give one's daughter to an insane man! And I still want to believe, in spite of the horrible misfortune that has struck me since then, that that appreciation of my reason was accurate. I want to believe that Gérald was a madman, and an impostor, above all . . . oh, yes, an infamous liar!

A few days later, I received an invitation from Monsieur de Solmes; I was careful not to be late, and I was one of the first to arrive.

"My friend," he said to me, "I've reflected at length, and I've also interrogated Camille . . ."

"And . . . ?"

He had the smile again that I had remarked before.

"That husband," he told me, "cannot suit my daughter in any fashion. Like me, Gérald's eyes frighten her, and your expression *demonic* appears to her to be absolutely accurate . . ."

"So that . . ."

"So that I shall signify to Monsieur Gérald today, with all the customary regrets, that he will have to address himself to another house . . ."

In an irrational impulse, I seized Monsieur de Solmes' hands and shook them forcefully.

"Good, good," he said, still smiling, "we'll talk about all that later. For the moment," he went on, more seriously, "I confess to you that the necessity I am in of confronting that evil gaze troubles me slightly. I'm not a nervous girl, but I'm in haste to be finished with that individual . . ."

"A madman who devotes himself to sorcery, to black magic . . ."

---

is a brief treatise or handbook; with a definite article the title usually refers to the *Enchiridion* of Epictetus, a manual of Stoic philosophy. The "worst" works of Paracelsus are presumably the magical treatises falsely attributed to the physician in question.

"In any case, who is not at all the husband that I desire for my daughter. I ask you not to lose sight of him . . . I can't say that I'm anxious about the consequences of my refusal, and yet, it seems to me that those eyes might cover stubborn rancor . . ."

"Count on me."

Gérald arrived; he was, in truth, very handsome, pale, with his long thin face, his blue-tinted black beard, and his thick hair, which a habitual gesture threw back in a flicker of flame.

We found ourselves beside one another, and chatted; he seemed at ease, as if he had nothing to fear that might thwart his projects. Toward the middle of the night I saw Monsieur de Solmes take him aside; I would have liked to hear the words exchanged, but I could scarcely see the two of them, half-hidden by a door-curtain.

Finally, they separated, and as Gérald went to the door his eyes met mine . . . a flash sprang forth. I felt something like a burn. In the distance, Monsieur de Solmes had addressed a furtive signal to me, as if to remind me of my promise.

I arrived in the vestibule a few seconds after Gérald. At first I did not see him, but as the lackeys were helping me to put on my overcoat, in a corner where other groups were nearby, I saw a singular scene in the mirror: on the steps of the perron Gérald was receiving something from a valet; an envelope that he slipped rapidly into his pocket, giving a handful of gold in return. Then he left.

I ran after him.

The night was cold, very bright under a white moon.

He was twenty paces ahead of me and marching quickly. I slid alongside the houses, muffing the sound of my footsteps.

Suddenly, at a street corner that the moonlight was blanching more brightly, he stopped, holding in his hand the envelope that he had received a little while before.

A shadowed covert permitted me to approach more close-ly, and I got close enough to touch him . . .

And I saw that he had opened the envelope and taken out a cardboard square: a photograph in album format.

Boldly, I leaned over his shoulder . . . and I uttered a cry of rage. Camille! The man had stolen a portrait of Camille!

I extended a hand in order to snatch it from him. He stepped aside abruptly, turning round, and we remained motionless for a moment, face to face.

"Monsieur," I exclaimed, in a voice in which I strove nevertheless to retain a note of courtesy, "explain to me why you have bought from a lackey the portrait of that person . . ."

He said nothing, keeping his eyes fixed on me: eyes that were sparkling like red-hot coals. Never have I seen in a human face such an expression of hatred . . . of ferocity . . .

"You have stolen that portrait," I went on, my anger rising to the point of rage. "That's a dishonest action . . . a disloyal action, for no one has the right to possess that image except the man whose name she will bear . . ."

"And you know that that isn't me . . ." he said, in a voice that hissed between clenched teeth.

"Yes, because it will be me, if it pleases God!" I said. "And I demand that you return it to me . . ."

As he sniggered, my hand rose to slap him . . .

What happened then? Today, I still ask myself whether I was not the victim of a hideous nightmare . . . and yet . . . and yet . . . !

I felt the pressure of his fingers on my wrist, circling it like an iron bracelet. Then it seemed to me that under that constraint, I was dragged away and lifted up. Around me, the streets, the houses and everything else passed with a vertiginous rapidity. Then walls opened up to give us passage, closing again behind us, silently . . .

I found myself in his home, in that man's home, in his laboratory . . .

Upright—magnified, it seemed—his face pale and his mouth contracted, he lifted above his head the adorable portrait of Camille, of my Camille . . . and he said: "You have believed, have you not, that one can toy with me with impunity. I have been rejected like a lackey. In his pride as a millionaire, that man has insulted me with his refusal. You are his accomplice. I know everything: your espionage, your calumnies, and your illusions too. That man is mad! Mad! Listen to this: I hate that arrogant father, I hate that daughter, and I hate you. I want to avenge myself on all three of you, at a single stroke . . ."

I did not reply; I would not have been capable of pronouncing a word, any more than of making a movement, as happens in dreams where the limbs are paralyzed and strength abolished . . .

But I saw around me all the grimacing apparatus of necromancy: retorts, furnaces, the athanor of the philosophers . . . And then, what attracted my attention most particularly were little figurines with human faces, which had needles in the form of swords stuck in their hearts.

He took one of them, and then, in a sneering tone, like that of a schoolmaster giving a lesson to little children, he said: "This represents to you a professor of mine, a grotesque incapacity who permitted himself, one day, to doubt my science. I tried out on him the antique practices of spell-casting. You must have heard mention of Ruggieri,[1] who accommodated so well in this fashion the enemies of the great Catherine de' Medici. I've restored them in their perfect exercise. I bewitch, torture at a distance and kill those I hate. I killed this man, but the effort of casting spells by means of wax images is too violent and dangerous for one's own security—which is easily understandable, since it's by an effort of will that one has to transport into inert matter the vivifying force on which the maleficia must be exercised . . ."

---

1 Cosimo Ruggieri (?-1615) was a favorite of Catherine de' Medici, who was arrested more than once for allegedly practising murderous sorcery, and thus acquired a great reputation as a magician.

I have not forgotten a single one of the words pronounced, and, strangely enough, they seem as clear to me, and as true, as if I were myself an adept of the criminal magic.

"I want now," he continued, "to act with less risk. I shall kill your Camille, in order that both of you, father and husband, will weep bloody tears over her grave, but I shall have no need to model a figurine, nor to infuse it, by borrowing from my intimate energies, with an artificial life, for I possess a parcel of her own life, of her vitality, in this . . .

"You believe, do you not," he continued, "that there is nothing, in this reproduction of a form, of a physiognomy, but a play of light? Ignorant fools! Between the body that places itself before the objective lens and the sensitized plate a current is established, removing from the being, as in a galvanoplastic operation, innumerable particles of its own matter, of it substance, of its life . . . Chemistry fixes them, nothing more, and—understand me well—between that representation, which seems dead to you, and the distant living being, a bond exists that can never be broken . . . between one and the other, innumerable threads subsist, like a network of electric wires. And when I strike, when I wound, when I lacerate that image, blows, wounds and lacerations, like a telegraph signal, like a voice on the telephone, will reverberate on the living being . . . who will not understand why she is suffering, why she is moaning, why she is dying . . .

"Yes, with this simple photograph, I have the right of life or death over your Camille, and I want to use it. No one knows that, no one has divined it, except me; I have understood that in nature, no bond is ever broken, and what is fixed on the glass is the vital dust; and it is on this that I am going to avenge myself . . ."

Suddenly, it seemed to me that the bonds that were holding me had just broken, and, in a paroxysm of fury I rushed at Gérald in order to snatch from his accursed hands the image of the woman I loved . . .

But he escaped me . . . and I saw that, leaning over the adored image, he was slowly plunging a point into the heart . . .

Then everything disappeared, and when I came round I was in my study with a volume by the necromancer Éliphas Lévi open before me.

It was broad daylight. I shook off the torpor that was oppressing me, and, remembering, I forced myself to laugh at what could only have been—I wanted to believe—a horrible nightmarish fantasy.

Someone rang my doorbell; a domestic came to look for me on behalf of Monsieur de Solmes.

Terror and dolor! During the night, Camille had died, as if struck down by an unknown malady.

I ran . . . and I fell into the arms of the sobbing father. He permitted me to see the adorable young woman, with her pale virginal face, and her hands folded over her breast.

Gérald! The assassin! Oh, I needed his life! I rushed to his house.

There I was told that he had not returned home; I cried that it was a lie; I knocked down the domestic who opposed my passage. I half-broke down the door of his laboratory in order to get through it more rapidly. He was not there, and yet, I recognized the vast room, with its retorts and its athanors . . . except that the wax figurines were no longer there.

And since that day, I have never seen the infamous Gérald again.

Camille is dead . . . dead . . . and I, shivering with anguish, wonder whether that man was mad . . . or whether I myself . . .

About the Author

Jules Lermina (1839-1915) was a radical journalist arrested more than once for subversion; he was in prison when the Prussia army closed in on Paris began in 1870, but was offered release if he would join the National Guard; although utterly unfit for military service he agreed, and was sent out of Paris to fight the invaders, thus being unable to join the Commune. Chastened by the experience, he took his wife and children to join an experimental Utopian commune, but soon became disenchanted and returned to Paris and journalism, writing Poesque short stories before becoming a successful writer of action-adventure *feuilletons*. When his daughter Marie-Pauline married the occult bookseller Henri Chacornac, Lermina became peripherally involved with the Occult Revival, writing several stories based on ideas fed to him by Papus and contributing several stories, including "L'Envoûteur" (1892), to *L'Initiation*; the translation is original to the present volume. Lermina had previously introduced occult elements into numerous stories for purely melodramatic purposes, and was personally skeptical, but his prestige as a writer and anarchist was sufficient to prompt Papus to ask him to chair the Congress of Occult societies that he convened in 1889.

THE EYE OF THE DRAGON

by R. de Maricourt

*To the Spirit incarnate in the personality
of Monsieur Camille Flammarion.*

I

"PARDON ME," said the intern, "but it's an urgent matter. Walk in the garden; I'll come to fetch you to visit the
epileptic ward."

It was hot—the white heat of those autumn days that rise
in the dew and set in the mist. Facing me, the establishment
extended into the distance its tedious symmetry of a barracks
of a royal château. I yawned and took a cigar from my case.

"Would you like a light? I'd be glad to offer you one."

A little old man, freshly shaved, brisk in manner, suddenly
emerged from a clump of rhododendrons and handed me a
box of matches. The apparition was so abrupt that I shuddered, as if at the unexpected explosion of a petard.

"Have no fear, Monsieur; although a boarder in the house
I'm not a redoubtable madman. At the most I could be accused of a touch of monomania. After having heard me, you
can tell me whether the reproach is merited."

I recoiled as far as the middle of the pathway, still holding the man under my gaze, whom I assumed to be an old gardener because of his blue apron with a large pocket. The sunlight was striking him full in the face and he frowned, little wrinkles forming at the corners of his half-closed eyes. He raised his arm in the air to shield himself, and as he was holding a spade the iron shone as it described a rapid semicircle nearby. A slightly mocking smile tucked up his lips.

"You're thinking, Monsieur, that in the hands of one of our inmates of the dangerous category, this instrument of labor might become a terrible weapon. In trusting me with it, the administration is giving me a certificate of harmlessness."

The old man had stopped a few paces away from me, both hands resting on the handle of his spade. He conserved the immobility of a bas-relief.

In a clear voice, expressing himself with the ease of a man of the best society, he said: "It's for hygienic reasons that I take some exercise by handling an implement with which my first education didn't familiarize me."

In him, rapid, even abrupt, gestures did not betray any incoherence; my interlocutor seemed perfectly sure of the direction of his movements.

He was short in stature, with a full, sanguine face, scarcely wrinkled, and he wore white side-whiskers, cut short, like his hair; he resembled a painted terra cotta statue. His small, keen gray eyes were deeply sunk beneath the brow ridge, itself surmounted by rough, thick eyebrows, darker in color.

Those eyes seemed to me to be a little too close to the nose, but I did not remark there the troubled, empty gaze that suggests a derangement of the mental faculties. Behind their soft expression, indicative of a fatalistic resignation, one sensed a slightly ironic disdain.

"Light your cigar tranquilly, then, and sit down here."

He guided me to a circular bench around the trunk of an araucaria that was already majestic.

236

"We might as well talk while awaiting the return of the intern—an amiable young man, an excellent fellow, although the theories of his school have stunted his brain. There's no amplitude in his ideas; so he'll tell you that I'm afflicted by delirious conceptions. Delirious conceptions! One of those terms that the ignorant invent to designate any mental operation surpassing their comprehension! My God, Monsieur, the fact is that I'm here because my family wanted to fatten themselves with the little money that remained to me. They thought that more practical than letting me squander it in perpetual voyages whose objective they didn't understand. That's the motive for my internment. Useful as it might be as a means of softening egotistical brutality, it's necessary to envelop it with a pretext, as one wraps an almond in sugar to fabricate a praline. In order to justify my reclusion, they have recourse to delirious conceptions.

"You shall know in what they consist.

"A bachelor, not owing anything to anyone, I made considerable expenses in searching for a certain breastplate considered as the masterpiece of Giorgio Staccone . . ."

"An innocent petty mania of archeology," I said, with a conciliatory smile full of indulgence.

"No, Monsieur, I'm not making a collection of antique weaponry. That breastplate—or, rather, that corselet—has a very particular interest for me. You'll understand it on learning that I commissioned it and supervised its execution personally in Milan in the winter of 1527."

"Ah! Damn!" I leapt to my feet, crushing a snail underfoot.

By means of a mild gesture, but full of authority, the old man made me sit down again. "Oh, Monsieur," he groaned, "you too, who inspired such confidence in me!"

While conserving its placidity, his gaze had become so dolorously suppliant that I was moved. His lower lip extended and his chin quivered like that of a child about to weep.

"You don't know, then, even as an eccentricity, the theory of successive incarnations? I say that I lived under François I. If I thought that I was incapable of demonstrating that fact clearly, I wouldn't permit myself to affirm it to you. I have, it's true, convictions that the majority of people don't share. Is that an absolute proof of dementia? Get away! Why that anxious and mistrustful expression? You'll make me doubt my own reason. I want, however, to believe in the plenitude of a lucidity that many proofs have not tarnished.

"Now, let's see, Monsieur; you'll grant me that, considered *en masse*, humankind is composed of imbeciles, and that the latter have established a level of vulgar ideas, narrow prejudices and stupid maxims, the ensemble of which is known as *common sense*. Below that level vegetate idiots; above it float madmen. Well, I flatter myself on being above you too; I hope so. The line of demarcation is as arbitrary as it is mobile; I'll even say that it doesn't exist. Properly speaking, it's only a nuance, and people perceive it through variously colored spectacles.

"Monsieur, Monsieur, please lend me half an hour of attention; when you've heard me, you can judge me."

Taking my silence for acquiescence, the fellow commenced.

II

"On a hot July evening I returned home harassed. Having thrown myself down on my sofa, I became drowsy almost immediately. The dying daylight left trailing glimmers that clung to the corners of the furniture. My eyes were fixed on my writing-desk, set against the window. When they closed I continued to see the objects garnishing my room, but they were bathed in a soft blue lunar light.

"At that moment the duality of the principle constituting our being appeared to me to be very gripping, because I saw myself lying on the sofa while I was floating above it. I saw myself down below, but I felt that I was higher up.

"Gradually, the light covered and veiled the whole room; it was slowly transformed into a thick fog that extended, taking on oceanic proportions; and in the immense sheet thus formed, a rip appeared, in the depths of which a landscape was framed. It was distant, minuscule, like one of those microscopic photographs enclosed in small objects that are sold in seaside resorts. It seemed to come toward me, growing, in the fashion of the phantasmagorias of a magic lantern. Perhaps it was me that was flying toward it with vertiginous rapidity; it seemed to me, however, that I wasn't changing location.

"Soon I was swallowed up in the details of a vegetation that took on natural proportions, and I found myself in the middle of open country. The fog was swept away, allowing the opaline transparency of moonlight to reappear.

"Around me I saw long, dry grass, very abrasive, lying down here and there as if after disorderly trampling. Blistered at intervals by hillocks, still covered by withered vegetation, the plain extended immeasurably as far as the eye could see. Above me the sky rounded out, full of stars, but to the left the silhouettes of large edifices rose up blackly against a fiery background. Immediately at my feet, against a steep slope, dirty yellow water was slowly carrying the cadavers of men and horses.

"I found myself in a clump of bushy trees; their foliage stood out with a perfect clarity against the horizon; I recognized elms. With my back to the trunk of one of them, I was gazing obstinately at the opposite bank. With feverish impatience, I was waiting for something, or someone.

"The conflagration grew; the red glow had invaded half the sky. A distant, dull murmur reached me, compounded from the cries of humans, the whinnying of horses and the clanking of iron.

"Toward the middle of the river a clump of reeds was leaning over and straightening up, tremulously, seized by a frisson at every ripple of the water, and the leaves collided, producing a monotonous clicking. From behind a trunk inclined over the river a frail, light boat emerged, which immediately drew level with me. I leapt into it from the height of my bank and I paddled with a furious urgency.

"'Oh! Gemma, Gemma.'

"That name, repeated twice, resounded in my ears as if someone else had pronounced it; however, I heard the sound of my own voice, but so hoarse and discordant that I hesitated to believe that it had emerged from my mouth.

"The slope of the opposite bank rose up as I drew nearer to it, plying the paddle. At the same time, the form of a wretched peasant hut built with reeds was outlined. It had the appearance of a slight eminence on an ocean of similar reeds, to such an extent that it could be mistaken for a simple accident of the terrain.

"From it emerged a woman, alarming by dint of a superhuman, impossible beauty: something unreal; one of those things that the imagination refuses to conceive. She took a few steps toward the bank. She was too far away from me for me to make out her features, in accordance with the laws of optics. Although plunged in shadow, her face shone radiantly by virtue of a luminous enchantment. That creature seemed to be kneaded out of light, as if, like certain precious stones, she bore a luminous hearth within her. Her eyes, the eyes of a statue, did not express any sensation or thought—nothing but a glacial calm, a tranquil indifference.

"I received a great blow and I felt the cold of a knife, with which I had been struck in the heart. I dropped my paddle. Immediately, the boat spun madly, drawing me away.

"More physiologist than psychologist, I could not make the autopsy of my soul. I can only affirm that my sensations were very complex.

"That Gemma, whose benefactor I was, I loved with a mixture of fury and adoration; she humiliated me, wounded me in my pride. The violence of the desire that pushed me toward her was complicated by hatred. I would have liked to bite her, to rip her with my teeth, but a force prostrated me before her as if at the feet of an idol.

"A tree trunk caused the boat of capsize and I sank to the bottom. Armored all over with steel plates, I did not even try to swim. Yes, Monsieur, that breastplate to which all the interest of my life is attached has already caused my death.

"The eddies pushed me toward the bank.

"In an instinctive struggling movement, I found myself, for a few seconds, with my head out of the water. The bank, now very close, had become a great black wall blocking the horizon.

"Above it, Gemma stood out against the sky, so high that her face seemed to rise radiantly in the constellation of the Pleiades.

"I made a supreme effort to cry again: *Gemma! Gemma!* No sound emerged from my throat. Still motionless, conserving her marmoreal rigidity, she had a placidly distracted expression while I died at her feet.

"The phenomenon of the doubling of the personality then presented itself with a poignant intensity.

"I was dying in the slow tortures of asphyxia, but at the same time I recognized myself lying on my sofa in the Rue de Fleurus.

"It was there, in fact, that I came round, my head somewhat heavy, at the moment when the sparrows ceased chirping on the rooftops; my absence had only lasted a few minutes."

✳

When the narrator had finished speaking, I said to him:

"It's simply a dream that you've related to me there."

"Yes, Monsieur, a dream exactly similar to the one you're having here as you look at me. Another moment of attention; as long as you're not a materialist, and we'll understand one another.

"Every visible action gives rise to an image that is inscribed in light, and which light bears away with a velocity of seventy-five thousand leagues per second. When the spirit, disengaged from the body, flies through space with a velocity equal to that of light, it witnesses past events as clearly as we witness, *in a material fashion*, those of present life. In either case there is a simple phenomenon of vision.

"You understand, therefore, that I can see again the places where I lived with the persons with whom my former existence coincided. Thanks to Flammarion, the astronomer, certain things anticipated intuitively have become realities for me, which are formulated with an entirely mathematical precision."

Taking a little notebook from his pocket, the old madman scribbled rapidly, and handed me the piece of paper on which he had written:

I died in 1527; it's now 1889. My spirit, in order to see the past again, must therefore have transported itself through space about 856,202,400,000,000 leagues from our planet.

"Don't let those figures stop you," he added. "For spiritual essences, time and space are absolutely chimerical. You'll know later that terrestrial life and matter are pure chimeras—fleeting shadows—themselves."

III

There was a silence. The old monomaniac's respiration had become gradually more rapid. He resumed speaking.

"Thank you for following me thus far. Now you'll find me a few years later, emptying a *fiascone* of Orvieto at the door of an *osteria* in Ponte-Molle.

"The thin, grotesque and tormented profiles of the statues on the bridge were outlined against the sky. The sun was disappearing behind the large coppery clouds of which Poussin was so fond.

"A heavy gust of wind passed, making the long grass undulate; the skeleton of a dead world seemed to tremble beneath the immense ocher carpet covering its bones.

"I remained there in inert contemplation, not thinking about anything, entirely enveloped by the solemn ennui weighing upon that yellow desert known as the Roman campagna. Sometimes an entirely mental oppression, a motiveless anxiety, a sort of confused presentiment, clutched my breast: the sensation of nervous people at the approach of a storm.

"A herd of buffalo engaged upon the bridge; their large hooves raised a rutilant dust in the fiery dusk. A man on horseback armed with a long pike was driving them before him, uttering cannibal howls. Entirely clad in animal skins, the man resembled an ancient satyr that the extravagant whim of a pagan god had maintained alive under that dead name. Was he not also one of those hairy onocentaurs feared by the ancients who galloped over the burning campagna in the sunlight?

"Instead of following the road I went along the Tiber in order to return to the city. I was not moving my legs; they were carrying me. A long distraction, an absolute unconsciousness, had rendered me incapable of directing my organism. If I was marching, it was by virtue of a series of those movements known in physiology as reflexes.

"Suddenly, I stopped, as if a powerful hand had been placed on my shoulder. It was impossible for me to lift a foot in order to continue. I was obliged to lean against a tree trunk, and I looked around.

"A quasi-fearful stupefaction petrified me. I rubbed my eyes several times.

"I was in the midst of the landscape of my dream; it was reborn completely with the clarity of an engraving scarcely paled by time.

"At my feet the slope descended steeply to yellow and sluggish water; a clump of reeds was vibrating with a continuous tremor, curbed by the current; facing me, a slight eminence in the grass took on the form of a reaper's hut. Was the woman about to appear? Was the little boat about to come around the bend?

"I breathed in air, filling my lungs; I was afraid, for I felt asphyxia gripping my throat, as before.

"The moon, slightly veiled, rose over the rump of the Sabine mountains. One by one the stars appeared in a softly blue-tinted transparent atmosphere.

"Saint Peter's, the Vatican and the Castel Sant'Angelo outlined their colossal masses against the ruddy background, but no longer had their contours. Was the conflagration not about to be ignited behind them?

"Gripped by weakness, I collapsed on the grass; on looking up I recognized fantastic designs traced on the sky by the gaps in the foliage.

"Then an internal phenomenon of a disconcerting nature was produced.

"I wondered whether all the surrounding objects were not illusions, mere reminiscences summoned during the dream I was having, memories of things once seen in reality. Like the sleeper in the *Mille et une nuits* I could not distinguish the phantom from the tangible, or know how to grasp objective reality.

"And in order to determine whether I was really awake I made grand gestures and spoke aloud.

"At the same time, confused images surged forth and were effaced, glimpsed in the fog of a remote distance. A buzz emerging from subterranean depths rose up, magnifying. I thought that I could make out human cries, the whinnying of horses, and metallic impacts.

"Then, immediately, I recognized the natural sound of the wind curbing the reeds in the plain.

"I cannot say at precisely what moment my spirit quit our planet to fly in light and revive there the time of my former existence. All the events of the preceding incarnation were retraced for me that night with a precision of detail that I don't find when I recall those of present life.

"Events are confused, entangled in my memory, to such an extent that it sometimes happens tome, before imbeciles, to make allusion to some anecdote of which I was the hero under Francois I. They do not fail to conclude that I really am mad and that my sequestration has been imposed by prudence. Oh, if only it were possible for me to imprison humankind in a lunatic asylum!"

"With things thus restored to their proper place, the world would be better," I said, affecting a profound conviction.

The old man's little gray eyes fixed upon me, with an expression that embarrassed me. "I'd like to believe that you're speaking seriously, Monsieur. In the meantime, I'll content myself with shrugging my shoulders and remaining silent."

"But no, please continue; tell me what you saw on the bank of the Tiber."

"Gladly, all the more so as the revelation of Rome clarifies and completes that of Paris, With it, my whole biography has been reconstructed. I'll summarize briefly.

"Very noble, bearing one of the finest names in France, fabulously rich, I had attached myself to the fortunes of the Constable de Bourbon.[1] I loved and admired that young hero, so superior to Francois I, a poor individual singularly disguised an exaggerated by history, a vulgar guttersnipe of mediocre intelligence.

------

1 Charles III, Duc de Bourbon (1490-1527) who was Constable of France from 1515-1521; he was killed during the sack of Rome.

"During the Milanese wars I had raised a company of men-at-arms: German and Italian adventurers, a few Frenchmen, a fine accumulation of gallows-birds. At the same time, I commissioned the item of armor that I've mentioned to you. With the boastful and puerile vanity of my epoch, I wanted my equipment to surpass in artistic magnificence all that had been done in that genre.

"I followed the Constable to the siege of Rome, I found myself beside him when he was killed in the breach at the Porta Cavalleggeri.

"After our entry into the city and the atrocities of the sack I pitched my tents on the bank of the Tiber, some distance from the Castel Sant'Angelo, to which we were laying siege. Messire Orazio Baglioni[1] was shut in there with the artillery that Benvenuto Cellini, a famous braggart, boasted of having maneuvered almost single-handed.

"I had just lain down, fully armed, on a few bales of hay, and I was beginning to fall asleep when I was woken up by loud clamors.

"Two disheveled women, their clothes in tatters, were running through the camp, pursued by soldiers. One of them, who seemed to be following the other, threw herself at my feet and embraced my knees. 'Illustrious captain, noble lord, in the name of the Madonna, save Dona Gemma. Her parents have been murdered, our palace is on fire. We have no refuge!'

"With my left arm I sheltered that Dona Gemma while, with my free right hand, I cut off a few heads of drunken lansquenets.

"When order had almost been restored I relaxed my arm in order to liberate the woman. Her face seemed to me to be illuminated simultaneously by the moon and the fire. Her face was all bloody. I thought that while fencing, I must

---

1 Orazio di Gianopaolo Baglioni (1493-1528) was put in charge of Rome's defences by Pope Clement VII during the siege of Rome.

246

have scratched her face against my corselet by an involuntary movement. I beg you, Monsieur, to note that detail.

"Madonna Gemma stared at me with a tranquility behind which I sensed a kind of disdain, almost scorn. Such an attitude, in our respective situations, was at least strange. I could have expected something better, if only thanks.

"The maidservant told me that she never spoke.

"Reapers, as you know, construct temporary huts in which to shelter during the hottest hours of the day. It was in a cabin of that sort near my camp, on the other bank of the Tiber, that I installed my prisoners. With the aid of valets, I took charge personally of bringing them provisions.

"Such bizarre conduct, in such conditions, given the ambient mores, can only be explained by a phenomenon rather rare itself among my peers. The fact is that at first sight I had fallen in love with Gemma, in love as no student had ever been with a prima donna or a valet with a princess.

"I had forbidden my men not only to molest the recluses but even to approach the hut, under pain of immediate death. The superhuman beauty of that woman petrified me in an astonished ecstasy. There was something enigmatic about her, attractive and repulsive at the same time, which exasperated my passion to the point of delirium. She did not speak, but could hear and understand. My most tender supplications and my most violent declarations had never altered that atrocious serenity for an instant. A stupid timidity held me barricaded within the limits of the most implausible respect.

"No bold word was ever able to emerge from my lips. Under her impassive gaze my eyes lowered as if I felt the shame of some unknown fault of which she alone had the secret.

"Oh, how I avenged myself in the depths of my thought for the tortures inflicted by that inert creature! In my dreams I treated her with the refinements of an exquisite cruelty. What debauches of savant ferocity! What profligacy of imagination for inventing tortures! She made herself a statue; it was with hammer-blows that I broke her into small fragments!

"It's necessary to pardon me. One becomes wicked by dint of suffering. An incredible thing: sometimes I believed that I recognized her features, her attitude. In darkness as distant as the depths of a well it seemed to me that a statue like Gemma was enthroned on a high—very high—pedestal . . . the edifice was somber . . . confusedly, I saw squat columns, monsters carved in the rock . . .

"Finally, one evening, determined to emerge from my ridiculous position, without waiting for the oarsman and the servants, I wanted to cross the Tiber. You know how I was swallowed up . . .

"That is all I saw under the elms beside the river. Without knowing when and in what manner I returned to my home, in the Via del Babuino, I found myself emerging from a long crisis punctuated with deliria.

"The fact was attributed to a miasmatic infection; I was made to take the eucalyptus syrup that Brother Alcide, a Trappist at the Trois-Fontaines-Saint-Paul had just invented."

The old man stopped, paused as if to reassemble his memories, and then resumed his narrative.

IV

"The day was ending, casting on the pavements the false yellow light that, in the towns of the Midi, allies a sensation of unhealthy heat with an opaque depression: a true sirocco day.

"After a long walk, exhaustion throughout my body but with a free spirit, my thought wandering, I found myself near San Giorgio in Velabro.[1] I was about to turn the corner of the

---

1 The church in question is located next to the Arch of Janus, on the spot where, according to legend, the she-wolf who suckled Romulus and Remus discovered them.

Piazza Bocca della Verita when I stopped suddenly, fascinated.

"On the façade of a house of sordid aspect I had just read, in red letters:

ANTICHITA—LOPALLINO DI NEATI

"I reread it several times, feeling—I don't know why—a frisson that shook me. 'Lopallino di Neatu,' I repeated, unconsciously, unable to prevent myself repeating the same syllables over and over. They returned, buzzing like an obsessive refrain, as I went up the two steps that led to the shop.

"It was a vast oblong room, low-ceilinged and dark, filled with the disorderly accumulation of disparate objects that one encounters in the shops of bric-à-brac merchants.

"A man sitting at a table was leafing through a large folio volume

"'I'd like to have . . .' I stopped, not knowing why I was there. After a momentary hesitation, I went on: 'I'd like to have a reduction in bronze of the little temple of Vesta,'

"I was speaking at hazard. The proximity of that charming edicule on the square had suggested an idea to me.

"The man raised his head momentarily, agitated his arm with the indolent majesty of an Oriental sovereign, and said: 'Serve Monsieur, will you.' Then he resumed his occupation. Old and stooped, coiffed in a Greek bonnet with black braid, enveloped in a dressing-gown whose cloth seemed to have been ripped from some antique tapestry, the man had massive, thick features. A little clump of hair grew on his nose, as hollow as that of Socrates; his ears were also hairy. Strong and russet, sprinkled with white, his beard masked his mouth and rose up over his cheekbones. His eyes disappeared behind round spectacles with smoked lenses. The accumulation of those trivial details did not, however, produce a vulgar ensemble. The physiognomy, evidently ugly, had a grandiose and gripping ugliness, so far above the mediocre that one could not see it without taking away an impression that dug into the memory like a coin embedded by a mallet.

"The man's gesture and appeal caused two women to emerge from behind the counter. One of them, of massive stature, inclined her head, searching for the requested object. I only saw a lock of gray hair escaped from the red headscarf that covered her head, knotted under the chin. The other, very young, was standing by the window through which a low daylight illuminated the curiosities in the shop teasingly. The light, arriving obliquely, enveloped the face of the young woman as it brushed it with the caresses of half-tones.

"I gazed at her. A wave of fever ran through my entire flesh; my arteries were throbbing madly, my teeth chattering. I held on to the counter with my clenched hands in order not to fall, and I murmured: 'Gemma! Gemma!' I was speaking in an extraordinary voice, devoid of vibration, which surprised me, inasmuch as it reminded me of the voice heard in the dream when, while drowning, I had implored the woman on the river bank.

"'Beatissima vergine!' cried the old woman. 'How do you know our Gemma?' And, addressing me directly: 'She only goes out to go to mass; that's where you must have seen her and must have asked her name. She's so beautiful, so beautiful that all strangers stop as she walks by; artists would pay dearly to have her for a model. In any case, if you had spoken to her she would not have replied, any more than she is replying now; the poor child is mute.'

"I repeated mechanically: 'Mute?'

"'Yes, Monsieur, mute since her accident. The scar that you see above her eyebrow comes from a fall; she has never spoken since. It was against an old breastplate hanging in the corner over there, directly below the Minerva . . .'

"Cutting off the old woman, I said with an excessive volubility: 'Yes, I know; a breastplate—which is to say, the part

250

of the breastplate called the corselet, damascened and nielloed steel; two gold bands rise from the belt to rejoin below the chin-guard, forming a chevron, at an acute angle. Among each band fantastic beasts are raised in black against the mat gold background. At the summit two dragons encounter one another, head to head, like two battling rams . . .'

"'That's right, that's right, but how . . . ?'

"'Oh, that accursed armor, who knows it except me, who was in command at Milan in 1527? The eyes of the dragons are formed by rubies sculpted to a point; one of those points tore her forehead . . . Do you remember, Gemma, oh, my Gemma? Don't look at me; you'll make me fall down dead . . . a nod of the head to indicate that you can hear me, that you've recognized me . . . !'

"Terrified, the woman recoiled, while the girl, with her serene impassivity, seemed to be looking around for the rotunda of Vesta with a slow and distracted gaze.

"The man had just stood up abruptly. Overturning the table and casting aside his book, he ran to me and took me by the arm. He drew me through the shop and made me climb a staircase whose steps seemed rickety and unequal to me, disjointed in places. We went along several very dark corridors.

"He opened a little door, closed it again with a key as soon as we had gone through it, and asked me: 'Are you an initiate of high grade?'

"The action was as rapid as it was unexpected; the question surprised me. Stupefied by all those extraordinary things happening in such a brief time, I remained motionless without opening my mouth.

The antiquary sat me down on a chair of bizarre form and I looked around without encountering the limits of the room. It was filled with a soft, discreet, attenuated light that seemed to be made of blue rays; the same mysterious ultraterrestrial light that had illuminated my visions. No source existed anywhere, with the consequence that the objects, illuminated equally on all their faces, did not cast any shadow.

"The things that I glimpsed appeared to me like images in a mirror over which human breath had extended a light mist. I perceived in that fashion great metallic plates, polished like mirrors, metal chains, tripods and certain objects that freemasons adopt in their pretentious images, symbols whose original significance they have lost. On a marble table a golden star with five points was encrusted, and placed above a wand, a sword and other instruments whose form and dimensions I could not grasp.

"The antiquary, who had followed my gaze, said, smiling: 'Here you are, dear colleague, in the magician's lair. I am acting without detours; do the same.'

"Having recovered a little from my amazement, I replied: 'In all sincerity, Monsieur, I have no idea what you're talking about. I believed in the magicians of the *contes de fées* of my childhood; I know that charlatans still exist who exercise in fairgrounds . . .'

"'Really? Well, so be it; I believe you, but you confound me. What! Do I only see in you a vulgar profane, stuffed with prejudices, kneaded by ignorance? Not even an initiate? But then the fact is even more admirable. Without any help other than your organization, you've become a seer? Yes, you've glimpsed mysteries, the knowledge of which we only attain after several centuries of ardent study and cruel proofs . . . You've perceived something beyond gross physical phenomena; you have, to some small degree, shaken off the temporary hallucination called organic life and grasped a few threads of the eternal verity. And you, thus privileged, sustain with the ignorant plebs of official science that magic is dupery or a chimera!

"'Know that our divine science has been transmitted from master to disciple since the world was created; as old as the world, it will only perish with it; it is what governs it by occult laws, directs it by means of invisible strings. The persecutions of blind governments have been able to oblige it to silence, but without it, nothing could steal its infinite power.'

"Lopallino had just taken off his spectacles and he was looking at me. His exceedingly brilliant eyes appeared to me to be circled with yellow like the eyes of birds of prey. Their disagreeable fixity caused waves of nausea to rise within me, with a general numbness, while a weight squeezed my forehead above the eyebrows, coiffing me like a lead skullcap.

"I would have liked to turn my own gaze away, but I could not; I was dominated.

"'How do you know about Gemma and the breastplate?'

"In spite of my desire to resist, an internal force obliged me to speak. I gave a complete account of the visions that had enlightened me successively in Paris and in Rome.

"When I said that I had found in Gemma a distant analogy of form and expression with a certain statue that I believed I recalled in the depths of a subterrain, Lopallino started slightly. His eyes lost in the void, slowly, he murmured in a very low voice: 'Yes . . . the Hindu temple . . . the brahmins . . . it's there that they began my initiation.'

"I continued my story, and I concluded it by saying: 'Now, Monsieur, since you claim to be a magician, tell me, if possible, how the Gemma by whom I was drowned in the spring of 1527 can be the Gemma that I rediscover today in the autumn of 1869 behind a second-hand dealer's counter?'

"Lopallino had listened to me without making a movement. He was still holding his chin in one hand, and seemed to be stroking his beard. When I had finished he folded his arms.

"'You are, I repeat,' he said, after a moment of silence, 'singularly privileged to have been able, without studies, to penetrate the mystery of successive incarnations; it is only revealed to the majority of humans after their death. I have certainly lived in another form than that of Lopallino the antiquary; sometimes I recall my anterior existences, but only by means of rapid intuitions like flashes of lightning that split the darkness during a storm.

"'It is even stranger that a Spirit has recovered its material form, and even its name, in the succession of its corporeal existences. That can be explained, though. Do you know what Gemma is?'

"I made no response, and the antiquary went on: 'Imagine a soul still in the period of incubation, an elementary spirit, an unfinished being attempting humanity. As it has to realize the prototype of feminine beauty on our planet, nature has not broken its mold; it would be difficult to assemble all material perfections a second time. That being, alas, lacks some of the seven principles whose combination constitutes human being. I wanted to complete Gemma, and you, whose fate is united with hers, could have aided me if we had not lost the Staccone breastplate . . .'

"*Either the fellow is infantile*, I thought, *or I'm drunk.* Habituated as I was to encountering singularities, my common sense had never run into such an extravagance. I tried to get up in order to look for the door.

"'Please listen to me until I have finished,' my interlocutor went on, 'and lend me the greatest attention.'

"I obeyed.

"'Thirty-five years ago. Lopallino, the shopkeeper of the Velabro, married a young and vigorous Trasteverine, who managed the shop perfectly. I therefore had an excellent wife. Now, she found a child abandoned on the steps of Ara Coeli.[1] No one claimed the child and we adopted and raised her; we named her Gemma because of her uncanny beauty, which became manifest during her earliest years. We had also observed in her a great difficulty in expressing herself, and the absence—apparently, at least—of all sensibility.'

---

1 *Ara coeli* translates as "Arch of Heaven"; the Basilica Sanctae Mariae de Ara coeli in Capitolio is the church at the summit of the Capitoline Hill.

V

"As I have said, the gaze of the so-called magician plunged me into a kind of torpor. His slightly dull voice and his slow and monotonous diction contributed to maintaining the numbness. It wasn't easy for me to follow his words, the meaning of which I tried to penetrate. As when one is falling asleep, I felt my thoughts escaping me, and I tried to grasp them, as a child tries to recapture a thread at the end of which he has attached a butterfly. I also felt humiliated by the fascination that the shopkeeper, charlatan or not, exercised upon me. I would have liked to interrupt him with some impertinent gibe, but it was impossible for me to say anything, and he continued, keeping his clear gaze riveted to my face,

"'Some time later, I made the acquisition of two objects precious to me: a steel corselet fished up from the bed of the Tiber near the Castel Sant'Angelo, and an engraved fragment of ruby. Having been able to distinguish the mark of the artist and the date of fabrication, I recognized a masterpiece of Giorgio Staccone executed in 1527.

"'The ruby interested me from another viewpoint. Independently of special researches necessitated by my profession, I had studied the hermetic sciences, toward which I was impelled by a taste that I can call instinctive. The knowledge I had acquired enabled me to recognize a fragment of the Gnostic *abraxas* of Alexandria, a Basilidean abraxas.[1] I still carry it about my person—here it is.'

---

1 The term *abraxas* results from a mistranscription of the word *abrasax*, originating in Gnostic texts associated with the Alexandrian preacher Basilides—whose writings have been lost but who appears to have been a believer in metempsychosis—and probably referring to the *megas archon*, the principle of the heavens, the seven letters corresponding to the seven classical planets; it is found engraved on a few antique gemstones, known for that reason as abraxas stones.

"Lopallino took a little case from his waistcoat pocket containing, on a soft cushion of white silk, a broken fragment of ruby, one of the faces of which bore the head of a cynocephalus on a human torso and some Greek letters, symmetrically disposed. The engraving must have continued on the missing fragment. 'If I could complete this piece,' he said, 'Gemma's destiny would be accomplished, at the same time as yours.'

"'I don't understand,' I said, wondering whether the poor fellow had the full use of his mental faculties.

"'Of course not! How can a wretched profane understand mysteries whose profundity escaped the hierophants of Eleusis? If your intelligence remains closed, at least open your ears. You know how Gemma, who was then four years old, was wounded in the head by falling on the point of the ruby mounted in the eye of the dragon. You have been told that that accident had determined her complete mutism. The day after her fall, the corselet had disappeared; I have never been able to recover it. By dint of labor I've made an important discovery: the ruby of the dragon's eye on the left of the corselet is nothing other than the second part of the Basilidean abraxas. That poor ignoramus Staccone, not suspecting the value of his treasure, simply sculpted that fragment in order to mount it in the steel of your breastplate.

"'A revelation of the kind that arrive in my rare flashes of extraterrestrial lucidity informed me of an even more important secret. The mystery of Gemma's fate is attached to the Gnostic talisman. That is why it's necessary to help me to recover the breastplate. Let that be your life's work. Consecrate to it the few years of existence that have been lent to you while awaiting another incarnation. Sooner or later, when the obscurities are dissipated, Gemma, having become completely a woman, will be yours.'

"Seized by vertigo, I felt my head spinning. 'Are you speaking seriously? How do you know these things?'

"In his calm and confident tone, Lopallino replied: 'Have you observed the significance of the name Gemma—which is to say, *precious stone*—that name designating the same individuality twice over? Have you also remarked the wound produced on her forehead by the same ruby? How do you explain the repercussion of an identical event at an interval of three centuries? What is the significance of the kind of chemical affinity between Gemma's carnal husk and a precious stone? An effect of hazard? Get away! For the sage, hazard doesn't exist. Seemingly random events have their reason for being by virtue of the immutable laws that regulate nature, but those laws escape terrestrial intelligence.

"'Gemma is an emanation of the universal soul vivifying everything created in the worlds that populate space. Everything in the universe is alive, even the minerals accused of inertia by our Academic scientists. They are composed of atoms that agitate in a perpetual turbulence. Their mode of crystallization is imposed by the same laws that delimit the form of animal organisms. Now, if they are alive, they have souls—rudimentary souls—principles of life destined for successive perfection. Know, then, that the Basilidean abraxas originated from the jewel mounted in the forehead of a Hindu goddess, and that the latter contained the as-yet-embryonic spirit of our Gemma. When that spirit is completed, the stone will soften and become flesh; a female heart will be able to beat within the magnificent frozen envelope.

"'Gemma will speak when language is necessary to express *sentiments*; thus far she has only known superficial *sensations*. Amour is a sacred mystery that, like the majority of humans, you have profaned in other existences, delaying your spiritual development. That is why you have collided with a block of marble, which you have not been able to visit spiritually. Purified by suffering, detached from brutal material instincts, you will determine the development of a heart in Gemma.

Perhaps further incarnations will be necessary for that. That is what the possession of the abraxas would have enabled us to accomplish.

"'You don't understand? To be intelligible, I would require other words than those of human languages. By itself, a talisman is nothing. The one I want to recover would be deprived of all virtue without the consecration of a mage who has inherited my knowledge, just as I have inherited the knowledge of Pythagoras, the Egyptians and the Brahmins.'

"Lopallino had stood up while talking; a transformation was operated within him. Of the Greek bonnet ornamented with gold braid nothing remained but a circlet of gold gripping his hair, which fell over his shoulders in long white undulations. Also white, his beard unfurled in Babylonian curls over the old dressing-gown, which had become a simarre laminated with gold. The blue radiance that had illuminated my dreams and now filled space was emitted by his shining eyes. Something immense was emanated by his entire being, which one sensed but did not know, which one wanted to grasp but did not dare: the radiation of an unknown full of majesty, an entirely psychic splendor.

"I murmured: 'Who are you, then?'

"The august individual smiled with the supreme condescension of a god descended to earth. 'Why did you stop when you saw my name inscribed above my door? Do you no longer know how to read?'

"Above me, in space, I saw again the letters on his shopfront: LOPALLINO DI NEATI. They fluttered and swirled, scintillating like a swarm of amorous fireflies on a beautiful southern night. They shone, paling and suddenly reviving, like phosphoric trails in the midst of darkness.

"Grouped in a semicircle they traced a nimbus around the head of the sublime old man; on his forehead blazed a luminous five-pointed star, the sign of the Microcosm. The

letters were arranged in such a way as to write: APOLLONIO
DI TIANE.

"Apollonius of Tyana! The great thaumaturge, the successor of Pythagoras, the pupil of the mysterious Brahmins of India!

"Conserving his smile, he said to me: 'I call myself Lopallino in the suburb of Velabro where I exercise my modest industry. Is it not singular that the letters of my name are those of the name that the ancient mage wore? You'll think that all this is illusion. In an instant we'll have had a dream . . .'

"Trembling, I murmured: 'Apollonius of Tyana! The divine Apollonius! Oh, my God—but I'm hallucinated; I've gone mad!'

"'You are already both. The light fascinates; it intoxicates like wine. You have seen the invisible; in the invisible alone, the truth resides. The world is not yet sufficiently spiritualized to grasp it. Yes, you will be mocked, persecuted, imprisoned with beings deprived of reason. The blind always treat as mad the man who affirms the light. Purify yourself, then, in order to rise within the spiritual hierarchy.'

"Overwhelmed, dazzled, crushed, I let myself fall back and closed my eyes.

"When I opened them again I was in an attic cluttered with an accumulation of old things. The debonair Lopallino was holding a lamp with three beaks; his back was arched beneath his old dressing-gown; a large cobweb was dangling from his Greek bonnet.

"He rummaged in all the corners. 'In truth, Monsieur,' he grumbled, 'I can no longer put my hand on what you're looking for.'

"I went downstairs rapidly, went through the deserted shop and found myself back on the corner of the Piazza Bocca della Verita. The light of the nearest street lamp hurt my eyes."

VI

The narrator stopped dead.

"And the end of the story?"

"There isn't one. I spent my years and my money in peregrinations, searching for the breastplate. My last voyage brought me here; I'm prevented from getting out. So I stay here, and let myself live here while awaiting a further incarnation. I'll quit you now, for the intern is coming, at the end of the pathway."

Picking up his spade, the old madman plunged into the clump of rhododendrons.

An idea sprang to my mind: the fellow's visions appeared to him to be yellow-tinted and their atmospheres a transparent blue. The wine of Orvieto, so sweet to the palate, is magnificently yellow. The facets of a crystal flask form a prism that the light traverses, casting on the tables of an inn certain rays of the solar spectrum in which the blue is dominant.

Was my illuminate simply a drunkard?

As I was asking myself that question, the intern arrived.

"Pardon me for having made you wait for so long. I've quit an agitated patient who isn't easy to calm down. I'm all yours now. Let's go to the epileptic ward; you'll see interesting subjects."

September 1889.

THE SARDONYX CHIMERA

by Jules Bois

IT was at the end of an exquisite and numerous dinner, at the hour when, according to Renan's expression, the stomach being satisfied, people talk about the immortality of the soul.

Several women had recounted stories of apparitions, and a naval officer a phenomenon of telepathy that had warned him, while at sea, of the death of a distant relative. Doctor Lanthoine, who had kept silent until then, with the slightly disdainful smile of psychiatrists habituated to caring for nervous maladies, intervened in the discussion.

"I beg the pardon of those who see marvels everywhere. I believe, on the contrary, that a natural cause, often very simple, is at the source of the most extraordinary events, but we don't always see it. That is the origin of the most foolish beliefs. Nevertheless, it seems that Nature sometimes wants to mystify us, she so often accumulates the most bizarre circumstances. I understand that imaginative brains, which do not have the habit of precise methods of investigation, let themselves yield, in such cases, to the craziest suppositions. I was even mixed up myself in the very modern story of a ring that one could believe enchanted, like the rings of the *Mille et une nuits* or the Nibelungen . . ."

Everyone fell silent, for the elevated situation of Lanthoine at the Salpêtrière, where he was regarded as Charcot's successor, and his lectures, already almost as illustrious as those of the master, designated him as the most competent authority able to cast a few glimmers of certainty on these obscure problems.

"I was at Cannes then," he commenced, "and I was giving my cares to Madame Ostidj, a neurasthentic Norwegienne of a complex beauty, in which Northern fluidity was lightened by an Italian quattrocentist charm. Her flesh seemed translucent, so pale was her epidermis. Her virginal tresses, her long, floating tunics, her green eyes and the eternal indolence of her poses idealized her as a creature of luxury and fragility. She had made one of those almost mystical marriages rather frequent in the lands of the North; her husband, aged and grave, enveloped her with a tenderness that one might have thought uniquely paternal. She played the harp, which completes characterizing her for your eyes. She often received the respectful visits of a friend of her family, Gabriele del Sogno, the son of a celebrated Florentine jeweler. Charming and very mild-mannered, the young man excited a sympathy all the more innocent because one divined him at first glance to be consumptive to the highest degree.

"I did not take long to perceive that he was smitten with the Norwegienne beauty, with one of those irresistible and platonic enthusiasms expectable in all invalids. While remaining the most virtuous of women, she had allowed her heart to be moved to a profound pity for the gracious youth condemned to an early demise. She comforted him by her presence and surrounded him with an affection that was both intellectual and seductive, which excited and consoled him.

"By virtue of a sentiment of superior charity, she had imposed on herself a kind of duty to charm that slow agony and render Gabriele's last hours delightful and beautiful.

She read to him, in her angelic, almost unhuman voice, the complicated and delicate poems of the latest school; with her slender and romantic fingers she played the harp until his anxiety was appeased. I received their confidences with all the more embarrassment because Monsieur Ostidj, who did not have the egotism or the jealousy usual in old men, consented to that obliging game. Their pure and enthusiastic intimacy augmented every day; the life of the consumptive was casting its supreme flame before being extinguished.

"He resided in the same hotel as her. In the evening, before quitting her, he always took with him one of her rings, a bracelet or a necklace, with which he slept, and which he returned to her the following morning. In her turn, she once took from him, in order to admire it, a strange ring of refined artistry, which never quit him.

"'Fortunately, I'm not jealous,' she said to him. 'This is a ring that doesn't come from me, and yet you always wear it.'

"He responded, smiling: 'I can't offer it to you now, for my mother gave it to me; my father designed it himself and created it to her order. I'm doubly attached to it, for art and affection are united in that.' And he added: 'I don't have long to live; will you permit me to bequeath you this souvenir? Promise me always to wear this ring after my death.'

"I can still see that marvelous and unique jewel: a Chimera whose head was sculpted in a sardonyx, colored enamels set in gold depicting the body, the claws and the wings.

"The poor fellow died suddenly one morning. His parents arrived in haste and I remember the anguish that traversed the beautiful Norwegian. By virtue of an excessive delicacy, she dared not reclaim from Madame del Sogno the jewel promised by her son, all the more so because the latter was insistent that her son be buried with that masterpiece of art, which maternal sentiment rendered sacred. I recall the bloodless and emaciated hands of the phthisic, his poor fingers clenched against one another, and the glaucous gleam of the sardonyx in the pale candlelight. After having seen him placed in the bier, the parents took the body with them to Florence.

"The next morning, at my consultation, I saw Madame Ostidj enter earlier than usual, very upset. I knew her great chagrin at that abrupt death and the bitterness combined with it in having nothing to remind her of that sad and pure tenderness. So I was stupefied when, mute and triumphant, she showed me the precious Chimera that I had admired on the finger of the dead man, and which, at that moment, ornamented her hand, by virtue of a sort of miracle.

"'How can you have that ring?' I exclaimed. 'Where did you get it? Who gave it to you?'

"An enigmatic smile passed over the Norwegienne's lips. 'Death has unfathomable mysteries,' she said. 'I believe that it's the soul of Gabriele himself who, faithful to his promise, sent it to me.'

"'And in what fashion?' I asked.

"'The chambermaid at the hotel ran to give it to me just now. When she raised the curtains of the bed in order to make it, she heard something clink on the marble of the fireplace; and it was that poor boy's ring that she picked up.'

"Then Madame Ostidj confided her scruples to me. Truly, had she the right to keep that jewel of art for herself? Undoubtedly it had been bequeathed to her by Gabriele, but no paper, not even a letter, furnished proof of it. To appease her, I advised her to go to Florence immediately. She went to visit the del Sognos, inconsolable at the loss of their son. All three wept together, but the father and mother could not believe their eyes when the Norwegienne showed them the ring and told them about the simple and mysterious fashion in which it had been found.

"'It's impossible,' affirmed Madame del Sogno, 'that we have all been the dupes of a hallucination. I clearly saw the ring on the finger of our child when the bier was closed.'

"The father looked at the jewel with the most serious attention, and wondered whether it might be a copy or an imitation—but no, there was no doubt that it was his own work; he recognized the slightest details . . ."

"Madame Ostidj continued to wear the sardonyx Chimera with a fidelity and a further increased respect, for she was now convinced that it was a relic of the beyond. No one could get it out of her mind that Gabriele himself, having not had time to bequeath her a souvenir in writing, had employed a supernatural means to transmit it to her. I did not seek to steal that illusion from her, which consoled her—and in fact, by what would I have replaced it? Nothing very sure, and, in any case, nothing as soothing for her heart."

Someone interrupted. "You don't admit, then, in spite of appearances, the intervention of the dead man?"

"It's necessary to abandon that hypothesis," the scientist said, "to those who believe. I imagine, rather, that a muscular contraction had abruptly relaxed the young Italian's clenched fingers. Then, the ring, too large, must have slipped from the emaciated finger without the people present, blinded by emotion, being able to perceive it, and it must have remained in the creases of the curtain until the maidservant found it."

"It's possible, in fact, that things happened like that," pronounced a young man who had not said anything thus far, in a slight British accent. We knew that he was a member of one of those scholarly societies in which the Anglo-Saxons, less frivolous than us, study mysteries methodically, without either skepticism or fanaticism. "The most extraordinary events follow natural paths in order to be accomplished. They are, however, no less extraordinary for that. In the story of the sardonyx Chimera there is the incontestable prodigy—whatever the method employed—of the will of the smitten phthisic reckoning with all obstacles and, as Gabriele de Sogno desired when alive, the ring returned after his death to the woman he loved."

"Coincidence," responded Lainthoine, with pursed lips.

"Coincidence is easily said, but explains nothing. You Frenchmen have the superstition of the word. When you have found a word you believe that all difficulties are smoothed out; on the contrary, it's then that they begin. This time, it's precisely in the coincidence that the mystery resides. It's the coincidence that you can't explain."

"We don't explain anything," said Lanthoine. "We try to show how things happen. Distant causes are metaphysical. To search for them is to get lost. We don't know them." And the successor of Charcot added, with a certain melancholy: "The Unknown overflows us everywhere."

In the emotional eyes of the women, and even in the anxious and indecisive expressions of some of the men, it was easy to discern that Madame Ostidj's belief in a sort of miracle of Tenderness was the preferred—and, in any case, the most attractive—explanation, so ready are we to admit, with the sage Oriental monarch, that Love is stronger than Death.

ASTRAL AMOUR

by Jane de La Vaudère

PHYSIOLOGICAL psychology has been very fashionable for some time. The phenomena of thought, the motor functions and their different phases have been localized with precision in one part or another of the medulla or the brain. The bizarreries of hypnotic suggestion have been explained and are not a secret for anyone. Some researchers have read the German studies of Weber on sensibility, those of Fechner on the measurement of sensations; the research of Helmholtz on vision and on music; various appreciations that have been combined and condensed by the learned Wundt, professor of psychology at Leipzig. France has the endeavors of Boca and Charcot, England those of Huxley, Maudsley and Carpenter. People are occupied with heredity and transmission; Ribot was the first to transfer that question from the purely medical domain into the philosophical domain.

"The question of suggestion," says Paul Janet, "raises many others: that of the relationship of hypnotism to hysteria; the question of hypnotic phases (lethargy, catalepsy, somnambulism); the question of passages from the normal to the suggestive state and vice versa; not to mention the philosophical questions more or less engaged in the debate; and finally, and above all, the question of the doubling of the self."[1]

The truth is that we are at the stage of hypotheses, and that the mystery that is within us and around us will last as long as our miserable reign. How can we explain what we do not understand?

Our imperfect nature deprives us of a host of enjoyments that beings better organized and more intelligent than us might experience. Our clairvoyance does not even embrace all the phenomena of creation; we do not have special re-agents for all natural agents. Our senses permit us to appreciate sound, form, taste, heat and light, but we do not know whether the air that we breathe contains free electricity or not. At the most, we have a vague sensation of malaise on stormy days. If the atmosphere of the globe had been devoid of lightning and thunder, perhaps we would never have had any presentiment of that force, which, says Monsieur Noegell: "plays such a great role in inorganic nature, which provokes chemical affinities, which, in all the molecular movements of organized beings, probably has a more decisive influence than any other force, and of which, finally, we expect the most important enlightenments in order to explain physiological and chemical facts still in the state of enigmas."[2]

Our eyes are sensible to the colors of the spectrum, but they do not grasp the ultra-violet that is distributed around us in vegetation. Thus, there are natural phenomena around us that escape us. Our present sensations only embrace a small number of the facts necessary to our existence. However, certain more refined, more vibrant, organizations have the prescience of invisible things, and sometimes the sudden revelation of some mystery hitherto unexplained. Light is cast,

---

1 The writings of the philosopher Paul Janet (1823-1899) were prolific; the quotation probably comes from *De la suggestion dans l'état hypnotique* (1884).

2 The reference might be to the German physician Hermann Franz Noegell, but the quotation is untraceable.

and becomes bright, in a moment. The contact of two exceptionally endowed intelligences ought to cause that wellspring of unsuspected good fortune to gush forth. I also believe that if I had not encountered Viviane, everything would have remained obscure in me, and that, following the example of other men, I would have sought to satisfy my despicable instincts, ignorant and disdainful of higher felicities.

I have always seemed bizarre to banal natures; the explosiveness of my imagination, my occasional invincible silence, or the surge of my speech, which escapes in sonorous or enthusiastic phrases, without apparent reason, all awaken mistrust around me. People have called me mad, but do we know, as yet, whether madness might be the quintessence and the sublimity of intelligence? Mad! Because we see that which will forever remain in darkness for other humans? Mad! Because the sensibility of our organism has developed to the point of exasperation, and that good as well as evil has become familiar to us? But where does good end, and where does evil commence? A common cowardice has fixed the limit of that which, in reality, has none; everything depends on the motive, circumstances and secret influences that are almost always inexplicable. Those who dream by day have knowledge of a host of things that will remain forever unknown to those who only dream by night. Visions are strewn with fulgurant lightning flashes that, at times, unveil eternity for us and permit us to retain a few scraps of the terrible mystery.

I was orphaned at a young age, and was taken in by an aunt who lived in the country with her daughter, a few years younger than me. Viviane had inherited the paternal fortune, which was immense; her education had also impelled her into the most elevated regions, which her remarkable intelligence explored without fatigue.

I associated myself with her studies, glad to be anticipated in the solution of a difficult problem, or to be able to converse with her about matters that are generally closed books for the majority of women.

In any case, Viviane was only a woman by virtue of the softness of her voice and the charm of her smile. She was extremely thin, her complexion almost diaphanous, and beneath the somber forest of her black hair, her pupils, in their blue enamel, resembled two coals that an interior fire sometimes ignited. She was tall, straightforward, and all her movements seemed harmonious. When I evoke her terrestrial image, I see her clad in loose, silky fabrics, leaning on the back of an armchair in an abandoned posture, her profound eyes half-veiled by the sweetness of a dream.

She did not awaken any desire in me. I loved her mind, her heart, her thought—in sum, what it is conventional for us to call the soul, not being able to define more clearly the second being that lives within us and commands slavish matter as a master.

Viviane was a soul, nothing more, and like a beautiful mystical flower, all dream and all perfume, I plucked that soul.

It happened on a foggy day in October; nature had the melancholy charm of fêtes that are about to end. A few yellow leaves dotted with crimson patches rolled at our feet. The sun, at times, appeared through the clouds like a feebly illuminated unpolished globe.

The spirit of things seemed to be weeping over the nullity of terrestrial splendors, and I thought that, like those leaves writhing on the damp earth, our youth would fall from the tree of life, and that cold winters would suspend their tresses of frost and snow there.

I searched around me for something a little more durable than the others, in order to support thereon my paltry hopes, which take so long to die, like all those born in the human heart. My gaze traveled through space, and, as if attracted by a powerful magnet, came to fix upon that of Viviane, who, silent and immobile, seemed to be lost in a dream. Suddenly, her eyes sparkled, a sort of electric shock was produced, the darkness that surrounded us was dissipated, and in the same way that two beams of light that encounter one another are confounded, our souls were no longer secret for one another. I felt myself warmed, comforted; I read within her, as in an open book, the infinite tenderness that she had for me. Her soul was radiant; I was dazzled by it, and such a flood of delight sprang from mine that she lowered her eyelids, delectably moved.

From that moment on, speech became unnecessary between us. I seized one by one all the vibrations of the heart that beat next to mine. My companion's ideas became palpitant and sonorous, if I might put it like that. Our two intelligences, in immediate contact, conversed with one another, understood one another, and, disdaining the efforts of conversation, so painful and so fruitless, rose to vertiginous heights.

There is nothing comparable to that divine fusion, that eternal caress, which never wearies, and which falls from the supreme limits of what a being can feel.

What did the years matter, old age and death? Our souls, forever infatuated, would dissolve in one another, would savor increasingly ardent ecstasies as they were purified and drew closer to the ineffable deliverance.

Until then, Viviane had remained the strange girl that I have described: too thin, too dark-haired, and too paltry; but even if she had been frankly ugly, I would not have been disquieted by it. Her body did not exist for me; I lived a completely intellectual life, so far outside common existences that nothing of what habitually charms men interested me.

However, the age of puberty was approaching; a change, insensible at first, occurred in my companion, and then, gradually, like a plant in spring, her young body filled with sap and developed; a livelier blood circulated beneath her delicate skin, and her gaze, her beautiful limpid gaze, became slightly troubled, like deep water at the approach of a storm. From that moment on, she ceased to belong completely to me. I made vain efforts to read within her, as I had done so easily before, and, gripped by hatred, I began to curse the expansion of the carnal envelope that was increasingly devouring the divine substance of her thinking being.

One evening, by the light of the flock of stars that hastens in the fields of infinite space, like as many lambs submissive to an invisible master who will slaughter them one day, I forced her to combine her thought with mine by an effort of will, as she had done so passionately before.

"Oh, stop tormenting me," she said. "I'm tired, horribly tired."

"What!" I cried. "It's thus that you withdraw yourself? Haven't you sworn to belong to me forever?"

She tilted her head, and tears rolled down her pale cheeks.

"Is it my fault that a strange force is drawing me away from you? It seems to me that there are sweeter things in life than those you have enabled me to know. Is it our role down here only to exist through thought, and are we not insensate to disdain what makes the happiness of the people around us?"

I contemplated her; she had metamorphosed, as if by a miracle. Her red lips were swollen voluptuously, and beneath the light fabric of her dress, her bosom rose and fell, moved by a new emotion. The lashes of her long eyelids put a soft shadow over her grace; she trembled before me, knowing full well that I was scornful of her now that she had revealed herself to be similar to other women.

"That's all right," I said, with a sigh. "You'll come back to me, Viviane, for everything that awakens your desire will wither, as you will wither yourself. I don't release you from your promise."

And, fixing my gaze on hers, I plunged into the utmost depths of her being, until a mysterious impact, followed by an infinite sweetness, had put us in perfect communication, one last time. She could not support the ardor of my will, and lost consciousness.

✳

Some time after that, the requests for her hand in marriage commenced, for she was very rich, and dowry-hunters would espouse a girl in her cradle if they could.

Viviane seemed the same for all of them: indifferent and slightly weary, waiting for her parents to fix a choice for her. I counseled her gently, astonished to find myself so calm and resigned. Is it the case, then, that our destiny is written in advance, and that, secretly in agreement, we were acting in accord with a ready-made plan, without even discussing that strange connivance between ourselves?

I would only have had to say one word to change the course of events. In that tightly-knit family, everyone's opinion was taken into consideration, and mine would have been heeded like the others. What did it matter to me? My torment was not of the earth; it was not a wife that I wanted, it was not her physical and palpable beauty that troubled me, but her hidden being, her astral essence, which, like a perfume in a sealed bottle, was dormant beneath her pale envelope of flesh.

That treasure of amour, I had once possessed, when, through the frail wall of her diaphanous body, it had sent me its radiance and its intoxicating effluvia. Now, that inebriating flesh had reclaimed its rights; that was the enemy; I detested it and, if I had dared, I would have annihilated it like a harmful beast.

That another would take it and make it suffer was acceptable; that the martyrdom of maternity would weaken it and twist it in slow convulsion was better still; for I, who demanded nothing of the despicable joys of life, was certain of being victorious one day. No, my ambition was higher; I was thirsty for ineffable kisses that never weary, mystical intoxications of thought that float in tenderness dazedly, like an opium dream or a divine ecstasy, like monks in prayer before their virgin, invisible but present.

It was necessary that Viviane's destiny should be accomplished; then she would come back to me more confident and tender, her soul would be assimilated to mine and would, so to speak, dissolve in me, a light vapor, an astral form, visible and yet embalmed like a smoke of incense. And my eyes, my nostrils and my lips would see her, respire her and drink her.

We spoke again about that supreme felicity. She shivered, and her soul sparkled in her eyes and palpitated on her mouth, but bonds attached her to her terrestrial envelope and I had the desire to squeeze that flexible neck with my clenched fingers, or cause the life of her ardent heart to spring forth in red droplets . . . But a dread, an obscure presentiment, retained me, and I awaited events without impatience and without disturbance.

Viviane was seventeen years old. Increasingly, the splendor of her beauty seemed to extinguish the radiation of her somber eyes. The soul escaped me, and I sensed it going to sleep in the wellbeing of health. She faded away, becoming disinterested in the long reverie in which we had once confounded ourselves. The woman had all her curiosities and her desires awakened; the troubling monster surged forth, with the smile of her red lips and the impudence of her pale flesh. I then had a sentiment of grim hatred, and in the fear of not being able to contain myself, I went away, certain that I would suffer less at a distance.

Viviane seemed happy with my sudden decision. My will still dominated her, and that power, which she could not vanquish, gripped her dolorously, like an obsession.

I remained absent for nearly six months, horribly tortured, without news of my relatives and without the courage to ask for any. When I returned, the peaceful dwelling was illuminated, peasants were pressing against the railings in order to see, through the high windows, the elegant silhouettes of women in silky ball gowns. A harmonious murmur reached me, and lackeys hastened to offer me their services.

I went into a vast drawing room, which bronze chandeliers charged with candles illuminated abundantly. Viviane was standing near a table, signing her marriage contract. Her shoulders, devoid of jewelry emerged like the flesh of a camellia from their long sheath of lace, her dark hair made a helmet of jet for her radiant face. She looked at me fearfully, and then went pale, and suddenly collapsed on the parquet.

I complimented her fiancé. He was a tall blond young man with a mild and attractive physiognomy. He had a meager fortune, but a great name; Viviane was not noble, and that equilibrated the advantages of the future spouses. By the urgency that he put into helping the young woman I saw that he loved her with all the impetuosity of his heart and his senses. In fact, she was so admirably beautiful that all men must have desired her. I conceived a more intense chagrin in consequence, and the Comte de X***, her fiancé, became particularly odious to me. He, on the other hand, had immediately taken me in affection, and I was obliged to promise him to go to see him often in a villa that he possessed on the Mediterranean coast, in which he intended to reside immediately after his honeymoon voyage.

The next day, when Viviane appeared in her long dress of white moiré silk, she could scarcely sustain herself.

"Go away," she said to me. "I've been happy since your departure, but now the strange madness that you once com-

municated to me seems to be gripping me again. I love the
Comte, I tell you, and it's to him alone that I want to belong."

"You're mistaken," I murmured in her ear. "You don't love
him, and whatever you do, I shall always possess you."

She shivered. "No, no! Go away, I implore you. I'm afraid.
I don't want to lend myself to your crazy imaginations any
longer. You're accursed! I hate you!"

She adjusted her veil, which quivered over her shoulders
and descended in light waves all the way to her feet. People
were arriving from all directions, and, drawing away indifferently, I went to install myself in the chapel, near the choir, in
order not to miss any of the ceremony.

Viviane knelt down on the red velvet prie-dieu, and although she did not turn round, she certainly divined my
presence, for her shoulders were trembling slightly, and the
missal that she was holding slipped from her hands and fell
on to the paving stones.

I summoned her thought with all the force of my will,
and at times I sensed it fluttering around me like a heavy
moth afraid of alighting. Then, suddenly, an impression of
emptiness and desolation invaded me; I found myself more
abandoned than I had ever been.

The newlyweds fled as soon as the ceremony was terminated, as if their happiness would only really commence beyond
the frontier. I did not enquire as to the itinerary that they had
mapped out; their actions were of scant importance to me,
and I knew that Viviane was too narrowly linked to me by an
immutable power to escape me thus, no matter how much
she might desire to do so.

After that departure, however, darkness fell upon my spirit; I lived mechanically, having no appetite for anything, bleak
and despairing. In my long feverish nights I evoked the absent
thought, but no secret voice responded to my sad appeals.
Had Viviane yielded, then, to physical amour, so incomplete,

so despicable and so disproportionate to the idea that one has of eternal ecstasy? Could she love that banal being made in the image of all, who held her in his arms as he had held many others, with the unique ambition of material pleasure? Could she desire that lover, who would go to sleep sadly over her quivering lips, already forgetful of past felicities, and who would find in the annihilation of his strength the annihilation of his amour?

How much sweeter were our old intoxications! We did not talk to one another, but we read one another like open books. Our hands scarcely touched, but our souls, all vibrant with amour, embraced one another madly. And that was the true, the only durable happiness, the one that religion has enabled us to glimpse as the supreme goal of our efforts, the one that, not being of the earth, can never end.

"Viviane! Viviane!" I cried in the night. "Come and place on my lips your divine form, white and as transparent as a cloud; let it press thereupon, dissolve therein, and give itself to me in a kiss!"

But the darkness thickened, an icy cold descended over my heart, and the ardent fusion did not take place.

Perhaps another had taken my beloved's soul!

At that idea, I shivered in anguish, and was haunted by ideas of murder. But could murder efface that which is ineffaceable? Would not killing those lovers give them to one another more surely, since it is only beyond life that the real and indissoluble union commences?

What other man could have penetrated those mysterious destinies?

Few human intelligences have that quasi-divine prescience, I said to myself, *and if it is sometimes given to them to perceive the truth, it is only a flash of lightning in their habitual darkness.*

※

It had been a year since the young couple had quit Paris, and if I sometimes received news of them, it was only indirectly, via the family.

One day, I learned that Viviane was a mother. I conceived a profound chagrin in consequence, for it seemed to me that the little being who was scarcely breathing would take all the solicitude of the woman. Nature has determined that there should be an infinite tenderness in maternity, in order that the torture of childbirth should be braved and desired even by those faint hearts who do not understand the futility of their mission and the cruelty of their obedience. An admirable folly that consists of making with one's flesh and blood sad and paltry beings whose life will be spoiled by the thought of death, and who will toil daily without a single moment of real happiness! A proud folly that consists of building temples and palaces that the wind will sweep away, and which will have scarcely more duration than the pygmies who constructed them! But human vanity is only equaled by human weakness, and until the end of the world, they will struggle in the void, commencing and recommencing their illusory labor.

Viviane was a mother! Her affectionate parents announced the great news to me joyfully, and, in order not to offend them, I wrote a letter of congratulation. The Comte de X*** replied to me that his wife was having difficulty recovering, although she was receiving admirable care, but that the child, on the other hand, was superb: the very portrait of his father.

I wrote to Viviane a second time, begging her to tell me about her life, her hopes and the plans. I did not obtain any response, and I understood that, if I did not make a supreme effort, the mysterious link that still attached us to one another would be broken forever.

From that moment on I extended all the power of my will toward the person that I wanted to reconquer. Not for an instant did I cease to think about her, to summon her irresistibly, to order her to manifest herself, so determined to convince her that it seemed to me that I could hear her timid objections in the distance. And I wanted her, I desired her madly, I was thirsty for her mystical kisses that did not touch the lips but fell upon the heart like a current of flame.

✳

One misty afternoon in April I was sitting next to the window in my large bedroom hung with pale golden-red Cordovan leather. The sky, not yet cleansed of the impurities of winter, remained a jaundiced gray, giving everything a desolate appearance. However, the almond trees and the cherry trees were beginning to flower; buds of a delightful pale green were bursting forth on the branches; but those promises of renewal squeezed my heart like a happy smile on a death mask.

I remained motionless, lost in my obstinate dream. Gradually, the shadows of night invaded my retreat, and my wide-open eyes could no longer distinguish things. I was indifferent to the present moment, to the world, to existence itself; a devouring fire rose in my breast, extending to my fibers, penetrating into the creases of my organism in waves of flame. And my soul agitated like a captive butterfly, ardent and feverish.

Visions of the past unfolded slowly, as diaphanous and light as the veils of the evening over which they were gliding. I saluted them with my heart and my lips, reproaching them for having fled me so quickly, and no longer being anything but phantoms of happiness. But they did not turn away from their route, for even our regrets escape us, and we cannot savor their dolorously bitter charm for long.

My childhood appeared pensive to me, so narrowly linked to Viviane's that I rediscovered her influence in the most insignificant details. In reality, she had been the complement to my thinking being, the reason and goal of my being. It was necessary that she return to me; she belonged to me as a tree belongs to the soil. She could not exist without me, and without her I remained somber and desolate.

The desire to receive the confirmation of my immutable rights returned to me more obsessively. I gazed into the darkness and I listened to the silence with so much intensity that my heartbeat accelerated and my muscles were violently contracted.

Suddenly, it seemed to me that I was no longer alone. I could not see anything yet, but a strange sensation alerted me, a sudden anguish, something like the rapid, soft and vertiginous fall that we believe we are making into the void in a dream. A pale light emerged from the depths of the room and vacillated momentarily on the wall like the projection of a lantern swathed with cloth. A slight creaking, and then a silky friction awakened my attention. I listened intently, in an anguish of superstitious terror, but the sound was not renewed. Resolutely and obstinately, I kept my eyes fixed on the mysterious light.

A few minutes went by, and then I saw a white form detach itself from the wall and follow the luminous path in my direction. I extended my arm to grasp it, but it retreated rapidly, seeming already to be extinguished by distance. I recalled it softly, and it regained confidence, swaying from right to left, still indecisive. It was nothing but a vague, almost transparent silhouette: the astral form of Viviane.

By a superhuman effort of will, I had obliged her to quit her carnal envelope and to obey me. I was in possession of a supernatural power and I took advantage of it to attempt miracles forbidden to all human beings.

I thought about those fakirs who, under the radiance of their astral fluid, summon objects that are displaced and come of their own accord to place themselves in their extended hands, of those yogis who have their eyes, nostrils and mouth blocked and who, after several months of sojourn in a tomb, emerge again alive and strong. Was I not the master of life and death?

"Viviane!" I cried. "I doubted you, but you have come to reassure and console me! Viviane, do you still love me?"

She drew nearer, and a soft and perfumed air struck my face.

I divined her response rather than hearing it.

"Come and take me back," she sighed. "I'm afraid of my weakness, and if you don't extract me from the hearth I'll be lost to you."

"I'll leave tomorrow, my beloved. Have confidence! Don't abandon me!"

I stood up impetuously and extended my arms toward her, but darkness fell, and I tried in vain to recall and to fix the fluttering soul. Suddenly, in the place she had occupied, I saw, distinctly, an open coffin, and in the funereal cavity a cadaver enveloped by its shroud. A fleshless hand dangled over the edge, and on the little finger shone a gold ring set with a ruby, which I recognized perfectly; it was the one that I had given Viviane at the moment of her marriage.

Stupefaction struggled then in my mind with the profound terror that I had felt at first. I sensed that my sight was becoming obscured, that my reason was fleeing, and it was only by means of a violent effort that I succeeded in steering myself to the mantelpiece and lighting the candles of the two large bronze candelabra that habitually illuminated my bedroom. The flame sprang forth, and the surrounding objects appeared to me in their customary order: the tapestries of fabulous individuals fell hermetically over the doors, and there was no draught from outside.

I got undressed and went to bed. One by one, the candles went out, and toward dawn, I fell into a profound and heavy slumber.

✳

When my valet de chambre, slightly anxious, woke me up, midday was chiming. Bright sunlight entered through the window, and things around me had an almost joyful aspect. In reality, my body alone had rested, for my mind had never ceased to evoke the strange nocturnal apparition.

"Make preparations for my departure as quickly as possible, and have the carriage ready in two hours," I said to the man who was awaiting my orders.

"Is Monsieur going to be absent for a long time?"

"Perhaps a week, perhaps a fortnight, perhaps a month. Don't forget anything that might be necessary to me."

Having dressed rapidly, I went to supervise my servants personally, who were making haste, being long habituated to my eccentricities.

The air was light, the sky a pretty turquoise hue. A large flowering pear tree sent me through the window the adorable perfume of its white corollas; I felt satisfied and resolute, as if the journey had been planned for a long time.

In the train, I closed my eyes in order to savor more fully the emotion that gripped me delightfully. An urgent but submissive appeal of my thought to a distant thought had sufficed to overturn the order of things: hearth, duty, and family would cease to exist for the soul that I had vanquished, if it pleased me to recall it to my power.

Life is nothing, I said to myself, *and it is not the comprehensible and logical causes that reign but the mysterious power that is within us, and which rises above all human plans. Like the pieces on a chessboard, we obey profound calculations of which we are unaware. We come and we go, sensate in appearance, but in reality unconscious of the mission that we are called upon to fulfill down here.*

When I rang at the Comte de X***'s villa, I had a sudden conviction that I had come to accomplish an irremediable action, the consequences of which would engage my entire existence. I had come guided by an irresistible force, and nothing would turn me away henceforth from what it demanded of me.

The gate was not locked; I pushed it, and as soon as I entered I saw my cousin at the end of a long driveway bordered by giant rose bushes and myrtles, paler and more tremulous than me. She had had a presentiment of my coming and had come to meet me.

Some distance from the gate she stopped, and her face contracted dolorously.

"You, here?" she said, in a muffled voice. "Why are you troubling my repose?"

"Have you not summoned me to you, dear Viviane?"

She put her hands together, terrified. "My God, protect me! He knows my dreams, he sends them to me! He still dominates me!"

"It was against your will, then, that you manifested yourself to me, in order to ask me to join you?"

"I want to love my hearth and my husband," she said. "I want to live as other women live, tranquil and honored. I want to do my duty as a Christian and a mother."

"You no longer belong to yourself, Viviane. Your body alone is here next to your husband and child, and whatever you do, your ardent thought will follow mine as a bee follows a perfume in order to drink at its source."

She drew closer, and her dark gaze, wide and profound, dared to fix itself on mine. Immediately, the strange and delicious commotion that we knew so well was produced within us, and the severe words that she had on her lips died away in a vague stammer. What did it matter? I had read once again in her beautiful eyes, those doors open to the soul!

The Comte de X***, alerted by his domestics, had joined us, and, smiling beside his wife, he extended his hand to me amicably.

"I'm delighted by your visit, my dear monsieur; I hope that you will prolong your stay for as long as possible, and not disdain our beautiful land."

I accepted the hospitality that he offered me eagerly, and that evening I was installed in a lovely bedroom with a view over the Mediterranean. The exquisite perfume of spring flowers rose up to my window, and my eyes went from the blue of the sea to the blue of the sky, dazzled by those two sublime and terrible immensities.

What remains for me to relate is so strange that few minds will understand me well enough to absolve me.

For long years I savored my triumph, and my happiness was complete.

Today, I doubt, I weep and I suffer.

May this sincere confession of my life bring a little calm back to my heart!

I installed myself, therefore, in the Villa des Roses, and from the very start, I understood that a struggle had been engaged between Viviane's material nature and the divine, exquisite, passionate individual that hid within it like a dragonfly in the heart of a lily. I neglected nothing that might increase my domination.

The presence of her child might have disarmed me, but I loved too intellectually to be influenced by human considerations, and the little being who loomed up between us inspired nothing in me but aversion.

My cousin avoided me, scarcely looked at me, and strove to fix her attention on the vulgar things of life. Oddly enough,

I only really rediscovered her when I could not see her; for although she remained mistress of her wakefulness, she was not of her dreams. Every night, her astral form quit the inert envelope that hid it from the profane and came to find me in the darkness of the closed room. A milky radiance struck my gaze, and the warm and perfumed apparition glided all the way to my lips, swaying like a flower of light. Her golden voice resonated within me; I was inundated by celestial joy, and until morning, I heard her sing her canticle of amour.

It was thus that, dissolved in one another, ecstatic and unsated, we compensated ourselves for terrestrial lies.

I was only living for those exquisite hours, disdainful of all the rest.

I was pale and feverish; Viviane also seemed to be wasting away. I rediscovered her now as I had known her previously: emaciated and indolent, with excessively bright eyes beneath the forest of dark hair that seemed to be consuming her thin face.

At times, she begged me to go away, to have pity on her and her child. But the unforgettable ecstatic memory of each night was too present in my mind to allow me to yield to her pleas.

A bizarre phenomenon occurred: I began to detest the woman that I saw during the day, who incessantly avoided me or begged me to leave, in order to redirect all my affective forces on the adorable individual who only lived for me and was only manifest in darkness. But that was too little, I would have liked to discover her incessantly, to possess her at every moment, to intoxicate myself with her mystical kisses, as a morphine addict savors his dangerous ecstasies at will by injecting a little of the poison into his veins. Those forced cessations exasperated me, and I confided my pain to Viviane's soul.

"Alas," she sighed, "like you, I detest that insensible body, which cannot quit the earth and enchains me to its obscure labor. I hate it with all the force of my love for you!"

"And will it always be thus?"

"Listen," she continued—and her voice vibrated in every fiber of my being—"Listen; I can, if you wish, belong to you without partition, dissolve in you for eternity. But it will be necessary to deploy great courage, and I fear that you might weaken at the decisive moment."

"Speak! What must I do in order not to quit you any longer? Tell me, I implore you."

She hesitated; then, gradually, I sensed that she disengaged herself, retaking possession of herself, and I saw her draw away, a light shadow, an impalpable and yet tangible form, like a snow-cloud.

In the very place that she had quit, the hideous coffin that I had contemplated before loomed up, with its funereal burden. I could not perceive the cadaver that it contained, the shroud covering it entirely, but the same livid hand dangled out of the bier.

Suddenly I saw it move, clench upon the shroud and tug it violently. I sat up in bed, shivering, my throat tightened by an inexpressible anguish, my soul desperately engulfed by a whirlwind of emotions, of which perhaps the least terrible, the least devouring, was a supreme terror. In the effort that it made, the hand dropped the ring that it bore on its little finger, and I thought I saw drops of blood falling with it along the bier.

Viviane's face now appeared to me, whiter than the sheets that surrounded her, and a breath as cold and damp as the exhalation of a tomb reached me. At the culmination of horror, I launched myself toward the frightful vision, but everything vanished.

Prey to an indescribable emotion, I dreaded understanding. Would it be necessary for me to become criminal to possess the dearly beloved fully? Did our strange amour require a human sacrifice in order to bloom in the sunlight? Certainly, I felt that I was strong enough to kill, and two victims were designated by my hatred: her husband and her child.

✳

The next day, Viviane was suffering and did not show herself.

"She's been very troubled for some time," the Comte de X*** told me; "an intense fever grips her during the night, and incoherent words escape her lips. I would have summoned a physician already if she had not begged me not to do so. What do you think, my friend?"

I dissipated his fears, giving him a host of good reasons.

"Your wife has never been very strong; she is greatly occupied with her child, and that is doubtless the cause of her fatigue."

He did not insist, but remained anxious.

I waited for nightfall with impatience in order to discuss the matter with my beloved.

She came at the usual hour, and as soon as I sensed her within me I begged her to deliver me from the horrible suspicion that had come to me.

"What are you demanding of me, then, Viviane?"

"A crime!" she replied. "My body is an obstacle to our complete union; that is what you must annihilate."

"Kill you! But I would never have the willpower or the courage."

"It isn't me that you'd be killing but the other, the obscure and suffering obstacle; it's the inert chrysalis that is keeping the butterfly of amour imprisoned."

"Kill you! But how? People will know, and imprison me; I'd be an object of scorn and horror for people!"

"No, it's my husband who will be accused. He alone has an interest in my death; he's poor and I'm rich; I've left him my entire fortune in my will."

"That's horrible!"

"No, it's human. Do you want to have me entirely and forever?"

I did not reply, bewildered by fear, and I sensed that the adored soul was disengaging from me. Then I made a supreme effort to retain her.

"I give in, Viviane, I give in! I'll be a wretch, a liar and a criminal, provided that you absolve me from baseness, deceit and crime. How can I kill you without betraying myself? How can I reach you?"

"Nothing is easier. You'll go along the balcony and you'll enter through the French windows of our bedroom. As the weather is very warm, I'll leave them open."

"But what about your husband?"

"You'll pour him a narcotic this evening, at supper. He won't wake up, and the next day, on finding him bewildered beside me, covered in blood, there'll be no hesitation in accusing him."

"So be it. I'll do as you order me to."

"You swear it?"

"I swear it."

"Until tomorrow, my love, and forever."

She glided away like a shooting star and was lost in the night.

I was still motionless, entirely intoxicated by the memory, when a sound of footsteps resonated on the parquet. The Comte had just come in, a candle-tray in his hand. He begged me to help him and to help Viviane, who was writhing in a crisis of nerves. I followed him, and approached the young woman, but as soon as she perceived me she hid her face in her hands.

"My child! My child!" she moaned. "Don't take me away from him. Have pity on him!"

I understood that a terrible battle was taking place within her, and I felt myself weakening in my resolution.

Throughout the following day, she held her son tightly in her arms; her lips trembled; she cursed me and begged me by turns.

I did not have the courage to resist her, and I went to bed early in order to hide my distress.

Toward midnight, her spirit arrived, as usual. The milky radiance departed from the depths of the room and the diaphanous form undulated toward me. But she did not press herself upon my lips or dissolve into my being like a delicious fruit. I begged and wept in vain.

"You've never loved me," she said. "Otherwise you wouldn't have hesitated to liberate me from the burden of life."

"Did you not implore me today to make me abandon my resolution?"

"It's the human creature who moaned, trembled and suffered! My soul remained impassive and scornful; it's her alone that you ought to consult."

"But I too am human, and everything human touches me!"

"Human life is nothing, it's the beyond that I envisage. What does it matter to us whether I disappear in a day, a month or a year? Time is of no account in eternity. And besides, are you not sparing me struggles, chagrins and malady? It's the sole means of proving to me the immensity of your tenderness. Leave the miserable body that is only able to tremble and complain to moan; our ecstatic dream is not of the earth; our souls, overflowing with desires, are thirsty or eternal possession. Afterwards, no more doubts, no more weaknesses: a sea of happiness, as blue as the sky, and likewise limitless; an abyss of sensuality in which our feeble bodies will be annihilated."

"Tomorrow! Tomorrow!" I cried, drunk on hope and covetousness.

The soul shivered.

"After having struck, you'll lean over the lips of the expiring woman," she said, "and you'll respire me, you'll drink me, in a supreme kiss."

From that nocturnal moment on, I was no longer my own master. I felt that I was driven by a mysterious, irresistible force and I was only living any longer for the accomplishment of my crime.

The first light of dawn caressed the surrounding objects; cockerels responded to one another, and soon a volley of roulades departed from every branch and a cloud of butterflies from every thicket.

I got up and went down into the garden to refresh my forehead in the morning breeze. The French windows of the conjugal bedroom were ajar. I saw that it would be very easy for me to penetrate therein via the balcony. A curtain was floating over the gap; everything therein was silent and calm.

I did not go in again until it was time for the morning meal. Viviane was waiting for me, standing by the table. She was frightfully pale; her convulsive hands came together at times, and her eyes were staring at me with an expression of terror and prayer.

Her husband noticed the alteration in her features, and spoke several times about going to fetch a physician, but I dissuaded him with a calmness that still surprises me today.

During the day we went to sit down in the shade of a plane tree of which we were fond. The child, lying in his perambulator, was looking around with his bright blue eyes at the leaves that a warm breeze was agitating softly, and Viviane, leaning on the Comte's shoulder, was weeping quietly.

She was so frail now that the light fabric of her dress creased around her shoulders and her wrists moved easily within their golden bracelets. A branch had caught in her hair, and in order to free it she had taken out the long tortoiseshell pins that secured it, with the result that the regal black fleece, darker than the night, undulated all the way to her feet. She was adorable and touching. No pity came to me, however. I considered her anxiously, and told myself that it would not be necessary to use a great deal of force to kill her.

Her husband left us alone for a few minutes in order to go and lift his fishing nets. When he had disappeared through the gate she threw herself at my feet and begged me to have pity on her, with heart-rending sobs. I picked her up without responding. Then she leaned over her son and contemplated him ardently, while two streams of tears ran over her cheeks and fell on to the infant's blond head.

I took her hands and forced her, by a supreme effort of will, to fix her thought on mine.

Her soul immediately sparkled in her eyes.

"Do you still want it, Viviane?" I asked her. "You can release me from my oath."

But she was transfigured.

"I want it! I want it! Take me and keep me entirely. This struggle between spirit and matter is horrible. I'd like to dominate myself, but I can't. Don't abandon me, my beloved!"

"If you put up the slightest resistance tonight, I'll be lost, for the Comte might wake up and accuse me of the crime."

"I no longer desire anything but death, I tell you, in order to belong to you, no longer to be anything but one with you, like your muscles and your blood. You will drink me in the only kiss that you will ever have given my perishable body."

Slowly, I turned my gaze away from hers, and, reconquered by matter, she knelt down beside her child and surrendered once again to her despair.

The day was exceptionally hot. At dusk, a storm was unleashed with extraordinary force. For several hours, the rolls of thunder and flashes of lightning succeeded one another without interruption. I was in a circle of iron, and my will to act, doubtless exasperated by the ambient electricity, attained such an intensity that I saw red, and had great difficulty containing myself.

Viviane retired to her bedroom early, asking that she should be allowed to repose. The Comte was, therefore, alone with me at the evening meal, and I deployed all the resources of my eloquence to distract him from his preoccupations. He was listening to me with interest, He drank mechanically, and I never left his glass empty. Hunting and fishing were his favorite pleasures, and I talked about them at length, inventing anecdotes, citing facts, and describing distant countries that I had never seen. My listener was under my spell; his dilated pupils were fixed on mine avidly.

At dessert, without him noticing, I poured a few drops of a powerful narcotic into his wine, and then I drank to the health of all the disciples of Saint Hubert.

He drained his glass in a single draught and replaced it on the table. By a skillful transition I then turned the conversation to Viviane's malady, and, suddenly recalling that she had been more afflicted than on the preceding days, he got up with alacrity in order to go and join her.

I remarked that he was very red in the face, and staggering slightly.

"I don't know what's wrong with me," he said. "I'm falling asleep."

I went up to my room in my turn. I could hear the domestics coming and going on the ground floor; then the noises faded away gradually, and everything fell into silence.

I had opened my window. The cooler air of the night refreshed my forehead, and over the narrow rectangle of the sky I saw innumerable stars scintillating, as if in a tabernacle. The tempest was still growling in the distance, however, and at times the trees writhed, and high waves jostled one another convulsively, like unsated lionesses.

The occult power that had dominated me since the morning still held me in its power. External facts had no purchase upon me. I was continuing my dream, speaking, walking and acting like a sleepwalker. And the obsession triumphed, lacerating, almost terrible in its intensity. If the evil spirit that was haunting me had ordered me to gouge out my eyes, tear out my tongue and slash my wrists, I would have obeyed without hesitation. Its empire was all the more redoubtable because it was excited within me by the most noble of sentiments, amour. I loved as no man had ever loved. I loved a pure spirit, and the idea of her eternal possession gripped me so ardently that I sensed myself fainting in an ineffable spasm.

Soon, she would be mine! A reckless ecstasy made me totter like a drunken man. Burning drops of light fell into my heart, and beyond the glimpsed felicity, nothing existed any longer; human conception was arrested, impotent.

I waited for another hour, a stranger to all reasoning, all dread. The thought of the crime was as intense as a burn. Finally, I sensed that the moment had come, and I slid on to the balcony, barefoot, in order not to make any sound.

The spouses' French windows were ajar, as they had been the previous night, and only had to be pushed gently; I slipped into the room, illuminated by the tremulous glow of an alabaster lamp suspended from the ceiling.

Viviane looked at me with eyes dilated by fear. Her entire body was quivering, and her teeth were chattering convulsively. The Comte, lying next to her, seemed to be plunged in a deep slumber.

On the wall of the room, draped in pale velvet, there was a panoply of Oriental weapons: helmets and bucklers of steel damascened with gold, sabers and daggers with ivory or jade hilts, sharp stilettos and krises with teeth like saws. I hesitated momentarily, and then chose a slender dagger whose blue-tinted blade cast a gleam in the shadow. I took the weapon down with a thousand precautions and, having tested it delicately on my arm, I approached the bed.

Viviane had sat up, as pale as a corpse, her face so distressed that I almost hesitated to recognize it. A feeble plaint escaped her discolored lips; in her immense eyes, the dilated pupils had devoured the iris. She tried to cry out, but her contracted throat would not allow any sound to pass. I tore the lace of her chemise, in spite of her convulsive efforts to push me away, and, with a vigor of which I would not have believed myself capable, I nailed her to the pillow with one hand while, with the other, I plunged the sharp weapon to the hilt in her breast.

She uttered a frightful, heart-rending, superhuman plaint, but I leaned toward her mouth and, applying mine to it, sucked in her soul, her ardent soul, frenetically, in an ineffable kiss. When I sensed it within me, it was like a liqueur that rises and fills a vase; my heart swelled with intoxication, and there was the anguish of a spasm in which I felt myself dying . . .

I was getting up with a triumphant cry in order to flee with my prey when a hand fell on my shoulder, and the Comte, almost as pale as the cadaver that lay beside him, sat up in the alcove.

Blood had spurted everywhere; we were both covered in it, and the curtains, the carpet and the wall-hangings seemed to be streaming with a sanguine flood. Then there was a dazzle, and as the domestics arrived from all directions, I allowed myself to be tied up without any resistance.

For twelve years I have been in an insane asylum. For eleven years, Viviane's soul remained faithful to me, and we savored indescribable ecstasies. Oh, I did not regret my liberty! For what greater happiness could I have been ambitious? Always alone with my dream, I found between the four narrow walls of my cell an entire paradise of intoxication!

If only I had died in my divine error! For, today, I doubt. My body and my mind have weakened, and as they weakened, I felt Viviane's soul withdrawing from me. The dreams that charmed me have vanished into a nebulous distance. I find myself once again in the midst of the miseries of life. My sky is veiled by livid clouds; I feel desperately alone.

The director of the asylum says that I am cured, and tomorrow, the doors will be opened for me.

Yes, but tomorrow, I will have ceased to live, for my divine madness raised me above other men; with reality, I am nothing more than a vulgar murderer.

THE SKELETON

by Gaston Bourgeat

IT was in November 1892. The night was profound, starless and moonless. The west wind, which was blowing a tempest, was detaching the last leaves from the tall trees that bordered the Seine, and, lifting the waves of the river, extracted dull plaints from them. I arrived with difficulty on the Quai du Louvre—I say with difficulty for I had to sustain an energetic struggle against the incessant gusts, but in that very struggle I found a charm that finished dissipating the disagreeable malaise that the spiritist séance from which I had emerged had left me.

As I turned the corner of the Pont-Neuf it seemed to me that someone was following me; on the Quai des Grands-Augustins I had the same impression; in the Place Maubert the impression was so strong that I turned round swiftly, but I sounded all the corners of the square in vain; I did not perceive anything suspect. In the Rue de Navarre someone touched my arm. Thinking that I was dealing with a malefactor, I got ready to defend myself; but the street was deserted.

I was directly opposite my domicile; I went in, closed the door behind me carefully, and it was with a relieved heart and mind that I climbed the first steps of the staircase, the thick carpet of which, stifling the sound of my footsteps, permitted me to hear midnight chiming in the concierge's lodge.

As I traversed the landing of the entresol several dry clicks, struck very rapidly, caused me to shudder; those raps were succeeded by a long, heart-rending plaint. What was happening, then, in that big new house, of which I was the first—the only—tenant? There was definitely mystery in the air, and the pink drawing room where I had spent my evening returned to my memory. I saw once again the large round table that shook lightly under the hands of the five persons sitting around it. The medium, a rather pretty red-haired young woman, had straightened up like a spring; she had drooled, foamed at the mouth, howled, and had finally entered into conversation with an invisible person—a skeleton, she said, the master of the Group . . .

Chasing away that bad memory, I continued to go upstairs, but my steps became heavier; it required a veritable effort to reach the first floor landing; having succeeded in that, I sat down on a bench and closed my eyes.

When I opened them again, I was absolutely amazed. Around me, the décor had changed; I found myself in a narrow and low gallery, the length of which I could not determine. The walls of the gallery were lined with human bones and naked skulls running from top to bottom, serving as paneling and cornice.

Believing that I was dreaming, I pinched myself forcefully and examined myself. I recognized the costume that I had been wearing only a moment ago; I took off my hat and I remember that a dry leaf fell from it, that I picked up that leaf, that I crumpled it between my fingers, and that I distinctly heard the particular little sound produced by the friction of the leaf. I rubbed my eyes; I bit down hard; I stood up; I examined the stone on which I was sitting; I sat down again and waited.

I experienced a great lassitude, and the cold of the place chilled me to the marrow of my bones.

Two brilliant dots, like two stars in mist, attracted my attention. I considered those two gleams attentively, which fascinated me, and at the same time filled me with an inexplicable repugnance. Soon, the luminous dots were very close to me; they were the phosphorescent eyes of a skeleton.

Seized by dread, I wanted to flee, but I bumped into the stone and fell heavily to the ground. An unknown force prevented me from getting up again; I dragged myself on my hands and knees, and with every effort that I made to advance, I seemed to be displacing a world. The terrible glow still surrounded me; I sensed the inexorable presence of the skeleton behind me; I heard atrocious clamors, plaints, threats, insults and, dominating them, the voice of the medium of the pink drawing room crying at the top of her voice: "Stop! Stop! It's *him*, the *dear Spirit*, the *Skeleton*, the *Master!*"

Now the gallery shrank and rounded out in the form of a tube; I continued crawling, believing that I was escaping by means of that slow, illusory flight, from a danger that I imagined to be imminent.

The tube shrank further as its icy walls compressed me like an iron vice, making my bones creak with a lugubrious sound; unusually, my head remained free and was still advancing, drawing my body, which I sensed elongating immeasurably, like that of an immense reptile.

How long did I slide like that, sticky and formless? I don't know, but every second must have seemed to me to be a century.

Finally, my forehead collided with an obstacle, against which my body curled up into a ball, like a wounded snake. The tube had disappeared; caught between two horizontal walls, superimposed, one of which descended slowly, I felt again the horrible sensation of being crushed—a sensation followed by that of a fall; then I suddenly saw myself, with my natural form, in the middle of a brilliantly lit temple.

I did not try to understand; what was happening to me was too prodigious.

I paraded a fearful glance around me. The temple was empty. Stout round pillars sustained its vaults. At the back, in the choir, an iron throne stood on a stone stage, which was shaded by long corroded drapes of gold crépine. To either side of the throne six low seats were disposed, three to the right and three to the left. Large candelabras aligned behind those seats and several chandeliers suspended from the vaults shed a vigorous light over everything.

Suddenly, a terrible sound troubled the bleak silence; it was like the bellowing of great organs, each note of which was false; a flute wept lamentably, oboes grated like a file biting iron; the Aeolian harp and *vox celeste* had vibrations and undulations that made one think of the plaints of the damned; the bassoon, the bourdon and the barophone roared like tigers, while the fife launched its shrill and viperine note.

A new spectacle brought my stupor to a peak. The walls of the lateral naves oozed ruddy vapors, which condemned rapidly and took on the aspect of different individuals, After only a few minutes, the temple was full.

I recognized the red-haired medium as well as various people seen in society or passed on the boulevard. There were men of all ages there, young and pretty women, old and ugly ones, and even children.

Reporting my gaze to the throne, I saw majestically seated there the skeleton with the eyes of fire. A brilliant court surrounded him. The flames of long candles undulating in the light smoke of incense caused the gold and precious stones of the costumes to sparkle. The organ did not cease bellowing, but its chords became suave and melodious. From the bosom of the temple, which progressively took on a magical aspect, rose an exquisite, divine song that reverberated from the powerful beams of the vaults. Everywhere there was nothing but light, perfume and melody.

At that moment, there was a movement in the audience, which divided and left a long empty space between the choir and the porch.

The skeleton stood up and descended the steps of its throne. Followed by a dazzling cortege and preceded by little girls who were almost completely nude, crowned with roses, some holding torches in their delicate hands that consumed a livid flame, others golden censers from which diaphanous blue-tinted ribbons escaped, it advanced into the vast nave. Under the unctuousness of its gesture of benediction the grateful crowd inclined. It approached the place where I was; an irresistible force made me bend my knee; the satiny and odorous flesh of the young thurifer-wielders brushed my face.

I bowed my head, fearing to see.

When I raised it, the skeleton had disappeared. I had before me a radiant angel, whose snow-white nudity was scarcely veiled by the furling of great wings. The visage of the celestial creature, of an ideal beauty, revealed a superb pride. Magnetic effluvia departed from his large eyes, which snatched my heart and made my blood boil. A sentiment of reckless amour for the adorable angel took possession of my being. I sensed myself dissolving into him, and that mystical union caused me an ineffable joy.

Nevertheless, obedient to an automatism acquired by a pious youth, I traced the sign of the cross over my breast. Then, in the midst of a formidable clap of thunder, the temple appeared to be swallowed up, and the angel, having become a skeleton again, uttered a sinister snigger.

Darkness enveloped me: thick, horrible darkness! A dolorous pressure was exerted on all the parts of my body; the slightest movement was impossible for me. However, I sensed that I was rising, drawn upwards. My ascension, sometimes slow and sometimes precipitate, gave me to understand that I was traversing superimposed layers of varying density.

I arrived thus in a gallery that I recognized as the one where my improbable adventure had begun. I followed that gallery for a long time.

I passed before a tomb where I read these lines, which were a revelation for me:

At the banquet of life, an unfortunate guest,
I appeared one day and I am dying;
I am dying, and on the tomb where I slowly arrive
No one comes to shed tears.

The catacombs, I thought, the catacombs of Paris! Why was I enclosed in those places? I was afraid.

I wanted to cry out, to appeal for help, but my throat would not produce any sound. I had the sensation of rising again, but rapidly this time. I passed through a bronze door without opening it. A dazzling light stopped me momentarily . . .

I was outside, in the Place Denfert-Rochereau. I only had one desire, pressing and anguishing: to return home. I took successively, the Boulevard Arago, the Avenue des Gobelins and the Rue Monge. I was not walking; I was gliding over the surface of the ground at a speed that gave me vertigo. The passers-by and carriages did not hinder me. I even traversed like an arrow, laterally, a tram full of passengers . . .

Suddenly, I fainted.

A sharp pain brought me back to my senses. When I opened my eyes I found myself in my stairwell; I had slipped from the seat on which I had gone to sleep and my knee had struck the floor, bruising it. It was broad daylight. I heard a sound of precipitate footsteps; it was the concierge, running up to investigate.

"Monsieur has fallen and hurt himself," he said.

"No," I said, "it's nothing."

"How weary Monsieur seems! Monsieur has doubtless passed a bad night."

"Yes," I said, "I slept very badly."

Then, to cut the conversation short, without really knowing what I was saying, I added: "I won't be back until this evening, and if, by chance, the skeleton comes to ask for me, tell it that I'm not in."

Leaving my concierge bewildered, I went into the street, but this time in the flesh and bone.

THE AMOROUS SHADE

by Maurice Beaubourg

To Jean Lorrain

I do not know whether you have shutters over your windows. Personally, I live in the country, in a remote spot, and I do not have them. My dilapidated little house would hardly tempt thieves, and all the peasants in the village—which is three hundred meters away—know that I live very poorly, cultivating my flowers and my vegetable garden.

My flowers are my great pastime; I water them in the evening and the morning. I possess simple ones and exotic ones, but I don't know which please me more. I have beds of majestic lilies and beautiful red poppies, and others, more modest, in which maidenhair ferns and bleeding hearts are mingled with forget-me-nots, resedas, sunflowers, carnations, lilies-of-the-valley and wallflowers. There are also bushes of white roses to either side of the door: climbing roses that already cover all the thatch of the roof, and which produce a delightful florescence every spring. Then my house is transformed into a hedge of white roses, and when the sun shines, bah! . . . in spite of my abandonment, I am inundated by true joy.

My vegetable garden is my great resource, and I ameliorate its soil by means of assiduous and persistent care. I grow all kinds of vegetables, which I take to market. The early ones, grown in frames near the left-hand wall, sometimes succeed.

Unfortunately, the field-mice and the worms give me trouble, and I observe a great deal of damage. I repair it, and I prune the trees in my orchard, which, every new spring, also become a second forest—a very sweet forest!—of white and perfumed flowers.

Perhaps, when dusk falls, I have felt slightly melancholy in my solitude, and a constriction grips my heart, with a desire to weep. It passes; to begin with, I'm a man, perhaps an old man, and I think that that melancholy comes from the decline of the daylight and all the green hues that pale in the Orient.

Then I go back inside . . . I light the lamp . . . I have supper . . . and when my frugal meal is concluded I remain for a while in the large square room that precedes the one where I sleep, and the pendulum of the clock swings in its case of varnished wood, tranquilly marking the seconds that go by.

I reflect . . . I walk back and forth, arranging this and that . . . and if it is a fine evening, I put my chair in the doorway in order to take the air, whistling an old tune, as I used to do.

I could keep chickens, or a dog, or . . . what do I know? . . . a little grey cat, turtle-doves in a wicker cage. I've renounced that, it's boring, and fatiguing, to begin with, and it leads me to sense that there is nothing living in my surroundings.

When I've taken the fresh air I lie down, in the depths of my bed, between coarse sheets of white linen, and I wait, looking through the windows that I mentioned just now, which have no curtains or shutters. Would you like me to tell you what I wait for? Would that interest you? I wait for the Moon to come and illuminate my bedroom.

Because I know that the moment she arrives, there, in the square to the right, the light shade, playful and amorous, of the woman I loved so much and whom I've lost, will also arrive, and brush my casements with the gauze of her divine mantle.

She flutters from lily to lily and strolls from poppy to poppy, seemingly taking a special interest in the forget-me-nots, picking the resedas, sunflowers and lilies-of-the-valley.

She respires them and throws them away. I often find the ground strewn with them.

And when, diaphanous and light in her white garment fringed with vague slate blue, she returns her smile to me, one might think that the passage of her dress over the window produces a discreet musical tambourine sound.

However, she doesn't want me to quit my bed in order to draw nearer, and the two or three times that I've attempted it—I even opened the window very wide one night—she suddenly flew away with a single wing-beat, all the way to the distant star where she resides, and where I've seen, alas, the light weave of her garment disappear.

So I no longer move . . . I never move any more, never—and, as chastened as a good little child who has just been told off, I remain quiet . . . in order that the little beloved, all crazy vapors and smiles, who flutters and frolics every evening, picks flowers and pecks along my window, will continue her sweet display indefinitely.

Today, though, I can no longer stand it! Must I confess it? Well, I've made a terrible resolution. I'm going to hide behind the window . . . and when she arrives, I'll stick her light mouth to the window . . . I have my means!

Outside, a very mild night extends, the perfume of which is suffocating; the sky, of a mysterious warn pink, seems to be entering into languor; it passes above my head, which is so feverish and so heart-breakingly exhausted, that I'm almost fainting. Pure stars are suspended there, and I tell myself that I adore the sway of the stars, which makes the trees sway, and makes the odors sway.

This is what I've disposed, and I've been working on it for a long time, for I don't want her to be able to escape. It's a net with a narrow mesh of imperceptible threads, woven in the lightest and most solid silk, which cost me three years of labor. That silk imitates the color of the blue and pink night, and I've taken care to introduce into it, in such a fashion that even a shade can't distinguish them, little blades of grass, diaphanous dewdrops, and a few silvery glimmers of glow-worms. I've coated all those tiny things and all the tenuous threads with perfumed liquid gum, and they retain everything that approaches them like magnetic iron.

There are nets surrounding the lilies, others the poppies, others the forget-me-nots, the lilies-of-the-valley, the wall-flowers and the climbing roses, and I hold the extremities of the threads in my hand, through a crack in the casements, not quite closed although they have the appearance of being from outside. As soon as she settles for an instant—a single instant—no matter where, her dress will be caught by that bird-lime, and while she makes vain efforts to escape, I shall leap out of the window and seize her.

But I'll shut up, for a corner of the Moon, nielloed with milky gold, is entering the window; she's going to slide into it gradually, and as soon as she's there entirely, I know that the one who follows her will appear.

She has entered by more than half now . . . and more . . . more and more . . . more and more . . . entirely.

And from the star up above, from the star that is opening, in order to let her pass, I see her . . . her . . . advancing madly . . . adorned in vertiginous lace . . . vertiginous . . . in a sound of silent and delectable thunder!

Lightly, she leaps over the garden gate, and advances like a plundering bee from flower to flower, without pausing at any.

Curiously enough, one might think that she's hesitating, suspecting an ambush, and she shows a desperate vivacity, hopping, coming and going, turning, running from one bush to another, here and there, everywhere, like a crazy little insect.

Already, she has passed close to me furtively, fluttering, and I was so moved, in the depths of my soul, and palpitating, that I didn't have the courage to quit my hiding place.

But this time she's coming back . . . she's coming back . . . and I want to surge forth suddenly, to throw myself upon her unexpectedly, to enclose her in the net, where she'll struggle in vain, and then I'll carry her into the depths of my room, and close the window again, which she'll no longer be able to get through.

Have you finished fluttering from lily to lily, nocturnal bee?

Have you finished bathing your wings in the water of the little reservoir, nocturnal demoiselle?

Have you finished, lover, sticking kisses to the window, when you don't want to give yourself to me?

Fly . . . ! Fly this way . . . ! Fly here . . . ! Zigzag, waltz, swim through the air! Never mind that I'm lying in wait for you, my flirt and my coquette, my divine and my divette . . . and as soon as you settle . . . as soon as you alight . . .

✳

Caught!

✳

Oh, how beautiful you are, my bride in tulle and muslin, so white in your garments, so white and slightly slate blue at the extremity . . . Forgive me for having tricked you . . . for having crumpled and torn your dress . . .

✳

You have no body, my sylph, my angelette, and yet, when I look at you, I follow your adorable forms under the airiness of your volatile costume . . . and when I hug you against my breast, I feel happy and consoled . . . but it seems to me, however, that there's no hurry at all . . .

It's a matter of recommencing.

And I want to recommence again . . .

Do you know what I'm going to do?

No!

I'm going to take you out of the silken net in which I captured you and lock you with a triple turn in the big cupboard at the foot of my bed, so that I have you with me incessantly, day and night, and you can no longer fly away!

You see, I was too unhappy, and martyrized for too long, and your immaterial kiss no longer sufficed for my thirst.

Come . . . come . . . the cupboard is open . . .

One turn.

"Aie! Aie!"

Two turns

"Aie! Aie!"

Three turns . . . locked!

"Aie! Aie! Aie! Aie . . . ! Blackness!"

And henceforth, I shall keep my ear to the wood of the cupboard where you're imprisoned . . . and always . . . always . . . always . . . without ever going to bed or getting up again . . . I'll listen to your heart beating!

"Well, what have you to say to me this morning, when the sun is born? Your voice is fading away, like distant crystal. Speak more loudly, my love . . . I can't make out your words . . ."

"*Cheri*, I'm getting bored inside this sad cupboard where you've shut me . . . I regret the heavens from which I've come!"

"Oh, my beloved . . . why do you want me to let you out? Why do you want me to melt my soul by depriving myself of you, since you make my happiness down here?"

"Your happiness! Your happiness! You no longer see me, and dare not open that door for fear that I might fly away before you can catch me."

"It's true . . . that I can no longer see you . . . it's even my living desolation, and I'm consuming myself only hearing the fugitive sound of your voice . . ."

"Once you lay in your dear bed with sheets of beige linen, and watered your flowers assiduously evening and morning . . . you were radiant with hope and you awaited my coming!"

"That's true . . . that's true . . ."

"You reposed on the doorstep from the fatigues of the day, whistling tunes . . ."

"That's also true . . ."

"And for the time that the Moon remained facing your window, I fluttered in your garden, nourishing myself on the nocturnal juice of lilies and poppies, and I deposited kisses close to you continually."

"Alas, alas . . ."

"I frolicked like a kid goat, leaping like a gypsy, as happy shades leap and frolic, and I sensed your passion . . . swooning behind the window . . ."

"I remember!"

"You were handsome, your face smiling and your eyes sparkling! By day you thought about the joy of the night! You were alive! You were alive!"

"Enough . . ."

"Henceforth, my gaze has ceased to encounter you . . . but you're ravaged, you have a fever . . . and although you say . . . you weep terrible tears . . . I sense your tears, which filter through the wood of the cupboard and drip desolately upon me! Oh, wretch! You wanted to imitate the people of earth, you whom, by virtue of my sublime commerce, rose above them. You wanted to padlock your happiness! You'll no longer see me . . . you'll no longer see me!"

"Shut up!"

"No! I won't shut up . . . on the contrary, I want to go on turning the blade in the bloody wound. I want to avenge myself on you!"

"Wicked! Cruel! Pitiless torturer in lace! I'm going to open the door . . . hold on! I've had enough of having hoped to keep you and feeling that you're slipping through my hands. And it's necessary henceforth that you return to the heavens that you love, swim through space again, rejoice eternally in your eternal liberty! I only beg you, little darling to come back sometimes by night, if you have nothing better to do . . . to loot the flowers in my garden, and coo as you coo . . . and I shall always hope that you . . ."

"I'll come back . . . I'll come back . . . I swear to you . . . open up!"

"I'm opening up . . . hold on . . . can you hear the key grating in the lock . . . three turns . . . that's one . . ."

"Ah! Ah!"

"That's two . . ."

"Ah! Ah!

"One more . . ."

"Ah! Ah!"

"I'm holding the door, and pulling the batten toward me . . ."

"Ah! Ah! Ah! Ah! The heavens . . . !"

"Well, no, I won't open it. I don't want you to leave me! I'm giving the three turns again. I'm going to brace myself against this old cupboard, to prevent you from escaping, and I'll stay braced against it . . . you see . . .

". . . for as long as I can . . .

". . . while I live . . .

". . . while I have a residue of vigor in my muscles, blood in my veins . . .

". . . against this old cupboard . . . against this old cupboard . . . indefinitely . . . Indefinitely . . . indefinitely!

"I'm odious to you . . . odious . . . I know it . . .

"But I prefer not to enjoy you and to hold you, my languid bride, rather than to know that you've departed again for the firmament I don't know, to make . . . perhaps . . . no doubt . . . it's more probable—for shades are extremely light and improper, so it's said—the happiness of Seraphim!"

THE OTHER EYES

by Jean Richepin

"BEWARE, young man," Abbé Garuby piped, softly. "You're wrong, I tell you, to want to attempt this redoubtable experiment. You'll expose yourself to sure and dolorous disillusionment. You'll see strange, monstrous things, to drive you mad, irredeemably mad, when, having closed your carnal eyes, I have opened what I call *the other eyes* for you."

"Have no fear," the young man replied, arrogantly. "My reason is solid; I'll answer for it. It has resisted the reading of all metaphysics. As for my heart, it's more solid still, if that's possible. It's absolutely safe from disillusionment, since it has no illusions whatsoever. You have, therefore, every freedom, and without the slightest scruple, to open for me what you call *the other eyes*."

"Consider," said the Abbé Garuby, slowly, "that the other eyes will permit you to look into the very souls of others."

"That's precisely what I'm avid to do," the young man replied, "if only to establish, conclusively, *de visu*, whether people really have souls."

"It really is *de visu*," said Abbé Garuby, smiling, "that you will establish it. I mean that the soul will appear to you as a form. But once again, believe me, the experiment is redoubtable—for that form is generally hideous. Now, let us suppose that you look, with the other eyes, at the soul of someone who is dear to you—your mother's, for example . . ."

"I have the good fortune," the young man interjected, "the inestimable good fortune, of being a foundling."

"In that case," Abbé Garuby continued, complacently, "let us say, if you wish, the soul of your mistress."

"A mistress, me!" the young man exclaimed, disdainfully. "I'm a virgin."

"Aha!" said Abbé Garuby, rubbing his hands. "You're stronger than I would have thought. Well, simply imagine that the other eyes reveal to you the soul of your best friend."

"Between the best and the worst," the young man declared, resolutely, "I don't know what the difference is, since I have no friends at all."

"In that case," Abbé Garuby proclaimed, raising astonished eyebrows, "you are, I confess, truly strong, and probably in a fit state to brave the redoubtable experiment. I shall therefore not refuse any longer to submit you to it, and I am at your disposal."

"My word!" said the young man, with mocking irony. "I confess in my turn that I find you very strong, and much stronger than I would have thought. For I won't conceal from you, mysterious and terrible Abbé, that I thought that, if you were refusing to open my other eyes, it was primarily for fear of letting me see, naked and in all its hideousness, your own soul."

"In which you are mistaken, young man," retorted Abbé Garuby with profound unction. "My own soul is, in fact, not one of those that can be seen, even with the other eyes. It is situated in infinite space, and even to perceive its scintillation requires a telescope that you do not possess, strong as you are. But let's leave my soul there, I beg you, and occupy ourselves, without further ado, in opening your other eyes."

So saying, Abbé Garuby had suddenly ignited in his usually dull gaze the pale and flamboyant phosphorescence that created there, when the occasion required, a magnetic nucleus of irresistible hypnotic effluvia. At the same time, he had imposed his icy hands on the young man's cranium, digging into his temples two thumbs that seemed to be drilling into his brain. And a moment later—a moment of fulgurant brevity—the young man sensed his carnal eyes closing, and the other eyes opening within him.

And then, before him, visible to those other eyes, the form of a soul surged forth: a form duly established *de visu*, as the Abbé had promised him; a strange and monstrous form, so hideous that the unfortunate nearly fell backwards in a faint of disgust and terror.

The form of that soul was, in fact, nothing but an ulcer compounded out of an innumerable conglomerate of ulcers, agglutinated with and engendered by one another, all copulating with one another in abominable and purulent leprous fungal growths, which seethed like clumps of vipers, sweating venoms, viruses, pus, putrescence, noxiousness: a living, pullulating death, all horrors blossoming in an apotheosis of horror. And in all those nightmarish figures, which really were established *de visu* as being the form of that soul, the other eyes also saw the symbolic significance; for every one of those ulcers, facets of the total ulcer, was a vice in action or in potential; and all the vices were there, with all their various nuances and combinations, multiplying endlessly in the prism of the infernal spectrum whose seven essential colors are the seven deadly sins.

Terrified, his heart in upheaval, his head crazed, trying in vain to close within him the other eyes that nothing could any longer close, the young man wondered who had delivered that vision to him, and thought, while his teeth chattered: *It's Abbé Garuby's doing, for sure. But what is he trying to do?*

Then, abruptly, the idea went through his mind, anguishing, atrocious, even more terrifying than his terror: *But no, no,*

Abbé Garuby wouldn't do that—for the soul that my other eyes see, that soul whose form appears to me, established de visu, *that soul of an unimaginable hideousness, is* his *soul, his own soul, Abbé Garuby's own.*

Suddenly, recovering his strength, drawing himself upright in his pride, feeling exalted to the point of heroism, the young man cried: "Terrible soul, hideous soul, soul of Abbé Garuby, it's not in infinite space that you are situated, and there is no need of a magical telescope to perceive the scintillation of your accursed star. I see you. It's you who are here, before my other eyes—but I no longer want to see you. I want you to deliver me from the horror of seeing you. You, your hideousness, the terror and disgust you inspire in me, and your ulcers, and your form with its facets of vices, and the blossoming of your abominations in the prism of the seven deadly sins, and you, finally, soul and body, you, mysterious, terrible and infamous Abbé Garuby, I shall annihilate you, being unable to annihilate my other eyes, I shall annihilate you, monster, monster, monster, filthy monster!"

In the young man's hand, between his fingers, which clenched upon it, the shaft of a weapon had been placed. Who had placed the shaft of that hatchet in the palm of his hand? He had no idea. He did not even think of trying to find out. His fingers clenched on the shaft. The hatchet was brandished. Already, it was whirling in the air, whistling, shining, fulgurant.

And while, from a corner of the room, Abbé Garuby watched that spectacle of dementia with his customary dull gaze, rubbing his hands together and sniggering silently, the bewildered young man, grim and heroic, his carnal eyes opened wide and stupidly terrified, contemplated the broken shards of the mirror in which his other eyes had seen, a moment before, the form of his own soul.

NECROMANCY

by Edouard l'Hote

A scholar of our time—and, which is rarer, a kabbalist, a necromancer—Éliphas Lévi Zahad, has written a curious book, which we believe to be dangerous, of which we shall not even pronounce the title, but a book assuredly of an uncommon force and audacity. Éliphas Lévi Zahad had studied to be a priest, but, by an effect of circumstances that we do not know, he renounced sacerdocy—or rather, instead of devoting himself to the science of God, he studied that of the Devil; which is not to say that in studying the one he had not acquired profound and elevated notions regarding the other.

In his quality as a magician, Éliphas Lévi has evoked, it is said, and *has seen*.

Evocation is, in fact, the touchstone of magical power. But before anything else, a few general notions regarding the doctrines of the master are indispensable to the reader.

Thus Éliphas Lévi, who does not lack potency in his boldness in posing axioms, affirms from the start this principle: "Nothing can enter the heavens but what comes from the heavens. After death, therefore, the divine spirit that animates a human being returns alone to the heavens, leaving on earth and in the atmosphere two cadavers, one terrestrial and elementary, the other aerial and sidereal; one already inert, the other still animated by the universal movement of the world, but destined to die slowly, absorbed by the astral powers that produced it. The terrestrial cadaver is visible; the other is invisible to the eyes of terrestrial and living bodies and can only be perceived by the applications of astral or *translucid* light, which communicates its impressions to the nervous system and thus affects the organ of sight to the extent of enabling it to see the forms that are conserved and the words that are written in the book of vital light—the great book in which, as Holy Scripture says, all of our actions are recorded."

There are aerial cadavers that can be evoked, it appears, by necromancy; but to see those strange forms it is necessary to put oneself in an exceptional state, which has something in common with sleep and death—which is to say that it is necessary, by means of certain preparations, to magnetize oneself and arrive at a kind of lucid and waking somnambulism.

Necromancy will therefore obtain real results, and its evocations, practiced in accordance with a formula, can produce apparitions: veritable visions. Modern science does not admit these empirical procedures, but how can one contest their power after what follows?

Éliphas Lévi, the author of the book mentioned above, had come to London to escape interior chagrins and to deliver himself without distraction to science. "I had," he said, "letters of introduction to eminent persons curious to obtain revelations regarding the supernatural world. I saw several of them and found in them, with much politeness, a great deal of indifference or levity. I was immediately asked for prodigies. I was a little discouraged, for, to tell the truth, far from being disposed to initiate others into the mysteries of ceremonial magic, I had always feared, for myself, illusions, fatigues and dangers; besides which, those ceremonies require expensive equipment difficult to assemble. I therefore absorbed myself in the study of the cabala, and was no longer thinking about

English adepts when, one day, on returning to my hotel, I found an envelope addressed to me. It contained half of a card, cut transversally, on which I immediately recognized the seal of Solomon, and a small piece of paper on which as written in pencil: *Tomorrow, at three o'clock, outside Westminster Abbey, you will be given the other half of this card.*

"I went to that singular rendezvous. A carriage was stationed in the square. I was holding my fragment of the card in my hand, without affectation. A domestic approached me and gave me a sign to open the door of the carriage. Inside the carriage was a lady dressed in black, whose face was covered with a thick veil; she made me a sign to climb in next to her, and showed me the other half of the card I had received. The door was closed again and the carriage set in motion. The lady having lifted her veil, I was able to see that I was dealing with an aged individual having, under grey eyebrows, extremely vivid dark eyes of a strange fixity; the lady appeared, moreover, to belong to the highest society. 'Sir,' she said to me, with a very pronounced English accent, 'I know that the secret law is rigorous between adepts; a friend of Sir B*** L***, whom you have seen, knows that experiments have been requested of you but that you have refused to satisfy that curiosity. Perhaps you did not have the necessary apparatus; I want to show you a complete magic cabinet—but I ask you before anything else, for the most inviolable secrecy. If you do not make me that promise, on your honor, I shall give the order for you to be taken back to your hotel.'

"I made the promise requested of me and I am faithful to it in not revealing the name, the quality or the residence of that lady, whom I soon recognized as an initiate, not precisely of the highest order but of a very elevated grade. We had several long conversations, during which she always insisted on the necessity of practices for completing the initiation.

"She showed me a collection of vestments and magical instruments, and even lent me a few curious books that I lacked; in brief, she determined me to attempt the experiment of a regulation evocation in her home: a complete evocation, for which I prepared myself for twenty-one days, scrupulous observing the practices indicated in the third chapter of the Ritual.

THE MAGIC CABINET

"Everything was concluded. It was a matter of evoking the phantom of the divine Apollonius of Tyana and interrogating him regarding two secrets, one of which concerned me and the other that interested the lady. At first she had counted on witnessing the evocation with a person of confidence, but at the last moment that lady was afraid, and as a ternary or a unity is rigorously required by the magical rite I was left alone.

"The cabinet prepared for the evocations was fitted out in a tower. Four concave mirrors had been disposed there, and a kind of altar, the upper part of which, in white marble, was surrounded by a chain of magnetic iron. Engraved on the white marble, and gilded, was the sign of the pentagram, and the same sign was traced, in various colors, on the skin of a newborn white lamb, which was extended over the altar. In the center of the marble table there was a small copper heart, with elder-wood and laurel-wood charcoal; a second heater was placed before me on a tripod.

"I was dressed in a white robe similar to the surplice of a Catholic priest, but more ample and longer, and on my head I wore a crown of vervain leaves interwoven with a gold chain. In one hand I was holding a new sword, and in the other the Ritual. I lit the two fires with the required and prepared substances and I commenced, at first in a low voice, which I elevated by degrees, the invocations of the Ritual.

"The smoke expanded; the flame caused all the objects it illuminated to vacillate, and was then extinguished. The white smoke rose up slowly above the marble altar; I seemed to sense a tremor in the earth; my ears were ringing, and my heart was beating forcefully. I put a few branches and perfumes on the heaters, and when the flame rose up, I distinctly saw before the altar the figure of a man, taller than natural, which decomposed and faded away.

"I recommenced the evocations, and came to place myself in a circle that I had traced in advance between the altar and the tripod. Then I saw the mirror that was facing me, behind the altar, clarify gradually, and a white form appeared there, growing and seemingly coming closer. Closing my eyes, I called to Apollonius three times, and when I opened them again, a man was before me, enveloped in a sort of shroud, which seemed to me to be gray rather than white. His face was thin, sad and beardless—which did not correspond precisely with the idea that I had initially formed of Apollonius, but was doubtless a proof that my individual was truer than the one I had imagined.

"I experienced a sensation of extraordinary cold, and when I opened my mouth to speak to the phantom, it was impossible for me to articulate any sound. I then made the sign of the pentagram with my hand, and I directed the point of the sword toward him, commanding him mentally, by that sign, not to frighten me, and to obey me. Then the form became more confused, and suddenly disappeared. I commanded him to come back, and then felt something like a breath pass close to me;[1] something touched the hand in which I was holding the sword and my arm immediately went numb all the way to the shoulder. I thought I understood that the sword offended

---

1 Author's note: "A similar breath makes itself felt in the evocations of Douglas Home." The name of the famous spiritualist medium cited was actually Daniel Dunglas Home.

the spirit,[1] and I planted the weapon by the point in the circle next to me.

"The human figure reappeared immediately, but I felt such great weakness in all my limbs and such a prompt enfeeblement take possession of me that I took two steps in order to sit down. As soon as I was seated, I fell into a profound torpor, accompanied by dreams, of which only a vague and confused memory remained to me when I came round. My arm was, however, numb and painful for several days.

"The figure had not spoken to me, but it seemed to me that the questions I had wanted to ask had been resolved of their own accord in my mind. Thus, to the one that the lady had charged me with asking Apollonius regarding the destiny of the man of whom she wanted to obtain news, an interior voice responded: *dead*. As for myself, I wanted to know whether reconciliation and pardon were possible between two persons in whom I was interested, and the same echo responded to me, pitilessly: *dead!*

"I am recounting here with the greatest exactitude the events as they happened, and I do not impose faith on anyone. The effect of that experiment on me was something inexplicable. I was no longer the same man; something of the other world had passed into me. I was no longer either cheerful or sad, but I experienced a singular attraction to death, without, however, being tempted to have recourse to suicide.

"I repeated the same proof twice, at an interval of only a few days, in spite of a very emphatic nervous repugnance. The

---

1 Author's note: "Spirits fear iron, especially swords. See the story of the shepherd of Cideville reported by Monsieur de Mirville in his scholarly work, *Des esprits et de leur manifestations fluidiques*. Aeneas, in his descent into Hell, drove away the spirits with his sword (Virgil)." Jules de Mirville (1803-1873) was a prolific author of esoteric texts who became one of the most influential converts of Allan Kardec's Spiritism, writing abundantly about a supposedly haunted house in the commune of Cideville. The title cited confuses the titles of two of his best-known books, first published in 1854 and 1863.

story of the phenomena produced differed too little from that one for me to add to this already length narration. But the result of those other two evocations for me was the revelation of two cabalistic secrets, which could, if they were known to everyone, change in very little time the bases and laws of society entire.

"Can I conclude from all this that I really had evoked, seen and touched the great Apollonius of Tyana? I am not hallucinated enough to believe it, nor unserious enough to affirm it. I affirm only that, without explaining by what physiological laws I saw and touched what I saw and touched, what I saw and touched distinctly, without dreaming; and that is sufficient to believe in the real efficacy of magical ceremonies. I deem, however, the practice to be dangerous and harmful. Health, whether mental or physical, cannot resist similar operations if they become habitual.

"Sine that evocation, I have reread with pleasure the life of Apollonius, which historians present to us as an ideal of beauty and antique elegance. I have remarked therein that Apollonius, toward the end of his life, was shaved and tormented in prison for a long time. That circumstance would doubtless have determined the unattractive form of my vision. I have seen two other individuals—there is no need to name them—and have found them equally different in their costume and their aspect from what I expected to see. Should I infer from that that it was the veritable individuals whom I wanted to see, that I saw?

"In any case, I cannot recommend too strongly the greatest reserve to persons who are tempted to deliver themselves to similar experiments; they result in great fatigue, cerebral disturbances and often in shocks profound enough to occasion maladies.[1]

---

1 Author's note: "'One day, during my operations,' says the cabalist Dupotet, 'I was jolted, rolled and bustled by an invisible power, in all the corners of my room, like a veritable elastic ball; not knowing the ter-

"I will not conclude without mentioning the rather strange opinion of certain cabalists who distinguish apparent death from real death and believe that they rarely occur together. According to them, the majority of people who are buried are alive, and many others who are thought to be alive are dead.

"Incurable madness, for example, would be for them an incomplete but real death, which leaves the terrestrial body under the purely instinctive direction of the sidereal body. When the human soul is subjected to a violence that it cannot support—chagrin, fear or despair—it separates itself thus from the body and leaves in its place the animal soul or the sidereal body, which make the human remnant something less alive than the animal itself. Dead people of that species can be recognized, they say, by the complete extinction of the moral and affectionate senses; they are not wicked and not good; they are dead. Those beings, which are venomous mushrooms of the human species, absorb as much as they can of the life of the living. That is why their approach numbs the soul and chills the heart. Such cadaverous beings—if they exist—realize everything that was once affirmed, and everything that is still affirmed today in certain countries, regarding *brucolaques* and *vampires*.

"Are there not beings in proximity with which one feels less intelligent, less good, and sometimes less honest? Are there not those whose approach extinguishes all belief and enthusiasm, who link you to them via your weaknesses, dominate you via your bad penchants, and cause you slowly to die morally, in a torture similar to that of Mezence?[1] They are dead people that we mistake for living ones; they are brucolaques or vampires whom we mistake for friends."

---

rain on to which I was venturing, I stopped and cut my operations short, and yet, you know, *I was not afraid.*'" Jules-Denis, Baron du Potet, alias Dupotet de Sennevoy (1796-1881 was an exponent of magnetic medicine highly praised by Éliphas Lévi, who also wrote *La Magie dévoilée et la science occulte* (1852), an important contribution to the Occult Revival.
1 Mezence is the French version of Mexentius, the name of an Etruscan tyrant featured in the *Aeneid*, where he is killed by the eponymous hero.

LIGHT-OF-SORROW

by Han Ryner

IN those days, life had become quite impossible on the frozen Earth. The last reindeer was dead and it was rare to discover any lichens beneath the equatorial snows.

A hundred humans, however, obstinately persisted in not dying. All day long they scratched in the snow searching for some edible vegetation—or, armed with enormous knives, they pursued a seal, which released lamentable, almost human squeals in its limping flight. In the evening, they came together in the same igloo, huddling together and warming one another up with their love—for they were good people. They wept when they cut the throats of the squealing seals, wondering what crimes their ancestors had committed that condemned them to kill in order to sustain their expiring existence.

Sometimes, though, in spite of their meekness, pressed by the madness of hunger, one of them would hurl himself upon another, kill him, and devour his warm limbs. Then, the horrible pangs appeased, he would recover his reason and die of grief.

Among these sad and gentle beings who were pursuing the fatality of an ending world, the saddest and gentlest of all was a man of thirty who was respected by everyone for his antiquity. There was nothing that could be known that he did not know, and every evening, he would teach his companions the science that had been rendered useless by the excessive cold. He told them about the ancient resources of fortunate humankind, and helped them to understand by means of strangely clear analogies. As his sterile knowledge made him sad, his companions called him by a musical and melancholy name that meant "Light-of-Sorrow."

✳

For five days, no one had eaten. They were all wandering around in groups, searching with terrible cries, but finding nothing. Light-of-Sorrow waved his large cutlass crazily. Everyone feared being killed by his famished fury.

One young orphan, however, whose name translates as Mother's-Tears, came to scrape away the snows by his side— and the orphan child smiled at the madman, whose strange eyes did not frighten him. It seemed, moreover, that the madness was gradually calmed by the smile.

Suddenly, Mother's-Tears uttered a loud cry of joy. He had discovered a lichen under the shifted snow. Violently, unconscious of what he was doing, Light-of-Sorrow precipitated himself upon him, tore the lichen from the little starveling's hand and ate it.

And his hunger was appeased—not sufficiently that he no longer suffered pain in his gut, but enough for him to recover his senses.

The weeping child looked at him and, vanquished by pain and disappointment, he fell into the white shroud of snow. Suffering in the depths of his soul for having caused suffering to one more unfortunate than himself, Light-of-Sorrow made a strange gesture of barbaric generosity. He extended his left arm on a block of ice and, with a sharp blow of his large knife, he cut off his hand. Then, presenting the bloody flesh to the child, he said: "Eat!"

The child made no move to take the bloody flesh—and the gaze of Mother's-Tears became a fixed, implacable, dead reproach . . .

※

That evening, with the exception of Light-of-Sorrow, no one in the igloo had eaten for six days.

"We're all going to die," someone said.

Isolated in a corner, lost in the memory of his time and the pain of his wound, Light-of-Sorrow murmured: "Life wants to live!"

In the cold night, they also heard someone move to stand up, and a woman's voice affirmed, courageously: "Life shall live!"

This bold statement had no effect on any of the dying people. No one replied. It seemed the bleak despair, heavier than before, descended upon the effort to express hope. Since the words had produced neither heat in the cold nor light in the darkness, was it all over, and the silence that had fallen the final silence?

Everyone, however, turned in the same direction. Something was shining in the night: a vague aureole around a gentle and valiant female face. And the woman said: "Shall we rise up, to love on Venus?"

"How shall we rise up?" asked Light-of-Sorrow.

"I don't know. Let's go."

The people went out of the cave—and those sad and gentle beings who had suffered so much and loved so much began to rise up into the air.

Light-of-Sorrow could not go with them. He sensed that he was attached to the Earth. "The weight of the crime," he sighed. But he looked at his handless arm, raised it into the air like a prayer, and began to rise, far behind the others.

326

His ascension was ponderous. He would never be able to catch up with his former companions. He saw them draw away, inexorably and forever. Then he lost sight of them—and to all his other miseries was added the misery of being alone.

Slowly, painfully, he rose up. He rose slowly, with a horrible sensation of effort, so long as he directed his injured arm toward the heavens. The arm seemed to be opening the space above him.

When the overtired arm fell back, though, Light-of-Sorrow, motionless in the infinity of the world and his anguish, felt space close around him again—and everything became black. It was as if he were in a tomb, and he felt that he was dying.

With an effort that became more painful every time, he lifted up his weary arm again, and began rising again into the suddenly brightened sky.

He rose up for millions of years.

He arrived on Venus. Venus resembled the Earth when he had left it. He did not find any trace of his companions there, or any trace of any living thing. Already, Venus was a dead world.

Light-of-Sorrow understood. Weighed down by his incompletely-expiated crime, he had remained *en route* for too long.

"I can ask no more than to suffer all the necessary suffering," he said—and, with his mutilated arm pointing directly at the heavens, he resumed his ascension.

He rose up for millions of years.

He arrived on Mercury—and he found that Mercury was a dead world.

I can ask no more than to suffer all the necessary suffering, he thought—but he did not say it, for he could no longer find words to express his thought.

He understood. In the long interval since he had last spoken, he had forgotten the words.

He did not weep, for he thought: *What use are words, since I'm alone? When I have found humans, they will teach them to me.*

And, with the liberating stump upraised toward the heavens, he resumed his slow ascension.

He rose up for millions of years.

As he rose up, it seemed to him that the sun was emitting less heat and light. Then the sun became no more than a kind of enormous moon. Light-of-Sorrow conjectured that the sun had become a habitable planet, doubtless inhabited. Perhaps he would find his companions there.

Surrounded by former planets that had become dead satellites, the sun-planet was probably rotating around a star in the constellation Hercules.

That was one of Light-of-Sorrow's last vague thoughts. Having lost words, he gradually lost thoughts.

Then he almost lost consciousness of himself; he was no longer anything more than an elevatory instinct.

He arrived on the sun, which was indeed a habitable planet. There he saw trees as stout and high as mountains, and animals that resembled moving hills.

In the midst of this gigantic vegetation, he recovered the consciousness of his distinct existence. He reflected, and recovered his memories.

On this warm and fecund planet the living was easy, especially for a being as tiny as a terrestrial human. Fruits were abundant, and the smallest fruit could feed him for a month.

Having a great deal of time to himself, he observed the new world as a child might, and ended up understanding life in the part of the sun where he was.

Among the unexpected creatures that he saw, some were particularly attractive to him. Even though they were very different from himself, and even though none of the words recovered from his memory were capable of describing their strange form, he understood that they were the humans of the sun. Often, by the variously soft light of the stars, they came together in the benevolent coolness and chatted.

At first from a distance, and then at closer range, hidden behind a leaf or between two pebbles, Light-of-Sorrow accustomed his ears to the thunder of their voices. He ended up understanding a few words of their language, and eventually understood everything that the articulated thunder was saying.

One night, by the variously soft light of the stars, someone whom Light-of-Sorrow understood, by distant analogies, to be respected for his antiquity said mysterious things.

These are the mysterious things that the respected old person said, and which Light-of-Sorrow, hidden within the calyx of a white flower, heard:

"According to the ancient sages, the planet on which we live was, for a long time, a star: a great fire lit in space. Uninhabitable itself, it gave light and heat to satellites that were the living planets, which our birth has killed.

"Again according to ancient tradition, the last inhabitants of the satellites migrated to our world. Traditions vary as to the nature and form of these beings, agreeing only in representing them as very small. Some books compare them to various species of our wingless insects.

"There is one other point on which all accounts agree: our ancestors, who were frightful barbarians, could not bear the proximity of rational beings of too different a form, and killed them all.

"Whether or not they carried out this murder, it is certain that the first humans of the sun committed many crimes. It is in punishment of those crimes that we have so much trouble slowly discovering incomplete truths.

"Perhaps the traditions regarding the emigrants from Mercury, Venus, the Earth and even further afield are themselves merely ingenious myths expressing the evident truth already suspected by our primitive ancestors: the eternity of life. We shall never know. The voyages to the satellites proposed by certain scientists will tell us nothing about this subject: any trace of life has long since disappeared from those frozen worlds."

Then, as if speaking to himself, the old person added: "Oh, to know, to know! I would gladly give my life for my people to know the fraction of truth contained in these myths."

In the scented calyx of the flower, Light-of-Sorrow waved and shouted with all his might. He shouted: "Those old traditions are true. Look! I am a man of Earth!"

No one noticed the flower-head move slightly. No one heard the feeble insectile murmur.

The enormous beings could not hear the loud shout of the tiny creature, because their ancestors had killed rational beings whose bizarre forms displeased them.

Light-of-Sorrow could not shout loud enough to make himself heard by them, because his egotistical folly had killed Mother's-Tears.

✳

He died of his futile effort. The next day, a bird found his little cadaver in the calyx of the flower. It carried him away in its beak and gave him to its chicks to eat, because the dead must make the living, and because it is inappropriate for corpses to be rotting in the scented calices of flowers.

THE COMMUNICATION OF WILLIAM TRYSTOR

by Emile Goudeau

AS soon as the table on which the evocative hands were resting had started to oscillate and pitch, thus indicating, according to spiritist belief, that a Spirit had taken possession of it, President Malbec declared in his fine grave voice: "Does the Spirit that is here wish to tell us its name? One rap for yes, two for no."

There were a few seconds of anxious expectation; then the table lifted slowly and struck two clear blows on the parquet.

"Damn!" exclaimed Georges Capitaine. "The Spirit is refusing to communicate with us."

And the six members of the spiritist group of Bois-Colombes, the *Pure-Lumière*, remained pensive, their hands extended over the round table whose assiduous knights they were, almost every evening. They were all equally forceful in faith and activity; for a long time they had been able, in numerous meetings, to evoke together from the bosom of the oak furniture, by means of their centralized power, the distant souls of Charlemagne, Jeanne d'Arc, Rabelais, Danton, and even the terrible spirit of Napoléon I. Now, under their previously irresistible hands, the phenomenon had become rebellious, and the spirits were remaining mute before their interrogation,

Their faces took on expressions of profound annoyance, and one of them murmured painfully: "Ah! William Trystor! William Trystor!"

That name, thus pronounced, rendered some firmness to President Malbec, in whose home the group of the Pure-Lumière met, on the first floor of his villa in the Rue des Carbonnets, at the back of a modest garden.

"Come on, come on, Spirit, whoever you are," he said, energetically, "reveal your name. By the sword of truth and the flamboyant pentagram, I adjure you to obey me!"

The table agitated madly in various directions, but without responding by precise raps.

"If it's you," said Malbec, then, in a mild, humble, insinuating voice, "if it's you, whose premature demise we regret so keenly, my honorable friend William Trystor, who is here in this table, don't refuse to communicate with your old comrades once more."

Immediately, the table began to execute a bizarre dance on its four feet, of an impatient vivacity. The six members of the Pure-Lumière were forced to get up abruptly, in order to follow the furious table's disorderly bounds across the room and the capricious zigzags of the four newly ataxic feet.

"Oof! It can't be our excellent friend Trystor who is playing with us like this," opined Georges Capitaine, who, in his quality as an employee of the gas company, loved to illuminate discussions.

"But then," said the president, with increasing energy, "whoever you are, Spirit, I order you to return to calm; if not, I'll afflict you with cramps in the astral light!"

That kabbalistically terrible threat made a sudden impression on the table, which, instead of running like a mad thing, bustling everything before it, recommenced swaying lightly in a placid rhythm. The six adepts of the Pure-Lumière, having picked up their scattered chairs, sat down again.

Their hands extended, without unnecessary pressure, they listened to the characteristic creaks groaned by the oak beams, and Malbec resumed the interrogation.

"One rap for yes, two for no; Spirit, are you our deceased and venerated William Trystor?"

The table rapped twice: *no.*

"I was sure of it," declared Capitaine.

"Would you care to say who you are?" added Malbec.

The table rapped one, curtly: *yes.*

There was an "Ah" of triumph in the audience.

"That's good," concluded Malbec, with authority. "Now, in order that you can reveal your name to us, I'll call out the letters of the alphabet. I'll begin: A, B, C, D . . ."

The table rapped once: D.

Having established the initial D, Malbec repeated his ABCD until the letter I, which a rap indicated. "Di," Malbec concluded.

And the integration continued, the raps succeeding one another punctually; finally, the unexpected word *Dindon* was constituted.[1]

A keen disappointment and an irritation contracted the faces of the spiritist friends of the great Trystor, gathered in order to evoke the spirit of that honorable gentleman, whose premature loss they deplored, and to which the facetious table had responded with a vocable devoid of respect: *Dindon.* There was an outcry. They demanded that the table speak in another tone.

The word that it proffered this time was: *Cretin.*

And as, in their exasperation, the members of the Pure-Lumière group abused the accursed spirit that was teasing them thus, the table started turning in an agile and brutal fashion, knocking over chairs and even crashing into the cup-

---

1 *Dindon* is the French term for a turkey, often used metaphorically, to imply stupidity.

boards, the walls, and the abdomens, backs and legs of the group—and ended up escaping from their impotent hands.

One of the members, mopping his brow, cried: "There's nothing more we can do! It's Balthazar!"

"It's Balthazar!" repeated the others, with chagrin.

And they all sat down sadly, abandoning the table, which settled down, creaking.

It is necessary to say that Balthazar was the pest of these meetings. They had named thus one of several "spirits of trouble, insolence and error" who disrupted their experiments. When the malicious Balthazar insinuated himself into the best-behaved item of furniture, that item lost its reason and went crazy, or if it consented to enter into communication, it was to spout idiocies, vulgarities or monstrosities. It was impossible to evoke the ancestors while that baleful influence was making itself felt.

Now, it was not the first time that such a misadventure had befallen the adepts of the Pure-Lumière, and every time, the discouraged group sat down and the evening terminated in depression.

That disastrous phenomenon is sometimes supposedly produced in the annoying presence of incredulous individuals or tricksters, who sneak into the most severe organizations, alas, but the Bois-Colombes group was sure of itself. On the other hand, the Spirit evoked, William Trystor, although very witty when alive, was incapable of playing practical jokes, and the respect due to his memory dispelled any suspicion of posthumous malevolence on the part of that gentleman.

It is necessary to say that the honorable William Trystor had been an indefatigable knight errant of international spiritism. As a traveler in champagne wines, that worthy man had carried the good news throughout the Old and New Worlds for thirty years while selling, in order to make a living, bottles coiffed in gold or silver paper. He had created in that fashion an undeniable and double popularity, as a prophet and an oenophile, from the north to the south and the east to the west, in London or Chicago, Saint-Petersburg or New York, in Amsterdam or Valparaiso, but above all in Bois-Colombes, that homeland of election to which, after each of his voyages, he came to repose his rheumatism and his love of propaganda. It was in Bois-Colombes that, weary of terrestrial agitations he had finally disincarnated, in the home of his friend Malbec, president of the Pure-Lumière group, on the first floor of the villa at the back of a garden in the Rue des Carbonnets, where his old and faithful companions gathered every evening: employees of the gas company, retired schoolteachers and others, desirous of still hearing, in the language of an oak table, the subtle information of the deceased master.

For several trimesters, the group had obtained few supernatural satisfactions, and the Spirit of Trystor had contrived important communications such as "Everything has an end down here," or "Be good to everyone, in order that they will be good to you." Those superior indications, descending from the darkness of the Beyond as far as the bosom of a table, and countersigned by Trystor, had given a veritable boost to the morale of Bois-Colombes group, when suddenly, Balthazar had intervened, in a nauseating fashion.

The group of the Pure-Lumière had felt disposed to dissolve rather than suffer Balthazar any longer, when Presidet Malbec, who would truly have had no idea how to spend his evenings—he did not like grogs, books, billiards, the theater or whist—had an idea of genius.

For several weeks the group of the Fraternité Solaire in Ternes had been cool with regard to the initiates of Bois-Colombes, but it counted among its initiates the most famous writing medium of the Seine—which is saying quite a bit. Writing mediums are those who write under the dictation of spirits, while in a trance. It was a matter, in the name of great principles, of abandoning any idea of rivalry and bringing off a great coup. So Malbec did not hesitate, and, mastering his pride, went to implore the superlative medium of Ternes, who deigned to accede to his request, for he held the name of Wiliam Trystor, who had appreciated his intellectual value, in high esteem. Then too, he was not sorry to humiliate the Pure-Lumière of Bois-Colombes a little; they have these rancors at Ternes, and even, it is said, in Passy.

One evening, Malbec, very grave, came along the Rue des Carbonnets in the company of an exceedingly singular man of indeterminate age, tall, brown-haired, thin and jaundiced, His ample, long frock-coat floated around his vague, emaciated body. His hollow eyes, shiny and mobile, did not look at anything, but seemed filled with mystery; he rubbed his hands together mechanically, or rather wrung them, with such nervousness that he seemed to be kneading an imaginary bar of soap between his fingers. Malbec testified to that bizarre gentleman a kind of veneration full of minute concern. He supported him paternally in order descend from the sidewalk and cross the street, and made a rampart of his body to protect him from any contact with passers-by, as if that fragile and precious being were at risk of broken by an unexpected shock.

He was undoubtedly the famous medium of Ternes, who, under the Hermetic pseudonym of Alkim, veiled the name of a simple taxpayer. No table could resist the simple digital pressure of the powerful Alkim; he knew, in addition, how to write directly under the dictation of the Spirits most devoid of orthography; he could sometimes incarnate disappeared individuals in his person, in such a fashion that their relatives and friends recognized the features of the deceased on the suddenly-transfigured face of Alkim.

In bringing that powerful evocateur to Bois-Colombes, Malbec counted absolutely on vanquishing the ill will of no matter what Balthazar, and also forcing the shade of Trystor finally to explain his enigmatic silence. Certainly, the procedure was violent toward a deceased friend, but did a Spirit of such superior essence have the right to keep quiet in the depths of limbo and to hide from the anxious questions of his friends?

Rubbing his hands energetically, Alkim approved of that way of seeing.

That evening, on the first floor of the villa in the Rue des Carbonnets, there was a remarkable séance.

Alkim asked that the lamps be extinguished, except for one, which, equipped with a shade, was placed on the floor in the corner of the room, in such a fashion as to leave the upper part of the room in a mysterious darkness, where only a single vague circle of light illuminated the black ceiling.

The six adepts were seated around the table, but instead of placing their hands on it, they united them, thus forming a magnetic chain in which Alkim, on whom all gazes were fixed, was the principal link. They all engaged to evoke mentally, doubtless with respect but also with great and fervent force, the spirit of the honorable disincarnate William Trysor.

A notebook and a sharpened pencil had been placed on the table.

Alkim, whose generally mobile eyes were fixed on his stomach, did not take long to shiver several times. The trance commenced; he sighed profoundly and murmured: "Write! Yes, write!" Then, abruptly releasing the hands of his neighbors, he extended his fingers toward the table, groped momentarily with somnambulistic convulsions, and, finally seizing the paper and the pencil, set about tracing lines, with his eyes closed, and more and more lines, casting aside pages filled by abrupt movements. In the oppressed silence of the witnesses, who continued to form a chain, nothing could be heard but Alkim's sighs and the friction of the pencil on the paper.

That lasted for quite a long time. Sometimes Alkim stopped dead, twisting the pencil between his nervous fingers, his head bobbing over to his breast, from which groans emerged; then he resumed writing with an incredible speed, in the dark. Finally, he ceased writing abruptly, leaned backwards, extending his arms in spasmodic fashion, let himself collapse in the armchair, and appeared to have plunged suddenly into a torpid fatigued slumbe

In a low voice, Malbec asked: "Is it finished?"

Like a scarcely distinct breath, vague and almost aerial, a very faint "yes" responded: a phantom "yes."

Someone tried to replace the lamp on the table, but Alkim suddenly started beating the air with his hands, as if that impure, brutal, terrestrial light was obfuscating him in his dream. Then, leaving the medium to his repose, Trystor's six friends went on tiptoe into the next room, taking with them the precious writing that had come from beyond the tomb, in spite of Balthazar, the trickster of the Beyond.

This is what they read:

"Very dear friends of Bois-Colombes, you are forcing me to reveal the truth; I am doing so, constrained, but glad, in sum, since I conjure you to communicate what I am going to say to all my friends, to passers-by, to the crowd, to mediums, to typtologues, those who write under the dictation of Spirits, and to those who listen to them, in sum, to all the living who, by virtue of suggestive force, table-turning, or any other means, put themselves, or try to put themselves, in communication with their departed friends, their disincarnate relatives or with the souls of the illustrious deceased whom the world regrets, with the heroes, saints, men of genius and demigods whom liberating death has carried away on her night-dark wing. To all those noble believers, salutation, and revelation!

"Very dear friends of Bois-Colombes, this is the truth that, for you, thanks to me, is erupting under the infallible pencil of Alkim, the very fervent and very honorable Alkim.

"So, perhaps three and a half days ago I was comfortably installed in my sepulcher. Ornamented with memories and regrets, I was commencing to savor a veritably reparative slumber, that I could have believed to be eternal, after so many terrestrial fatigues . . . voyages . . . speeches . . . controversies. It was vague and mild, that repose earned by numerous sweats in sleeping-cars, fiacres, steamers and the furnished hotels of the Two Worlds! What an inestimable moment of quietude between two existences, the terrestrial and the other! The cadaveric rigidity on my body, like dead meat, was perfect, and my tranquil perispirit, like a voyager between two trains, was sleeping, while my flowering immortelles and my wreaths of pearls were swaying up above in our modest cemetery of Bois-Colombes. That appeared to my soul, through its somnolence, to be absolutely delightful, when—*bang!*—I was abruptly woken up . . . oh, very abruptly . . . my spirit even oscillated under the shock and suddenly bounded into space.

"For a moment, I was able to believe that, promoted to some new planet—Saturn or Uranus, perhaps Venus or Mercury—I had been launched through chaos in order to attain a new vital garment and reincarnate myself, in accordance with the laws of metempsychosis . . . but it was nothing of the sort. Drawn by an irresistible force, like a nacelle lifted up by a balloon, I felt myself projected with an extraordinary velocity all the way to Fifth Avenue in New York, on the ground floor, and precipitated into an oval walnut table six feet long and four wide, on which a dozen people—gentlemen, ladies and misses—were leaning their powerful hands.

"Scarcely awakened from my mortuary sleep, I was immediately obliged to make that heavy object oscillate. I was asked if it was really the celebrated William Trystor who was thus enclosed within those planks . . . oh, those planks, a new coffin, a funeral bed, less restful than that of my sepulcher—where, at least, I had nothing to do. Immediately, I was obliged to reply *yes* by means of a violent blow.

"I heard one brute, full of humor, declare: If *it's Trystor, he's going to sell us a few cases of champagne!* I was about to get annoyed, and I shook the table violently, bustling everything in order to thump that impolite individual, but he was made to shut up. Then I was asked whether I was well, whether the future life was agreeable, etc. I responded as best I could, tapping on the parquet with one or other of the four legs that the table offered me.

"I would even have smiled at that unexpected quadripedal state if I had possessed a mouth and lips. But I did not even have time to resolve the question of knowing whether disincarnate Spirits can smile, and how, for a very stupid young miss, who was voluntarily obeyed in that milieu, asked me abruptly whether I had seen Washington. I replied *no* by striking two blows with my four wooden feet. Then she commanded me to go and search for the spirit of Washington.

"Immediately, I was expelled from the table and projected into black space, scarcely illuminated here and there by a few souls more luminous than the others. I could not find any Washington . . ."

At this point in the manuscript there were indistinct zigzags, obscure hieroglyphs that the members of the Pure-Lumière could not succeed in deciphering. Then, in neat enough handwriting, the communication of William Trystor resumed:

"On evening, in Bordeaux, the various questions that were addressed to me were so particularly inapt that the famous word of Cambronne was about to escape me[1] via the typ-tological alphabet when I thought that the Spirits of higher grade, especially those who hope to be reincarnated in good conditions, always retain their *sang-froid* and maintain them-selves within the limits of an exquisite politeness.

---

1 Portentous historians recorded that when the beleaguered General Cambronne was invited to lay down his arms at Waterloo he replied: "The Guard does not surrender!" but members of his unit reported that what he had actually said was "Merde!"—a stronger expletive in French than its lit-eral English translation. He denied that he had made either remark, but it did not stop "the word of Cambronne" becoming a popular euphemism.

"You can imagine, my friends of Bois-Colombes, how many times in a month I was awakened from my eternal sleep to go into occasional tables, chairs, top hats and various objects, to predict a future that I do not know, to give information on operations on the stock-exchange, to proffer my advice regarding a projected marriage or a necessary divorce, to announce rain or fine weather . . . it's frightful; oh, simply frightful!

"But in truth, the most tenebrous torture to which I was delivered was when I was no longer sufficient for the curiosity of the audience, who sent me in search of another Spirit, Napoléon I or Henry Monnier, Voltaire, Danton, Marat, or even Saint Louis, Alexander the Great, Aristotle, Pythagoras . . . How should I know where to find those famous Spirits, among the innumerable crowds that populate the atmospheres—me above all, newly arrived in those immense salons of the invisible?

"I returned to lie down in my penumbra. Only, in the end, I perceived that I was wasting my time during these multiple evocations in the furniture of the Two Worlds. I was not advancing in grade. Every time I was woken up I imagined that an angel was going to take me to a new world where I would enjoy the promised recompenses, and every time I was drawn again to the earth by a few more or less intelligent spirits.

"Fortunately, I encountered an evil Spirit who said to me: 'I'm condemned to spend a thousand years in the terrestrial atmosphere because I was a practical joker—a trickster, if you wish—during my life; as I can't hope for any mercy, I continue to play jokes on humans. When people evoke you, do as Alexander the Great, Charlemagne, Napoléon I, Jeanne d'Arc, Voltaire and all the geniuses and heroes do, who are weary of humans, and send me into the table in your stead when you're summoned. For a start, that amuses me; I say stupid things to them, sometimes solemn, sometimes vulgar, and in that fashion I render a service to the great men, who, in their new lives on new planets in the scintillating skies they have entered, have plenty of better things to do than predict rain and fine weather to rheumatic rentiers or exiguous silly girls.'

"Such was the speech of that Spirit you call Balthazar, whom I have sent to you and will send you henceforth, as all the wise disincarnate do whose presence you solicit for no good reason, instead of blessing them and praying for them.

"Know too that, by virtue of a recent decree, I have just been promised the estate of an inhabitant of Saturn, and must enter those functions next week. So, dear friends of Bois-Colombes, do not count on me any longer, and believe in my regrets . . . Aie! Aie! What's happening? Who is pulling me like that? What is it? Aie! Aie! . . . !"

At this point a long streak of pencil striped the manuscript.

"Someone's calling me to another table! Lord! In Chicago! I'm running there, to tell those Yankees what I've just declared to you here. Adieu, then. Adieu! T . . ."

The final T had a strange form, and truly implied a signature of the Beyond, a definitive P.P.C.[1]

The members of the Pure-Lumière group contemplated that reading in silence.

One of them suggested: "Perhaps it's Balthazar who dictated that."

Another declared: "What does it matter? Perhaps one ought not to disturb the Spirits at the moment of their solar ascension."

And they all remained pensive, while Alkim, who had finally woken up from his lethargy, appeared on the threshold, pale and grave, his eyes mobile, nervously wringing his hands, and said: "I'll gladly take a little cognac with sugar."

And the group went into the terrestrial dining room, where a supper was served.

---

1 *Pour prendre conge*—i.e., a polite goodbye.

ABOUT THE AUTHORS

MAURICE BEAUBOURG (1859-1943) was a journalist and dramatist prolific in the *fin-de-siècle*, particularly associated then with symbolist periodicals. Some of his early fiction was collected in *Les Contes pour assassins* (1890) and *Nouvelles passionnées* (1891), and his work continued to exhibit a preoccupation with crimes of passion; "L' Ombre amoureuse" was the first of a series of "Contes pour les ames mortes" published in Arsène Houssaye's *Grande Revue de Paris et Saint-Petersbourg* in April-July 1891. He was a member of the advisory panel for the literary section of Papus' *L'Initiation*, presumably having been recruited after the success of his "idealist" drama *L'Image* (1894), in which some critics found echoes of neoplatonism.

SAMUEL-HENRI BERTHOUD (1804-1881), who attached a variant signature to his works because his father, a printer by profession, had used their common forename on his own publications, edited a local newspaper in his native city of Cambrai before founding a periodical of his own, where he published much of his early fiction, including his pioneering *contes cruels*, collected in *Contes misanthropiques* (1831; tr. as *Misanthropic Tales*). That endeavor brought him to the attention of Émile de Girardin, who employed the technical skills he had learned while assisting his father on the editorial staff of *La Mode* and *La Presse* when he relocated to Paris in the early 1830s; he also worked for *La Revue de Deux Mondes* and *La Revue de Paris*—then the two central organs of the burgeoning Romantic Movement—as well as *L'Artiste,* before he was entrusted by Girardin, first with the sole editorship of the revamped *Mercure de France,* and then that of the pioneering didactic "family magazine" *La Musée des Familles.* He must have lived in Paris before then, presumably as a student in the early 1820s, because he was already acquainted with Honoré de Balzac, with whom he had collaborated on various projects. He had also attempted to collect the folktales and legends of his native region and to write stories in a similar spirit, many of them, including "La Bague antique," collected in *Chroniques et traditions surnaturels de la Flandre* (1831; greatly expanded 1834; partially tr. in *Martyrs of Science and Other Victims of Devilry and Destiny,* 2013, and *The Angel Asrael and Other Legendary Tales,* 2018). During the Second Empire he did various editorial jobs, often uncredited, and wrote many articles for newspapers as "Dr. Sam," mostly popularizing natural history and science, before becoming prolific again under the Third Republic, extending his variegated career into the 1880s.

JULES BOIS (1868-1943) obtained a considerable reputation as an occult scholar via his mystical poetry and his friendships with the likes of Joris-Karl Huysmans, whose research for *Là-Bas* (1891) he assisted, Jean Lorrain and Gilbert-Augustin Thierry, although he was not as credulous as those quoting him often assumed. He first obtained literary success with the "esoteric drama" *Les Noces de Sathan* (1890), and his further ventures in occultism included a survey of *Le Satanisme et la magie* (1896). His sociological treatises, including *L'Eve nouvelle* (1894), anticipate an end of anthropocentrism and the genesis of a new woman. Bois' contributions to periodicals were mostly non-fictional, but they included the novel *Le*

Vaisseau des caresses (1907 in *La Nouvelle Revue*; book 1908). "La Chimère de sardoine," was first published in the literary supplement of the newspaper *Le Figaro* on 5 May 1906; the translation is original to the present volume.

JEAN-GASTON BOURGEAT (1864-?) published several books on the occult sciences, including *Magie* (1895; expanded as *La Magie*, 1904) *and L'Empire de mystère, essai philosophique sur le phénomène du sommeil, avec explications exotérique des songes* (1910, in collaboration with Abbé Julio), and treatises on the Tarot and "psychic culture." His collaborator, the renegade priest Ernest Houssay (1844-1912), alias "Abbé Julio," published numerous volumes on the magical uses of prayer, exorcism, etc. "Le Squelette" (September 1908) was the first of several contributions that Bourgeat made to Papus' periodical *La Voile d'Isis*. The translation is original to the present volume.

ALPHONSE BROT (1807-1895) made his literary reputation as a historical novelist and dramatist, although he was also employed for many years as a civil servant managing the printing press of the Ministry of the Interior. His early short fiction was written while he was a member of the *petit cénacle* alongside Théophile Gautier, Gérard de Nerval, Petrus Borel and "P. L. Jacob le Bibliophile" (Paul Lacroix); much of it, including his baroque recapitulation of the legend of "Faust," was collected in *Entre One heures et minuit II: Un Coin du salon* (1833). The first volume of the couplet in question, *Devant la cheminée*, had featured work by Brot's mentor, Émile Marco de Saint-Hilaire (1789-1887), perhaps the most scandalous of the Romantic historians by virtue of his pseudonymous authorship of *Biographie des nymphes du palais royal et autres quartiers de Paris, par Modeste Agnèse, l'une d'elles* (1823), a fanciful detailed history of the city's brothels. The fantastic element of Brot's work was eliminated thereafter, and he never wrote anything else as surreal as "Faust." The translation is original to the present volume.

ALPHONSE ESQUIROS (1812-1876) was another member of the *petit cénacle*, who must have been familiar with Brot's "Faust." He published some poetry in the early 1830s and his first novel was the occult historical fantasy *Le Magicien* (1838), but almost all of his subsequent work was non-fiction; his remarkable occult novella "Le Château enchanté" (1846); tr. as *The Enchanted Castle*, 2021) first appeared in *L'Artiste* after that periodical's acquisition by Arsène Houssaye, and was rapidly reprinted in the *Revue de Paris*, which Houssaye had also taken over, probably having been commenced in the 1830s and belatedly completed at Houssaye's instigation. Esquiros' early interest in occult science had rapidly given way to an intense interest in "magnetism" and protopsychology, on which subjects he contributed scholarly studies to the *Revue des Deux Mondes*, but he subsequently devoted his efforts to political activism, his election to the Legislative Assembly following the revolution of 1848 being swiftly followed by exile from France after the 1851 *coup d'état*, although his political career went on to greater success after 1870, "Ebn Sina" (1849; tr. as a supplement to *The Enchanted Castle*) also appeared in *L'Artiste*.

ÉMILE GOUDEAU (1849-1906) was a journalist primarily remembered as the founder of the Hydropathes literary club, which re-formed in 1881, after a hiatus, in the Chat Noir, which its members made famous; he edited the magazine named after the café from 1882-84. His own work, including the novel *La Vache enragée* [The Mad Cow] (1885), was mostly humorous. He had a regular column in *La Grande Revue de Paris et Saint-Petersbourg*, in which he included the present story in 1891; the translation is original to the present volume.

ÉDOUARD L'HOTE (?-?) published a volume of poetry, *Les Primevères* (1836) and contributed art criticism to Arsène Houssaye's version of *L'Artiste* in the 1840s. Houssaye described him in his memoirs as a friend, and recruited him again to write for his *Grande Revue de Paris et Saint-Petersbourg* in the 1890s, to which he contributed the present item in 1891. As a friend of Houssaye and Alphonse Esquiros, L'Hote might well have met Alphonse-Louis Constant before he became Éliphas Lévi, and could have kept in touch with him thereafter. The translation is original to the present volume.

JULES JANIN (1804-1874) began a lifelong career in journalism as soon as he left school, soon working alongside Charles Nodier at the *Journal des Débats*. He became Nodier's closest friend during the last two decades of the latter's life. He contributed to the first incarnation of *L'Artiste* and worked for Émile Girardin for a while as an editor, but remained something of a literary butterfly, never settling long in one place and aborting many of his projects. His initial reputation was made by his novel *L'Âne mort et la femme guillotiné* (1829; tr. as *The Dead Donkey and the Guillotined Woman*), an extended *conte cruel*, the critical success of which he never repeated. Much of his early fiction was fantastic, and he titled his first collection *Contes fantasiques* (1832) although, like his other collections, it mingled tales of various kinds. "Le Mort magnetisé" first appeared in the *Revue pittoresque* in 1845, several weeks before Edgar Poe published the first version of his own story describing a similar experiment, usually known as "The Facts in the Case of M. Valdemar." The translation first appeared in *The Magnetized Corpse and Other Paradoxical Tales* (2014).

GABRIEL DE LAUTREC (1867-1938) was, for a while, one of the more flamboyant lifestyle fantasists of the *fin-de-siècle*, advertising his occult interests, his friendship with Paul Verlaine and his fondness for hashish in his literary works, his dandyism and his decadence tastes in the décor of his apartment, but he worked by day as a schoolteacher, and eventually toned his act down considerably, becoming a prolific proto-surrealist humorist under the influence of Alphonse Allais and aiming most of his later publications at the juvenile market. A series of quasi-autobiographical items published in Papus' periodical *L'Initiation* in 1907-8 as *Le Feu sacré* (tr. in *The Sacred Fire*, 2019) offers details of his intro-duction of occultist lifestyle fantasy, but waxes more lyrical about his experiments with hallucinogenic drugs, claiming that they provided the raw material for most of his *Poèmes en prose* (1898; tr. in *The Vengeance of the Oval Portrait and Other Stories*, 2011 and *The Sacred Fire*). "Le Talisman" was also reprinted in *L'Initiation*, presumably because of its repre-sentation of "revelatory slumber."

RENÉ DU MENSIL, COMTE DE MARICOURT (1829-1893) was a historian and archeologist, whose serious interest in Gnosticism and the Hermetic tradition was reflected, in combination with this interest in contemporary psychic re-search, in his supposedly non-fictional *Souvenirs d'un magné-tiseur* (1884). His previous imaginative fiction had included *Marcien, ou Le Magicien d'Antioche* (1866; probably based on William Tandy's 1860 drama *Marcion; or The Magician of Antioch*), the satirical *Souvenirs d'un hirondelle* (1870) and the remarkable futuristic fantasy *Au bout du fosse!! La Commune en l'an 2073* (1874; tr. as "All the Way; The Commune in 2073" in *Nemoville and Other French Scientific Romances*, 2012). His son André (1874-1940) followed in his footsteps, writing numerous historical biographies. "L'Oeil du dragon" (1890) was the first of three novelettes serialized in *L'Initiation*; the translation is original to the present volume.

HENRI MARTIN (1810-1883) spent the bulk of his career producing a *Histoire de France* (13 vols. 1833-36; updated and expanded to 19 vols. in 1865), initially planned and begun in collaboration with "P. L. Jacob le bibliophile" (Paul Lacroix). In the latter part of his life, having been elected to the Académie, he served as a senator. The early volumes of his history put a heavy influence on the alleged Druidic contribution to the pre-Christian history of Gaul. He published the novel *Wolfthurm* (1830) before contributing a series of stories to *L'Artiste* in 1831, including "Le Mauvais oeil," which were never collected in book form. The translation was first published in *Isuren and Other Stories* (2023).

VICTOR-ÉMILE MICHELET (1861-1938) was a childhood friend of Stanlias de Guaita, and collaborated with him and "Papus" (Gérard Encausse) in the formation of their new Martinist Order in the 1880s—a crucial event in the course of the French Occult Revival; he was also a fervent admirer of Édouard Schuré, whose writings also made a crucial contribution to the Revival. He shared Joséphin Péladan's interest in Symbolist Art and his first book was *De l'ésoterisisme dans l'Art* (1890), published more than ten years before his first collection of mystical poetry, *La Porte d'or* (1903), although the material therein mostly dated from long before; his collection of fantastic short stories and prose poems, *Contes surhumains* (1900; tr. with additional material as *Superhuman Tales*, 2018), from which the present story is taken, beat it into print, as did its companion volume *Contes aventureux* (1900), but they too recycled some material written much earlier.

CHARLES NODIER (1780-1844) was the most signif-icant pioneer of French Romantic prose, and the literary salon he founded in association with Victor Hugo and Alphonse de Lamartine, which became the *cénacle* he host-ed at the Bibliothèque de l'Arsenal, was the powerhouse of the Movement during the crucial but problematic years of the late 1820s and early 1830s. Always inclined to depres-sion and anguish, his troubles were intensified when he was banished from Paris after publishing the satirical ode *La Napoléone* (1802; tr. as "The Napoleonad") and it was while leading a peripatetic existence that he published *Les Tristes, ou mélanges tirés des tablettes d'un suicide* (1806; tr. in *Outlaws and Sorrows*, 2021), in which "Un Heure, ou la Vision" first appeared. It was the first of his many supernatural fantasies, but its basic pattern was repeated in many others throughout his life. The defense offered by himself and others for his error in writing *La Napoléone* was that his mind had been disturbed by emotional traumas, compounded by his medicinal use of opium; his longest and most bizarre work of occult fiction, *Histoire du roi de Bohème et de ses sept châteaux* (1830; tr. as *The Story of the King of Bohemia and his Seven Castles*, 2023), takes the form of a surreal opium dream experienced by one "Théodore"—that being the forename by which the German writer of hallucinatory fantasies E. T. A. Hoffmann is called in stories written in homage by Alphonse Brot and Jules Janin; the latter signed a story in *L'Artiste*, in which Nodier features as a character, derived from the text of the novel.

JEAN RICHEPIN (1848-1926) achieved a *succès de scandale* with his collection of verse *Le Chanson des gueux* (1876), serving a term of imprisonment after its successful prosecu-tion. He became one of the most flamboyant members of the Parisian literary community, performing his own songs in *Le Chat noir* and appearing on stage with Sarah Bernhardt in a play he wrote for her, prompting her to opine that he was a bigger ham than she was. Bizarrely, he was elected to the Académie as a result of a cabal formed to block the entry of the symbolist poet Henri de Régnier (whose election was merely postponed.) He joined the stable of writers assembled by Catulle Mendès to write short fiction for *L'Écho de Paris*, and transferred with the other major members to *Le Journal*, where "Les Autres yeux" appeared in the 21 December 1899 issue; the translation first appeared in *The Crazy Corner: Horrible Stories* (2013).

HAN RYNER was the version of his name used after 1896—when he became a fervent Anarchist—by Henri Ner (1861-1938), a prolific journalist, novelist and short story writer. Almost all of his work embraces his own idiosyncratic brand of mystical "individual anarchism," supposedly derived from the Greek cynic philosophers, whom he considered to be the inventors of the method of teaching by means of parables, which he tried to continue. Samplers of his work in translation are *The Superhumans and Other Stories* (2011)—which includes the translation of "Lumière-de-douleur," the original having appeared in *Demain* in 1897, *The Human Ant and Other Stories* (2014) and *The Son of Silence and Other Anarchist Fantasies* (2016); the title short novel of the third volume, an account of the initiation of Pythagoras into the Hermetic mysteries, is perhaps his most significant work of occult fiction.

"X. B. SAINTINE" was the pseudonym of Joseph-Xavier Boniface (1798-1865), who was conscripted to the National Guard in 1814 and met the writer Eugène Scribe in barracks during the Hundred Days, when the two collaborated in a writing a vaudeville—the first of many for both of them. His first major project was a series of linked short stories begun in the *Mercure du dixneuvième siècle* in 1823, of which "L'Enfant du sorcière" (1824) was the fifth. The initial series was reprinted in book form in two volumes as *Jonathan le visionnaire, contes philosophiques et moraux* (1825), the eponymous immortal being the notional narrator of the stories. The series was further augmented twice, firstly by a striking novella, "Histoire d'une civilisation antédiluvienne" published in the *Revue de Paris* in 1832, signed "Jonathan le visionnaire," which describes the entire history of the society in question from its prehistoric origins to its collapse as a result of reckless and excessive technological progress. That story was not included in *Les Soirées de Jonathan* (1937), which added half a dozen new stories to items reprinted from the original collection, nor in an 1853 reprint, perhaps because of fear of the censors, although it was included in a posthumous edition of 1866. The entire series is translated in *Jonathan the Visionary* (2018). Saintine ventured into occult fantasy more whimsically and more ingeniously in another series of works based on journals he kept of his dreams, which he did not collect until the final years of his life, as *La Second Vie* (1862; tr. as *The Second Life*, 2018), although many must have been written much earlier. The present story was published before the production of *Le Monstre et le magicien* at the Porte Saint-Martin theater in 1826, but Saintine might have read Mary Shelley's *Frankenstein* (1818), on which the spectacle in question was loosely based.

GILBERT-AUGUSTIN THIERRY (1843-1915) changed his signature to Gilbert Augustin-Thierry late in life to emphasize his kinship with his paternal uncle, the famous Romantic historian Augustin Thierry. His father, Amédée Thierry, was also a historian, who was forced to make a living from journalism when sacked from his academic post during the Bourbon Restoration because of his Republican opinions. Gilbert followed closely in his footsteps, becoming a pillar of the *Revue des Deux Mondes*. That periodical picked up a series of stories launched in the *Nouvelle Revue* under the title "Histoires de Mort et de Vivant," of which the present story was the first. This translation first appeared in the collection *Reincarnation and Redemption* (1919), which was followed by two volumes aggregating four later items in the series, *The Blonde Tress and the Mask* (2021) and *Stigma and the Pompeiian Fresco*. The intensively-researched historical backgrounds of the stories, most of which are short novels, and their earnest tone, entitle the later ones to consideration as some of the finest examples of nineteenth-century occult fiction. An earlier novel in the same vein was *L'Aventure d'une âme en peine* [The Adventure of a Soul in Torment] (1875).

JANE DE LA VAUDÈRE (1857-1908) was baptized Jeanne Scrive; she was the daughter of the Surgeon-General of the Army, but lost both her parents while she was a child. She was raised in a convent and married off by her relatives, soon after she completed her education, to Gaston Crapez, who inherited the Château de La Vaudère from his mother and added its name to his own. His wife also adopted it, retaining it when she left the family home to live in Paris, where she attempted to seek fame as an artist before switching her attention to poetry, drama and eventually to fiction. Her early publications include a good deal of material based on her experiences in the occult underworld of Paris, much of it—including the present story, originally serialized in *L'Univers illustré* in 1890-91 and reprinted in *Les Sataniques* (1897) as "Viviane"—published in translation in the collection *The Double Star and Other Occult Fantasies* (2018), part of a series that also includes several other occult novels, including the best-selling *Le Mystère de Kama* (1901; tr. in *The Mysteries of Kama and Brahma's Courtesans*, 2019). *Le Harem de Syta* (1904; tr. in *Syta's Harem and Pharaoh's Lover*, 2020) and *La Sorcière d'Ecbatane* (1906; tr. in *The Witch of Ecbatana and the Virgin of Israel*, 2021). The last-named story, allegedly dictated by a Chaldean mage, is framed by an account of a Spiritist séance that the author claimed in a contemporary article actually to have attended.

"CLAUDE VIGNON" was the pseudonym of a writer and sculptor baptized Marie-Noémi Cadiot (1828-1888), who was briefly married to Alphonse-Louis Constant, alias Éliphas Lévi, after 1848, although the marriage did not last long. In the early 1850s she published detailed accounts of the artwork displayed at the annual Salons, but in 1856 she broke new ground with a collection of fantastic stories entitled *Minuit!! recits de la veillée* (tr, as *Midnight!!*, 2021) The collection was reprinted the following year as *Contes à faire peur*, with a prefatory note saying that its distribution was permitted in foreign territories but prohibited in France, implying that the first edition had been seized by the authorities and most of the copies destroyed; at any rate, the collection remains little known in France, although it is a landmark work of French fantastic fiction. By the time of its publication, Cadiot was married to the Marquis de Montferrier, and she went on to become a successful writer of sentimental novels—a career that she continued during her third marriage, in 1872, to the Opportunist politician Maurice Rouvier, who was assisted by the support of her salon to be appointed to serve two terms as President du Conseil. A great admirer of Balzac, she adopted her pseudonym from his novella "Béatrix" (1839), where it is attributed to an art critic based on Gustave Planche. Her regular reportage of the Salon must have brought Cadiot into contact with Planche, and also with Charles Baudelaire; *Minuit!!*, although published before Baudelaire's collection of translations of Edgar Poe, seems to show the influence in its later inclusions of Poe stories that Baudelaire had translated for periodicals. "Le Convive des trépasses" is, however, much more obviously affiliated to the Gothic tradition of Romanticism, and is one of the most extravagant examples of that kind of horror fiction.

OTHER BOOKS IN THE SERIES

The Zinzolin Book of Occult fiction (edited by Brendan Connell)
The Vermilion Book of Occult fiction (edited by Brian Stableford)
The Zaffre Book of Occult fiction (edited by Brendan Connell)
The Viridian Book of Occult fiction (edited by Brendan Connell)

A PARTIAL LIST OF SNUGGLY BOOKS

G. ALBERT AURIER *Elsewhere and Other Stories*
CHARLES BARBARA *My Lunatic Asylum*
S. HEZOLNRY BERTHOUD *Misanthropic Tales*
LÉON BLOY *The Tarantulas' Parlor and Other Unkind Tales*
ÉLÉMIR BOURGES *The Twilight of the Gods*
CYRIEL BUYSSE *The Aunts*
JAMES CHAMPAGNE *Harlem Smoke*
FÉLICIEN CHAMPSAUR *The Latin Orgy*
BRENDAN CONNELL *Metrophilias*
BRENDAN CONNELL *Unofficial History of Pi Wei*
BRENDAN CONNELL (editor)
The World in Violet: An Anthology of EnglishDecadent Poetry
RAFAELA CONTRERAS *The Turquoise Ring and Other Stories*
DANIEL CORRICK (editor)
Ghosts and Robbers: An Anthology of German Gothic Fiction
ADOLFO COUVE *When I Think of My Missing Head*
QUENTIN S. CRISP *Aiaigasa*
LUCIE DELARUE-MARDRUS *The Last Siren and Other Stories*
LADY DILKE *The Outcast Spirit and Other Stories*
CATHERINE DOUSTEYSSIER-KHOZE *The Beauty of the Death Cap*
ÉDOUARD DUJARDIN *Hauntings*
BERIT ELLINGSEN *Now We Can See the Moon*
ERCKMANN-CHATRIAN *A Malediction*
ALPHONSE ESQUIROS *The Enchanted Castle*
ENRIQUE GÓMEZ CARRILLO *Sentimental Stories*
DELPHI FABRICE *Flowers of Ether*
DELPHI FABRICE *The Red Sorcerer*
DELPHI FABRICE *The Red Spider*
BENJAMIN GASTINEAU *The Reign of Satan*
EDMOND AND JULES DE GONCOURT *Manette Salomon*
REMY DE GOURMONT *From a Faraway Land*
REMY DE GOURMONT *Morose Vignettes*
GUIDO GOZZANO *Alcina and Other Stories*
GUSTAVE GUICHES *The Modesty of Sodom*
EDWARD HERON-ALLEN *The Complete Shorter Fiction*
EDWARD HERON-ALLEN *Three Ghost-Written Novels*

www.ingramcontent.com/pod-product-compliance
Lightning Source LLC
Chambersburg PA
CBHW060619100726
47907CB00006B/1688